THE
SACRISTAN

BRIAN PENTLAND

Order this book online at www.trafford.com
or email orders@trafford.com

Most Trafford titles are also available at major online book retailers.

Print information available on the last page.

ISBN: 978-1-4907-6057-5 (sc)
ISBN: 978-1-4907-6059-9 (hc)
ISBN: 978-1-4907-6058-2 (e)

Library of Congress Control Number: 2015908011

Trafford rev. 09/18/2015

 www.trafford.com
North America & international
toll-free: 1 888 232 4444 (USA & Canada)
fax: 812 355 4082

This book is dedicated to dearest Fozzie

CHAPTER ONE

Home Base

CHAPTER ONE

Home Base

'I am not going.'

'Oh yes, you are, young man, or there is going to be serious trouble.'

'Emotional blackmail won't work on me,' replied a defiant Emmanuel over the breakfast table.

'Emmanuel, please! Your father will be terribly upset.'

'Really?' was the rather haughty reply. 'You do realise that I received a telephone call this morning from my mother, who has also been invited to the wedding.'

'Well, seeing that it has been an afterthought, I should be very surprised if Angela is interested.;

'One is as bad as the other,' said Kerry, putting her cup down and heading for the toaster. 'Would you like another slice?'

'No, thank you. Angela, and I are out to lunch. I don't want to ruin my appetite.'

'Charming! My mother is a very poor influence on you.'

'Not at all! Angela and I just happen to get along famously.'

'That is exactly what I mean,' replied Kerry, as Emmanuel stood up and gave her a kiss.

'See you later. I'm off with Angela to check out a fabulous pair of French chairs.'

'I can just imagine!' said Kerry, settling back into her chair and being very aware that she was applying twice the amount of butter to her toast than was necessary. It had always been like this, she thought. Emmanuel and Angela against the world, and the thing Kerry found most annoying was they always won. Angela was very much the matriarch of this family. She had come from a wealthy background and followed the usual social rules to marry a man of suitable means. They had been given this enormous double-storeyed Victorian mansion as a wedding gift from his parents and it also came with two large Victorian double-fronted houses with huge bay windows that sat side by side. One of them, the furthest away, No. 10, was where Emmanuel headed, two doors down to his grandmother's mansion. Kerry had been very dubious about accepting this house when she married, feeling that an overbearing mother so close was perhaps not such a good idea. The other house next door and beside the mansion was No. 8 and that was now the property of her only sister, Mary, but she was rarely resident as she had a large country property.

Kerry looked at her lukewarm tea and sighed. It had been almost thirty years ago that she and Salvatore had married and despite a few moments it had been an extremely happy marriage. Kerry had gone to a school ball and there she had met a young man who also attended a good Catholic school. He invited her out and so a slight relationship formed, but on being invited to lunch at his family's home in a suburb the other side of the city, in a zone one could not call chic, but honest, Kerry met and fell in love at the first introduction, to Salvatore, the brother of the gentleman who had invited her to lunch. Her mother, Angela, thought the whole thing just too silly to think about, but for Kerry and Salvatore this was it.

Angela's husband had died many years before when his daughters were in their early teens and Angela had inherited everything. She immediately took all in hand and the companies that were her husband's she merged with her own, never selling anything, just expanding ruthlessly. She never lost a night's sleep from forcing somebody's company into bankruptcy. She was only concerned about profit, so when Kerry had put her foot down about marrying Salvatore, who obviously had a very limited financial background, Angela being Angela took over. Salvatore had worked in a family business of stone masons and Angela simply did her homework and found a large stonemason's business in financial trouble, bought it out at a low price and installed Salvatore as manager. On the agreement that the figures were met each month, eventually the business would be handed over to him. So 'Lampedusa Stonemasons', a large gilded sign, heralded one's entrance into what was now one of the largest of the businesses in Melbourne, and was seen as the right place to get exactly what one wanted. The marriage also went with No. 8 Ashfield Avenue, which was put in Kerry's name, not Salvatore's, something that he never managed to come to grips with. Although he had been handed the opportunity of his life with the stonemason's complex, he always lived in his wife's house, not his.

He and Kerry had had two children, both boys and as different as daylight is to night. Vincenzo, who went by the name of Vince, was quiet, hard-working and at school a very high achiever. At the age of eighteen he entered Melbourne University, completed in record time a degree in theology and entered a seminary, much to Angela's surprise, as well as of the rest of the family. 'Oh well,' was her reply on hearing the news and offering Vince a glass of champagne, 'your uncle is a Monsignore so I guess it runs in the family blood,' and gave him a kiss. Salvatore was not so excited about the situation. He had automatically assumed that Vince would take over the enterprise that he had worked on for more than thirty years and so their relationship became much more formal.

But Vince had a brother, eight years his junior, Emmanuel. Needless to say, Salvatore was adamant that he choose the name of his sons and Kerry allowed him this right in a world where her mother controlled all, financially and socially. Chalk and cheese is an expression used to describe extreme opposites and Vince and Emmanuel were just that. The only thing they had in common was their extreme good looks. Vince was taller than Emmanuel and with a shock of short cropped black hair and dark brown eyes, very similar to his father. He was also blessed with an olive skin. His handsome features made him a great loss to the social scene when he accepted his vocation. But if Vince was extremely handsome Emmanuel was a show-stopper, tall, black bushy hair cut into a mane, olive skin, an inheritance from his father's Italian background, a very fine face with a determined forehead and jawline and a strong nose. But the impact of Emmanuel was the eyes, a blue shade that defied identification. In the harsh sun they turned to a strong cobalt; in the evening light they seemed a little lighter, but the combination of all the features was, as Angela said, 'just marvellous'.

It cannot be said that Emmanuel studied very hard at school. Both he and Vince went to the most expensive Catholic boys' school in Melbourne, not so far from where they lived in Hawthorn and, needless to say, Ashfield Avenue was the smartest address in this suburb. Whereas Vince applied himself, Emmanuel did not. At a very early age he spent a good deal of time with his grandmother. She adored him and he her, so this relationship from his teens on developed into a very sophisticated friendship. Angela forbad Emmanuel to address her as 'grandmother' and so Angela and Emmanuel were always seen at smart restaurants, the theatre, the races, anywhere where it was the place to be and have fun. There they were, together, laughing and joking, generally at someone else's expense. Salvatore disliked this take-over of his son and in the confines of his home was not short on expressing his feelings. He and Emmanuel had a poor relationship but both made a little effort for the sake of Kerry.

At an early age, when Salvatore at the dining table one evening reprimanded him, he simply stood up, ramming his chair in sharply against the table and informed his father he could be contacted at Angela's and despite threats he stalked out of the house, slamming the front door. He walked down two doors, entered the large double gates and rang the doorbell, while admiring Angel's meticulously cared-for garden. When the maid opened the door, he simply announced he was there for a few days and would be having dinner with Angela. She knew deep down that at fourteen years old this was probably not the best way to prepare Emmanuel for a responsible future life, but as she absolutely adored him she could never refuse him anything. Needless to say, Salvatore found this constant interference in the upbringing of his son very annoying, but due to the business arrangement he had with Angela he was in an awkward situation. The person who was trapped in the middle of this terrible family situation was Kerry, who found she had to placate her husband and plead with her mother to arrive at an equilibrium that equalled survival. But it was Emmanuel who inevitably controlled all. He had worked out very early in his life that life owed him a living and so he aimed at the top. It was not that he hated Salvatore. He found that his constant insistence that he do and think like him to be repressive. He had pieced together that, having met his paternal grandparents, this type of behaviour was considered normal. He rebelled and with Angela two doors away and a very sizeable bank account, why on earth did he have to put up with it all?

Whether he assumed everyone drank champagne as Angela did is not quite certain but after many rowdy discussions about drinking, Kerry gave in and a large supply of domestic champagne was installed. To her surprise it needed topping up regularly.

'I don't know why you indulge him,' said Salvatore one evening, sarcastically.

'Darling, I purchase for you the red wine you really prefer; Vince won't drink, but Emmanuel will, but he prefers another type. Where's the problem?'

'The problem is your mother,' he replied, looking at the television.

'Don't start, Salvatore!' warned Kerry. 'If Emmanuel liked beer, for you it would be fine. The fact is that he likes champagne – I don't honestly see the difference.'

'Have it your way then,' he said, in a defeated way.

Salvatore was now coming up to his forty ninth birthday and was still a very handsome man. Like his sons he was blessed with that beautiful olive skin and his thick black hair was now taking up a grey tint on both sides, giving it a theatrical effect as of two soft wings of grey either side of his handsome face. Despite his reliance on Angela business-wise, she had not looked at a statement from his business for years, but had seen him as a man who had taken an opportunity and made it work. He had expanded the business from constructing grave stones to importing marble and travertine from all over the world. He was aggressive. Salvatore, as a business man, knew how to make one dollar do ten dollars' worth of work and Angela was most pleased with her investment. But he was engineered socially by women, two of them his beloved wife who bore up well considering Emmanuel and Angela, and his mother-in-law, who controlled all, completely.

In his own family, things were anything but tranquil, when a Sunday lunch was organised for all his extended family. He found it very tense and very artificial. His mother, Nella, was also a matriarch but on a very different level from Angela. Nella struck on the very level of 'family' and made no allowances at all. Every boy, every girl would be married and she would be delighted receiving the offspring, the more the better. But nothing could have been further from Angela's view, considering all this family stuff ridiculous. Yet she also dealt in this currency. Vince was to Angela the perfect man and deciding to become a priest for her was a great achievement, but Nella saw this as a lack of fulfilment, no children. Angela had said, when hearing this, that she thought Nella should open a lost dog's home. Salvatore smiled weakly. These Sunday lunches where the whole of Salvatore's family got together (he had three brothers and a sister) turned out to be noisy, with too much food: with any excuse possible, he and Kerry left, leaving room for criticism about both. Salvatore liked seeing his relatives but there was the problem of his older brother, Mario, who had never forgiven Salvatore for taking the rich woman he thought he was destined for, so family get-togethers always produced an electric tension, even though Mario was now married with three children. The beaten-past-the-post syndrome had never left him.

Emmanuel loathed these occasions: it was under great sufferance that he would attend them. He found the conversation trite and boring. Vince supported it all, but Emmanuel no. So for Emmanuel to attend one of these family turns now became a thing of the past. He and Angela always had another appointment here or there and so he never attended and Salvatore always felt out of this tight family group. His mother had never approved of Kerry and so she always blamed her for never bringing Emmanuel to her dining table, as well as for the tension between the two elder brothers. If these occasions were boring for Emmanuel, they were a genuine nightmare for Kerry and in amongst all this was a family wedding to resolve.

Emmanuel was determined he was not going to suffer an afternoon with his cousins and that was that, but hearing that Angela had received a late invitation he went down to see how the lie of the land was socially. At twenty years old, he was nothing short of magnificent physically, and he knew exactly how to use this appearance.

Angela had worked it all out much before the rest: her coterie of male friends was nearly all gay and she would not have had it any other way. When Kerry and Mary grew up in this fine mansion, it was rare any other woman was seated at the table, and Kerry and Mary accepted very early in life the funny repartee that never left them and the friends of Angela whom both of them still continued to see. Salvatore had no problem at all with this and when he was first married to Kerry enjoyed the attention that Angela's many male guests paid him. He was the perfect social attachment to Angela's dinner parties. He should have had his eyes open, but conceit sometimes clouds things successfully.

Emmanuel and Angela had a rapport that was based on fun and honesty. Neither ever felt that it was necessary to lie to the other. The one or the other might do something the other might not think appropriate, but honesty was the complete basis of their relationship and it remained so for all of their lives. So at the age of fourteen, Emmanuel confessed with a certain amount of pride and with a glass of champagne in his hand at a private evening with Angela that he had finally managed to have sex with the captain of the football team but was a little alarmed that the next year he would be gone and so he would have to search about again. Angela downed a whole glass of champagne with the realisation that Emmanuel was the only person in the world she understood completely. She did, however, caution against announcing this to the family, but praised his ability to get what he wanted. It was probably this, for Angela, that made him unstoppable. He wasn't afraid of anybody or anything and if in his distant mind there was a problem, forget it – Angela would work it out, and inevitably she did. So Emmanuel managed to enjoy school to the utmost and it had very little to do with academic achievement.

'Well,' he said, when seated with Angela, 'what about this wedding?'

'Well, darling, you do realise it's the races at Flemington, don't you?'

He laughed. 'Great! We are not going.'

'Mrs Christie, your daughter is here,' announced the maid.

'Thank you, Eva . . . Come in, Kerry,' and Kerry entered and joined them at the table.

'You are both coming to this wedding whether you want to or not.'

'Not is the answer,' replied Emmanuel.

'Your father will be very upset,' she replied.

'I am not going,' insisted Emmanuel, 'and that's it, and nor is Angela. We are going to the races.'

'Oh mum,' she said, exasperated, 'I don't ask much but just this once, for Salvatore's sake. Come on – I loathe these occasions as well.'

'So why do we have to suffer?' asked Emmanuel.

'Because once in a while we do things for duty, not because we like them.'

There was a silence that meant as usual Angela would decide.

'Is Vincent attending?' she asked. The fact that she had used 'Vincent' and not 'Vince' meant that she was stalling a decision.

'No, he can't get away.'

'Hmm,' was all the reply. Again, silence.

'Come on, my for sake. This is the least the pair of you can do.'

'Why do you think my invitation was so late?' asked Angela, in an off-hand way.

'Someone shot the pigeon,' quipped Emmanuel and began to laugh.

'Very well, we shall attend his wedding but on the condition we can leave when we want. Is that clear?'

'Perfectly,' replied Kerry.

'You will notify Nella as to this, of course?'

'Of course,' was the reply and with a weary sigh Kerry rose and left.

'Oh, what a bore,' Emmanuel said.

'Well, sweetie, you never know who could be at this do,' and Angela smiled. 'Besides we have a dinner engagement at eight and this starts at midday so let's see what happens, and by the way don't go wandering off with a good looking long lost Italian cousin and leave me sitting talking to someone about bringing up children in the Montessori method.'

'Would I?' said Emmanuel, with a wicked smile.

'In one word, yes,' she smiled.

Salvatore was genuinely surprised that Emmanuel and Angela had decided to attend this family wedding and was very pleased, but at the back of his mind was the thought of them passing social comments about the wedding that were probably not going to be very kind. He was dead right.

Angela's Mercedes followed Salvatore's. 'Good heavens, darling,' she said. 'I hadn't any idea that the suburbs stretched out so far. I don't think I have ever been out this side of town for years.'

'Lucky you!' he smiled at her.

'What am I going to tell my relatives when they ask me what Emmanuel does for work?' asked Salvatore, looking at Kerry who was very elegant, complete with a hat.

'I haven't a clue, darling. Make something up. Goodness knows, Emmanuel will.'

This had always been the real problem between Emmanuel and Salvatore, work. Salvatore had assumed, when Emmanuel left school, that he would go to the university or come and work with him, but Emmanuel had a very different idea and Angela raising the limit on his credit card assured him that work was rather silly when he didn't have to earn a living and was Angela's constant companion. No amount of arguing or screaming or even pleading was any use. If things got rough at home, Emmanuel simply left the house and moved in with Angela. He had a whole suite and Angela had had a great time decorating it at her expense. Nowadays he was generally more resident there than at No. 10.

'I don't understand why he just doesn't have any sense of responsibility,' complained an exasperated Salvatore, pulling up at a red traffic light, 'and what exactly happens if and when Angela dies. He will literally be out on the street.'

'Darling, that is exactly where he won't be. I know my mother very well and I am certain that in her will she'll leave Emmanuel one of the richest young men in Melbourne, so don't let's worry on that account.'

The cars pulled up in front of a nondescript gymnasium that went by the name of St. Joseph's Catholic Church or so the sign went. 'Oh, another architectural disaster,' gasped Angela as she and Emmanuel waited for his parents to join them.

Nella, having seen them, quickly moved over, gushing about how happy she was to see them both. 'A circus tent in citrus lemon chiffon,' said Emmanuel, when she had left.

'Careful,' warned Kerry, sharply. 'This wedding hasn't even started.'

It was Mario's oldest daughter that was to be wed, so Mario strutted about, saying the right thing to everyone, but when he saw the four of them together he stiffened. 'Hello,' he said, 'I am so glad you could make it.'

'Thank you,' replied Kerry, who was the only one making conversation. It had not gone unnoticed by Mario that the two latest model Merceddes were parked just down from the church.

The wedding over, everyone moved toward their cars and on to what is politely called 'a wedding reception'. This was held in a local centre that catered especially for these occasions. From the minute Emmanuel entered, it became a social hunting season. To his great annoyance, he and Angela had been separated and he was seated with other younger members of the family, each place seating being allocated as Nella and Mario's wife thought appropriate. Herein lay the problem. Emmanuel made it quite clear he was not sitting with a group of cousins he did not know well or like, so he took his name tag off the table and placed it beside Angela's and duly sat down beside her. This upset all the arrangements and it was Mario, who if he had no time for Salvatore, had even less time for what he saw as an over-indulged twenty year old who did nothing.

13

'Sit where you have been allocated,' Mario said, sharply.

'I'm surprised you know what the word 'allocated' means,' ' spat back Emmanuel, sarcastically. Mario had always thought a good slap would not go astray with Emmanuel and was very very close to going through with it. Kerry was the other side of this table and with Salvatore was beginning to feel very uneasy. For Mario it was a stalemate: he either made an issue of it or gave in to – in his mind – an arrogant twenty year old. Foolishly he chose to attack Emmanuel verbally. The room suddenly became very quiet as Mario's voice became louder and Emmanuel's replied sharper.

Nella dashed across the room to placate the situation and said seating was not such a problem, so Emmanuel got what he wanted. Mario was black with rage but toned it down due to the fact it was his daughter's wedding. So after the speeches, the meal began. Emmanuel was in top gear, sending the food back as inedible and complaining loudly as a result of the wine. Even Angela moved uncomfortably. Halfway through the reception Mario had had enough. Noticing Emmanuel's performance he swept across the room and seized Emmanuel's shoulder. Emmanuel spun round and forcefully knocked his hand away.

'I think you had better leave,' said an over-excited Mario. Quick as a flash, Emmanuel replied, 'Thank God! I thought you would never ask.'

Mario was stunned and stood back, not knowing how to reply. Salvatore wiped his brow with a table napkin.

'Come on, Angela. Let's go, shall we?' They stood up, crossed the entire hall and went out with everyone chattering on about what had happen at the other table. Mario suddenly felt that he had over-reacted and sought to right things with Salvatore and Kerry but the more he tried the more tacky everything became.

'Let's just leave it, Mario. It's your daughter's wedding. It's her day. Let's make it as pleasant as possible.' Kerry smiled and reached under the table to hold Salvatore's leg, whose hands were both clasped very tightly around a wine glass. Mario retreated to his table with the bridal couple and it was Nella who, when she discovered what had happened and realised that Mario had ordered Emmanuel out, began to move the drama forward. It took some effort from her immediate family to settle her down, as she considered Mario's handling of the situation totally exaggerated and she knew very well that this beautiful grandson of hers was probably never going to darken her doorstep ever again.

'Darling, the food was ghastly,' complained Emmanuel, driving back to the city. 'I loathe these occasions. Thank goodness we got away. Actually I'm starving. Shall we call into our favourite restaurant? We may just be in time for something.'

'Why not?' smiled Angela.

She had seen Emmanuel angry with his father often, but this social exercise today made it very clear to her that this twenty-year-old was someone to be reckoned with socially. She also realised that a return to his paternal grandparents and cousins was now very much a thing of the past.

Driving home, Kerry looked at Salvatore. 'I don't suppose it could have been worse,' she murmured in a dejected way.

'They could have thrown bottles at one another!' said Salvatore sarcastically. 'Why, oh why is Emmanuel always so difficult?'

'Darling, they shouldn't have sat us at different tables. I suppose I should have told Nella that he was coming with Angela and would want to remain seated with her. I just never thought of it. Oh well, the wedding finished smoothly, thank goodness.'

'Mario is an arsehole as well,' spat Salvatore. 'To order my son out of the reception is unforgivable.'

'Even if what Emmanuel did was unnecessary,' sighed Kerry. 'It will be interesting to see how the future wedding invitations will be worded.' She laughed. 'Come on, darling, it's not the end of the world.' She squeezed his arm, and though he turned to her the movement on his lips could not be described as a smile.

As usual, Kerry caught the flack. The next day her telephone rang constantly from her in-laws, saying how shocked they were with Mario's performance and how terrible for poor Emmanuel. Not one word was said about Emmanuel baiting Mario. It was, of course, Nella who was the most upset and had called both Kerry and Salvatore to explain how upset she was about everything and her poor beautiful grandson. Salvatore did not elaborate on Emmanuel's social behaviour. Emmanuel continued the following week as if nothing had happened and even Salvatore decided that it was probably the best way to handle it.

Emmanuel had also learned how to handle an auction room. He was a very aggressive bidder and at a recent sale showed this. Angela had seen a painting in a large house sale that was to be auctioned the following Thursday. They had been twice to see it; the catalogue read 'in the French 18th century manner' and the estimated price was marked beside it. 'I'm sure we can get it for much less,' he said with a smile.

The day of the action saw a particularly packed sale room but both Angela and Emmanuel were sure the byers were there for three very important modern Australian paintings. There were 220 lots and the one they sought was 112 in the category marked 'European Paintings'. They arrived early, just to gauge the market and found the prices high. Angela gave Emmanuel the limit she would bid for this canvas and eventually, in the early afternoon, the auctioneer announced 'Lot No. 112, a painting in the 18th century French style' and the bidding began. Emmanuel was very aggressive and the bidding petered out, leaving only him and a woman sitting uncomfortably close to them. He bid quickly. Every time the woman raised her hand, Emmanuel's was instantly lifted, taking the bids higher. 'Against you,' said the auctioneer, looking at the woman, who glanced sideways at Emmanuel with his arm ready to lift again. She shook her head, the hammer went down and Angela was the proud owner of this 18th century painting. Emmanuel's aggressive bidding had saved Angela a vast amount of money. The painting had only just reached the reserve and so a smiling pair headed off for drinks at a smart hotel, satisfied that all had gone well.

This love of French things was the result of Angela taking Emmanuel to Paris for his school holidays when he was about fourteen years old. A deluxe apartment and all of Paris, it seemed, at his feet, and for the first time in his life he genuinely began to learn. Angela was an excellent teacher, as were her friends in Paris. Emmanuel had found an art field and he became totally devoted to it, the French 18th century. Versailles for Emmanuel was nothing short of paradise, even though it was winter: in Paris he didn't feel the cold. He absorbed this magnificent culture and just drank and drank from it. With Angela's friends, their days were spent going from one magnificent house to another magnificent palace. It never stopped. The gilt furniture, the exquisite silk fabrics, the marvellous bronzes and the porcelain. Oh the porcelain! How he loved it all and he learnt for the first time. It was a subject he was interested in; all the decorative arts from this period were for him magic and as he had a very retentive memory he never forgot anything.

The flea market in Paris was for him wonderful. Here not only could you look at beautiful things, you could also acquire them and this Angela and Emmanuel did, with Emmanuel instantly grasping the process of bargaining. So once again Angela spent, but with Emmanuel's keen sense of getting a good price she spent much less.

They were the perfect travelling companions. They needed one another but they never smothered each other. It was indeed the perfect balance. Emmanuel also had fun but discreetly. A beautiful creature like him never had to wait long for anybody, especially someone to share his bed. But he never prolonged a relationship. It was like purchasing a piece of furniture: the drama to get it at the right time, with the quality right. It was the same with men; once he had had them it was particularly rare he would have sex with them a second time. Needless to say there were many broken hearts scattered around Emmanuel's feet. Once Emmanuel left school these trips to Paris became more regular. At least twice a year Emmanuel and Angela were seen heading off again to France. They never went anywhere else: Emmanuel just wasn't interested in going anywhere but just to Paris and so that was where they went and spent.

The oddest thing, according to Kerry, was Angela's big dinner parties, which occurred generally twice a month. The large dining room in cream and gold, obviously in the French manner, was filled with eight other people apart from Emmanuel and her. She sat at one end of the huge table and, if available, Kerry at the other. If she was not there then Emmanuel sat there but generally he sat on Angela's right hand side. It was only men that made up these deluxe evenings, and Salvatore fitted in remarkably well. As Kerry could never fathom, on these evenings, father and son never crossed swords verbally. Both allowed the other his point of view, with perhaps just a few gentle jibes but showing a complete harmony. Even Angela found this odd as well and many a time when alone with Kerry this subject came up. Perhaps, mused Angela, this was due to Salvatore being in Emmanuel's world, all gay men, and he felt there was no need to take his usual aggressive attitude with his son. Or was it, thought Angela, that just by Salvatore being present and having a good time Emmanuel saw it as his father's acceptance of his sexuality? Salvatore had never broached his view of Emmanuel's sexuality; Angela and Kerry had always spoken openly about it. Both were genuinely concerned about who would end up being Mt. Right for him. However, Salvatore chose not to see it or perhaps it was easier to assume that he was just going through a phase, supported by a very rich and dominating grandmother. Not even in those moments when Kerry and Salvatore were alone, no matter how Kerry moved the conversation, Salvatore never seemed as if he understood what she was talking about. She came to the conclusion, as she said to Angela, 'There are none so blind as those who won't see,' and that was that. So the subject of Emmanuel's sexuality at No. 10 Ashfield Avenue was extremely different from it at No. 6.

Every so often, Angela, being Angela, demanded that Kerry and Salvatore attend a dinner. Needless to say Emmanuel was always present when the only one of her relations she ever received was able to dine with her. Monsignor Michael Christie was her first cousin and they had always been very close. The jokes and smart repartee never stopped and if Salvatore felt a little formal, the rest definitely did not. Kerry and Mary had grown up with Mons, as he was called, and adored him. As time progressed, this early affection had cemented itself into an immovable love. He thought both Vince and Emmanuel were splendid and was extremely happy when Vince first went to him about accepting his vocation. Needless to say, all doors were immediately opened to him.

From when he was a very little boy, Emmanuel and the Mons had been inseparable. Emmanuel adored him. He was a very handsome man, Monsignor Christie, of medium height with a very fine face with strong features, but he had the softest green eyes that gave a hint of knowing a great deal more than he was letting on. It was a regular occurrence now that every second week, when 'the Mons' was not so busy, a Mercedes would ferry Emmanuel and him to a very smart restaurant in the city for lunch and lots of funny stories. Repartee would be the result. It turned out with time that Emmanuel and Mons became closer and closer as friends. Although the Monsignor had been delighted with Vince's acceptance of his vocation, he had known right from the start that Emmanuel was not going to follow the same path. Sometimes Emmanuel would exasperate him with his ideas and Emmanuel was completely honest with him. But come the end of a luncheon or dinner party and he always looked forward to seeing him again.

Monsignor Christie had had an excellent noviciate and in a very short time had moved up the hierarchical ladder. He had been a priest in a small country parish for five years, Sitwell by name, and it was a place that was to have a profound influence in the future on Emmanuel's life. He had been recalled to the Cathedral as he was an expert in Latin and ceremonial and had never moved from there for the rest of his life. When one of the old monsignors died a year later, the Archbishop installed him as Monsignor Michael Christie at a very early age: not all in the ecclesiastical world thought that this rapid promotion was really something he deserved but obviously the Archbishop had other ideas. He had gone from strength to strength and a magenta cassock at Mass with beautiful Irish lace over it assured all that his position in the Cathedral was not be under-estimated. He always had fond memories of his first parish at Sitwell, which now seemed like a hundred years ago though he was still connected to it due to Kerry's sister, Mary. She had married Keven O'Shanassey, who had, or should we say his parents had, a large property about six kilometres out of Sitwell. Whenever he saw Mary, this was always a subject that was brought up again and again, with Monsignor Christie ever curious to know what was happening in this rural district.

This evening at Angela's, with Kerry and Salvatore, drinks were held in Angela's elegant drawing room. The staff, when Monsignor was present, were always very nervous. They never relaxed when he was present whereas with Angela's other male friends this never occurred. Bang went the front door. 'I'm sorry I'm late!' cried Emmanuel as he rounded the corner of the hallway into the drawing room and kissed everyone. He had always used this Italian form of greeting and many of Angela's friends waited patiently for it. 'I have to change. It's been a dramatic day,' at which he laughed as he dashed upstairs.

'What are you doing for Christmas?' asked Angela, looking at Michael.

'Oh, I think we shall all be exhausted.' He laughed. 'Midnight Mass and then three more Masses in the Cathedral – a full day.'

'I don't see why you can't dash over here, cassock and all, and have lunch, or if that's not convenient, come for dinner.'

'I'll let you know.' He smiled at her and went on, looking at the painting on the wall, 'Angela, is that a recent acquisition?'

'Yes, it is. Emmanuel and I got it at auction last month. I was very happy about it and the price. Emmanuel is really fabulous at auction.'

'Not only at auction,' came a shout from Emmanuel as he entered and automatically refilled their glasses with a big grin.

'I think you get worse every year,' joked Michael.

'Oh, I do. Isn't that seen as progress?'

'Depends,' Michael replied. 'And how's business, Salvatore?'

'Good. Needless to say, Christmas rushes are always the same. Not all of us have Emmanuel's lifestyle.' Michael noticed the comment.

'Eat your heart out!' was Emmanuel only reply to his father and Kerry immediately changed the conversation.

'Mum tells me you are going into vestment restoration.'

'Me personally? No. But times have changed and the wheel of fashion for the church is returning, so we may as well be ahead of things.'

'What change in fashion?' Emmanuel asked, seating himself on a French chair that he drew up closer to Michael.

'Well, the cathedral had a big collection of fine vestments but when the new style came in, the casula, the old chasubles, just got stacked away and now out they come and the repairs begin. Some of them are in a shocking state,'

'What's the difference between a casula and a chasuble?' asked Emmanuel.

'Good taste!' was Angel's sharp retort and Michael laughed.

'My cousin is a traditionalist and so hates change,' and before he could explain to Emmanuel the difference between these two vestment types Kerry did so in layman's terms.

'A chasuble is a vestment that was used here in Australia and basically all over the world until after Vatican Two. It is cut away at the shoulders and a piece of fabric hangs at the back and front of the priest. Often these panels were embroidered. Then, later, the fashion changed and instead we got these floppy things you see now at Mass, where this tent-like thing reaches down to the end of the arms.

'Oh, someone else who doesn't like casulas,' laughed Michael.

'You all look like overweight mums at the supermarket,' said Angela, which had Emmanuel in hysterical laughter. He had a very deep laugh and it was very infectious.

'Darling,' chipped in Angela, addressing him, 'don't you remember when we were in Paris and went to the Museum of Notre Dame. You saw the vestments donated by the Empress Eugenia?'

'Oh yes, I do. Oh, so that's what you're talking about!'

To Salvatore this subject made no sense at all.

'Well, Mons,' smiled Emmanuel, I take it you are going to be the trail blazer in the vestment world, returning to grandeur and chic?'

'You never know,' was the reply.

The maid announced that dinner was served and with that they all moved to the dining room.

'How's Mary?' asked Michael. 'I received a Christmas card only yesterday from her.'

'The same, it appears,' answered Angela. 'I have no idea why she spends so much time in that dry landscape when she has a house right next door. It isn't that she has a family to look after.'

Kerry knew very well that Mary and Angela were so similar that they did anything but complement one another. Mary was extremely outspoken and this often annoyed Angela, who could be blamed for the same approach as Mary.

'Well, what was the exhausting day?' Angela asked.

'I met and had a drink with Nella in town. She was so insistent.'

'How is she?' Salvatore asked, realising he had not spoken to her since the wedding episode.

'The same,' was the offhand reply. 'She tells me Mario is having problems with your father,' he continued to Salvatore, who commented, 'It's their own fault. Neither has the foresight to expand properly, so little by little, if they don't re-organise themselves, they are going to end up in economic hot water.'

'I'm sorry for granddad, but Mario can die with his secret.' Michael turned his head a little but did not pass a comment. 'Anyway, I've said to Nella that perhaps you may invite her over for a Christmas drink as I am not going over there.'

'Thanks a lot,' Kerry replied and Salvatore just sighed. This push and pull with his family exhausted him and he knew very well that Emmanuel inflamed the situation. He was more than happy to see his family but now, preferably, without Mario. But to invite them all over for a drink was the last thing in the world he wanted before Christmas and he knew that Nella would be waiting for him to telephone her for the time and date.

As Salvatore lay in bed, he looked at the large chandelier suspended from the centre of the room. Kerry always knew that this was a sign that he was not content. She slipped an arm around his broad shoulder. 'Let's get it over and done with as soon as possible. Look, if we have them for drinks, here, there can't possibly be the blackmail of having to go to your parents' for Christmas lunch.'

'Want to bet?' he said slowly. 'And you know Mario's going to come.'

'He may not, after the wedding situation. He may just lie low.'

'He won't,' Salvatore argued, knowingly. 'And what the hell are we going to do about Emmanuel? Have you thought about that?'

'Darling, if Mario is at No. 10, Emmanuel is sure to be a No. 6. There is no love lost between either of them.'

The date and time was set for the drinks, and Salvatore booked an Italian restaurant close by, so everyone was free to attend or not. For

Kerry, trying to organise numbers and tables with Nella did not turn out to be the simplest thing in the world. But if Kerry was surprised at Emmanuel's help and assistance, Salvatore was astounded. He knew Emmanuel did not get along with his family and everyone blamed that on Kerry, not on Angela as it should have been. She point blank refused to have anything to do with them except Salvatore, to whom she was very attached. Salvatore had this uneasy feeling that Emmanuel knew more about this coming evening than he was letting on, and he was dead right!

The afternoon when Emmanuel took it upon himself to invite Nella and her immediate family over to a drink in a smart hotel in the city, he spelt out very clearly to her that if Mario put a foot in No. 10 Ashfield Avenue, then he, Emmanuel, would never speak to any of them again. This placed Nella in the most difficult of situations, and to explain to her elder son, who was a regular visitor to her home, that the twenty year old Emmanuel had barred him from taking part in a family celebration for Christmas at his brother's home. This drove Mario into a rampage of screaming and banging his fists down on Nella's table, upsetting a glass of wine and sending food in all directions. The expletives he used to describe Emmanuel really do not deserve to be translated from Italian into English! Nella's tears eventually quietened the situation down, but if Mario was jealous of Salvatore's financial success his hate for Emmanuel knew no bounds.

Emmanuel was charm personified, helping all, checking that the waiters were efficient, speaking to everyone, even those in the past he had cut dead. It was then that Salvatore realised that as Mario had not attended this evening and Emmanuel had the look of the cat that had got the cream, that all was not as it seemed. He noticed a very nervous Nella, but as the evening moved on everyone relaxed and a good-looking, tall, blonde waiter slipped into Emmanuel's pocket his address and telephone number.

'Well, it wasn't too bad,' said a contented Emmanuel, with a smile, when the evening was over. 'And just think, Salvatore, you won't be forced to put up with a raucous Christmas lunch.' Emmanuel always used Salvatore's Christian name when addressing him. It had annoyed his father originally but now he just accepted it as normal.

'I noticed Mario wasn't present,' said Salvatore as he had a drink with Kerry after the evening was over. He looked directly at him. 'Wise man,' he responded in a rather superior way. 'Emmanuel, what did you organise with Nella for this evening? I noticed she was a little agitated.'

'Oh, you know Nella. She is impossible to organise.'

'She's not the only one!' replied Salvatore sharply and he knew very well that his elder brother's non-attendance had most certainly had something to do with his son.

Angela as usual took over when Christmas lunch arrangements were made. Salvatore and Kerry surrendered and just went along with the tide. Kerry received a call from her sister to find out how the lie of the land was as she had not given Angela a yes or no for this Christmas lunch.

'Oh, do come, Mary. At least I shall have another woman to talk to,' knowing very well what Angela's table arrangements would be.

'How did the wedding go?' Mary asked curiously.

'The wedding was exactly what one would expect, 220 rowdy guests and Emmanuel and Angela stalking out. Oh, I can't tell you! Salvatore was furious at everybody. Anyway, I'll tell you all when I see you.'

'OK. The day after tomorrow. It's completely dead up here.' Mary hung up and then made two calls, one to Angela, announcing her arrival and another to Mrs. Browning, saying she must have No. 8 Ashfield Avenue in tip-top condition, then hung up.

Mrs. Browning actually lived at No. 8. Behind the large house had been a stable and this had been converted into a very pleasant flat where Mrs. Browning controlled all at No. 8. She had worked for Mary for nigh on thirty years and although Mary was rarely resident, the house and grounds were kept in immaculate order. The expression 'tip-top condition' simply meant fresh flowers for the two reception rooms.

Mary's and Kerry's houses were identical but the interiors were not. Mary's house was furnished in a grand Victorian manner, with damask and good quality antiques. The house was noted for the extremely abundant curtains throughout: whereas ten metres would have been sufficient for Mary or Mary's decorator, needless to say a great friend of Angela's had used twenty so the house had a very formal deluxe look about it, with chandeliers everywhere. But this house, in contrast to Angela's mansion next door, was seen as quite tame. Angela had decorated her two storeyed mansion in the French style and the abundance of gilt furniture was amazing. Despite the vast quantities of it the house seemed much lighter due to the gilt and there were mirrors and paintings everywhere. Huge Aubusson carpets lined the floors in soft beiges and rose and the whole effect was of an easy grandeur. Emmanuel adored it. His suite upstairs was in the same style as the rest of the house but he had insisted on something a little more dramatic and so it was in shades of raspberry, cream and gilt, just the thing for a twenty-year-old, if your name happens to be Emmanuel. Of the three houses only Angela had a pool in the back garden, neatly and tastefully landscaped and Emmanuel was often seen in this hot season splashing about, with Angela taking a drink on the side under a large umbrella.

Kerry and Salvatore's home, although matching on the exterior with Mary's was completely different inside. It had been physically altered and a huge section added across the back which virtually became the area that they lived in. The great glass expanse overlooked a lush back garden that Kerry was very proud of. It was a space that she spent hours in and it showed the result of a careful, loving hand. The large area across the back was floored in white marble, giving the maximum contrast between a lush green space outside and a cool architectural interior. The house was furnished inside in a very modern, international way, modern Italian furniture from Milan mixed with antique Chinese pieces and ceramics. The whole space was a calm co-ordinated, sophisticated space that was very easy to live in. As Emmanuel grew older, he would accept this style but as he said to Kerry, the French interior of No. 6 was just him. She did not reply. But this house was where Kerry and Salvatore spent most of their time. They had no staff, although they could have afforded them. A woman came twice a week and cleaned but that was it. Kerry was the home-maker and loved it. In a certain sense she was glad Angela had taken over Emmanuel as it left this large space for her and Salvatore, who loved nothing better than when they were alone to cook for them both. It was his special love and he was very good at it.

'Darling, do come and have a drink,' cried Angela, and Emmanuel hauled himself from the pool. Grandson or not, Angela firmly believed he was the finest, most handsome man in the world and walking towards her only clad in a small swim brief this vision only convinced her she was right. The tanned skin which became quite dark, the shock of black thick hair, those electric blue eyes, and his ease of movement gave Angela this odd thought that Mr. Right was going to be the happiest and luckiest man in the world.

'Darling, did I tell you Mary has deigned to join us for Christmas?'

'Great!' was his reply. 'How long will she be here for?'

'I haven't a clue. You know her, here for a week and then back to the bush. Really, I don't know what she does there all alone. It's been years since Keven died. Oh well, at least she will have a pleasant time with us this year. Kerry tells me Vince is also coming and so is the Mons. I got a call this afternoon. It all sounds just perfect.'

'I think Mum and Salvatore are planning a light dinner in the evening, so that should be OK,' said Emmanuel, as he stretched his long dark legs out in front of him and helped himself to a drink. 'Something casual after the formal lunch sounds perfect,' he went on, in an off-hand way.

'Really?' Angela spoke sharply. 'Do you realise that it's less than a week to Christmas and that wretched restorer has not returned the dome. I shall be furious if it's not all ready for Christmas lunch.'

The dome Angela was referring to was a large gilded structure that sat on a glazed octagonal base that had all but two of the sections glazed. It looked like a small temple but it held Angela's pride and joy, a Neapolitan Christmas scene. She and Emmanuel had this year, as they had every year, taken from two large trunks all the little figures and animals to construct a Nativity scene, but due to an accident in one of the storerooms of Angela's home the large dome that surmounted this extravaganza had dropped and a section of the carving had been broken and the gilding chipped. The Nativity scene was all complete, but there was no dome, and as Monsignor Christie and Vince were to be present, this tended to make Angela all the more agitated. Salvatore had worked out years ago that the perfect gift for Angela was another figure to add to this scene and as he had a contact who had a lot of them for sale he had bought them all, mostly in poor condition, and sent them out a month or so for restoration, one at a time, for Angela's birthday and Christmas gifts. It was unlike Angela to get carried away about gifts but she was like a small child, ever so anxious to see just what was in Salvatore's present each time. Needless to say, this large structure that held all the figures had had to be enlarged twice and it gave Angela many hours of worry to organise and design the case so it could be enlarged to take yet another figure or animal.

'Mrs. Christie!' came a call from the house. 'There's a man at the front door with the lid for the Christmas figures.'

'Coming!' shouted Angela. 'A lid! Really, I don't know what staff are coming to these days.' She stood up to go out, leaving Emmanuel laughing at her indignation.

'Mary, come in,' Kerry greeted her sister, as Mary swept through to the living room overlooking the back garden. 'A drink?'

'Need you ask?' Kerry went to the far side of the living area that contained an ultra-modern kitchen and in a moment was seated with her sister, catching up with all the family gossip.

'How has Angela been behaving herself,' Mary asked bluntly.

'Just the same. She and Emmanuel are really unstoppable.' She repeated the wedding incident.

'Sounds ghastly,' Mary commented.

'Angela is a terrible influence on Emmanuel. It often has Salvatore exasperated.'

'How do Emmanuel and Salvatore hit it off?'

'Well, it's a bit better now, as he virtually lives full time with Angela. Sometimes I don't see him for a week or so. You know what Angela's like.' Mary certainly did.

Both Kerry and Mary were tall but there the family resemblance stopped. Kerry was light blonde with a beautiful face, soft classic features, slim and dressed with a great sense of style, though very low key. This could not be said of Mary, who was dark, with an extremely sculptured face always heavily made up, also slim but perhaps a fraction more solid than Kerry. She was never without high heeled shoes that made her seem even taller. She could only be described as theatrical in attitude, appearance and dress sense. Needless to say Emmanuel adored her. Her one-liners were deadly and she made every comment a winner. She was quite fond of Kerry's handsome husband but hadn't seen him for almost a year; nor had she seen Emmanuel and she was looking forward to doing so. The same cannot be said about Angela, whom Mary found suffocating and extremely bossy. It didn't take long before the two of them crossed swords verbally, and as usual, at times like this, it was Kerry who was the go-between peacemaker.

'What are you doing for dinner?' Kerry asked.

'Nothing. Can I take you and Salvatore out for a meal?'

'No. Listen, Angela and Emmanuel are off to a so-called smart pre-Christmas dinner party somewhere, so why don't you join Salvatore and me here for dinner – unless you want to get back into the social swing of Melbourne!'

'I'd love to join you both, but I had better go down and check in with Mumsy first.' She laughed. Mary had a full-throated laugh, almost masculine, and when in full flight socially you knew exactly by this particular laugh where she was.

'This way, please.' Mary was shown into Angela's large reception room, with Angela arguing about the dome not fitting properly.

'Well, nothing changes!' commented Mary. 'How are you?'

'Don't ask. I have a logistic problem on my hands. Go through. Emmanuel's at the pool. I'll join you in a moment,' and with that dismissal Mary headed out to the pool.

'Mary, you look divine,' exclaimed Emmanuel and rushed over to hold her in his arms.

'Darling! And don't little boys grow up!' as she surveyed his near-naked body. 'Someone will kill for you, sweetie,' and he laughed.

'A drink?'

'Just a glass or two,' she smiled. I believe you and Angela are out tonight.'

'Why don't you come with us? I can telephone. It won't be a problem. Oh, do say yes.'

Mary looked at this vision as she accepted a glass of champagne. He was beautiful, she thought, and everything was in the right place. What a stunner! 'Darling, I can't, but I will tell you what, you can take me to lunch tomorrow.

'I'd love to. Oh, how marvellous that you've come to have Christmas with us.'

'Mario's not joining us,' Mary teased.

'Hardly,' was his sarcastic reply. 'He is definitely someone or something in the past.'

'Well, darling, I'm dying to hear your side of the story. Lunch tomorrow. I'll let you go and get changed.'

'Good heavens, is that the time?' he exclaimed, emptying his glass in one gulp. He gave Mary as kiss. 'I'll see you tomorrow for lunch. Glad you're here.' Off he sped across the lawn toward the house in his swim briefs, with a towel draped over one shoulder. Mary just stared after him. They were quite close, Mary and Emmanuel. When together, they complemented one another and Mary's theatrical appearance and gestures endeared her to Emmanuel all the more. Therein lay a great problem, namely Angela, who was extremely jealous of Mary's rapport with him, and if she felt threatened as regards someone moving in on what she considered exclusively her territory, sparks began to fly.

Mary moved back toward the immaculately kept mansion and into the reception room where it appeared the large gilt dome was finally in its correct position, with Angela surveying the final result.

'I'll see you the day after tomorrow,' said Mary. 'If you want me to do something to help the festive lunch along, give me a call. By the way, I believe unless you scurry off you are going to be late for a dinner engagement.

'God! Is that the time!' gasped Angela, looking at the magnificent French clock on the marble mantle. 'Fine! Fine! I will catch up tomorrow,' and with a final look at the Nativity scene, she hurried upstairs to change so as not to keep Emmanuel waiting.

Mary went next door to her house and unpacked her things, then walked slowly through this beautiful home, just drinking in the atmosphere, as she had not been there for almost a year. 'Yes, it is beautiful,' she thought, confidently. 'A pity Angela's next door~!' She then showered and changed before going to Kerry, calling Mrs Browning to say that most likely there would be a dinner party or two but she would give her ample notice, and if she needed assistance to simply hire it. As she moved down her tessellated front path and closed the big cast iron front gate, she noticed a Mercedes pull up right beside her because of limited parking further on, and Salvatore hopped out.

'Well, how are we, handsome?' Mary smiled on recognising him at once.

'I'm fine,' at which he moved around and embraced her. 'You have been away for too long.'

'Thanks. Can I give you a hand with the parcels?' she asked, looking at the back seat of his car, littered with things.

'No, no, I have it all organised,' and he led her into the house arm in arm.

'Kerry!' he cried and she came up the corridor to his beck and call. She kissed him and then looked perplexed, 'but Salvatore, the food!'

'It's all organised. Have a drink with Mary and I'll get going.'

The two sisters sat in the living area, overlooking the garden, while Salvatore ferried supermarket bags and parcels from his car to the kitchen. Then he disappeared into the shower, changed and was back with them.

'Don't worry; Salvatore is the chef tonight, so you won't starve.'

'I'm sure I shan't,' she agreed. 'I saw Emmanuel at Angela's pool this afternoon. He really is a good looking young man and just as quick as ever.'

'It's a pity his interest doesn't match his good looks,' commented Salvatore, who also thought his son beautiful.

Mary picked up the sharp comment. 'I wouldn't worry, Salvatore. It appears Angela has everything in hand.'

'That is exactly the problem,' he said sitting down with them. 'She indulges him in a most terrible way. Everything he wants he gets.'

'Lucky him' Mary said. 'I think he is terribly brave. Personally my experience of living with Angela comes very close to the word 'purgatory'. She is just impossible, and I am sure age has not tempered her at all.' She finished her glass, which Kerry refilled.

'He has no sense of business, or of doing anything useful, just dashing off with Angela to another opening, an auction or a restaurant. He is simply a cricket in summer. When the winter comes he'll know all about it.' Salvatore stood up and went to the kitchen and continued the conversion across the bar which was high and visually hid the working of a sophisticated kitchen.

'I don't think winter will ever come for Emmanuel,' Kerry said. 'He is just too well insulated with Angela and if something ever happened to her I am sure No. 6 and everything in it plus the finance to keep it all going will be handed on to him. Personally I couldn't bear living in that gilded cocoon but Emmanuel loves it.'

'She has ruined him,' insisted Salvatore, banging a saucepan down.'

'If that is your definition of ruin then Emmanuel's a lucky boy,' said Mary. 'Oh, by the way, how's business, Salvatore?'

'Actually, it's great. I have brought out a whole new range of prepared flooring tiles, you know, the marble square with cut-off corners and a small square of generally black marble set into the void. Well, I have found a deep honey gold Persian travertine which looks great with the white marble, as does the terracotta marble, and I have just signed a contract a week ago for a hotel in the city. They are re-vamping, so the business is booming, thank goodness. I'm afraid it's not so good for my family's business. Mario refuses to change or update his merchandising, so I am told, via Emmanuel, they are not doing well at all.'

'I've heard a whisper that Emmanuel and Mario are not exchanging Christmas cards this year,' Mary offered, wickedly.

'Don't start me!' Salvatore warned. 'By the way, you do like seafood, don't you?'

'I adore it, darling. Kerry, when does Vince arrive?'

'Christmas Day, and he's staying with us for two days and then he's back to the seminary.'

'But I thought he was ordained,' said Mary, in a surprised way.

'He is, but as he was outstanding they held him over for a year to do extra study and to help train the new novitiates. Vince is more their age, and it seems to be a formula that works. But he is breaking his neck for his own parish, so if you see him and the Mons chatting quietly, you can bet Vince is trying to put pressure on him to get a parish of his own.'

'You know, I haven't seen Vince for literally years,' Mary commented. 'How does he look?'

'He's very handsome,' interrupted Salvatore, 'and in clerical garb looks very impressive.' He smiled like a proud father, thought Mary. 'And what about your life in the country? You must be very busy, as we see you so rarely nowadays.'

'Oh, I keep myself busy,' Mary replied, smiling, 'and while I am down this time I just might pop out to your yard and have a look at some marble flooring. I think it's time to smarten up the bush homestead.'

'Well, you are in for a surprise,' said Kerry.

'Really? Why ?'

'Well, Salvatore has purchased the huge block of land beside his business and built a new showroom and offices. It looks very smart.'

'Well, I shall be delighted to have a look. I'm having lunch with Emmanuel tomorrow. Perhaps I can make arrangements for him to escort me to have a good look around the new showrooms.'

'It'll probably be only the second or third time he has set foot in the place,' Salvatore said, sharply. It was then that Mary realised that Salvatore believed quite firmly that Emmanuel's place in this life was working with his father in this now thriving business, but the sharpness of his tone indicated that Emmanuel had other ideas about his future.

'You know, the thing I hate about Christmas is buying gifts. I never know what to buy,' Mary complained, 'and I am sure when everyone says it's just divine they can't wait to throw it in the rubbish bin. I think this year we should discuss about giving this gift thing a miss. If we want to do something, the money we would have spent could be sent to a charity or something. What do you think?' She tilted her head to one side.

'There is going to be trouble from Angela,' answered Kerry.

'There always is!' was Mary's retort.

'Well, you know how she just lives for Salvatore's gift of a figure or an animal for her Italian nativity scene. I'm certain she is not going to give that up.'

'Suppose not. By the way, Salvatore, what happens when the figures run out?'

'I guess I shall have to have someone import them for me from Naples. You know there is a whole street that just sells these figures and objects for these Nativity scenes. It's quite amazing. I saw it on the television a couple of weeks ago.'

'I'm surprised Angela hasn't hopped on a plane and dashed to the spot to buy.'

'It's unlikely,' said Kerry. 'Emmanuel and Angela are Francophiles and so it's only to Paris for them.'

'Come on! Dinner's ready,' called Salvatore. They moved to the prepared dining area to enjoy Salvatore's splendid meal and to compare notes as to who would be present at Angela's the day after tomorrow, as she had insisted on keeping it all a secret.

CHAPTER TWO

Emmanuel in Love

CHAPTER TWO

Emmanuel in Love

'Come in! Come in!' cried Emmanuel, playing host to all. Eventually the last guest, being Vince, arrived. 'How are we all?' he asked, as he kissed Kerry and then Mary and obviously Angela. There were handshakes for the men but a hug for Salvatore.

Salvatore was right, Mary thought. In clericals, Vince looked divine. After drinks and the obligatory admiration of the Nativity scene, she was seen sitting between Vince and Monsignor Christie, and her forceful laughter took over that side of the table. Before they began, Angela motioned all to silence and Michael smiled. 'This year I shall renege on my responsibilities and hand the honour to Father Vincenzo.'

Vince rose as automatically did the other nine guests. 'Benedictus benedicat per Christum Dominum nostrum.'

'Amen,' chorused everyone, and sat down. The noise became louder as the guests attempted conversation from one part of the table to the other.

'Paul, I need your help,' shouted Mary, looking amazing all in black, with the most electric red lipstick and heavy eye make-up.

'Mary, for you anything, but only on one condition.'

'Oh, sweetie, what's that?' she asked.

'That this time, as you have finally hit civilisation you dine with Anthony and me or no help. Oh, and by the way, what do you want?' he asked. Paul and Anthony were an institution. They were a little older than Kerry and Mary but not much. They had been together for years and constant guests at Angela's table. Paul was a decorator and Anthony worked – or it should be said correctly – owned a very successful real estate business.

'Darling,' Mary continued, 'you must simply come to the bush. The homestead really is the pits. I need a new outlook on life.'

'Ever thought of a man?' chipped in Emmanuel, to everyone's laughter.

'Been there, done that,' was Mary's swift reply. 'I am this week going with Emmanuel to have a look at flooring at Salvatore's so we shall see what happens.'

'Mary, it will be a pleasure,' and he turned, as he was sitting next to Angela, to describe a beautiful French chair he had seen and was she interested in it. From the intense interest in this subject, she was obviously in the affirmative.

'Well, tell me about Sitwell. What's happening up there?' asked Michael.

'It gets worse and worse,' moaned Mary dramatically. 'Cattle, sheep – I don't think anyone thinks anything else. So boring ! The men are tiresome, the women vipers, so it doesn't leave a girl much to think about.'

'How is the local priest working out?' asked Michael, knowing full well what the answer was going to be.'

'Him!' Mary's voice was raised as she emptied yet another glass. 'He is so mediocre as to be totally forgettable. Not a clue, Mons, not a clue. And as for that Deacon – enough said.'

Michael had heard this from Cathedral circles and Vince listened intently to Mary gathering pace in her description of one parish problem after another.

'I say, Vince,' she said, turning to look at his handsome face. 'What's your Latin like?'

'OK, he replied. 'I can say a Latin Mass, if that's what you're asking me about.'

'Wearing what?' asked Emmanuel. 'Hopefully not those ghastly casula things?'

'Since when were you interested in ecclesiastical vestments?' responded Vince in a surprised way.

'We all have standards.' Emmanuel came back.

Vince narrowed is eyes. 'Careful, little brother!' he warned, and so the lunch continued in Angela's elegant cream and gilt dining room, with sharp repartee from all. Even Kerry had a few sharp but funny words to keep the social ball rolling.

The other two gentlemen that made up this table of ten were Robert Anson and Keven Tilley, again friends of Angela, but Robert was also a very good friend of Keven. Whenever a dinner party or a group function was organised these two separate men joined in. But it was Keven who was totally besotted with Emmanuel. He thought that only once in a lifetime could one see and obviously discreetly touch a god and here he was, the most gorgeous, lovable, adorable – and if one let Keven go on with adjectives to describe the one person in his world he adored he would continue all day. Kerry and Mary had also known Keven for years and always bolstered him up when he thought he might never live through another day without seeing Emmanuel, 'the most beautiful thing in the world, that just gets better every day', being his plaintive cry. Salvatore thought it all a bit silly but he didn't find it a problem, and Keven was also a guest at their home. But for Keven it was generally when Emmanuel wasn't present. Kerry worked

41

out it was the only way to get any sense out of him. But today he could gaze like a Labrador waiting for his master to take him for a walk.

'Mons,' said Vince, as in this casual situation it was how he addressed him, as he had all his growing years, 'I don't suppose you have put a word in for me for a parish?'

'Vince, don't you think you would be happier at the cathedral?'

'No, not yet. I think I need some real experience with people. At the cathedral it's all very formal – not that I don't like that, but I would like to take it step by step.' He stopped, had a drink and continued, 'Just like you did.'

Michael smiled and reached into his jacket pocket. 'See if this suits you, Father.'

Conversation at the table dropped and Vince took an envelope from Michael's hand. He looked at the address on the front: 'Fr. Vincenzo Lampedusa'. He duly opened the unsealed envelope and read the contents.

'Wow!' was his only response and he stood and walked behind Mary and embraced Michael from behind. 'Thanks, Mons, thanks very much.'

Well,' Mary asked, 'what's it all about.

'It's my first parish.'

'Congratulations Vince. Where?'

He handed her the letter, smiling from ear to ear.

'God!' was Mary's loud exclamation. 'Sitwell. Darling, how divine! At least one intelligent soul! Oh how divine! Oh, Vince, you can't possibly live in that hovel by the new church. You must come and live with me. It's only six kilometres away. Oh yes, you must live with me. Paul, darling, the renovations to 'Bantry' must be started at once.'

'It will be Vince's responsibility to live in the canonica,' said Michael.

'Canonica!' Mary screamed, very loudly. 'It happens to be a substandard flat, nowadays, Mons, not as it was in your time. Low ceilings, the rooms as small as a matchbox and in summer basically a torture chamber of heat. Oh no, darling, that just won't do at all. I will get on to Sarah Higgins this afternoon. Don't worry, darling, all will be well.'

Salvatore had the overwhelming feeling that no matter what he did in this world, his sons were never his. Emmanuel was Angela's and now Vince was moving into Mary's orbit and it left him with the feeling of abandonment in a certain sense, that the two sons in his own way he loved were being drawn further and further away from him. It was Kerry who sensed Salvatore's loss as Mary continued to take over Vince. She took hold of his hand and was aware of a firm grasp in reply.

'Now, Vince,' said Emmanuel, teasing him, 'only chasubles. Remember style, Vincenzo,' and laughed. They had an indifferent relationship. Vince and Emmanuel, and eight years difference never saw them together much. Although they liked one another and never argued, it could never be said to be a close, brotherly relationship. Salvatore had made the error that as they did not argue they must automatically be good friends. This assumption he drew from his own background. It was not that he thought he had been a bad or uninterested father, and as such his logic was confused, so that now his sons were moving away from him, yet still oddly remaining in the tight family group, well organised, but by women.

One side of the table was now well geared up with Mary in control, giving Vince the advice obviously with her bias about Sitwell, with Michael chiming in about how he remembered it.

'Oh, forget it, Mons. Your vision is long gone. This priest we have now has very much seen to all of that.'

'What a great pity,' was Michael's reply, and so the noisy meal continued, with Angela holding court at one end of the table, Emmanuel at the other, and Mary in the centre, between Vince and Michael.

'Just so exhausting,' commented Kerry, as she flopped down on a long black leather setee.

'So Vince is to go to Mary's, is he?' asked Salvatore.

'Darling, thank goodness he is going somewhere where he has a friend. Some of these priests are sent to who knows where and are totally alone. Surely you wouldn't wish that on Vince, would you?'

'Of course not,' he answered. 'I'm going to have a lie down for an hour. What time do the wolves arrive?'

'No one is here before 8.00,' and she stood up and walked with him to their bedroom. Then she realised that he was like a little boy who had lost his way.

The late afternoon had seen Vince and Emmanuel at Angela's splashing and swimming in her pool, chattering on about everything and nothing at the same time. Even Vince noticed that his little brother had become quite the good looking young man.

Whilst this was happening and the maids were clearing up, Angela had taken it upon herself to unlock the door of the large case that held her Nativity scene and put in place Salvatore's latest gift, a little fat man in pink silk with a turban and wearing a necklace of pearls with green silk shoes and in one hand a chain which was attached to a carved monkey looking ever so surprised. It is quite the nicest of all of them, she mused, just the nicest of them all, but this case just has to be changed. It's now far too small. You can't see all the figures properly. Yes, I must change it. And with that word 'change' Angela was about to alter a piece of furniture and, without her realising it, at the same time, Emmanuel's life forever.

The evening passed as noisily and as happily as the lunch but much more informally, but between these two Christmas festivities Mary had been on the telephone to Sarah Higgins at Sitwell explaining that her nephew was to be taking over the parish as the other incumbent was to be moved elsewhere. Sarah, her mother-in-law, and Annie, were probably the only three women Mary spoke to and she enjoyed their company immensely, Sarah being as forthright as Mary, so together they were seen as a formidable proposition. They had many years ago taken an interest in the local parish activities but politics, due to another family, had seen both of them wash their hands and just forget about it all. They attended Mass but that was it. Nothing more. And they could not be conscripted to help in any way at all, due to a mutual loathing of Betty Howes, whose family had more or less in the last fifteen years taken over the running of St. Bridget's Church, and it seemed the priest himself. So Vince's appointment as parish priest was, in Mary's and Sarah's minds going to turn all this around and be very much to their advantage. Country town politics have never shown mercy.

'Michael,' asked Angela, as Emmanuel handed her another drink, 'who did you say did all the restoration work in the sacristy of the cathedral?' Here, Angela was referring to the repair of the old pieces of furniture, the plan presses that had once held, and in some drawers still did hold the chasubles.

'He's a very young man but extremely talented,' answered Michael. 'The repair and re-polishing have been splendid. I can genuinely recommend him. Why? Do you need some piece of furniture repaired?'

'No, I need a talented person to redesign and construct a new case for my Nativity figures. The old one has been altered twice and it is just too small.'

'You know, Angela, I don't know of anyone in Melbourne with a finer collection.'

'Thank you, but it's due to Salvatore.'

'What's due to me?' Salvatore was just passing behind Angela.

'Darling, your fabulous gifts to me. I have been speaking to Michael and he seems to know of a brilliant cabinet maker. I need a larger container for them all. This year's gift of the little man in pink with the monkey was just divine. I think I like him more than all the rest.'

'I'm glad you liked him,' Salvatore said, and passed with yet another tray of food from the kitchen.

'Shall I give him your telephone number, then?' continued Michael.

'How kind. Yes, that would be lovely.'

'Oh,' he said, 'I see Mary is giving Vince all the background to his new parish.'

'Yes,' was the flat reply, and she excused herself to find and tell Emmanuel that a cabinet maker was to present himself at No. 6 to organise a new home for her Nativity scene.

And so the festive period continued like this from Christmas through to the New Year. Emmanuel accompanied a very buoyant Mary to Salvatore's work site and was genuinely surprised at the landscaped section in front with the very modern showrooms set amongst trees. She took a long time to decide what she wanted and in an odd way Emmanuel thought the details she wrote down on several sheets of paper were somewhat exaggerated, but he stood silently listening to Salvatore explain to Mary the difference in qualities and prices.

New Year celebrations saw everyone in different places doing different things.

'Darling, it's not a problem. If you want, we can go to Nella for New Year's Eve. We have spent Christmas with Angela and the boys, so for me it's fine.'

'Thanks, but would you be upset if we just had a quiet night at home?'

'Salvatore, you are divine,' Kerry replied, using Mary's favourite adjective. 'I couldn't think of anything I would like more.'

'Shall we ask Mary?'

'I know, from listening to Emmanuel, that he and Angela have drinks, dinner and then are going on to yet another party. I can't believe the two of them actually enjoy it all. I just find it a bit repetitive.'

'Me too.'

'I'll ask Mary and just see what she says.', so it was that after a drink with Paul and Anthony Mary joined them for a light meal – or that was the initial description – and a quiet, relaxed night of remembering and laughing, but that electricity in the back of Mary's mind was accelerating a thought pattern that she was sure was going to stimulate her and the power base at Sitwell, via a certain Father Vincenzo Lampedusa. Mary remained for another two weeks, dashing from place to place with Emmanuel as a guide and companion, or, as ever, in the company of Paul and Anthony, discussing changes to 'Bantry' in the country.

It must have been a month after the Christmas festivities had settled down and with a certain amount of family pressure that Salvatore and Kerry made the trip to his parents' home for a dinner that was pleasant, until Mario's late arrival and then the tension set in. Any advice Salvatore offered to save his family's sinking business Mario took as arrogance from someone who had made it. Needless to say at the end of the evening, and having said their goodbyes to Nella and the usual extended family, Salvatore had to agree with Kerry that perhaps Emmanuel had worked out this family social scene well before them.

'Mrs Christie is expecting you, Mr. Collins. This way, please.' The maid showed Richard Collins into Angela's exquisitely decorated sitting room. He sat down and just glanced around. It was really quite a sight. He had never seen so much gilded furniture and fabulous objects, all complementing one another, and through the doorway he could see yet another sitting room in reds and cream and gilt. He began to feel a little uncomfortable, looking at the enormous crystal chandelier, which reigned supreme suspended from the ceiling. It was now February and outside was just so hot, but indoors here the silent air conditioning tended to convince you that you were in an enchanted space.

'I'm so sorry to have kept you waiting,' said an elegantly groomed Angela, wearing, as usual, a display of fine jewellery. She was a very handsome woman, thought Richard Collins. 'My cousin said he would give you my telephone number. How kind of you to wait until the festive season was finished.' She pushed a button near the marble fireplace before she sat down.

'Yes, Mrs. Christie,' came the reply from the maid.'

'You will join me in a glass of champagne, I hope.' she asked, smiling.

'Thank you.'

He was good looking, thought Angela, mid-twenties perhaps, beautiful face, flawless skin with a tiny hint of a beard line, a thick mop of slightly unruly light brown blonde hair and eyes – yes, she thought, he has magic, green eyes like a cat. He had on a short sleeved white polo shirt which showed his tan off to perfection. He had very well developed arms and a large strong chest that was tightly covered by his shirt. Well, she thought, a very good looking young man. 'You come highly recommended,' she went on, for some reason enjoying this social introduction. 'Monsignor Christie tells me your work is excellent.'

'Thank you,' he replied. 'He is very kind.'

'Oh, he has always recognised fine workmanship,' she chatted on. 'I have asked you here to solve a problem for me.'

'Yes, Monsignor Christie explained that you need a very large display case.'

'Oh no, Mr. Collins, I want a masterpiece and nothing less.' Richard had the odd feeling that he was being drawn into something that he was going to have little control over.

'Would you?' Angel smiled at him, tilting her glass, and Richard duly stood to refill it for her. 'And you own, please.' He wondered if they would ever get down to business. 'You see that large drape in the corner of the room. 'Would you be so kind as to very carefully remove it?'

He stood again and carefully, as instructed, removed a large sheet of white cotton, and to his utter surprise saw the whole Nativity scene, crammed into this glass case with a gilded dome on top. He just stared dumbfounded. He had never in his life seen anything like it. Fifty – or were there sixty – little figures of about 25 cm all dressed in faded silks, going about their daily tasks, whilst the Holy Family sat in the centre, seemingly unaware of the activity round them.

'It's fantastic,' was his only response as his eyes ran over the crowded scene. 'Are they very old?' he asked.

'They come from different periods. The Holy Family is the oldest piece, eighteenth century Italian.' She stood up and joined him at the case. 'The rest vary, age-wise, but they all complement one another. Even before you begin this work for me, I am going to lend you a book on these Nativity scene from Naples, so you have a sound understanding of what you are doing.'

It sounded a little patronising, but he accepted it. 'You see, they are so packed in you can't see them very well now, and I just know it could be better if we had more space, but you see the problem is this, it has to be packed away each year, as it's on show for about a month, so I'm not sure what to do. A larger case is an easy solution but what do I do with the large empty case for eleven months of the year? So you see it really is a problem. Do you have any ideas?' She returned to her chair.

'Well,' replied Richard, but before he could continue the banging of the front door announced another arrival.

'Angela, where are you?' came a strong masculine voice.

'In here, darling.'

Emmanuel spun into the room without realising that Richard was sitting across from Angela.

'Everything's organised for this evening,' he began, and suddenly spun around like a spring unravelling. He said absolutely nothing. The instant vision of Richard had for the first time since Angela could remember dumbfounded him.

She took over. 'Mr Collins, may I introduce you to my grandson, Emmanuel: Emmanuel, Mr. Collins,'

'It's Richard,' came the very quiet reply.

'How are you?' asked Emmanuel with his deep blue eyes surveying the most beautiful things he had ever seen in his life. This sensation was completely reciprocated by Richard – he had never seen anything like Emmanuel in his whole life. It was like a model from a chic magazine but here he was in three dimensions, sitting now between himself and Angela. She watched this play and to say she was surprised was not incorrect. Emmanuel had the social confidence of ten men but here he was stumped for words. Well, well, she thought . . .

'Now, getting back to my project,' she began, and then realised the only thing that held any interest for Richard was the beautiful young men sitting between her and himself. 'Do you think you could design a case that could be just taken apart piece by piece?' she asked.

Richard suddenly turned his head and looked at her as if it was the first time he had ever seen her. Oh, she thought, this is not going to go anywhere. Richard rallied, perhaps to prove to Emmanuel he was capable of making decisions.

'In this large house, don't you have a service room that could be fitted up permanently with these little figures? It seems to me if they are always packed away the silks and velvets must get crushed.'

Angela placed her glass on a side table and just stared at Richard: he suddenly felt very odd.

'A permanent exhibition,' she said. 'Hm . .'

'What about the service room between this room and the dining room?' suggested Emmanuel, coming into the conversation for the first time.

'Is it very large?' Richard asked him.

'Come and have a look.' Emmanuel was now regaining his social skills and they moved to a door off the corridor. It swung open to reveal a long, narrow room with shelves down both sides and a small rectangular window right up near the ceiling. 'It would be no trouble to build a permanent structure here, in fact with an electrical system you could do all kinds of things to illuminate the figures, or if you wished I could make a large display case that simply came apart in pieces and you could store it in here.'

'Let's think about it,' said Angela, in a slightly calculating way. 'I shall call you tomorrow morning. I presume you are free to start work here at once?'

Richard smiled. 'If you call me tomorrow morning, I'll start immediately. If you don't call, I shall have to accept other work.'

'How kind you are,' said Angela, grandly. 'Shall we say tomorrow? Goodbye, Mr. Collins. Emmanuel will show you out. Oh, don't forget the book.' She stood up, shook hands formally and moved to the case with the figures, picking up the cotton cover.

'I'm looking forward to seeing you tomorrow,' said Emmanuel, with a broad smile.

'I think that will depend on your grandmother,' was the reply.

'Oh, not at all.' At which Emmanuel kissed him on both cheeks.

It was an elated young cabinet maker that passed through a very well-kept garden and out of the gate, thinking only of a beautiful young man with electric blue eyes. 'Oh, sorry,' he exclaimed,' I wasn't watching where I was going.'

'No harm done,' and Kerry watched a young man who seemed to be lost or was it confused? She didn't know, but having come from Angela's home, she knew either could be the case, knowing Angela so well.

'What do you think?' Angela asked Emmanuel, glancing again at the crowded case of figures.

'I think he's beautiful,' Emmanuel grinned.

'Oh dear, this had better not interfere with my building programme. But you are right, he is very handsome.'

Angela made straight for the telephone, as Emmanuel went out and changed in the dressing pavilion for a swim.

'Paul Stratford Decorating,' came the response.

'Darling, it's Angela. I have an emergency. Can you come over?'

'I'll be over later for a drink. I'm expecting a client now but after that I am free. See you then. Bye!' He had known Angela for years and every now and again she called for an emergency when generally it meant she had purchased another piece of furniture or a painting and one or the other needed restoration or she took it upon herself just to change the drapes in this room or that.

At ten past five, Paul was shown in and through to the pool where Emmanuel was in the water and Angela had the ever present glass in her hand.

'Darling, do sit down and have a drink. Do help yourself.' She smiled and then went on to describe Richard Collins's suggestions for her ever-growing Nativity collection.

'Hi, Paul!' cried Emmanuel settling himself into a chair. Oh God, he is beautiful, thought Paul.

'What do you think of his ideas?' he asked Emmanuel, admiring the near-naked god.

'I think he's fantastic.'

'Really?' replied a surprised Paul. 'Well, this should help public relations when he starts work. Come on, let's have a look at this service room. I must confess I don't think I have ever thought about it.'

'What will you do with all this dining room stuff?' he asked Angela.

'It can all go to the storage rooms off the kitchen. It's probably more convenient out there.'

'What was this narrow room used for originally?' Paul asked, as he noted Emmanuel's well-tanned body.

'I don't know' replied Angela. 'When I moved in many years ago it held a single bed on one side but why the window was so high up I haven't a clue.'

'I think you should put it in this room. It obviously needs proper ventilation. What's why it smells a bit, but a huge case at one end in fact covering the entire space under the window, some good decorating touches and off we go. But be careful with the design of the case. You don't want it looking out of place against the house.'

'Absolutely,' agreed Angela, and looked about the space again. 'Hm, I'll have the staff empty it out at once. Good. Now that is decided I want you to oversee the design of the display case and have a few ideas for tomorrow.'

'Tomorrow!' cried Paul.

'Of course, darling. Mr. Richard Collins starts tomorrow.' And Paul noted a broad smile on Emmanuel's bronzed face.

The next day, at 9am, saw the four of them present to discuss this new building project. It was Emmanuel who took over, insisting on this and that and in the end the design for the case was arrived at. It would cover the entire end wall and would stand on legs in pairs, to give it just that much more style, as Paul explained, and they would add wainscoting to the room and a heavy damask wallpaper. Richard just stood back and watched the three of them, not necessarily correcting one another but refining the details to a point that he genuinely thought was exaggerated, including, the two long benches either side of the room that he would also be required to make and have painted in cream and gold. It all seemed to him as though he was required just to do the work. He had very little input at all, but generally in a situation like this he would have said something, but a beautiful young man beside him who constantly smiled at him kept him from feeling out of things.

'Now, Richard,' as Angela had been asked to use his Christian name, 'you can take all the measurements and off we go. Emmanuel can help you.' She smiled as she and Paul moved to the sitting room, discussing the merits of purchasing antique benches for the sides of this narrow room, or having them made anew.

'Well,' began Emmanuel, confidently, 'it seems that we shall be seeing a lot of one another.'

'So it seems,' was the quiet reply. Emmanuel naturally assumed that Richard would be totally overwhelmed by the offer of being with him and was genuinely surprised when he offered him the end of the tape measure and began to take measurements, with the only conversation being, 'No, from there – that's right.' No matter how Emmanuel tried to draw Richard into a social conversation, he resisted and continued taking measurements and drawing small sketches of the project. It wasn't that Richard would not have killed to have Emmanuel in his arms; it was that the person employing him for the moment took precedence. This was a prestigious job and being recommended by Monsignor Christie, Richard had no wish to confuse issues, well, not at this point anyway. And this was the bait for Emmanuel. He had never been 'put off' like this in his life, and he couldn't understand it at all.

'I don't understand what's wrong with him,' he stated to Angela, after Richard and Paul had left.

'Why? What's wrong?' she queried.

'Well, he seems only interested in the building of the display case,' he said, in a miserable tone. 'I don't think he even noticed me.'

'Oh darling, he will, he will. Now come on. Paul tells me that there are some gilded benches at an antique shop at Hampton of all places. I thought we might as well have dinner at one of those beach front restaurants. Oh, come along, Emmanuel, he will be in your arms before you know it! She laughed, but the only reply was 'Hmm . .'

Mario, in his attempt to haul his family's business out of trouble, made an extremely foolish move and that was to float a mortgage on the business to purchase an enormous amount of marble to floor and lay an entrance area and bathrooms in the renovation of a city hotel. He should have been more astute and checked more carefully the people behind this project. But a certain arrogance and pride pushed him forward and he accepted the contract.

Salvatore had also been approached by this company but had been warned off it, simply because the company had no collateral to pay as they had underestimated the cost of the renovation and with a little homework and two telephone calls he said that unless the money was paid up-front or there was a guarantee of payment thirty days after the completion date he was not interested, as the outlay was not an indifferent amount. He never heard from them again and he was totally unaware that Mario had accepted the work, as they now rarely spoke to one another. Mario had spoken to his parents and brothers, insisting that this be kept a secret until the profits were safely in the bank. But in order to complete this large project it was necessary for Mario to employ more men to complete the task which obviously meant a larger cash outlay. The work started well, with Mario, his father and brothers working almost ten hours a day in an attempt to complete the task.

Salvatore, meanwhile, was waiting for Paul's return from Sitwell, or more precisely 'Bantry', Mary's large country house, for all the measurements for the new flooring. Salvatore's business had gone from strength to strength and his new flooring project of cutting large numbers of white marble tiles and inserting different coloured squares at the corners of each made this mass production quick and easy. It had been very popular with decorators and home-owners and so he was feeling just a little proud of his venture, not to mention the handsome financial return.

Each morning for Emmanuel it was exhilarating to see Richard. Each day was something new to him, the anticipation of descending the grand staircase and walking past the drawing room to hear the hammering of nails into timber meant very surely he was there, but no matter how Emmanuel angled or twisted his social offers a refusal, polite though it was, was always a refusal. Emmanuel was exasperated; never had he been refused; hundreds would have killed for the opportunity, but here it was, with Richard, nothing but polite conversation, a casual joke, but that was it.

'I am sure he hates me,' he said dejectedly as he sat himself opposite Angela at breakfast.

'Of course he doesn't,' replied Angela. 'It's just that he is a very professional worker and that has to be admired.'

'Does it?' grumbled Emmanuel, and drank his coffee, wondering why life was so cruel. He later had to go to Kerry's to see if she and Salvatore were coming to dinner that evening and he noticed the strength of the sun as he left the house and walked up two doors.

'Hi!' was Kerry's cheery cry, 'another hot day.'

'Who cares!' came the reply. Kerry swung around to see a very dejected son.

'Emmanuel, what's wrong?' she asked, anxiously, never having seen him like this before.

'Nothing,'

'Emmanuel, what precisely is the problem?' she insisted, sternly.

'It's Richard. He isn't even a little bit interested in me.'

'You mean the boy that's building the case for Angela? Well, really!' She thought to make light of the situation and then a look in Emmanuel's direction showed her ever so clearly that he was suffering terribly.

'Oh, darling,' she said, holding him in her arms, 'there are lots of Richards in this world and you are sure to meet the right one.'

'I'm not,' was his dejected reply.

'Darling, sit down.' He dutifully obeyed her. 'Emmanuel, you are the most beautiful young man in the world. You can have whoever you want, but, darling, has it ever crossed your mind that this Richard may like you but that he prefers girls from a sexual point of view?'

'Emmanuel turned his head and looked at her in sheer disbelief. 'What! A girl !!'

'Well, darling, believe it or not, quite a few good-looking men just happen to be heterosexual.'

'I don't believe it,' he said, arrogantly.

'Well, darling, you may have to, whether you want to or not. Oh, by the way, tell Angela that we shall be there about 7.00 tonight.'

With that, Emmanuel rose and left the house, not even saying a goodbye. He can't be, he thought, as he re-entered Angela's house, meeting her crossing the hallway.

'They'll be here at 7.00' he said, in a lacklustre way.

'Emmanuel, come with me.' She led him into the sitting room and rang the bell.

'Yes, Mrs. Christie?'

'A bottle of champagne.'

'Certainly,' was the maid's surprised reply.

Angela glanced at her watch, which said 10 to 10. 'Now, Emmanuel, I can't have you like this at all.' And as she poured the drinks, she went on, 'What exactly do you want from Richard?'

'Love,' came the reply, without hesitation.

'Well, let's see what we can do about that.' When Emmanuel repeated what Kerry had said, she replied,' Oh, what nonsense your mother goes on about! She wouldn't know it was a tiger until it had ripped her arm off,' which had Emmanuel in hysterics. She continued, 'I have two daughters and one as silly as the other, although I must say Kerry married a very handsome man. This cannot be said for Mary, still it takes all kinds. Now, darling, everything is going to be just fine. Tonight, I think you can introduce your Richard formally to Salvatore and Kerry. Now, darling, do pop down to the wine merchant and get me these things on the list.' She handed him a sheet from the desk top. 'Off you go!'

He headed out through the house, glancing into the room now well underway to hold the extended nativity scene, only to see a broad set of shoulders levelling off the top section with a spirit level. Emmanuel sighed and made for the garage. A moment later a black Mercedes was seen heading up the Avenue toward the well patronised wine merchant.

Angela finished her glass of champagne and then crossed the room. She hoisted the cotton cover that hid the Nativity scene, glanced at it and then noticed her latest addition. It was the monkey with his odd expression that convinced her what she was about to do was absolutely essential.

'Richard,' she said, and he climbed down the ladder.

'Yes?' he replied, cheerfully. 'Is something wrong?'

'Oh no, Richard, quite the contrary.' He looked at Angela, assuming this was a comment in his favour about the work he was attempting. 'Now, Richard, don't you think Emmanuel is extraordinarily beautiful?'

Perhaps it was the suddenness of this comment that caught him off guard, but his reply was a simple 'Yes'.

'Oh, fine. This cat and mouse routine just won't do. You are staying here for dinner this evening, and after work you and Emmanuel can have a swim together before dinner.'

'But I haven't anything to wear!'

'Oh, for heaven's sake! Emmanuel will see to that. Good. Now all that's settled. I must say the fact that you have made the case much higher is a very good idea.'

'Well, I had a good look at the book you lent me and if we stagger the levels you will be able to see all your figures quite clearly.'

'Exactly. I think seeing things clearly is so important, don't you?'

'Yes.' The reply was very quiet.

Angela made her way back to the large drawing room, finished her drink and then went toward the kitchen to make sure that an extra place setting was organised for the evening meal. Richard could not believe what was happening. The whole direction of his life had been taken over by Angela; not only did she employ him at this moment, she was also, it seemed, offering him something he wanted desperately. He couldn't believe it! It just wasn't possible! He had refused Emmanuel's offers only because he was very certain that this matriarch would cancel his employment immediately and here she was offering him Emmanuel.

Emmanuel himself was ecstatic when he returned from the wine merchant, only to be told of the organisation for the evening. 'Angela, you are adorable,' he chanted, moving to the room where Richard was working, but, instead of being grateful for the turn about, Emmanuel began another game and Richard, being a step ahead of him, played along with it.

'How nice you are dining with us tonight.'

'Yes, isn't it?' and the small talk continued. Then Emmanuel made an error. He turned the conversation around so that it seemed that he was doing Richard a favour. Richard knew exactly what Emmanuel was doing and quietly said, 'I don't have to come this evening.' He turned to return to his work and a shot of fear swept up through Emmanuel as he had never felt it in his whole life. Richard stopped what he was doing and turned to see a very different Emmanuel.

'If you don't stay this evening, I shall die,' he murmured. He moved toward Richard and stood very close. He was aware he was breathing irregularly and then he placed his arms around the other's broad shoulders and drew him close. He was very aware that Richard had not reciprocated, but continued to hold him and then he felt it, as two very strong arms encircled him and held him tightly. For the very first time, Emmanuel felt a surge of adrenalin through his whole frame. He rested his head on Richard's shoulders. 'You're fantastic,' was his only comment. Then he lifted his head and a pair of cobalt blue eyes looked directly into a pair of soft green ones and at that very moment they both knew without a shadow of a doubt that they had found something that was going to develop totally. The kiss that followed cemented it into a reality.

It was not only Richard who noted, while swimming with Emmanuel, that he had a good body, it was also Emmanuel, who was very pleasantly surprised with Richard's physique, a well-built body with strong shoulders and very muscular arms. The torso was broad and, at the top, covered in soft blond brown hair. His legs were extremely well-developed, and Emmanuel noticed that this was not the only region that was very well developed.

Salvatore missed the plot completely. He could not understand what all the glances were for that evening, and Angela being ever so gracious, it seemed to him. But Kerry had caught it at once. She knew Emmanuel only too well but she had never seen him besotted like this before. Floating, yes, she thought, he is floating, and she turned and looked at Richard whilst the others were talking about Vince, now in residence at Sitwell and definitely under Mary's wing. He was very handsome, Kerry thought, almost as handsome as Emmanuel, but then it would take someone like this to finally hold Emmanuel and she noticed also in his conversation an intelligence and a form of deliberate reasoning that she admitted later she liked much more. But, oh, if this became a serious relationship how was she going to explain this rationally to Salvatore? She sighed and then looked toward the end of the table where Angela was holding court and smiled. Angela will do it, I suppose, then reached over, took her glass and looked again at a young handsome man called Richard whom she was sure was to become for Emmanuel a very important part of his life. She was not wrong.

At the end of the evening, Emmanuel asked Richard to remain for the night.

'I won't,' he smiled and then kissed him at the front door, after the others had left, 'but if you're interested, and tomorrow being Saturday, you could come over and join me early in the morning. You know the address.'

'How early?'

'That's entirely up to you.' Richard kissed him again and turned to head toward the front gate, very aware of the sound of the front door closing. He pulled his van out onto a silent Avenue and then onto the main road, surprisingly empty for a Friday night, and drove home. As he closed the front door of his terrace house in Richmond, he was for the first time in his life aware of a loneliness. He undressed, went to the bathroom and then to bed, being ever so aware that in this large double bed there was only one person. This was a totally new experience for him; he had always been independent and, like Emmanuel, not short of bed companions. It was this independence he prided himself on, but somehow, under this smart, static façade, a beautiful young man called Emmanuel had slid and all his careful plans for the future suddenly had no basis at all.

It was a similar situation for Emmanuel, except that he was sure, except for the initial setbacks, that everything would work itself out and obviously in his favour, but this was a very different relationship that he was about to enter, and willingly. For the first time in his life he was dependent on another person in a loving relationship. He had always called the shots, but with Richard this was not to be, and even he, with all his conceit, saw this as the future. As he rolled over in his gilded bedroom, he sighed and smiled. He wouldn't have it any other way.

The alarm clock screeched 6.00. Emmanuel slammed his hand down on the button, silencing it immediately. He rose, shaved, showered and dressed and a black Mercedes nosed its way from Hawthorn to Richmond, hardly 15 minutes away. He parked at the end of Elm Street and in a space of twenty metres, with a firm hand used the large brass door knocker at No. 6. In a few moments a sleepy voice cried, 'Who is it?'

'Open up! It's your life.'

Richard opened the door to a buoyant Emmanuel. 'What took you so long?' Richard asked with a smile.

Both of them had had quite a deal of sexual experience, but somehow this was different. Somehow all the ends tied up neatly. For both of them, this was what they wanted for the rest of their lives, simply one another.

This was also a period when they began to explore one another, to understand and on this basis began to slowly lay the foundations for a stable relationship. Both realised that neither really controlled each other; it was a game of give and take, and for Emmanuel it was new. He found, to his utmost surprise, he liked it. They spent most of Saturday in bed, laughing and making vague plans, but mostly making love and sleeping.

'Tonight you must sleep at my place,' insisted Emmanuel.

'I'll feel a bit awkward,' Richard replied, lifting his torso up and resting his head on the palm of his hand.

'Why? Angela is not judgemental. What's the problem?'

'I don't know,' Richard replied, pulling Emmanuel back on top of him.

'You will have to get used to Angela sooner or later, so the sooner the better.'

'Hmm, I suppose so.'

'We're having dinner with Angela tonight, but first drinks with Paul and Anthony. They're great! You've met Paul. Come on, let's have a shower and go to Angela's. I am starving.'

'Oh,' came a sharp reply. 'I'm quite capable of preparing a meal. You don't always have to depend on Angela.'

Emmanuel noticed a narrowing of Richard's eyes. He immediately threw his arms around his neck. 'Oh, Richard, that's not what I meant. I would be delighted to have lunch with you. Please don't get me wrong.' He felt slightly embarrassed.

'I'm sorry. A case of over-reacting.'

Emmanuel snuggled in against his naked body. 'You know, Richard, you have a great body.'

'You're not too bad yourself. Now, come on and I will organise lunch.'

'With or without clothes?' Emmanuel asked chirpily.

'Please yourself!'

As they left No. 6 Elm Street, Emmanuel said, 'Did you bring a jacket and tie?'

'Yes, just as you said. I take it that the evening is going to be smart.'

'Oh, don't worry about that. It's for tomorrow morning. Do you want to come in my car?'

'Why not?' He seated himself next to Emmanuel and again brought up the subject of dressing. 'What do you mean, a jacket and tie for tomorrow morning?'

Emmanuel looked at him and frowned. 'Why, for Mass.'

Richard took a deep breath. This whole world Emmanuel lived in was so very, very different from his and he had the feeling that in a short time he was going to be moulded into it, whether he wanted to or not.

'The Mons says an early Mass at the cathedral. We all go.' It was his assumption of things that Richard found a little difficult to grasp. Doesn't everyone go to early morning Mass when one's relative, a certain Monsignore, is saying it? He noted Emmanuel had never even asked him if he was Catholic or not. Richard was never to overcome these comments. He found as he moved in this tight circle that one just had to accept things, especially if organised by Angela in the background. He was a Catholic, but by no stretch of the imagination could he be called practising. There it was, a cocktail party at Paul and Anthony's, then back to Angela's for dinner with Kerry and Salvatore, to bed and that exquisite pleasure of love-making with Emmanuel and next morning off to early Mass, with, to his surprise, the same guests as at the table the evening before. Then a casual lunch for twelve, or perhaps more, at Paul and Anthony's. Richard was not used to living like this and undoubtedly without Emmanuel he would never have contemplated it, but in a short time he was drawn in with a fine net and even though occasionally he fought to free himself he eventually gave in. The thought of being without the man he now loved desperately was just simply out of the question.

It wasn't that Emmanuel was insensitive to Richard's situation, he wasn't. But he had been brought up in a world that accepted impossibilities being possible and this was where he fitted Richard in. He knew he could not live without him. His sensual personality, his exciting love-making were all part of, to his mind, the world in which Angela controlled or organised everything.

An example of this just before the now-enormous case and surrounds were completed occurred on Saturday lunch time, when a group of friends of Angela's were having drinks around the pool. It was probably going to be the last time the pool was used, as a slight autumnal breeze made itself felt.

'Richard,' came Angela's voice above the noisy crowd. The chatter died away. 'Darling,' she said, having now accepted him as family, 'is your passport valid?'

Richard looked at her as if she were asking for a blood donation. 'Yes, I think so. Why?'

'Oh, darling, how divine! We are all off to Paris next Thursday. Won't that be great? Springtime in Paris! Emmanuel and I adore it. No, darling, not a word. It's all organised.' She swept off to speak to Paul about transport of goods between Paris and Melbourne.

Richard immediately made his way to Emmanuel. 'Look, I haven't got the money for a holiday in Paris.'

Emmanuel just kissed him in front of all, and it was at this moment that Salvatore realised that this new addition to the 'family' was more than just casual. 'Darling, don't you understand?'

'You're damn right I don't.' Richard was suddenly becoming angry.

'Richard,' came a voice from behind. He spun around, freeing himself from Emmanuel's arms. He now felt totally out of his depth. Kerry linked an arm through his, having been very close when Angela was making her travel arrangements. 'Shall we find a drink?' She steered him toward a quiet part of the garden as Angela cried out for Emmanuel. 'You'll never get used to her,' she laughed. 'As my mother, she was a pain. My sister and I never knew what day it was. One day the theatre, one day a cocktail party – it never finished and still hasn't.'

'I haven't the finance to keep up with this,' he replied, quietly.

'Richard, do you love Emmanuel?' He turned red with embarrassment. This was Emmanuel's mother asking if he loved him.

'Yes,' he said in a whisper, looking at his empty glass.

'Great! Now you are part of this crazy family. You are going to have to accept Angela. There is no problem with money. Angela will continue to pay your weekly wage as she is now doing, whether you're in Paris or building her display case. She has a large apartment in Paris and you have been invited, all expenses paid, not just because you are Emmanuel's lover but because she genuinely likes you. You will notice that Emmanuel just takes all this for granted. Well, that's because from when he was a little boy his grandmother changed and became his fairy godmother, and more than that his closest female friend, and you, it seems, fit neatly in beside them. Don't worry, Richard, your life with Angela and Emmanuel is destined to change. Oh, do you think we could have a top-up?' She squeezed his arm. 'Just enjoy it, darling. Life is short.' They turned to find Emmanuel coming towards them with a champagne bottle.

'Refill, anyone?' He winked at Richard. 'You'll love Paris. Oh, by the way,' he looked at Kerry, 'I have this odd feeling Salvatore is going to be questioning you this evening. Come on, Richard. Angela wants me to introduce you to a friend of hers. She has given tours all day of your work. You have become quite the star.'

'Always have been!'

'What do you mean, 'special friend'?' asked a straight-faced Salvatore as he prepared the evening meal for Kerry, who sat back looking vacantly out of the window.

'Oh, Salvatore, please! What are you going on about?'

'Richard.'

'Don't you like him?'

'Yes, of course I do. He seems to be one of Emmanuel's more stable friends.' He looked at Kerry as she returned the glance. The answer to all his questions and one in particular was answered. He sat down beside her, filled up their glasses and just looked ahead in silence. Then he reached and held her hand. 'I suppose I have always known, but somehow today when he kissed Richard and seemed so very happy – I don't suppose I would want any more for him, would I?'

'No, darling, neither of us would want any more than Emmanuel's complete happiness and it seems at last he has found it. Let's hope he is mature enough to handle it.'

'He will. Don't forget there's Angela right behind.' He smiled, withdrew his hand and placed his arm around Kerry's neck. He had this blank feeling, no pain, no unhappiness, just an acceptance that no matter what he thought or said Emmanuel would do exactly as he always had done, exactly what suited him. And now, publicly, his lover was aided and abetted by Angela, so even if he had had a few words of warning they would have been totally negated by a much more dominant force in his son's life – Angela.

The display case was now finished, as was the wainscoting, so with the exception of the interior of the case Richard's work was more or less completed. It was the different levels and the lighting for him to finish off, the rest of the room was Paul's responsibility, who was not unhappy that he could have the room painted and papered without Angela hovering about like an anxious vulture. But before the three of them left for Paris a very nasty scene took place which placed Salvatore in a very awkward position. As they were to leave on Thursday, and Saturday was Nella's birthday, Emmanuel was persuaded to go with his parents to see his paternal grandmother on Tuesday evening.

'Oh, what a bore!' he exclaimed to Angela. 'We have to eat and drink like workers and that blasted television in the corner just screams all night. I can't bear it.'

'Darling, it will be over in a flash. Don't worry.'

In due course, after much small talk, Salvatore pulled up in front of his parents' house and they went in to an excited Nella exclaiming that the gift he brought her was exactly what she wanted. The clatter of plates and glasses, the noise of Salvatore's brother and wife speaking all together and the television blaring in the corner was such a contrast to Angela's set and organised world that Emmanuel became brittle and just helped himself to a drink, not speaking to anyone. It was just as they were about to be seated for dinner that the back door slammed shut and Mario swept in. He was well prepared for Salvatore and Kerry, as he had seen their car in front of the house, but he was totally unprepared for Emmanuel, who chose to ignore him. To say conversation was stilted was an understatement, but it was Salvatore's quiet father who 'let the cat out of the bag' about Mario's new business venture.

'What?' exclaimed Salvatore. 'What guarantee do you have for payment?'

Mario was furious that Salvatore was questioning his venture as he spat back some sharp reply. Nella immediately attempted to quieten things down, ordering all to the table and adding another place setting as far away from Emmanuel as possible. The first part of the evening was relatively calm, with Nella taking over, talking about grand-children. It was when Nella announced that she was so happy that Emmanuel had come to her early birthday party and asked him to send her a postcard from Paris that Mario said, 'It would be a better idea if he got off his arse and did some honest work.'

'Oh,' retorted Emmanuel, 'don't tell me you think you are a good example of an honest worker. You look ten years older than you are and you're in debt.'

Mario was furious. It took very little on Emmanuel's part to excite him and being quite vain the age comment hit home. He was just about to start when his younger brother, not taking much notice of the usual table banter and watching the new headlines suddenly lurched forward.

'Fuck!' was the word used to display his disbelief.

'Cocomming & Co have been handed into receivership. This large company, with eight major projects in the city, are to declare bankruptcy . .' and so the report went on. Mario went white. This was the company Salvatore had been warned about, and this same company Mario had mortgaged everything to finance the lay-out for the marble. There was dead silence at the table.

'Turn the television off,' demanded Salvatore. 'Now, exactly what investment do you have in this company?

Mario said nothing, but his younger brother furnished him with enough detail to show how serious the financial situation was.

'My advice is to get as much of your material out at once, and then see if you can sue for the amount of work you have completed. Why the hell didn't you telephone me first?'

'Why should I?' responded Mario, adopting an attacking approach. He sat back arrogantly in his chair, staring at the plate of pasta in front of him with the sinking feeling that the world was about to swallow him up.

'So this is an example of intelligent work is it? My grandparents bankrupted by a foolish son!'

He should not have said it, but Emmanuel never or rarely thought first. He did see clearly as Mario grasped the plate of pasta and hurled it in Emmanuel's direction. He ducked and the plate flew across the room to smash against a wall, spilling its contents down the wall. It was Kerry who now took over. 'Mario, this violence is not going to save the business. You now need clear and precise advice and no drama if you're going to salvage anything.'

Mario pushed his chair back roughly and made for the door, slamming it behind him. The rest of the evening was one of attempting on Salvatore's part to find out exactly how much money Mario had borrowed and whether it had all gone into this project or not. Neither his father nor brother could shed any light on the situation. It appeared that Mario had taken it upon himself to organise everything, but had taken no-one into his confidence. The three of them left a very distraught family group wondering what tomorrow was to bring.

On the way home, the conversation was very much about saving the family business but with Mario at the head of it it was going to be very difficult. Neither Salvatore nor Kerry mentioned what they thought was Emmanuel's very inappropriate remark, even if there was some truth to it.

'I'll drop you off here,' said Salvatore as his car drew to a halt in front of Angela's mansion. 'Tell Angela I shall be in in a moment.'

Emmanuel went in and found Angela with a sketch pad, drawing different versions of the interior of her display case. 'How was the evening?' she asked.

'Don't talk about it. That cretin Mario threw a bowl of pasta at me.'

'What!' Angela put her pencil down. 'What happened?'

'Oh, Salvatore's here in a moment. He can give you the gory details. Such a creep, that Mario!'

A rap on the front door heralded Salvatore's arrival; he found the pair of them with the obligatory glass in hand.

'A bit of drama?' asked Angela.

'A bit.' He placed his laptop on the desk where Angela had been working, and began to explain the family predicament. Angela showed no emotion at all. She just listened very carefully.

'What are they planning to do?' she asked, when Salvatore had completed his version of the financial fiasco.

'No one seems to know, since Mario has kept most of this a secret.'

'I see.' She motioned Emmanuel to refill her glass. 'What do you wish to do?'

'I should like to help. It is my family.'

'What work does the Company have that has not been started?'

'We have three jobs,' he answered, and opened his laptop. Angela studied the three projects, one being a hotel foyer, another a complete modern set of apartments and the third an 80s renovation of an apartment block of all the bathrooms.

71

'Salvatore, listen carefully. Offer the family the last of these options with the marble they have recovered. This should be a good cash job, but you will not, under any circumstances employ any one member of your family.'

Salvatore was quite taken by surprise and his face showed it. 'I will not have your position as manager undermined and that is that. If you wish to hand your private money to your family, that's your business but I warn you very strongly against it, as it will never stop. I suggest that you recommend a good solicitor and see what he can salvage. By the way, Salvatore, what is your collar size? I know this divine shop in Paris that has such beautiful shirts.'

Emmanuel noticed – as did his father – that the business voice of Angela was without much pity and the moment she changed to another subject she was charity itself.

On returning to Kerry, Salvatore recounted what Angela had said without passing a comment on what he thought was a tough approach to his family's predicament.

'For once, darling, I have to agree with Angela. These are adults that entered into this arrangement and the fact that not one of them queried Mario's right to take out a mortgage or look at the consequences of it does not show too well for your family.' Here she stopped.

'I know,' he agreed. 'Well, I guess we shall now have to wait and see what the solicitor says.' He had to agree again that Angela was right, even if he was surprised at her insistence that none of his family were to be employed in the business. Mario was totally predictable and at a family conference several days later with Salvatore present put on the full family drama.

'Oh, it's fine for you to pass these comments,' Mario spat at his brother, 'with the rest of the family and extended family watching on. You happened to marry money.'

Salvatore was becoming very angry. He had arrived here this evening to try to help the situation and had not anticipated Mario's sarcasm.

'I can offer you a good cash job, seeing you have recovered a good percentage of the marble from the hotel. Take it or leave it.'

Mario thought the offer patronising, considering Salvatore's secure financial situation and said so. Salvatore was furious and spoke sharply to his father: 'Who is in charge here?'

There was silence, except for Nella, who was sniffing into her handkerchief.

'I am,' was his father's slow response.

'Well, do you want the work or not?'

'We are in a very bad way.' His father scratched his chin. 'Of course we shall accept it.'

'Why can't all of you work with Salvatore? It would be very good for everyone,' added Nella.

Salvatore gasped. Oh, he thought, here goes. 'That is impossible.' He spoke quickly and did not elaborate. Even Mario knew that Angela was behind that statement and probably the nephew he loathed most in the world. 'I suggest you all sit down and discuss these matters together carefully first. I was also offered this work but I did some homework and it wasn't difficult to see they couldn't pay.'

'So easy in hindsight!' Mario commented, sarcastically.

'This is not my business, but if it was, brother or no brother, I should fire you at once. You are a liability in this business and the chip on your shoulder doesn't help.

'Fuck you!' was Mario's educated response.

Salvatore stood and said goodbye to all, with the exception of Mario, and left. He had an odd feeling it would be some time before he returned.

CHAPTER THREE

Paris and Home Again

CHAPTER THREE

Paris and Home Again

'Fasten your safety belts; all seats into the upright position; landing in ten minutes.'

Richard lent over Emmanuel and peered out of the window. An early morning glow with strong sunlight was illuminating the whole city. Richard had never been to Paris before and so it was for him a new adventure. The flight had been fine: 23 hours, but first class was, he considered, not bad at all, with seats that lay back and so sleeping was easy, even if Emmanuel sometimes made sleeping difficult. Here he was, whisked away from work in Melbourne to hovering above the most beautiful city in the world. He couldn't believe it. The Eiffel tower, the Arc de Triomphe – he could see them clearly on this early spring morning.

Emmanuel hailed a taxi and off they went in the direction of central Paris. The taxi sped in the direction of the Arc de Triomphe, around a corner and right again into Rue Anatole de la Forge. No. 10 and they all alighted with Emmanuel paying the driver as Richard moved the luggage to the pavement. Angela spoke fluent French, but Emmanuel only survival French and Richard none at all. The apartment was, of course, ready for Madam and her friends and a sharp young man sprang to Madam's every need. Angela always employed someone to look after her and Emmanuel in Paris and this glorious apartment she had purchased twenty five years ago was now ready yet again for her. It was furnished exquisitely, obviously in the French 18th century style, with fine paintings, furniture, beautiful Aubusson carpets and what seemed to Richard an over-abundance of chandeliers and crystal sconce.

'Home again!' Emmanuel exclaimed, with a smile. 'You know we must keep going all day, otherwise we shall be awake all night.'

Richard just smiled as Emmanuel showed him to their room and the unpacking began. But Emmanuel had not brought much due to the fact that the wardrobe here held quite sufficient clothing for him. Twice a year for six or seven years he had made this deluxe apartment a safe haven. He went to the window and looked out at the apartment block on the other side of the street.

'What are you looking at? Richard asked.

'Oh, last year there was a young guy who was always at the window in his underpants, speaking on the telephone. A bit more interesting than watching pigeons!' He turned to walk to Richard and held him in his arms. 'I love you,' he said, and kissed him.

Richard did not reply, but the firmness with which he held Emmanuel made it clear that he was also of the same mind. Angela could be heard in the large drawing room, telephoning friends and making all sorts of arrangements for the two week stay. 'Boys, do dash out and have a look around. I expect you both back at 6.00. I have a few friends coming in for dinner then tomorrow we can start to really show Richard Paris.' She kissed them both and reminded Emmanuel of the code to press that opened the principal glass and wrought iron door that led into the apartment foyer.

It was a gracious apartment, every room except the two bathrooms and the kitchen Angela rarely saw had beautiful marble fireplaces with huge gilt mirrors above them. The first room on the left on entering was the dining room and through huge glass doors this opened into the sitting room. This was, as with the other rooms, fitted with a magnificent, and what was probably the most important, fireplace in the apartment. There was a comfortable camel-back settee in cream silk and chairs in gold and crimson silk damask. As always there was a chandelier in rock crystal, which gave the room a feeling that time just did not change. The whole apartment continued in this vein. The walls in all the major rooms were divided into panels and everything but everything was symmetrical. The panels in the dining room were hung with many small paintings of horses, each balanced against another, and the gilt 19th century French chairs, of which there were ten, stood sentinel around the beautiful table with its inlaid marble top.

The bedrooms were generous, but irregular in size, with walls tapering in on one side to make way for a bathroom or another service room. Both bedrooms had grey marble fireplaces.

As Richard and Emmanuel left the apartment and walked around the corner to the taxi rank, it struck Richard that to arrive in Paris after a twenty three hour flight and to arrive at an apartment like the one he had just left, with a fire in the grates in the two principal rooms and the apartment filled with fresh flowers, was probably as close to paradise as he was ever going to get. Emmanuel looked so much the model on a day off, with an overcoat, as it was still very early spring, side by side with the man he believed was without a doubt the most handsome man in the world.

The first day they just strolled about, looking at everything from a tourist's point of view: the in-depth stuff would start as from tomorrow. What a beautiful city – and the thing Richard noted was the use of gold leaf. It was everywhere. It was in this early spring light positively gleaming. This first impression was magic.

They had lunch in a tiny restaurant Emmanuel remembered in the Latin Quarter, just across from the front of the Louvre over the Seine, and there they were. It was dark inside but warm, and Emmanuel ordered for Richard, joking he had ordered elephant steaks, and laughed. The wine, the atmosphere and Richard knew now why Emmanuel and Angela loved this city. Neither, it appeared, was going to live here permanently, but it seemed that neither of them could live without it. It was like a magic oxygen supply that one always needed in order to survive.

After a late lunch and a stroll around Place du Vendome, looking at all the most exclusive jewellery shops in the world, Emmanuel hailed a taxi and they returned to the apartment to find the young man who cared for the apartment organising a chef for the evening, as Angela had decided a table of eight was just the thing for the first night in Paris. But half way through the meal, Emmanuel began to flag and so directly after the splendid meal he and Richard retired. Not so Angela, who, with her guests, finished up at about one in the morning. Emmanuel climbed naked into bed to be followed by an equally tired Richard. They held one another and then slowly drifted off to sleep with the expectation that tomorrow was going to be a very well organised day because of Angela, and they were not wrong.

Angela was dynamic as a person and with a social strength to keep up with anyone. She had very carefully monitored this relationship between Emmanuel and Richard, exactly as she had controlled Salvatore's business originally. She liked Richard: that was sufficient for her, so she let out the reins on Emmanuel just far enough so that if something went the way she did not want it to she could pull him back under her control at once. Hence this trip to Paris. It had been very interesting for Angela to see Emmanuel in love as opposed to infatuated for a fortnight, and she was very pleased with his performance. This was what she had always wanted for him, a man who could mentally look after him and according to her Richard was the man, not pretentious, but kind, intelligent, not pushy. Even she had to agree with Emmanuel that he was very beautiful. So Angela was content, assuming she had organised this very well and the end result would pay dividends.

The next day being Saturday obviously meant the flea market at Porte de Clignancourt. Richard was totally overwhelmed. He could not believe it was so enormous and the thing that surprised him was that Emmanuel and Angela seemed to know everyone. The flea market was vast, and whatever you wanted you could have, depending if your pocket could stand the strain. Richard's eyes just danced from one object to another. At one o'clock, Angela said to the boys, 'Lunch!' and whisked them off to a noisy restaurant at the beginning of Paul Bert, where the dealers and buyers over lunch spoke only of prices. Angela ordered for them, even though the smaller print under everything on the menu was in English. They charged their glasses and drank to a successful find at the market.

'What have you seen that you like?' Angela asked Richard.

He tilted his head for a moment and then smiled. 'He's right here.'

'Excellent choice,' laughed Angela, as Emmanuel simply glowed with pride, 'but those small rock crystal chandeliers – I think the price is too high.' She had reverted to the full business woman again. It took Richard a long time to get used to this dual personality, but Emmanuel accepted it as normal.

They returned to the market once again and spent the early afternoon searching for hidden treasures. Angela had found what she wanted by being an expert at this market, playing cat and mouse with the price. She did not purchase the light fixture and two sconces even though the man had dropped the price considerably after half an hour's bargaining. Richard and Emmanuel, whilst Angela was doing this on one side of the alley, crossed and went into a crowded interior selling academic drawings and for $50 Richard purchased a beautiful pencil drawing of a naked youth that had great similarities to Emmanuel and it was with some pride he later showed it to Angela.

'Yes,' she said, studying the drawing back at the apartment, 'it's a very competent drawing.'

'I am bigger than that,' said Emmanuel.

''Well, your hands are, anyway,' Richard laughed, receiving a sharp slap on the shoulders. Angela chose not to hear anything.

That evening they went to a restaurant close by that, when in Paris, they always patronised, and Richard was surprised that the owner from the thousands of people that must have passed through his restaurant doors remembered Angela and Emmanuel. The next morning all were bidden to rise early.

A taxi collected them, and it being Sunday morning, took them to the church of St Nicholas du Chardonnet. They arrived half an hour early to see that the last Mass had not finished. Richard thought that odd but sat quietly with them, waiting for it to finish. When it was over, he was astonished at Angela and Emmanuel's behaviour: they stood instantly and pushed through the exiting crowd, and found three seats in the second row. Angela adjusted her mantilla and Richard noted that most of the women had either hats or mantillas, but he was quite unprepared for the following Mass. He had gone to a Catholic school, and Mass was Mass as far as he was concerned, but suddenly, as everyone rose, a procession entered and a pre-Vatican Two sung Mass began. He had no words to describe the sensation but what he witnessed was a tradition and a precise rite in Latin that rather overawed him. When he swung about to glance at the priest at one stage in a pulpit, clinging onto the side of a column, he was stunned at the packed cathedral. A soprano and tenor, as well as a swelling organ, filled this building. He was very aware of being so close to the sanctuary, of the precise rite of genuflecting and moving from side to side of the priest by the assistants. At the completion of Mass, Richard was aware his eyes had not stopped for long on any of the many parts that made up the ceremony. It was almost exhausting in is strength, he thought. At the end, the crowd moved out; two principal doors had been flung open and the organ was in full peal. He found it difficult to concentrate for the next few minutes.

'As it should be done,' said an ever-confident Emmanuel.

The three of them had a late lunch at the apartment, with a great number of oysters being consumed and washed down with copious quantities of champagne, followed by pheasant and roasted vegetables. Quite a day, he thought. He and Emmanuel rested after lunch and at five o'clock were ready yet again for Angela's programme to whisk them off to a cocktail party, then dinner. Richard decided it wasn't a matter of keeping up: one was just swept along with the rush of energy that was Angela.

On Monday, she alone returned to the market and then met the boys for lunch and an initial attack on the Louvre. Returning from this exhausting exercise, it was Emmanuel who noticed two packages in the entrance.

'Congratulations,' he said to Angela. She smiled and settled down as he immediately filled three glasses with champagne. Richard looked at Angela and then Emmanuel, who laughed. 'Angela returned to the market this morning so the chandelier and two sconces are now in the packages.'

'They are just what we want for the room with our display case,' she informed him. He knew he was never going to get used to this whirlwind life, but then he wondered who cared when it was so great. Emmanuel left them to telephone Kerry about a handbag she wanted, and Angela took the opportunity of being alone with Richard to speak to him.

'Richard, how much a week would you get for renting your terrace house?'

He was quite taken by surprise. 'I don't know. Why?'

'Well, you obviously enjoy Emmanuel's company so I see no reason why, when we return to Melbourne, you just let your house and move in to No. 6 Ashfield Avenue. There is loads of space and the pool in summer – everything you could want.

'Thank you very much.' He was aware he felt awkward. 'You are extremely generous.'

'Not at all.' She smiled, but this had been a very calculated move on her part. Here in Paris the boys slept together every evening. This they had not done in Melbourne and Angela was absolutely sure she was not going to tolerate Emmanuel moving out of her home and moving in with Richard, so she sought to fight fire with fire and jumped the gun. Richard knew that the moment Angela proposed this offer to Emmanuel he would be trapped. He would have to trade his independence for the man he loved.

Day after day museums and galleries, lunch on the Seine on a boat – it did not stop. The only thing in the two week period that was repeated was the Mass at St. Nicolas du Chardonnet, and all too soon it was time to pack their bags and take a taxi to the airport.

Angela had indeed spoken to Emmanuel about Richard moving in to No. 6 and he joyfully agreed, never for a moment expecting Richard would be anything but delighted. So on the long flight back to Australia all the pros and cons of taking up residence in Angela's home were thrashed out. Angela had won yet again. If Richard thought the move was going to be difficult, he was wrong. Angela organised everything, even to the point of taking Salvatore aside and explaining as diplomatically as possible the new lie of the land. Salvatore was not blind. He had seen his son elated in the company of Richard and he thought him a fine young man, a sentiment echoed by Kerry, but to have Angela explain specifically what were to be the future living arrangements – and also sleeping – did very little to assure Salvatore that this was the correct path for his son. But with Angela's strong persuasion he gave in, even if his arguments were, as Angela said later to Kerry, rather macho and extremely silly.

It might have been macho and silly, as Angela put it, but Salvatore was anything but happy about the situation. He thrashed it through in his mind day after day; all Angela's friends were gay, so were a great number of Kerry and Salvatore's closest friends, but this issue sat very uncomfortably on his shoulders. It wasn't that he didn't like gay men; he loved their attention and their outlook on life. Heaven knows, it was Paul who steered him into this new flooring system, that was making him a fortune and he knew he couldn't have worked something quite so simple out that would have done so well, so why was he upset? He knew he was, and so did Kerry. She was glad that Angela had spelt it out so clearly as only she could, thought Kerry, so what about Salvatore's attitude? He liked Richard very much and before Angela had said anything they were developing a fine relationship. Now Kerry sensed the problem and telephoned Angela first, then Emmanuel and lastly Salvatore.

'Darling,' she said to him, 'we have two guests for dinner this evening, special ones. I will leave it all up to you,' and hung up.

A sprightly bound up the hallway announced Salvatore had arrived and depositing everything in the kitchen and the fridge he turned to see Kerry dressed for a special evening. He noted the table was laid with white damask and the best silver.

'Wow!' he exclaimed. 'You look great.' She thanked him. 'Now, who do we have for dinner?'

'Your son and Richard.

Salvatore looked across the room but saw nothing. He went into the kitchen area to prepare without a word. Kerry had the knowing feeling that there was going to have to be a little conversation, bitter or otherwise, before the boys arrived.

'Salvatore,' she began, 'let's have it. What's wrong?'

'Nothing.'

'Oh, darling, I know you're hurting inside, but for what?'

'You don't understand,' he said, giving a lobster a hard time.

'Oh, but I do. If you are worried about your son's sexuality, forget it.' He looked down at the bench top as he organised the meal, almost as if he were afraid to catch Kerry's glance. 'Salvatore, the boys are due here in half an hour. If in that time you cannot verbalise what you are concerned about I shall collect them and take them to a restaurant in town without you. Are you listening to me?'

'Yes,' came the muttered reply.

'Well?'

'It's just that I seem to be incidental to their relationship. No one asked me anything. Angela tells me that Richard is my son's lover and moving in with her. What do you expect me to feel like?'

Kerry gave an audible sigh. 'Salvatore, if, and only if, Emmanuel had come to you and asked if he could bring Richard home here as his lover, what would you have said?'

'I don't know,' he replied, quietly. 'I don't know.'

'So why are you torturing yourself now?'

'Because no one asked me.'

'Darling, what the hell are you talking about?' Kerry was becoming angry with him. 'He is our son. He has been in Angela's orbit for years. He is an adult. He is not fifteen years old, but I am sure at fifteen Emmanuel was having sex with men and this is the first time in his life he feels confident enough to bring Richard to dine with us and you don't approve. I just don't believe it. Hopefully, Salvatore, this is not some macho phobia that is about to surface because your son – and let me make this clear – *my* son as well, has decided to have dinner with his boyfriend.'

Kerry it's not like that, I promise.' He looked down at what was to become the dinner. 'He's impossible, absolutely impossible. Emmanuel is beautiful, intelligent and I can go on about the negative adjectives, but- - -' Kerry completed the sentence for him, 'but there's always Angela?'

'I don't know, and I probably can't live without either.' He turned on the tap to wash his hands.

'Haven't you seen the change in him since his return from Paris, now he is living with Richard? He's a different young man. He thinks now, before passing one of his sharp one-liners. He is more considerate.'

'I know. It's easy to see the change in him and it's for the better, I agree.'

'So, darling, where is your fear, or what is your distress that you are acting like this?'

He placed both hands down on the marble bench top and dropped his head.' 'I can't bear the fact that I am going to lose him to Richard,' and tears began to form. Instead of rushing to his side, Kerry waited. This was the only way Salvatore was going to clear away this problem. 'He will leave us, and we shall only see him occasionally.' More tears began to flow.

'Oh, Salvatore, how similar you and Angela are! He wiped his eyes with a tea towel. 'What do you mean,' he sniffed.

'Why do you think Angel took Richard to Paris with her and Emmanuel? Why do you think she has organised that Richard is now resident at No. 6? She thinks the same way as you, she wants to keep Emmanuel with her for as long as possible and she is prepared to do anything to keep him with her and happy.'

'Yes, you're right,' he admitted. 'I know, deep inside, if he's happy with Richard, then so am I. It's just that I seem to be an afterthought in this situation. Everyone has gone and done what they wanted and no one thought of what my opinion was about Richard.'

'Well, what is it?' Kerry emptied her second glass.

He sighed and looked at her. 'Exactly the same as yours.'

'Well, darling, I shall be the proudest woman in the world if you tell him that this evening.'

'You're wonderful. You know all these things instinctively. For me, it's much harder.'

'You're wrong. With Vince it was very different, but Emmanuel, I tell you honestly, this is the first friend he has had that I think will work for him in a relationship, a mature relationship, and for that I am grateful to Richard. I wonder if you and I, in the same situation as

Angela, would have offered Emmanuel and his lover the suite opposite ours to live in?'

'I should have needed convincing,' and here he stopped to look at the dining table set for four.

'But she didn't, did she? She was prepared to give them both her home and her love unconditionally.

'I'm not sure about 'unconditionally', but Angela was, I feel, a step ahead of us.'

'But let's see what we can turn on this evening, darling. We just might find we have two beautiful young men dining with us regularly.'

So that was it; all hurdles jumped and Richard two days after his return to Melbourne had taken formal residence at No. 6 Ashfield Avenue, much to Angela's satisfaction and Emmanuel's delight.

Ten days later, a well-padded, large wooden box was delivered and Paul called in to organise an electrician to hang the new purchase from Paris. Richard had begun to paint the interior with sky and clouds and the different levels had little stairs connecting them with columns and ruined buildings. The movable miniature spotlights were hidden in the ceiling section of the case. And so came the big day of Emmanuel and Richard bringing in the fifty or so figures and Angela taking great care to arrange them, with Richard moving the lights to exactly the spot where she wanted them – altogether a great success. Angela was ecstatic and a large drinks party was organised so her friends could see the finished result, chandelier, sconce and all.

Richard had a small studio from where he worked, basically a shed he rented. This both Angela and Emmanuel decided just would not do, so as one of Angela's investments was a row of Victorian shops, and one with a good rear access being vacant, Richard was moved in and a very smart sign on the window read 'Fine Furniture Restorer'. The front window always showed some of his finer efforts.

Life did not change much for Emmanuel, except he had Richard every evening. His days were well filled up with Angela and, to his way of thinking, he was the happiest young man in the world. But a dinner party at Angela's one evening opened up for Emmanuel a new and, to his way of thinking, a nasty sensation, jealousy. It had never been part of his life ever, but this evening one of the male guests made a play for Richard. Emmanuel was so used to men doing this to him he never thought of it and just basked in the attention but to see it happen to the man he loved set all the alarm bells ringing at once. The green dragon of jealousy bit hard. Emmanuel's instant sarcasm, not to mention sharp words, were sufficient to warn the predator away but he genuinely suffered and in bed that evening held Richard very tightly.

'You didn't really think I would do anything with that guy, did you?' To his surprise he saw tears in Emmanuel's eyes. 'Oh, come here,' and Richard held him closely and ran his hands through his thick hair.

'You don't know how much I love you,' Emmanuel said, brushing his tears away.

'You're wrong. I love you with all my heart and soul, and will do until the day I die.'

There was no further comment. They snuggled down together in one another's arms. But Emmanuel never forgot that moment of jealousy and in the future was extremely careful at these dinner parties who sat beside Richard.

And so the seasons passed and a whirlwind organisation by Angela saw Emmanuel and Richard seated together on a plane in late spring, heading for Paris.

'Darling, you will love Paris in the autumn.'

Vince, at Sitwell, had telephoned Monsignor Christie several times for clarity on certain points, as it was not all easy going in the town. Sitwell was a sleepy country town in the Mallee in Victoria. The large flat plains seemed to extend for ever, extremely hot in summer and bitterly cold in winter, as the wind swept mercilessly across the plains. It was a grazing and wheat belt area and very little had changed since the 1920s.

Sitwell claimed a main street which ran the entire length of the town and either side were late Victorian shops of varying quality but all had large façades above the verandas, stating who they were and what they sold. Once, the street must have had a charm, but in the seventies a council with no foresight had felled all the century old plane trees, claiming they were too big, and took too much cleaning up in autumn. They planted Australian native trees: the result was predictable and pathetically sad. So Main Street - and it did not matter what time of the year it was – always looked tired, but especially in summer, with the glistening bitumen that shimmered in the heat.

Behind Main Street, both right and left, spread out the township in an orderly grid system and vague attempts at suburban gardening had been attempted by the owners of the dwellings that dotted the streets. Most of the houses were pre-1920 but a few of the more nasty ones poked their noses out at the others, claiming to be modern and, as such, very much more up to date. Half way down Main Street was a ragged palm tree that determined the division in this town geographically and financially. The street was called Sutton Drive and it cut Main Street in half, running at right angles to it. On one corner stood a weatherboard church with the palm tree; it had been the Presbyterian Church and was now functioning as the Uniting Church. Diagonally opposite was a red brick church which, by way of notification, had a modern sign stating it was Anglican.

If one entered the town from the highway (and Sitwell had been by-passed in the 1970s), one drove down Main Street and to the left passed the now Uniting Church. With paint peeling off there was a row of moderate suburban houses and the old Methodist Church that in this day and age was used as a badminton hall. If one turned right, past the Anglican brick building, with its orange terracotta tiled roof, one entered into what is generally acknowledged in all small towns to be the smartest street in town, and at the very end stood the Catholic Church and school.

Half way down this street, lined with Australian native trees that were lifting all the cement guttering, was a magnificent Victorian mansion, the largest house in Sitwell. It was inhabited by the Higgins family. Three generations ago they had built it and still inhabited it. It was one storey and very ornate, with the traditional verandas surrounding it and set on a very large plot. A tower on the side stated most definitely that the inhabitants were to be respected or else. Two doors up on the opposite side stood the most ghastly modern structure that went by the name of a 'house'. The resident was the architect that had designed it as his family home. Every type of architectural cliché could be used to describe it, a flat but irregular roof, huge windows, just the thing for long hot summers, one part in cream brick with feature walls in roughhewn stone and the huge glass windows that always had the curtains drawn. The front fence in itself deserved description: about a metre and a half tall, made of a mixture of free form cement, now with peeling paint, cream brick sections, irregular and again the roughhewn stones. The total effect was alarming and in this house resided the architect Anthony Howes and family.

If these two largest of the houses on the street were completely different, so too were the relationships between the two families. 'Disdain' is the word that comes to mind.

But if Anthony Howes's house screamed out as one passed, the Catholic Church he designed at the end of Sutton Drive was an exercise in just as bad taste. The old weatherboard Catholic Church was still in place and was used by St. Bridget's School as a hall and gymnasium. Right in front of it was Anthony Howes's 'masterpiece'. It is difficult to find adjectives to describe this monstrosity. It had an irregular roofline, from very low to extremely high in the front and was basically constructed in stratas of white cement, brick and crazy paving stone. There were skylights let into the irregular roof system filled with the crudest coloured glass designs possible in the harshest reds and oranges, which were perhaps the fashion in the seventies but where, one would never know. The front section had a vast wall of this shocking glasswork, so the interior took on the effect of a furnace, especially in summer. The roof had always leaked and the water stains were easily noted on the side wall.

The interior was something again. It had a worn apple-green carpet wall to wall; with the red windows this complementary colour scheme gave no rest at all to the eye. There was, needless to say, no high altar, just a huge concrete block with a wooden top on a raised dais. Our Lady's chapel was constructed near a side door out of glass bricks and to make an exit from this door one had to file around it. But the sacristy was so small that the priest dressed first, followed originally by the altar boys, as there was room only for the bulky inadequate furniture to take two people at a time. Just beside this barn-like structure was the priest's apartment, and it was exactly as Mary had described it to Vince that Christmas almost a year ago, a small matchbox of a building with low ceilings and a furnace again in summer, as it was long and narrow, the longest wall facing west.

It was to this that Father Vincenzio Lampedusa had come and to say he had been shocked was an understatement at the architectural mish-mash of the New Church and school buildings, all surrounded by a sea of black asphalt. For the first month he had stayed with Mary at her large homestead six kilometres out of town, but he found the logistics difficult so an arrangement was struck that at weekends, which were his busy periods, he remained in town in the apartment but at the first opportunity he fled to Mary's, away from this depressing architectural heap.

The Higgins and the Howes families had been the founders of this town, both wealthy with properties. When the elder members of the families handed the properties over to the younger generation they moved into town. The Higgins family had at this time much more financial power. Needless to say the huge Victorian mansion was proof of this. As they had built and paid for the original Catholic church, now wedged in behind Anthony Howes's monstrosity, it was this that divided once good friends into a situation now where the Howes and Higgins refused to speak to one another. In the seventies, Anthony Howes, as a result of a successful marriage, found his bank account in a very healthy state and as a result demolished the original Howes mansion in Sutton Drive and built the present construction, but this was not enough. He decided a new and powerful design was necessary to lift the Catholic image in Sitwell, so with the help of a few people he knew, especially the priest of the time and with the bishop's permission, he was foolishly given carte blanche : the present day St. Bridget's was the result.

Mary and Sarah Higgins were the closest of friends and spent quite a bit of time together. Mary was often a guest at the Higgins home on Sutton Drive and with Sarah's mother, still the matriarch, she passed her only social time, as she was considered an odd woman locally and dressed, to their way of thinking, strangely. She was quickly labelled a snob: small country towns never change.

The thorn in the side was the church. The Higgins family had built and paid for the old one and the Howes had completely built it over with their monstrosity in front and it was a subject that Nancy Higgins returned to again and again. Now there was hope of resolving the problem with Vince in charge, but how – that was the problem? And so was money.

Mary had married a man eighteen years her senior and it was said cattily that it was to escape Angela. He was a kind man, Keven O'Shanassey, tall and very thin, with a mop of grey hair perched on top and a very sculptured face, hollow cheeks, broad shoulders and very much the countryman. He had cared very much for Mary and indulged her every whim. Perhaps he was afraid she would become tired of the country life and return to the city. He need have had no fear, as Mary loved Bantry, an enormous property that she now had run like clockwork for the past seven years, due to the fact that Keven had just quietly died in his sleep, without pain or illness. He just went to bed one evening and quietly passed on. They had no children, so Mary inherited all

It was the homestead at Bantry that was the jewel. It had been built in two periods by the O'Shanassey family and the old part was absorbed into the new section built in the 1860s. It was a huge, red brick structure of two storeys. It boasted two towers and a double-storeyed veranda that encircled three sides of the main building. One arrived at the house through a now mature park of ornamental trees. In fact Mary had only re-opened the original front drive four years before, as a quick exit from behind the house and across a paddock saved two kilometres of the drive into Sitwell. But she was determined to restore Bantry to what it must have been at the turn of the century, even if she had no intention of returning to eight indoor staff. When she had arrived at Bantry, which seemed now like a century ago, she had found it in poor repair, a working house but with much to be done, and so with determination she set about dealing with it. There were many things that set Bantry above the local homesteads. One was its vast size and another, and perhaps more important one, was its location.

Whenever Vince returned to Bantry, his black Mercedes smoothly moved between the huge iron gates that, at a touch of a commander, swung open, and he drove through this beautiful park. The drive was straight but at regular intervals symmetrically large pedestals in brick rendered in cement rose and were topped with large urns with lids. They were never meant to have plants; their form alone spoke for them. And then as Vince, in a spring downpour, pulled up in front of the largest tower, he looked to his left as he always did to a series of three large terraces that finished at the river below. The terraces were so broad that the top one on the right held a tennis court and it never failed to impress him, with steps going down to each level, with pedestals topped with urns. It truly had a magical effect, especially in this soft spring rain.

Some time ago now, Paul Stratford had arrived at Bantry to assist Mary with a few ideas and the renewal of the pavement in the hallway. Paul was a very handsome man, cultured and very aware of his clientele. He was tall, with black hair swept back and going grey, and splendid grey blue eyes just like smoke coming from an autumn fire. He had skin that was flawless, not a mark on it, and after a shave he had the appearance of never having had a beard line. He breathed elegance and as he had furnished Angela's house, now three or four times over, he knew the family very well. There was never a dinner party at Angela's that Paul and Andrew were not present.

'Darling,' he said to Mary, having surveyed the exterior all in the most immaculate condition from the palm house to the tennis courts, that Mary never used, the terraces that fell away to the river below, and the exterior fabric of the house. 'Perfect!' was all he could say. He was not so complimentary about the interior, however. 'Mary, darling, it is too old hat.' When she asked why, he went on, 'Just look around you. It's ghastly!' He helped himself to a drink as she gazed both right and left.

'I don't see anything wrong with it,' she insisted.

'Mary, it is so left-over I can't tell you. I'm prepare to take a bet that if I seized one of those dowdy brown curtains and attempted to close it, it would drop to the floor in a pile of dust.'

'Really?' Mary replied frostily.

'Yes, really.' He stood up, walked across the large drawing room (of which there were two in this mansion), seized the curtain and attempted to close it, not that in the middle of the countryside this is necessary. There was an odd sound and half the top section, after a ripping sound, hung limply from the top. 'Told you so! He smiled and returned to his chair.

A sigh acknowledged defeat. 'Is it really that drab in here?' she asked, never quite having noticed the interior.

'Yes, Mary, it is. The outside of Bantry is stunning. There's not another house in Australia with the view and the terraces to the river, and the outside of the house is pristine. But, sweetie, inside it's definitely awful.'

'Oh well, have it your way,' at which she filled her glass. 'Anything you want, but not too much gilt furniture. I would hate to wake in the morning and feel I am at Angela's.' They both laughed. Although Mary found Angela insupportable and was not short of saying so, she had inherited from her her business acumen. When times had been good at Bantry, Mary took the money and invested it in an air-conditioning factory which she and Keven purchased. They brought in an American engineer and in four years had doubled the initial investment. So she continued, but never on the stock exchange, just like Angela. She did not trust it or perhaps it was that neither of them could control it, so they just passed it by. On these ventures, Mary could do no wrong, so a very healthy agricultural capital was multiplied many times over with many other worthwhile investments. To refurbish the vast mansion entirely was no problem for Mary, therefore. The only thing that perplexed her was how she had never seen the interior before as wasted or left over from another era, and, as Paul pointed out, 'not smart'.

'In here, darling,' cried Mary, as Vince in clericals entered the drawing room. 'You look as if you could do with a drink. Bad day?'

'No, not really, but just trying to change the smallest thing seems impossible.'

'Don't worry, Vince. Nancy Higgins is prepared to insure the new church well, dowse it with petrol and set fire to it.'

He laughed. 'Not a bad idea. I just don't see the point of putting money into repairing this monster. I have spoken to the bishop and he says that if there is not the money at hand then it has to stay. Oh, what a bore!' At that point, for the first time in her life, she saw Vince as Emmanuel – or was it the other way around? She didn't know.

'I'm having such a problem with the Deacon. I am undermined at every turn.

'Fire him, darling. It's the only way.'

Mary knew very well this Deacon and loathed him. He was a very close friend of the Howes so that made the borders even more defined. Andrew Symonds was the appointed Permanent Deacon, on a contract, and as he saw Vince and Mary with the Higgins he assumed that Vince was a problem and so made life as difficult as possible for him. Andrew Symonds was short, approximately 66 years old, of no features worth mentioning; he had grey hair, a grey beard and was super-territorial. Perhaps the washed-out eyes that were always covered with heavy black-framed glasses said it all. One never knew from his eyes what he was thinking, and as Mary often said, for the Deacon to think as opposed to make problems was something again. They never spoke. Every Sunday the Deacon would make an effort to slide up to Mary and Sarah Higgins and pass banal comments. Mary took to turning her back on him and as both she and Sarah still insisted on hats or mantillas they vexed the Deacon enormously, knowing that neither of the two, or for that matter, Nancy Higgins, ever attended Mass without a head covering.

This Deacon was well grounded in the sixties when this particular permanent position was instituted in the Catholic Church. It had never existed before; a permanent Deacon was generally married and always tedious. It seemed to be the pre-requisite. But on a power basis, they are a dangerous race and Vince was now finding this out.

'Nancy, you look divine!' exclaimed Mary, after Sunday Mass. Back at the Higgins Mansion down the street for lunch, 'Vince will be here in a moment. Where did you get that beautiful mantilla?'

'Thank you, Mary. It was a gift from my husband when we went to Europe for our honeymoon. I have always liked it.'

Nancy Higgins lived with Sarah and her family – or was it the other way around? The house was so large it didn't really matter.

To Michael, Mary said, 'Darling, you look more handsome every day.'

'Thanks, Mary. You should get a job in public relations!' He was Sarah's youngest son. At twenty three he was handsome, smart but not interested in anything but laughing and drinking with Mary. His older brother Gerald, who managed the family property, Mary found dull and terribly predictable and if he was such, the wife was obnoxious. Mary and Sandy, as she was called, decided it was better for everyone just to ignore one another. 'Overweight and over-opinionated,' was Mary's diagnosis of Sandy, which had Michael in hysterics. 'Mary, you are great!

'Thank you, darling. I hope you're sitting next to me today. We don't want fatty taking up too much space.'

He laughed again. He was indeed a handsome young man, as handsome as his elder brother was plain. His long, wavy blonde hair and electric green eyes and perfectly tanned skin gave him the look of an international tennis player, and in shorts he had a blonde down that covered his very muscular legs. Altogether, according to Mary, stunning.

Vince finally arrived, breathing fire about the size of the sacristy, where everyone had to wait to change. 'The waste of time is just stupid,' he complained.

'Oh, Father,' Nancy smiled, 'I am sure they wouldn't jail an elderly citizen for burning that monster to the ground. A heavy insurance, Father, that's the game.' Everyone laughed, but Vince had seen prior to entering the Higgins Mansion the Deacon's red car in front of the Howes house. He let it go.

When Paul had been here, Mary had initially called him for new flooring in the enormous entrance hall, as the tessellated flooring was broken and missing lots of pieces, but although this was important there was another reason she wanted him at Bantry. It had to do with an event two months earlier. It had been Nancy Higgins's birthday and she asked Vince for a big favour. Would he say a Latin Mass for Nancy in her private chapel? The answer was in the affirmative and they had all crowded into this small room with a magnificent rose window that had come from a demolished church in Melbourne years before and an altar under it that Vince faced to say the Mass. At the end a very generous lunch was laid out. Nancy had said to her invited guests after thanking Father that 'we threw all this out for polyester.' There was laughter but the truth of the matter was there.

It was after this lunch that Mary returned to Bantry. She went to the side garden on the level above the tennis court and stared at the part of the homestead that was different to the rest. The fabric was red brick but the two long windows had Gothic tracery. She had with her a key which unlocked a door at the end and poked her head in. It had been the chapel of Bantry. It was a largish rectangular room with a tray ceiling that made it look taller, in pine lining, and two windows with the Gothic tracery on the right-hand side. Half the flooring was tessellated octagonal tiles, many cracked and for some odd reason the other half of the flooring was wooden. At the far end in this cold structure was what was left of the altar. As Mary moved closer, dodging sacks of potatoes and broken furniture, she looked closely at the altar, completely destroyed at one end by borers and what must have been an attachment like a large frame with an ornate pediment which was in several pieces on the floor. There was an extremely damaged painting of St. Michael that once had been held inside the cornice. Altogether it was a very sad sight. It was to this that Mary had taken Paul, to see what he could do.

'You don't really expect Vince to say Mass here, do you?' he asked, in surprise.

'Not really. I think it needs some work. I guess I was prompted by the private Mass for Nancy Higgins's birthday and as Vince is here five nights a week I suppose it's the least I can prepare for him.'

'Darling, it's no better than a storeroom and a bad storeroom at that.'

'Now, darling, don't go on about it. Just do something about it.

He did. Two days after he had returned to Melbourne with a sketch book filled with notes and measurements, a van drew up in front of Bantry and the driver and gardener loaded onto it the damaged altar and cornice section, the broken pews and what was left of a wooden platform and altar rails, and said goodbye. Three hours later it pulled up behind Richard's shop and the two of them offloaded the contents.

'I'd burn the lot,' commented the deliveryman. 'It's all junk.' He pulled out into the heavy peak hour traffic and drove off. Richard had to agree with him; it really was second rate junk.

The next morning, Paul had an appointment with Richard to discuss the repairs. 'But it's not worth it,' moaned Richard.

'Be that as it may, here is what you are going to do. Rip out all those ghastly painted panels, take the measurements and Salvatore will cut marble for you. I have phoned him so he is ready. Install the marble instead.'

'But, Paul, one side is eaten way by borers.'

'Get rid of it. Replace any part that is damaged and I think you may as well re-make the gradines. They don't look as though they could hold one candlestick, let alone six.'

'All this stuff virtually has to be rebuilt'.

'You've got it in one. Oh, by the way, this is a rush job. We can't have Father Lampedusa saying Mass on Mary's kitchen table, can we?'

'Suppose not,' came the forlorn reply. He handed Richard a set of dimensional drawings and headed out of the door, leaving Richard totally bewildered as to where to start.

The following week Salvatore sent two men who stayed with Mary and began the immediate task of re-flooring the chapel with white marble, with honey-coloured tiny squares let into the corners of the large white ones. Mary was most concerned about the rubbish and debris that was hauled out of the chapel. 'If the wood is borer-ridden, burn it. In fact, burn everything that doesn't serve.' A large bonfire behind the service buildings was testament to years and years of useless junk.

'She's doing what?' exclaimed Angela.

'Setting up a chapel for Vince.'

'Well, well, I would never have believed it. What's the altar like?'

'It's totally rotten. Two thirds of it has to be re-constructed.'

'Well, give me the measurements of the top and I will have the linen cloths made. It's the least I can do for Vince.' With that she changed the subject and spoke about the opera that they were to attend the following evening.

A bang of the front door announced that Emmanuel had returned. He kissed them both. 'Well,' he began, with an arm around Richard's neck, 'I believe you are to restore the chapel fittings at Bantry.'

'Restore! Rebuild, you mean.'

'I must have a look tomorrow. I didn't even know Bantry had a chapel.'

'Have you been to Bantry?'

'Yes, but not for years. Vince and I went there when we were kids for a holiday but when I began to enjoy it he was too old and it didn't interest him, so I went alone three or four times. It's great. It has a river at the bottom of a terrace system. There used to be a boat with a canvas roof. I wonder if it's still there. Would you like to go and see it?'

'Love to,' was the reply.

'Well, when the altar is fixed -'

'- and the rest!' Richard grinned.

'When it's all fixed, we can all go. What do you think, Angela?'

'I'll think about it.'

The next morning, a call to Mary confirmed Angela's opinion that she had absolutely no idea about getting this chapel ready for Vince and Angela said she would take over – and so she did.

Angela and Emmanuel began a hunt in the antique shops and auction rooms for all the items necessary for a Mass.

'I don't like them – they are too heavy,' Angela insisted, as they were shown a set of six ecclesiastical candlesticks. 'But we'll think about them.' They left the shop. 'I think I just might give the Mons a call. Perhaps he can help us out.'

'But, Angela, I thought those candlesticks were great.'

'Yes, they are, darling, and I am sure tomorrow the price will be much more reasonable.' The pair of them headed back toward the car arm in arm, laughing.

'Richard, you're not going to work today,' said a sleepy Emmanuel.

'Come on, beautiful, I have to finish all these things for Bantry.'

'Forget it. Today we must go to the zoo.'

'What! The zoo! What for?'

Emmanuel drew him closer and then announced: 'You know, Richard, you are just perfect.' He kissed him. The acceptance of this wonderful complement meant without a doubt that the zoo was it. Richard had grown up in a family where every dollar counted and now he was suddenly swept away by the man he most loved in this world, where money or the survival on it, just wasn't important. 'Of course, it's Thursday. Doesn't everyone go to the zoo? And, besides, Angela is joining us at the restaurant at one o'clock.'

Richard could never get used to this, as much as he pretended to. It was a world that didn't stop. There were no slow moments at all. He had an altar to finish off; as one does, he thought nothing made sense. A month ago, because it was autumn in Paris, well they had to go, declared Angela and that was that. The only concrete thing in his life now was this beautiful young man now sliding up on top of him, which, without a doubt, meant they were going to be late for breakfast, but they would be exactly on time for Angela at the restaurant and the zoo.

'You know,' Angela said, addressing Richard, as Emmanuel knew the story, 'when I was a girl there was a huge triumphal arch, obviously a miniature of the one in Paris. You entered up a circular staircase inside it and came out on a little platform. The elephant arrived and you were settled into the howdah. They did up the leather straps and you went for a tour of the zoo on the back of the elephant. Oh, it was simply marvellous. I was very sorry about the other animals living in those awful conditions, but you see now,' she went on with a sweep of her hand, 'it's all so up-to-date. But I must confess I would so like a ride on the elephant.'

'So would I,' enthused Emmanuel. 'Don't you think we could get Mary to keep elephants?'

'Darling, she doesn't know the first thing about a chapel, so God help the elephant!' So between 'essential' luncheon at the zoo or a newly discovered restaurant, Richard attempted to finish the work. When Paul asked about the progress over the telephone, Richard simply replied, 'Oh, but we had to go to the zoo!' As the answer was simply accepted, he never got used to it. Why would Paul just accept that he was a day or so late with the work he was waiting for? Then it struck him – Angela. Paul dined with Angela and the boys, but while having pre-dinner drinks and waiting for Salvatore and Kerry he went on about Bantry. 'The best room in the whole house is the library. It is quite splendid. The joinery is fabulous. With new wallpaper and curtains it will just simply take over the whole house.'

'Really,' Angela said in an offhand way, 'and what precisely are you planning to do with it?'

'I plan to use a heavy embossed paper in strong greens and then I'll match it with some silk damask from Casserta.'

This is where the largest palace in Italy is located, and behind this enormous complex, in a myriad of tiny disorganised streets are the silk mills. They had protection under the Kingdom of the Two Sicilies and even under the Unification of Italy in 1861. They survived and today, in this quasi-republic, they are living proof that beautiful things can still be produced as they were in the eighteenth century, even if mechanisation has come along. All the silks are faithful copies of the antique ones and the prices at the factories are good. If they are purchased in Rome, in smart stores, one pays five to eight times the price.

Paul, always thought he had his clients' best interests at heart, the two or three times a year he went to buy, and spent a lot of his time with a certain Luigi Veltoni, who supplied not only accommodation but everything else that went with it. The two of them saw one another twice or three times a year for a week or ten days but the passion never subsided with time. It became mature but the passion was always there. Anthony never knew about Paul's other life and even if he had it would not have changed their relationship. Anthony and Paul had been together for basically all their lives. They were almost an institution. Anthony being in Real Estate had gone up and up and up, so that now he had a very large mansion in George Street, East Melbourne and it was here they decided to stop.

Richard had decided to stop feeling overwhelmed but this house in East Melbourne in its own way rivalled Angela's, different, but the impact was the same. Paul had worked for and with Angela for years but a part of him he had kept quite private, the jokes, the repartee, everything smart but . . . If only, he thought. Emmanuel was the closest thing to paradise on this earth, but he never made a wrong move. There was simply too much at stake and he knew Emmanuel could not be trusted to keep his mouth shut, especially with Angela: no secrets, fine, but for Paul this also equalled no work.

'Emmanuel, would you give me a hand!' cried Angela. He put down his glass and moved to her ever-imploring voice.

'What are you doing?'

'Help me out with this trunk which was hidden at the bottom of a closet in the upstairs corridor.'

Emmanuel drew out the wooden trunk which was not easy, as the handles were trapped at the side of the closet. Finally it came out.

'Well, do we get the pirate or the treasure?' he teased.

'No pirate this evening.' She smiled as she opened the lid. It did indeed hold a treasure but not the sort that sparkles like diamonds, but the value was equally high.

'Angela, it's full of lace!' He at once withdrew a roll and unravelled it. 'Wow, it's beautiful!'

'Yes, it is,' she agreed. 'What you have in your hands is late eighteenth century Brussels lace. Do you like it?

'Angela, it's fabulous.'

'You know, Emmanuel, that the greatest collectors of lace are men, not women. It is the same with dolls.'

'I can't bear them,' he replied. 'I hate dolls. I don't care how much they cost. They are spooky. They sit back, pass judgements and never ever help anybody.'

Angela was surprised that he had taken this sharp point of view, and the fact that he saw them as judgemental. She had never thought of it before, but they were soon forgotten as the rolls of lace were withdrawn from the trunk.

'I thought to use some of this for the altar cloths for Bantry, but on seeing it all now, I shan't do it. To cut this beautiful lace up is just unthinkable.

'What was it used for?' he asked

'Well, a great deal of it by the length once was ecclesiastical. It trimmed albs or cottas and what is here has obviously been stripped from those garments.'

'Look at this.' From half way down the trunk he extracted a one metre wide length of lace that made a skirt.

'That is the bottom of an alb and those two bits sewn onto the bottom are the ends of the sleeves.'

'Angela, how long have you had all this lace here?'

'Oh, it must be years. I suppose I occasionally think of doing something with it. I open it up, look at it and then pack it away. I suppose I should give it all to Vince, but not yet. Help me put it back.' They returned it to the bottom of the closet.

'Darling, I am going to have a rest. Richard should be back soon, so now the pool's ready I hope only to hear the splash, not the intimate details.' She laughed as she stood up and walked to her room.

Summer had come suddenly and every evening before dinner, and occasionally after dinner, depending on Emmanuel's sense of adventure, they used the pool – much to Angela's satisfaction.

CHAPTER FOUR

The end of the world

CHAPTER FOUR

The end of the world

Some months had passed since Richard had finished the work for Bantry and it was now all in place. The work inside the homestead was well underway. Mary was elated and had invited Richard and Emmanuel to stay to see Richard's work installed, plus the restored canvas of St. Michael, but with work and social plans, this seemed to be difficult to organise. There was always some little problem time-wise that said 'next week for sure'. Richard's business was great; he had never had so much work and Paul, being very pleased with the standard of his work, sent him material for restoration and new work to be constructed from his designs.

Life plodded on the same at Sitwell with Mary and Sarah Higgins putting a spoke in the wheel of the Deacon at every turn. Vince still found things anything but easy. He had, on his arrival, dismissed the woman who was the housekeeper for the Canonica, namely the nasty residence beside the church, for the previous priest. Jan Roberts had cleaned and supplied lunch and dinner for the priest. Nancy Higgins put a stop to it at once and said to Vince that to have a friend of the Deacon preparing food for him and second rate at that was tantamount to waiting to be poisoned. So Vince now took all his meals at the Higgins's house when in Sitwell, which meant Saturday and Sunday evening and all the lunches. Sarah had said to Mary that her mother had never been happier or the two girls who worked for her more exhausted. Nancy always now for lunch had the large dining room prepared. In the past they had all eaten in a room overlooking the garden, close to the kitchen. Now, every lunch, or when 'Father' was here, Nancy went all out. Previously this vast room with seating for fourteen had been a forgotten space. Now it came to life. In winter the fire was always ablaze in the marble fireplace; the candelabra, which had been like all the other silver crated up, were now alight; and the silver gleamed, much to the maids' exhaustion. Mary was always welcome at this table and with Michael and a few drinks the two of them took over.

The room itself was enormous, with a high vaulted ceiling which was covered in a riot of plaster work and needless to say a huge crystal chandelier hung from the centre; two matching sideboards either side of the fire breast were the recipients for food and an abundance of silver. It was indeed a fine Victorian room, totally complete, but it was Mary who said to Nancy that she was sorry but she could not possibly attend another meal in this room. Nancy was shocked, feeling that in some way she had offended her.

'Oh no, darling. If you don't get a dimmer for that crystal monster I am going to start to have to wear eye shades.' They all laughed. 'Vanity, vanity!' cried Michael. Needless to say, the following day the electrician arrived.

Vince was definitely the star in this household and many of the parishioners were not all that happy about Nancy and the family's monopolising 'Father'. The funniest afternoons or evenings at the Higgins's home, which revelled under the name of 'Shannon', was when Mary and Michael, after a few drinks, would mimic and send up the Deacon and his wife.

If the Deacon could be described as a non-event, and grey at that, even though no-one underestimated his cunning, his wife, Bronwyn was something again. The standing joke was always 'Dolly and the Deacon', which now took a singsong tone to it and nothing annoyed the Deacon more. Perhaps, as one of the parishioners said cattily, 'If it had been the Deacon and Dolly, perhaps he would be happier with his name first.' But it was always 'Dolly and the Deacon' and 'Dolly' because Bronwyn shared a bust measurement something like Dolly Parton, the American entertainer. But the Deacon's Dolly made the most of it. At 56 she should have looked into a dressing mirror from behind, but our Dolly was mad for stretch jeans and tight cotton interlock tops, a mop of orange-red hair and an over-abundance of make-up. Her presence in church never altered. 'Oh, here is Dolly and the Deacon!' even if he wasn't present it was a rhythm that everyone caught on to. If Dolly's make-up and clothing were, to say the least, adventurous, her footwear was unbelievable. Where Dolly found these platform numbers remained a mystery and she was not telling a soul, but the platform soled shoes which elevated a shortish, over-weight matron another seven or eight centimetres in the air were all in denim in every design known to man or woman. She had them covered in denim – she even had a pair of denim-covered golf shoes as she played golf with Betty Howe on Wednesdays, which was ladies' day at the local Sitwell golf course. Michael always called Betty Howe 'Butch Betty' or 'Betty Bulldike', much to his grandmother's disapproval, even though she loathed Betty Howe.

Betty was tall and angular and always wore a type of man's haircut, no make-up ever at all and always men's shirts or polo shirts, with trousers. She had never been seen in a dress in the history of Sitwell gossip. She was a great contrast to her husband, the dreaded Anthony Howes, who was now close to seventy, short, very overweight and dressed like a country fob, in velvet trousers, flannel shirts and sports jackets, the tweedier the better. But of all these oddities it was Dolly who won the award for just sheer bad taste. She was completely oblivious to it. She had it or them and she flogged them, much to the local parishioners' annoyance, as they saw this flaunting for what it was, inappropriate, especially in church. She teetered down the aisle and attempted to genuflect, it being impossible considering the shoes, and so she did a sensible glide into the closest seat to the front. She never made the mistake of taking the Higgins's pew; not even Dolly was that brave. But it did annoy her, and she and the Deacon were not short of saying so, that considering their imagined status an invitation to dine with Father at the Higgins home, Shannon, or at Bantry just simply never arrived and when she had invited Vince once for lunch he declined graciously, saying he already had a standing arrangement.

111

At Mass, Mary always sat in the Higgins's pew and as always beside Michael. The contrast between the two of them was always commented on, Michael the blonde, beautiful young man from Shannon and Mary, impeccably dressed in black, always in frocks, never trousers, and her usual trade mark of a large black hat and electric red lipstick. Sarah quite often, as did her lack-lustre husband, thought that Mary, although her closest friend, was perhaps not the best influence on Michael, but be that as it may, they always sat together, laughing and sending up the locals. But the sending–up now was in the dining room, and at Shannon was always the same. Here was the odd thing: Nancy sat head of table with Vince on her right, but always on her left sat a young man who was not a part of her family.

Philip was twenty three years old, a very beautiful creature, but delicate and very shy. He had had an extremely difficult life and one which had left him always extremely cautious with people, though with Nancy he felt secure. Bev worked for the Higgins and had done all her life; at forty she looked as if she would keep this large household in order for eternity but she had one morning approximately five years before disturbed Nancy who found her in tears. Nancy was so surprised – nothing moved Bev, so what was wrong? It was then that Bev explained to Nancy that her only brother, who was very dyslexic, had been beaten by his father and she was at her wits end to know what to do, her mother having died many years before. Nancy just looked at Bev and demanded to know why she had not said anything before about Philip. Bev answered that it was her problem and she just did not think it appropriate to trouble her employer with family matters. Nancy immediately dispatched Bev to collect Philip and all his belongings.

In the long servants' wing Nancy had an old bathroom updated; the local plumber was surprised as was the builder when Nancy rang at once to say she had an emergency and was waiting for them. Nancy had Bev's accommodation and the part where Philip was to live joined together with a big living room in common. The servants wing had originally held seven people with indoor and outdoor staff, so accommodating Philip was not a problem. In record time, with a diminutive, dynamic Nancy Higgins giving orders to everyone, Philip's apartment was completed and she insisted for every meal he eat with them, while Bev served at table. Philip and Nancy played cards together and painted. She was a hard taskmaster, but Philip respected her and probably for the first time in his life began to put things mentally in some form of order.

Needless to say, he formed part of the Higgins family group at Mass on Sundays. And he adored Vince. He thought him the most special person in the whole world and it had taken all Nancy's training for Philip to finally gain the courage to say, 'Good morning, Father' or 'Good evening.' Vince described him to Mary as like a frightened deer, beautiful and terribly timid but with the same huge brown eyes that seemed to look straight into your most inner thoughts. Mary agreed: he was indeed a beautiful creature but although she always spoke to him he never replied. Michael, who virtually lived with him, could joke and perhaps be understood and laughed with, but he kept his own counsel and stayed very close to Nancy and, if he had the opportunity, Vince. Little were they all to know that a scene where Philip played leading man was to completely galvanise the Higgins and O'Shanassey group to such an extent that change was inevitable, especially for the Deacon.

Before this occurred, it was Mary who was riding high. Vince was with her at least five nights a week; for the other two Nancy Higgins had taken it upon herself to have the best guest room totally refurnished and with an air-conditioner for the long hot summer nights. Father Lampedusa was well looked after. Needless to say, the bitching letter sent by the Deacon to the Bishop about a priest not residing in the Canonica was not replied to. Vince was also having problems with the school. Apart from it being an architectural mishmash, the powers within this educational institution were well trained in the Deacon's direction, just as the previous more conservative administration had been under the previous priest, and the Deacon moved on but with exceptionally bitter feelings: the relationship was anything but co-operative.

The same had happened with the music in the church. An electric organ, at one side of the altar accompanied by two guitars, belched out the most extraordinary mediocre church music that was possible. This was the first thing Vince stopped, working on the assumption no music was better than kitsch ecclesiastical stuff, and said so. The Deacon reported back to everyone that Father was getting above himself a bit and had no contact with the parish at all.

The Deacon was right into the concept of ecumenical co-operation and this took the form of once or twice a year the three churches had a ceremony together. Needless to say, the Higgins did not attend.

'Go if you want, Father, but don't forget the last time,' said Nancy, very formally. The whole Higgins family used Vince's Christian name in the privacy of their home but never outside. Vince was always referred to there as 'Father'. 'If you think you can follow up behind Dolly and the Deacon,' she went on, in a sing-song fashion.

'He'll make a fool of you in public, like last time,' Mary added, entering into the conversation.

'She's right,' chipped in Michael. 'He will use you as an understudy. I saw him do it one night with the previous priest. He is only after promoting himself. Why the hell can't you fire him?'

'It's a bit more difficult than you think,' Vince replied. 'I would have to prove that what he was doing was detrimental to the position he occupies and that although it is obvious it's difficult to prove it before the Bishop. But his contract is up in about fourteen months. I looked at the sheet the other day and I can assure you, despite what the Deacon thinks, it will not be renewed, or the Bishop will have to find another priest for Sitwell.'

'Well,' said Nancy. 'Aren't we all at Bantry for Saturday dinner? Drinks, perhaps, on the terrace?'

'Drinks anywhere!' joked Michael. He looked back toward his grandmother and noticed she sat in a privileged position at the head of the table as head of this family, but it was the man on her right he thought without a doubt, without that clerical collar, not to mention the rest of his clothing, who would be the closest thing to perfection he had ever seen. The more Michael saw of Vince, the more he wanted him and the knowledge that he couldn't have him fuelled the flames of desire higher and higher.

And so it was, on Saturday evening, instead of the usual Mass, this ecumenical event took precedence.

'We shall start at 5.30,' announced the Deacon, in a knowing way.

'Start whenever you wish. I shall not be there. I have a Latin mass to say at Bantry.'

To say the Deacon was taken aback was an understatement. 'But you have to be there,' he said in an authoritarian way.

'I don't have to be anywhere. You consider yourself the representative of this parish. You go, if you think it's wise,' and Vince closed the conversation, leaving the office and heading out to his car. He pointed it in the direction of Bantry.

The Deacon was black with rage. 'I'll telephone the Bishop,' the usual threat that he never went through with. 'Who does he think he is?' he yelled and screamed to Dolly. 'Without the priest at this event it just doesn't work. If the parish gets hold of this and they will, no one will attend.'

And so it was, for the first or second time, Vince put his foot down and instead of attending this inter-church service said a Latin mass at Bantry for Mary and the extended Higgins family in the newly completed chapel. Later, as planned, there were organised drinks on the top terrace overlooking the river, then they went in to the dining room, completely overhauled by Paul, for a pleasant evening of eating, and, as Michael always commented, 'and drinking!'

The odd thing about Bantry was that Paul overhauled all of it in record time with good quality antique furniture, beautiful textiles and rugs apart from one room off the landing, a small room with a high, tiny window and an old single brass bedstead with a mottled brown and beige wallpaper that was stained by a water leak at some stage; a tiny table beside it with a thirties lamp on it and a religious engraving in a black frame on a plain wall; and that was Mary's bedroom, for all the finery in this vast mansion. When she closed her bedroom door she saw none of it and equally missed none of it as well. This was in sharp contrast to Vince's room, which had a dressing room. It was decorated by Paul in burgundies and gold in the most subtle faded shades with a huge canopy bed draped, as were the windows, in silk damask and in the centre of the ceiling a magnificent Venetian chandelier was splendid.

The Deacon now began to feel that all was not well. How dare this upshot of a priest in this, his first parish, refuse to take responsibilities? Of course as, the Deacon saw it all. He was not blind to the renewing of his contract in fourteen months' time, but his conceit was that this young priest would not last the distance. He spat fire at a dinner at the Howes, with Dolly explaining that what they all sacrificed for the parish this tall dark priest was slowly tearing apart.

Vince had called his treasurer in to find out, as he did every second Tuesday, the exact financial situation of the parish, and on taking a look at the sheets handed to him was shocked at the final balance.

'That's not possible,' he said, sharply. 'Even I can add and deduct. Where is this money going?

The treasurer, a certain Simon Thomas, said nothing, but looked blankly at the sheet he had handed Vince, who literally threw the sheet back at him.

'Simon,' he said in a calculating tone, 'I will give you until our next meeting in fourteen days' time to come up with a correct balance sheet for this parish for the last ten years or I shall call in the tax department and cry fraudulent handling of the parish's money. Do you understand me?'

'Yes, Father,' was the slow reply, 'but it's not my fault.'

'Well, whose fault is it and where is the money?'

Simon looked down at the desk where Vince had now clasped his large hands together. 'Who else has the right to use the parish cheque book?'

Vince took a deep sigh. 'The Deacon.'

'Yes, Father, the Deacon.'

'You will go to the bank and make arrangements immediately that only I have the right to touch this account. Do I make myself clear?'

'Yes,' smiled Simon. 'It will be a pleasure. Will I find you here in twenty minutes?"

'Yes. Why?'

'You will have to sign two documents. I shall go to the bank and get them a once.'

It is not surprising that Dolly and the Deacon were more popular with the non-Catholic community, due to the Deacon's capacity to inveigle himself on to local committees and especially his and Dolly's performance every Thursday night. What a performance it was. Behind the red-brick Anglican Church was a large hall and every Thursday evening there was 'line dancing'. Our grey Deacon took off, bumping into women, making innuendos, with Dolly staggering about in time to the music. This hour and a half every Thursday evening assured the non-Catholics that this was the face of the progressive Catholic Church. Nothing could have been further from the truth.

A furious Deacon swept into Vince's office, which was at the back of what had been the old Canonica, a grand Victorian house of which now the front half was used as art rooms for the school and a computer room, so that there was always a din in the background.

'What is this supposed to mean?' shouted the Deacon, waving a cheque that the bank had refused to honour. 'I have kept this parish in order for years. How dare you refuse to allow me to handle the financial side of things? I shall telephone the Bishop at once.'

Vince turned his telephone around and pushed it toward him. 'Do you want the number?' he asked.

The Deacon threw his now useless cheque book at Vince and stormed out, slamming the door.

Emmanuel had had lunch with Richard in his workroom, surprising him with champagne, paté, roast chicken and all sorts of goodies he had purchased from the local delicatessen. They joked and laughed together, saying that this celebration must be about eighteen months after they did it. Emmanuel laughed and Richard drew him near, knocking over a glass of champagne and kissed him.

'I love you more now than I ever have,' he said.

'Me too,' was Emmanuel's reply.

'Oh, I knew I had something to show you. Look, I found it in the bottom of a cabinet. I think it must be the early sixties - the colour printing is terrible.' Emmanuel looked at a large photo of a funeral Mass, a High Mass with priest, sub-Deacon, Deacon, master of ceremonies and a myriad of altar boys. The whole scene appeared to be dressed in black velvet. 'That's the way I want to go,' Richard laughed, 'with the lot!' Emmanuel looked at the photograph again, then left it and kissed Richard once more. 'Next weekend, Bantry at last,' he smiled. 'You'll love it. I spoke to Mary yesterday and she said all is ready for us. It's going to be great. I know you will love the place.'

'I am sure I shall. Is Angela coming?>'

'No decision as yet, but I guess so. She wouldn't miss out on the fun, darling. Now I have to run. I promised her that I would collect a catalogue from the auction rooms for the painting sale on Tuesday. See you at home.'

They stood up and held one another in their arms tightly.

'I'll see you later.' Emmanuel headed out to the car and on to the auction rooms.

When he returned, having collected a few things for himself and Richard, he was very surprised to see Salvatore's car parked right in front of Angela's. He parked the Mercedes in the garage and with a paper sack of oddments he had purchased, with the catalogue on top, headed indoors from the back of the house.

'Hi, I'm home,' he called out. 'I got your catalogue. Number 162 is just us.' He rounded the corner of the red and gold sitting room to see three people rise to their feet, Angela, Kerry and Salvatore. All three were silent. It was Emmanuel's sixth sense that made him freeze. He just stared at them, waiting for one of them to say something.

'What's wrong,' he eventually asked slowly, and noticed that Angela had tears streaming down her face and was making no attempt to dry them.

'Darling, she said, 'There has been the most terrible accident.' He did not move his eyes off her. 'It's Richard,' she went on and the tears flowed again.

Emmanuel turned his head slowly around. 'What are you talking about?' He directed his question to Kerry.

'Emmanuel, there has been a terrible car accident. Richard has been killed.'

Emmanuel immediately put his hands over his ears as if he did not want to hear anymore and so it wouldn't be true. The bag with its contents crashed to the floor. He was completely numb. He felt nothing at all. He looked at them all again and the silence was deafening. He moved his head from person to person with his hands still over his ears and then he let out a cry that was nothing short of terrifying. He sank to his knees and began to weep in gasps.

'It's not true. It's not true,' he repeated again and again. Salvatore quickly crossed the room and knelt down to hold him. His whole body was trembling and the tears now began to flow. Angela watched the scene and prayed she would never see it again for the rest of her life. Salvatore embraced his son, somehow feeling that this might help but he knew in his heart that Emmanuel was never going to be the same young spontaneous man ever again. He wept with him. Any attempt to console Emmanuel was useless and Kerry called Dr Harris, who arrived and with a great deal of difficulty injected him so as to put him into a deep sleep. They left his bedroom and went downstairs.

'You may as well stay for dinner,' said Angela in a lost way and for the first time in her life Kerry saw Angela as a fragile old lady, an image that she had never seen before, weeping for the pain that Emmanuel was suffering. It must also be said that the three of them were going to miss Richard enormously. He had been part of their family for eighteen months; he had lived and dined with Angela every day, if they were not rushing from one restaurant to another. If he made a void in their lives, for Emmanuel it was a chasm that could never be filled.

'But something so stupid,' moaned Kerry, as once again they went over the tragic accident. After lunch with Emmanuel, Richard had discovered he had run out of a certain glue and had gone to the local hardware store that sold it. On his return to his shop he waited at the lights and when it was green crossed with others, but a car, in attempting to beat the lights, spun around the corner and hit the few people crossing, Richard being one of them. The other two people suffered a broken shoulder and an arm as they fell to the roadway but Richard had fallen and hit his head violently against the car and then the road itself. There he lay motionless. It had been one of those things that should not have happened, but had, and a young man sedated up stairs was to carry this image for the rest of his life. It was Kerry who realised that it was not only Emmanuel who needed help in these days. She had a mother and husband that this shocking accident had affected profoundly.

Emmanuel walked down the stairs, having shaved and showered, but whilst shaving the only image he saw in the mirror was himself, with no chatty naked figure behind him collecting a towel or speaking about the day's adventure. Nothing, this was the word, nothing. His life was completely finished. There just wasn't any point contemplating a future as it was not going to happen. He sat in his usual place for breakfast but had this blank feeling that there was a thick glass wall that separated him from the rest of the world. Eva had worked for Angela nigh on twenty years and had taken quite a shine to Richard, who, on her birthday, had brought her twenty yellow roses and they had had a drink and a laugh with Emmanuel in this now empty room called 'the breakfast room'. Eva entered to ask what he wold like for breakfast but the sight of him so alone propelled her forward and as he stood up the two of them burst into tears. It was Angela making an entrance, dressed completely in black, who saw the extreme sadness felt by both. Eva excused herself, bumping into a chair as she left. 'I am sorry' she said, as she passed Angela.

'There is no need to apologise,' was the reply. 'Emmanuel, is there anything you would like me to do for you?'

He wiped his eyes. 'Yes. I want to see the Mons.'

'Just a moment,' she replied and turned to go to the telephone in the passageway.

'I am sorry. Monsignor Christie is preparing for a meeting,' came the reply.

'Get me the monsignor now,' came the icy reply. 'This is Angela Christie and we have an emergency.'

After a moment, Michael answered, 'Angela, what's wrong?'

'Get over here at once, Michael. Richard has been killed in an accident.'

'And Emmanuel?' he asked.

'He wants to see you now.'

'Twenty minutes.'

'But Monsignor, the meeting begins in fifteen minutes.'

'You chair it.'

'But Monsignor, they expect you . . .'

'Even priests have families,' was his reply and he fled down the corridor to his car, heading as quickly as possible to Hawthorn.

A knock at the front door and Eva in tears gave Michael the feeling that this was going to be the most difficult moment in his life. He was shown into the breakfast room where tea or coffee was ready. Emmanuel stood up, ready to say what he wanted to and then a glaze covered those electric blue eyes, and all Emmanuel saw was the white ecclesiastical collar. As they moved to one another, Emmanuel simply lost control and wept bitterly in Michael's arms. Michael held him for some time with his strong arms around him, not saying a word. It was Emmanuel that slowly pulled himself away and sat down, as did Michael. Angela rose to leave them.

'Stay,' said Emmanuel. 'Mons, is it possible that someone can see their destiny or future?'

'Why?'

'Well, yesterday, when I was with Richard for lunch he showed me an old part of a magazine that had a funeral, a High mass, with everyone in black, and he said if he went,' he began crying again, then righted himself, 'he wanted a funeral like it.'

'What are you asking me, Emmanuel?'

'Will you give him a funeral like that, in Latin?'

Michael sighed and looked into two beautiful blue eyes, rimmed with red.

'Yes, Emmanuel, I will but' – and here he stopped. Both Angela and Emmanuel waited. 'Only if you give me a promise.'

'Emmanuel frowned. 'Yes, he said, quietly. 'What do you want?'

'In the near future, Emmanuel, I am going to want you to do something difficult for me.'

'OK. I promise,' said Emmanuel.

'Would you like Vince to be part of this Mass?

'Yes, I would.'

'There is a church quite close here that still says Latin Masses and the high altar is still in place. We shall have the Mass there. Is that all right?'

'Yes, perfect,' was the reply and Angela took over as Michael stood up to leave.

'Mons!' was the cry and Emmanuel was again in his arms in tears.

Richard's family had no objections to the very formal Mass and Angela began, as she always did, arranging everything. It was all smoothly organised and to all Emmanuel's friends who were in fact Angela's as well, the summons went out as well as the dress code.

Vince left Sitwell with Mary as soon as Michael called him, as the funeral was the day after next and the Deacon was left in charge. They spoke again and again about this tragic accident, but the thing both of them were most concerned about was Emmanuel, as Mary and Vince had immediately telephoned Kerry who said that Emmanuel was shattered and Salvatore was not bearing up well at all.

The moment they arrived in Melbourne and found their way through the traffic to Hawthorn, they first went to see Kerry, Mary having already alerted her household, to see how things were, and then it was

Vince who went two doors up to No. 6 to see his brother. Emmanuel was in his bedroom, with a photo clasped in one arm. A knock on his door announced Vince, who gently opened the door into this amazing room of reds and gilt, and on the bed saw the littlest person in the world folded neatly up around a photo frame. Vince moved forward and sat on the edge of the bed. The pair of them looked at one another but the moment Vince placed his hand on Emmanuel's shoulder - that touch he was never going to feel from Richard again – he just gave in. The heart-rending sobs as Vince drew him into his arms was something Vince would never forget, his little brother completely alone in a certain sense. Although his family were gathered tightly around him at this moment, he was totally alone and felt it so badly. Vince had telephoned the Mons and a quick exchange of directions the following day prepared Vince for the Mass as Master of Ceremonies.

It was an overcast day, which threatened rain, but it held off. It was a large gathering of all Angela's friends who had known Richard and Emmanuel together in this last eighteen months. When Angela said that she would organise things she was not fooling. Her great friend a florist had decked out the church in white roses and lilies. The High Altar was a blaze of pure white. As they all entered the church, Emmanuel walked between Angela and Salvatore, all in black. Angela was aware that Emmanuel was shaking and linked arms very tightly with him, but it was half-way down the aisle that Emmanuel saw it. In one moment it seemed enormous and then in a split second his mind began playing tricks on him. The coffin had been covered with a black velvet embroidered pall and Richard was underneath all of it, the man he loved and was never going to see again. Then the church became a blur and he couldn't see anything clearly. He reached for a handkerchief but before he sat down all the gathered group noticed Angela take his arm and direct him to his seat. Before sitting down he noticed a bunch of eighteen white roses bound with white ribbon. He looked at them and then said, 'Angela.'

'Yes, darling. Put them on top of the coffin,' and the beautiful young man moved like a ghost, silently, across the floor before the altar rails and placed the bunch of roses on the coffin. He froze for a moment and Salvatore went to stand up and assist him, but Angela raised her hand. Emmanuel returned to sit between them, the bell sounded for the beginning of the Mass and everyone stood. It was indeed a fine Mass, and if Richard had thought that the dusty page he withdrew from the cabinet was the way he wanted to go he was indeed the recipient of exactly what he wanted. Oddly it had a great calming effect on Emmanuel.

At the completion of the Mass, the coffin was taken out and placed in the hearse which slowly drew away from the church gates, this being the signal for all the invited people to move to Angela's for a luncheon.

Emmanuel moved through the large group of friends on Angela's arm, not seeing anyone. Salvatore and Kerry moved to the other side of the church and offered their condolences to Richard's parents, who were completely surprised as to who were all the smart people and did Richard know them all, they wondered? Everyone moved to No. 6 Ashfield Avenue and it was there that Kerry noted Paul in deep discussion with Monsignor Christie. Obviously she noted by the nodding of heads that something had been said and at that point Paul spoke to Angela and left. The rest of the large group took drinks and moved about, chattering to one another.

'I think we'll start,' said Angela, and everyone after a few scuffles of 'no, you here, no, no, you here' all seated themselves with an empty chair that was obviously for the absent Paul. The smoked salmon came on silver trays and in silence everyone helped themselves.

It was at this point that Mary took over. 'Darling,' she said, as she was sitting next to Emmanuel, with Salvatore on the other side, 'fill it to the top.' Emmanuel was, to say the least, surprised at this statement, but duly did as requested. 'I'm sorry, Emmanuel,' she went on, taking a gulp from an over-filled glass, 'but I'm not going to have a luncheon like this where everyone is afraid to say something that might upset you. I suffered once in my life a luncheon like this when Keven died and I swore before all the saints I would never do it again, and I am not prepared to do it for you.'

Angela was black with rage that Mary had taken it upon herself to dictate the behaviour at her table.

'If you think, Emmanuel, that Richard would be happy with all of us sitting together and afraid to laugh or joke, I don't think you knew your lover at all.'

Everyone gasped, except the Mons, who was most interested how this conversation was going to complete itself. 'When Keven died, I sat at a table like this, with all his relatives, and the most the conversation got to was ram prices. All I wanted to do was scream 'Get out! I don't need you!' I just want to be with someone who understands.'

Here she stopped. Emmanuel reached over and held her hand with its well-lacquered nails.

'You're absolutely right,' he said. 'He would have hated an afternoon where everyone wasn't themselves.'

'Emmanuel', she replied, 'at a certain point you are just going to want to be alone. Just get up and go. Do you understand?'

He smiled and said yes, though it was clear Angela was not smiling. But the luncheon picked up and soon conversation was buzzing all around the table. The first course being finished, the main course was being served as a ring on the front door bell announced Paul's return. He was genuinely surprised at the spontaneity of the table, having previously noticed nothing of the kind. He put down, away from the table, and in front of the bay window, a parcel, rather a large parcel, about seventy centimetres all around, and moved to the table.

'Don't tell me,' he said looking at Eva, 'that the smoked salmon is finished?'

'We might just be able to find you something,' she answered with a smile, and disappeared into the kitchen to return with a small plate and a silver serving plate with seven large pieces of salmon.

'Eva, you're a saint!' he cried, as the others were moving onto the main course.

'Well,' asked Salvatore, 'what's in the parcel?'

'Oh, it's for later. It's for Emmanuel.'

'Really,' murmured Mary. 'Do top me up.'

Vince had kept quiet during this lunch but now he chatted on to Paul and Anthony but found a block in speaking to Emmanuel. He wanted to tell him one hundred things but realised that what Mary had done was infinitely more appropriate. Michael thought the same, but his punchline was to come sometime later.

Salvatore gently plodded out into the waves of conversation and was soon engulfed in funny stories and laughter was just impossible to contain. At a certain point Mary put her hand on top of Emmanuel's and he looked at it, not her face.

'It's going to take longer than you think,' she said, softly, 'but whether you believe it or not we do make it. All of us have this capacity to renew and that's what life is about. By the way, if someone had said that to me when Keven died, I would have cheerfully throttled them, but here we are, darling, and the only way out of this is forward.'

He held her hand tightly and gave a weak smile. 'I suppose you're right,' he replied, in a dejected voice.

'Don't worry, darling,' she continued in a whisper, 'you have a lot of tears to shed yet,' and lent over to kiss him.

As dessert was being served, Salvatore again asked Paul what was in the package. Paul looked nervously at Angela: she and Michael both looked very calm. Paul took a deep breath and began in short sentences: 'It's for you, Emmanuel. It's a bit early. Under the circumstances I've been advised it's the right time. Yes, go on, open it.'

Emmanuel stood, walked across the room with every eye following him, and removed the brown paper wrapping. There is was, the most exquisite gilded stool one could imagine: the legs were carved like lengths of rope and it was twisted in all directions. On top was a highly buttoned silk damask cover in a cherry red, which gave this beautiful piece of furniture the finish it deserved. Emmanuel ran his fingers across the damask covering and then looked back at Paul. 'I don't understand,' he said, with a frown. 'What is this for, and from whom?'

Paul took a deep breath and half a glass of champagne. 'Emmanuel, this is your birthday gift from Richard.' Emmanuel began to breathe very deeply. 'It's early but I think perhaps it's appropriate today.'

Emmanuel ran his hands over the gilded legs and then back over the highly buttoned seat. 'It's beautiful,' he whispered. 'It's so beautiful,' and then he rose with tears streaming down his face. He looked at Paul for an explanation, as he found his way back to his chair, looking across at this extraordinary piece of furniture. Mary filled Emmanuel's glass with champagne. 'I had a job about three months ago. Richard came with me to take some measurements for a bathroom cupboard and on the way back I had to see a friend of mine who has a warehouse full of junk and stuff. There is was, so damaged not even I would have taken it. But Richard saw it and was absolutely positive you would love it, so he spent hours re-carving all the missing pieces and gluing it all together again. We had it re-gilded and re-upholstered so here it is. This is what he knew you would like.'

At this stage, tears were forming in Paul's eyes and he stopped his conversation abruptly. With this, there fell a silence across the table.

'It's beautiful,' was Salvatore's comment, breaking the awkwardness.

'Yes,' added Mary, taking over with her hand on Emmanuel's. 'Darling, what a divine gift. You must be very happy.' Her words were well chosen. The grief of losing the man he loved was countered by Mary demanding that Emmanuel be happy as a result of the selection and restoration of something that was just for him.

'Yes,' he agreed, 'it's fantastic.'

'You don't have to stay all afternoon,' said Mary. 'I think you now deserve a little time all for yourself.'

The smile was weak but the opportunity to exit was very welcome. With the gilded and padded stool in his arms he thanked everyone and disappeared upstairs to find just a little space where he could empty his heart with tears for someone he was missing terribly. Looking across at a very decorative Victorian stool he had, in an odd way, a tactile object that was something his lover had restored, just for him, so this stool was to become, for Emmanuel, a symbol of love, a real object that he could gaze at, touch, drape his shirt over, no matter what. It stood on its four gilded rope-like legs. It was a concrete reminder of the man he loved and missed desperately.

Emmanuel was inconsolable the following week, in tears for most of it. The slightest thing, a hint of the past and he was to be found weeping. If he was not in his room, it was certain he could be found sitting in Angela's small room, gazing at her display case that held her Nativity scene, for it was here he had first held Richard and he had in turn been held by him. Kerry was extremely worried about him, as were all his friends. She insisted he come to dinner on Wednesday night as he had always done with Richard; it was her way of trying to make him cover his old tracks, but this time alone. He had to do it, but he was finding it almost impossible. He remembered Mary's words, 'the more people try to help you, the more you either want to cry or scream,' and it was exactly that, except screaming at people he loved and who loved him caused him yet another dilemma, so he began to take a stand that was fatal. He began to bottle everything up inside. He kept all the moments that could have been expelled with an outburst of tears inside. He became a much more formal person, stiff and obviously without joy. Every social function Angela took him to was without feeling. He was polite, made conversation but everyone was aware he just wanted to go home. Angela was now very worried and discussed it with Kerry and Salvatore, as Mary and Vince had long before returned to Sitwell.

'I think we should be looking for some professional help,' admitted Angela in a distressed way, and went on talking. Kerry excused herself and went to the bedroom where she picked up the telephone and dialled Monsignor Christie's private number.

'Hello, Mons, it's Kerry. Emmanuel is not coping at all.'

'Are you all at home now?' he asked.

'I can organise it that Emmanuel is here, if that's what you're asking.'

'Yes, and also Angela. This concerns her as well. Give me half an hour.' He hung up and made two telephone calls to Sitwell.

Emmanuel, at Angela's persuasion, joined Salvatore and Kerry and to his word, in half an hour from the phone call Salvatore opened the door to the Monsignor. They both walked down the corridor and Michael realised that Salvatore was extremely agitated.

'A drink?' he said, as they entered the large room with its view of the garden.

'Why not?' He smiled and being duly seated looked across at a pale-faced Emmanuel.

'Emmanuel, do you remember you made me a promise?'

'Yes,' was the simple response.

'Well, I am now here to keep you to your word.' Emmanuel turned his head to one side and frowned. 'Emmanuel, you are going to Sitwell for twelve consecutive months, where you will assist your brother as Sacristan. I did exactly what you asked of me and now you will do what I am asking of you.'

Emmanuel showed no emotion whatsoever. He sat as if the bus conductor had asked him for his ticket. It was Angela and Salvatore who began the attack.

'It has nothing to do with you,' Michael said to Angela, who was the more vocal. 'This is exclusively between Emmanuel, Richard and me.' This quietened everyone. 'And now I must go.'

'Oh, do stay for dinner,' appealed Kerry.

'I'd love to, but I have a meeting in exactly thirty five minutes at the Cathedral.' He stood up and looked at Emmanuel, who rose to his feet. 'You begin work at Sitwell on the last day of January, which gives you a little less than a week. Remember this date, Emmanuel. After one year of serving Holy Mother Church and your brother you will find that the enormous weight you are carrying for Richard will have been removed. Mary and Vince are expecting you.'

Emmanuel accompanied Michael to his car and instead of returning went slowly to No 6 and up to his room. He had made a deal but he had never for a moment thought that it would cost him quite so dearly. 'Sitwell! What the hell am I going to do for a year?' He lay on his bed, this time, for the first time, thinking of his plight and not of the loss of Richard, but the words that Mons had said earlier spun back and forth in his head. 'This is exclusively between Emmanuel, Richard and me.' If these thoughts passed slowly around his mind, two doors up the street at No. 10 the fireworks had been well ignited. Angela was irate that Michael had made this deal with Emmanuel and said very forthrightly to Kerry and Salvatore that it was blackmail of the worst type; that Michael had taken advantage of Emmanuel at a weak moment and was now using this to suit his own ends. Salvatore agreed completely and so the argument heated up. It was Kerry who just watched this discussion and then realised that both Angela and Salvatore were talking about themselves, not Emmanuel. They both wanted him with them and it was they who were the centre of the discussion.

'He's right,' Kerry interrupted, stopping their conversation. 'The Mons has it all worked out.'

'From his point of view,' countered Angela, sharply.

'The Mons is not sending Emmanuel to Sitwell as a punishment or even to pay a debt to him. He is sending him there to face a new challenge and that may well be what Emmanuel needs. He can't stay here in tears for the rest of his life.' She went on softly, 'Heaven knows I shall miss him like crazy, but if these twelve months give him the opportunity to turn around and see the world as he saw it before, with Richard, I for one am all for it. Let's not be selfish here. He has to have something to work for and with Vince and Mary there I think . .' She stopped and then went on, 'No, I don't think, I am certain the Mons is right. This is what Emmanuel needs. Besides we can visit him whenever we want, can't we?'

Salvatore saw the sense in this Sitwell move, but not Angela, who still berated Michael's handling of the situation.

'The stool is beautiful,' said Kerry. I think it will be with Emmanuel all his life.' She looked at Angela.

'Yes, I'm sure,' Angela replied, much more quietly, and then told Kerry and Salvatore a little story about the stool. After the funeral lunch, Angela had called Paul aside and reached into her desk drawer for her cheque book, assuming rightly that the gilding and upholstery costs had not been paid, due to this shocking accident, and asked Paul for the account. He had lent over and kissed her.

'No, Angela,' he said, firmly. 'Richard and I will organise the accounts, thanks.' He left Angela with tears in her eyes.

* * * *

'I don't care. I must have it delivered Monday morning before eight o'clock. Certainly I know it's difficult and you can bring all the papers over to me tonight.' Angela slammed the phone down as Eva passed. 'People today, you pay them money and they think they are doing you a favour. I can't believe it.' She stormed out to the breakfast room for a cup of coffee, still muttering under her breath. Things were indeed frosty between Angela and Michael, and their usually long chats on the telephone were short and to the point. Michael was not worried.

He had known Angela all his life and she had never changed. She was a winner and to lose caused her great annoyance, to the point where she could become quite nasty. But from the past he knew that with time she generally forgot about it. This time, though, for Angela it was different. She was losing not an argument or a piece of furniture at auction, she was losing the one human being in the world she loved unconditionally. No matter what Emmanuel did that she sometimes found trying, she forgave him immediately and she knew very well no matter how she plunged herself into frantic social situations it was going to be an extraordinarily long twelve months.

It was all arranged for Emmanuel to take the train and Mary would drive to the next big town with a railway station and collect him. The following weekend Kerry and Angela would drive up with the rest of Emmanuel's things, plus a well-packed gilt stool. But Angela, being Angela, decided she would have the last say, so as Salvatore and Kerry joined Angela and Emmanuel for his last breakfast for a while in Angela's breakfast room, it was that after talking quietly to them, feeling the awkwardness, he looked down at something that caught his eye on his plate, assuming that Eva had mistakenly left it there.

'No, darling, they are yours.' Angela smiled. 'I couldn't possibly have you travel by train, It's so tiresome. Besides you must have your own transport in the country.' She looked at the set of car keys with the Mercedes symbol on them. 'Your new car is in the side drive.' She spoke nonchalantly and he immediately raced out to see what it was.

'Well, that seems like the old spirit,' commented Angela. 'Do sit down.' She motioned Salvatore and Kerry to take their seats.

'Angela, Angela!' he shouted as the back door slammed, 'it's fantastic. A Mercedes sports! Oh, 'Angela!' He embraced her. 'It's the tops.'

'I'm glad you like it, darling. Now, shall we have breakfast?'

At exactly nine o'clock, the black Mercedes sports, well laden and with a stool on the front passenger side strapped in a seat belt, and after many kisses and tears, left in the direction of Sitwell. Angela returned to phone Mary at the last moment, to alert her to the change of plan, as well as give her unnecessary advice about how to handle Emmanuel. He drove through the suburbs and out onto the freeway. As he drove the houses became fewer and fewer. It was the beginning of February and even at 9.30 in the morning it was very hot. His car moved smoothly into a shimmer of heat as he tackled the open road. He strangely felt free – or did he, he wondered – or was it just that a change of address was giving him a different perspective on his life? He didn't know but he didn't feel too bad and for the first time, concentrating on an almost three-hour drive meant no tears.

About half way or so as he thought, he stopped at a roadside service station and filled up with petrol. He asked the overweight girl at the petrol pump how much further it was to Sitwell, the response being 'haven't a clue'. He then thought it was time to telephone Mary.

'Oh, thank goodness you called, darling. It appears Angela is being territorial with your telephone number. Where are you now?'

He again asked the petrol pump girl, who begrudgingly gave him his present whereabouts.

'Darling, you have been moving! Listen, you are about an hour away. When you leave the freeway, not the old sand road we used to use but continue on for about a kilometre and turn left and go on until you see the big gates. Press the intercom and someone will let you in. I'll see you in an hour.' She hung up.

He had indeed made good time and it had everything to do with the new Mercedes sports which glided down the freeway effortlessly. He stopped the car in front of an imposing set of metal gates well over two and a half metres high, supported by curved brick walls. A press on the brass button, the words 'Emmanuel Lampedusa' and the enormous gates swung open, virtually at his command. He had never entered this way before, so he was very interested as he drove down through the park in a straight line that was every twenty-five metres punctuated by yet another pedestal with a covered urn on top, in pairs right and left. Then, in the distance he saw it, the huge brick mansion standing stoically in the hot February sun. The closer he came the bigger it seemed. He hadn't been here for years, when he had he was quite a small boy, so his memory of Bantry was much distorted. Then his memory was jogged: those strange fountains ! As he rounded the circular drive he saw one of these fountains in the centre. It had a very ornate basin set in the ground but a column of very rough brickwork with, half way up, a sort of shelf or basin set around the column and another at the top. It was certainly the work of an amateur, if not the local handyman many years ago but they were still there and this one right in front of the immaculately kept house and gardens.

'Darling, how divine! You have arrived!' Mary exclaimed, embracing him. 'How was the drive?'

'Good – no real traffic at all.' He looked around the three large terraces that finished at the river below.

'Before you unpack, sweetie, come with me,' and he stepped onto the broad veranda. They walked right around the front of the house.'

'It looks great, Mary.'

'Thanks. I have a couple of things to show you.

As she walked arm in arm with him in the shade of the veranda it was the smell that Emmanuel noticed, a dry, slightly eucalyptus smell, or was it just the earth giving up a perfume due to the scorching sun? As they rounded the last corner, there it was, the second fountain, identical to the one in front of the house.

'I remember the fountains,' he smiled.

'Oh, darling, don't talk to me about them. Paul has been giving me a really hard time about them. He hates them and is considering dynamiting the brick columns. I told him he could do what he wanted but he is so insistent.'

'Do they work?'

'Not really. One definitely no and the other just dribbles water everywhere. They haven't worked for years really, so I guess they will have to be totally re-plumbed. I personally never see them. Vince says he hates them, so I guess Paul will have to get going.'

'Perhaps they looked all right when they were originally working.'

'No idea, but in my time neither ever worked properly. Oh, here we are!' They moved out of the shade into hot, late morning sunshine. Mary crossed the lawn and opened the door of the chapel. She said nothing and Emmanuel entered the cool of this room, and there it was, in place. He had seen the altar in sections at Richard's workrooms but never all together. Mary had been wise to show him this at once as she knew he was probably thinking of it. He said nothing but just kept staring at the large structure now with the painting in position.

'It's beautiful,' was all he said.

'Come on, darling,' she replied, softly, and they turned to head out into the blinding sun, putting on their sunglasses at once.

'It's over here,' she said, not allowing Emmanuel time for sentimental thought, and what had been an old Palm House had been converted into a large dressing room and outdoor living room with a kitchen, bathroom and what had been an empty paddock before, now a swimming pool Paul had installed. The hedges around it served as walls for an outdoor private garden room.

'Wow!' was Emmanuel's comment. 'It's new.'

'Yes, I had it put in when I knew Vince was coming, so now the two of you can escape the country summer. Come along, darling, let's get you settled and we can have some lunch. Oh, Emmanuel, it is divine to have you here.'

'It's great to be here,' he replied, and meant it.

His bedroom and bathroom were equally as grand as Vince's. The rooms were enormous and to cross the room from side to side emphasised this. The French windows opened on to the upstairs veranda and from the corner of it you could see right to the bottom of the terrace system and just a little of the water.

'Mary, it's fabulous.' And indeed it was. It was Paul at his most adventurous. It was all in shades of dark green and gold. There was also a huge canopied bed in gleaming brass, draped with metres of green silk, the curtains held in position by big gold cords and tassels.

He unpacked a few things and placed his stool by a very fine boulle writing table: the red of the boulle tortoise shell and the red of the stool's damask upholstery were a perfect match. He stood back and admired the two pieces together. 'Hm,' he thought, 'not bad at all.' He then changed his shirt and made for downstairs, where Mary was waiting for him in the big drawing room that was sumptuously decorated with Victorian furniture and, like the rest of the house, metres and metres of fabric had been used in upholstery and extravagant curtain arrangements. They chattered on over a bottle of chilled wine and Mary was surprised that he was so chatty and not at all depressed about Richard – or so it seemed. 'It's living with Angela,' she thought, 'that's enough to depress anyone.'

The maid announced lunch was served and they moved to a small dining room where they were accompanied by the sound of a discreet air conditioning unit.

'Vince is back this evening. I believe he is having problems with the school. Really that Deacon is a shit,' she said, refilling Emmanuel's glass.

'Who is he?' Emmanuel asked. Mary, in full flight, went on to describe in vivid detail Dolly and the Deacon, which had Emmanuel in gales of laughter. She also gave him a rough layout of the land, telling him about the Higgins and the Howes, but in her descriptions of the Higgins family she intentionally left one out, that being Michael. This was a card she was holding back for the moment.

After lunch, she gave Emmanuel a quick tour of the whole house and introduced him to the staff, a husband and wife team and a gardener.

'Mary, where's the boat?'

'Darling, I can't begin to tell you. It sank. Can you imagine it? One morning, it just was at the bottom of the river. You have no idea the trouble everyone had bring it up. Really, darling, the Titanic would have been easier.' He laughed. He loved Mary's dramatic way of speaking and he had always enjoyed her company. 'Well, they told me it couldn't be repaired or wasn't worth it, so I had to get another and I am told that every winter it has to be hauled up with a winch and put in a shed at the edge of the river. Such a bore, darling! I mean, what if we wanted to use it in winter? It would have to be unwinched or something. Anyway there it is – there.'

'It's quite big – and it has windows.'

'Not only that, darling, a motor as well, so you can chug up the river whenever you want, and, darling, something ever so much smarter than the old boat. Can you believe it? It has a refrigerator, essential, I should say. Wouldn't you?'

'Oh yes, of course,' and they both broke into laughter.

'Darling, why don't you park your car in the garage? There's space for everyone and then have a rest. The pool is at your disposal and just poke around as you wish. Drinks, darling, are at 5.30 in the drawing room. I'll see you then.'

As they headed back to the front of the house, she disappeared inside and after parking his car he noticed yet again the strange, rough brick columns with basins in what appeared to be broken slate and also what a great contrast they were to this magnificent mansion that was now his home for the next twelve months.

CHAPTER FIVE

St Bridget's

CHAPTER FIVE

St Bridget's

If Emmanuel was becoming adjusted to Bantry and finding it all a bit of an adventure, the same could not be said for the occupant of No. 6 Ashfield Avenue. Angela had the feeling that she was walking about in a tomb. It was the silence that she found insupportable and the void Emmanuel had left was just getting larger and larger. Over dinner with Kerry and Salvatore she confessed that if the twelve months were not over soon she was genuinely considering entering a convent. 'You have no idea how empty the house is,' she complained to them. 'I even feel cautious about making a noise.'

'Last Wednesday night we went out to dinner,' answered Salvatore. 'To just sit here and look at one another, when every Wednesday evening we shared it with Emmanuel and Richard – it was just too sad.'

'Oh, Salvatore, with all this sorry situation I forgot to ask you about the family's business.'

'It's been declared bankrupt, but because Mario took out the mortgage he has had to bear the brunt of it all. My father and brother found work at once in a cousin's stone masonry business. My father is an expert at carving, so he didn't have any problem. My brother fitted in quite well. I think if the truth be told they are happier working without Mario drifting about criticising.'

141

'And Mario?

'Well, I'm not sure but I do know my cousin refused point blank to employ him, even if he is short of skilled labour and as I haven't spoken to him for some time I haven't an idea.'

'Oh well,' she said, as if to close the conversation. 'I believe Mary is giving poor Paul a difficult time. How inconsiderate of her. She has both the boys and wants more of Paul's time. She has always been the same.'

Both Kerry and Salvatore picked up a jealous edge to this comment but decided to let it lie. Discussing it later by themselves, they decided that indeed Mary did appear to be the winner, with both Vince and Emmanuel firmly under her wing.

'Emmanuel, where are you?' came a cry, after the black Mercedes came to a halt at the front door of Bantry.

No reply meant a search, and at the pool Vince found him lying in the sun. Emmanuel stood up and embraced him, something he had never done with Vince before.

'How was the drive up?'

'Fine. Want a drink?'

'Not now. It's almost 5.30 and drawing room time.' He laughed. 'Just a minute.' And disappeared into the dressing room part of the new pool house, removed his clericals, changed into swimming trunks and returned to dive into the pool. He was taller than Emmanuel and much broader across the shoulders, like Salvatore, and he had very powerful legs, with well-developed muscles, along with his arms and chest. Emmanuel assumed that it was all the result of strenuous sport when he was at school. Sport was something that Emmanuel had loathed but he thought the end result for Vince was not bad at all, and joined him in the pool with a splash. The yelling and fooling around made it quite clear to Mary that she just might as well start the evening at the pool, so the staff were told and drinks and nibbles were transported to the pool house, with a very decorative Mary claiming, 'This new brand of bubbly is just divine. Boys, come and have a taste.' As they drew themselves from the water, Mary cooed appreciatively at two exceptionally handsome men. 'Hm,' she said to herself, 'one untouchable, but the other not.'

'What's the plan for tomorrow?' she asked Vince.

'Well, I thought I might take Emmanuel in and show him the ropes.'

'Good idea. Nancy is just so excited at meeting you, darling.' Mary looked at Emmanuel, who asked, 'Listen, Vince, what am I supposed to do?

'Serve at Mass for me. Why?'

'Well, what does this Deacon guy do?

'Not much, except play the fool,' chipped in Mary, 'and also stand in front of Vince as much as possible.'

Vince sighed.

'Tell him to drop dead,' said Emmanuel, helping himself and Mary to another drink.

'Easier said than done,' was the reply.

Mary looked at Emmanuel. 'Don't worry, darling. 'Half the parish are more than willing to chip in for half a kilo of bunny bait.' Vince and Emmanuel both laughed.

The boys changed and the three of them headed back to the house for dinner. Mary as well as Emmanuel always saw Vince in clericals and to see him only in a small swim brief oddly changed their perspective of him. When he dressed, he changed yet again – or was it what they expected of him? Mary wasn't sure, but beautiful he was.

When they were seated, Mary said, 'I can't wait for tomorrow. Sarah will be able to give us a running report about last evening.'

'What happened last night, then?' asked Emmanuel.

'Well, darling, there is at Sitwell this musty old club. Once, years ago, I attended a function really just ghastly, all those old crocodiles dressed in beaded cardigans. Not for me! But this year, for the annual dinner, poor Sarah was obliged to attend. Nancy said she refused to go.'

'Is this the social highlight of Sitwell?' he asked.

'Almost,' came Vince's reply

'Oh come, Father,' said Mary in a send-up tone, 'we have the St Bridget's ball in a month or so.'

'So when you came here, Bantry was a very different place?' asked Emmanuel.

'The physical structure was the same but the building and outbuildings were in poor condition and what you see now inside is due to Paul's work. I just gave up after all those years. I just mentally refused to see anything inside. You see, when I married Keven and moved here, his ancient parents were here as well as Florence, who was his mother's sister and his sister Anne, a real bitch. The golden oldies were OK - oh well, Keven's father was a real gentleman of the old school, but my mother-in-law was ghastly and dominating, just like Angela but dressed ten or twenty years out of date and with a face that could split rocks.'

Here, both the boys began laughing. Vince had heard the story before but each time it was repeated Mary embellished it a little so it became even more amusing.

'She was right into old-fashioned protocol. What a bore! And with eight indoor staff you felt as if you were at a cinema all day. She wasn't fond of me.'

'Funny about that,' quipped Emmanuel, laughing.

'Careful, darling,' warned Mary. 'The worst part of the day was eating. If lunch was a trial, dinner every evening was murder. Everyone had to wait until mumsy-in-law was ready and then we trooped in from the drawing room, the ladies having had a sherry and the men a whisky or two. We had to stand behind our chairs until Alice, as her name was, sat and then we could all do the same. It sounds funny now, but at the time it was excruciatingly boring. Alice dictated when one began and finished and with the second glass of wine she feigned shock every evening. But her elder unmarried sister, Florence, was the best She was hysterical, far gone, totally confused about everything. She would begin telling the same old story again and again, then branch out to the mating of sheep. Needless to say Alice missed the joke, but Florence would always arrive, especially in the evening, in the most amazing clothes. Where she got them from I have no idea. One evening we had sat down for dinner without her. 'I have had a tray sent up. My sister is out of sorts.' We started the meal and of course in silence. Florence was the only one who chatted. Then there was a dreadful thud.' Here Mary stopped and broke into laughter that would not stop.

'Fill up the glass,' said Vince, 'the story's worth it.'

Mary immediately stopped laughing and glared at Vince. 'As I was saying, the staff went into the hall and helped Florence up. She was dressed in a ball gown of the turn of the century with tulle and sequins. She had stood on the hem and cascaded down the stairs. 'I thought I would have a bite to eat before I went to the ball,' she said, if I remember correctly. You have no idea how she looked. Her grey hair was everywhere and she had found some white face powder, so her face, hair and the front of this frock - or what was left of it, because it was all in shreds – was covered in this white powder. Women don't use it now but at that time rouge was the thing and poor Florence had applied it, obviously without the aid of a mirror and the lipstick as well. Alice highly disapproved of both. Florence looked like something out of the circus but the odd thing was the family and staff went on as if it was completely normal. For me it was the highlight of everyday.

And then Florence went into a nautical period and from the upstairs balcony could be heard crying out, 'Look at the dolphins! Oh, there she blows!"

'Didn't you find it all just a bit much?' asked Emmanuel.

'Darling, growing up with Angela wasn't all that different.'

Vince went into hysterical laughter, Emmanuel less so.

'What happened to Florence?'

'Well, one evening, we all went to bed and in the morning there she was in a turn of the century bathing costume, mop hat and all, and had obviously fallen from the top of the staircase in the night and broken her neck. For me, it was a very sad period because after that if things had been terrible before they now became much worse. Keven's sister, Anne, was a cross between Dracula and Godzilla and I am not exaggerating. She was what is called 'an unclaimed treasure'. She was older than Keven and had that tight little face and extremely narrow eyes, almost oriental, and a real bitch she was. If one said anything, she always interrupted. She had a dowdy dress sense, and no charm at all but harboured the great illusion that she and Dame Margot Fonteyn were identical. I tell you, you think Florence had problems –' here both Vince and Emmanuel were hysterical with laughter as these descriptions of Mary's in-laws were done with a great amount of hand movement and flinging back the pitch black mane of her hair, which emphasised the story no end – 'Anyway, here is the funny bit. Alice finally realised the angels were about to come, so she had a chalice made, set in diamonds. She had a bracelet – nowadays you would call it a tennis bracelet – there must have been thirty six or so quite big diamonds. Alice was very proud of it. And so she sent the bracelet to Melbourne, to have Dunklings set the stones into the base and lower section of the bowl of a chalice. It remained here at Bantry, because in those days the priest came out here to say Mass for all the staff and us, and the chalice was used here. But always Alice took it after Mass up to her room.

'What happened with Anne?' asked Emmanuel, filling up the glasses again.

'Well, that's the funny thing. Keven's parents died within a month of one another. They were what one would call very senior citizens and then the power game commenced. I personally couldn't care where I sat at the table but with Alice and Keven's father gone, I immediately re-organised the whole set-up, especially the wine cellars, which, by the way, you must have a look at, Emmanuel. They are enormous. Why they constructed such a vast cellar I don't know but eighty per cent was undrinkable, especially all that ghastly Rhine wine – so sweet! Anyway, I sat in Alice's place with the table still extended to take twenty, with Keven at the other end and Godzilla halfway down the middle. Can you imagine anything quite so stupid? When I insisted the staff close the table down so at least I could see Keven, Anne refused to eat with us and took to eating in her room from a tray. I personally was elated and couldn't think why I hadn't done this before. Anyway, after Alice had died, the chalice disappeared. We searched everywhere but to no avail. It was gone. And about a year after, I suppose, the golden oldies packed it in,' and this even put a smile on Emmanuel's face. 'One morning Keven and I got up, went to breakfast but there was no Anne. Keven was quite concerned but I said we would check her room in a month or two.'

The boys were again in fits of laughter.

'Well, where was she?' Emmanuel insisted.

'No one knew. She was listed officially as a missing person or something, but she never appeared again. Whether she had just left with a gardener or someone had murdered her - no Vince, don't look at me – but believe me, given the opportunity I would have drowned Godzilla without a qualm – a real bitch. So to this day Bantry has lost a crocodile and a chalice.'

'Do you think she took the chalice and fled?' asked Vince.

'No idea. It's odd because all the other jewellery was intact, nothing missing. I wear some of it occasionally but it's very heavy stuff and I am not one really for broaches and there are dozens of them, all that heavy gold with turquoise and diamonds, which was the fashion at the turn of the century. But there are some good rubies. I must have them reset. Oh, and. of course, Alice's famous rope of pearls – well that I have worn, but the rest . .' with a swish of her hand, '. . . is far too theatrical for me,' and then wondered why there was a burst of laughter.

'But what about the ballroom? You started telling me about it.'

'Oh, well, the roof leaked badly and the ceiling is vaulted. Even in Keven's time we still only patched it here and there. The cost of renewing the whole slate roof was astronomical then, so it's probably much the same now. It's filled with coloured plastic buckets that were placed under specific leaks to catch the water. Later we had the whole roof redone when finances picked up but the golden oldies had left a shocking financial mess and Keven for most of his life worked at trying to put everything in order. But getting back to the ballroom, after the new roof was installed, one afternoon in summer, if I remember, there was a shocking noise whilst we were having lunch. We rushed into the ballroom and the ceiling or at least a good half of it had crashed to the floor. I said to Keven just to lock the door, and have a drink. He was divine. And that's it.'

'But how long ago did it collapse?' asked Emmanuel, curious.

'Oh, at least twenty years ago, I suppose. I don't remember exactly.' It was her hand movement that virtually suggested that everyone just left ceilings on the floor.

'Paul's hysterical about it and has had three different plaster companies in to return it as it was but they say it's extremely difficult and it's going to cost a fortune. Now, darlings, when are we going to use this vast ballroom?'

'Line dancing with Dolly and the Deacon,' responded Emmanuel with a grin.

'Hardly, darling. I think I would much prefer to breed ferrets in there. Anyway, boys, plans for tomorrow?'

'Emmanuel can come with me in the morning and have a look around, and then you, I have heard, are joining us at the Higgins for lunch. He can return with you. I will give him a few lessons for Sunday, and then off we go. So, little brother, breakfast at seven. Do you think you can be ready?'

'Absolutely.' And everyone said their goodnights, heading for their respective rooms. It was on the top landing whilst Mary was still downstairs talking to the staff that Vince held Emmanuel in his arms. 'I am really glad you're here,' he said, releasing him for a moment. 'I need you to help me through this mess.'

As they drew apart, Emmanuel said, 'Don't worry, Vince, we shall take them in hand.'

They headed off to their bedrooms and as Emmanuel closed his door he was very aware, leaning back against it, and looking at this marvellous room, that this embrace with Vince was the first physical contact he had had with a man since Richard had died, and although it was his brother and a priest at that it felt a very secure sensation. As he lay in bed with the moonlight streaming in through the window, making odd shadows on the walls, he was aware for the first time since Richard had died that he wasn't in tears. He still felt an enormous loss but as this was his first evening at Bantry and everything was new in his mind, before he dropped off to sleep, his brain was filled with images of Mary's stories of the past, an eccentric on the balcony who saw dolphins and whales and a diamond encrusted chalice that probably lay hidden somewhere at Bantry

* * * *

'You were up bright and early,' commented Vince as they ate breakfast. Mary rarely rose before nine. He and Emmanuel walked out into the warm morning that looked as though it was destined for high temperatures. 'I don't know why Mary just doesn't take the thing down – it's so ugly,' he said, as they passed the fountain on the way to the garage.

'Do you think that after building the mansion they ran out of money, so they just slapped something up?' Emmanuel suggested.

'No idea.' Vince backed out and then headed up the drive.

It was strange to be next to his brother in clericals and Emmanuel decided he liked it, but if he liked Vince's appearance, he was in for a real shock and the word 'like' could not be used.

Vince turned into Sutton drive and there is was: even from there, with the morning sun behind it, it was an aggressive statement.

'Vince, is that it? It's hideous beyond belief.'

'You don't have to tell me,' Vince replied. 'I have to work in it.'

'It's ghastly. I thought perhaps Mary was kidding but she's not.'

'No, she isn't, this time.' He pulled up in front of the church.

Emmanuel was shocked. The whole complex had a rundown appearance about it. And the other thing he noticed was that there was not one tree.

'Come on. If you're shocked at the exterior you had better hold on when I unlock the door. The interior matches more or less the outside.'

It was the sea of worn patches of apple green carpet that spread itself everywhere and the harsh red and orange glass in the windows with crude designs that made the whole thing look like a gaudy airport terminal.

'I suppose that thing in front is the altar,' commented Emmanuel, feeling instantly depressed. Then his eyes roamed to a glass brick structure with a statue of Our Lady in it. 'You're kidding!' was his sharp remark.

'Oh come on, I'll show you the rest. It gets worse.'

'Impossible,' cried Emmanuel as he noted all the water stains on the side wall.

'Yes,' answered Vince, 'this has to be sorted out before winter. The quote I got to repair the roof is astronomical.'

'Bulldoze the lot! I would.'

'If only! But you see that leaves us without a church.'

'Try hiring a circus tent. It would certainly be more aesthetic.' Emmanuel could not believe how tiny the sacristy was. There was a huge plan press built in under a wall system, so even removing it still would give no space.

'And to make it more stupid,' Vince said, 'the plan presses are empty, as I use casulas here and these, like all the white wear, are hung. Come on, let's have a look at the school before the students arrive.'

Growing up in Ashfield Avenue, in a leafy suburb where every rate payer made an effort to improve their surroundings, they saw that here, it seemed, it was exactly the reverse. The asphalt was everywhere broken or cracked badly and there were papers that had not been collected, weaving themselves into the bottom of the wire netting boundary fence, with orange peel scattered like confetti.

'Don't you have a cleaner?' Emmanuel asked.

'Oh yes, but what a problem! Eddie does as little as possible, as you can see. I put the feelers out to find someone to replace him but the Deacon and Headmaster threatened to strike if their friend Eddie was fired, so you see, Emmanuel, I have been blocked at every turn. The only thing I have managed to do is get rid of the guitars as musical accompaniment to Mass, and there were hails of protest'

Directly behind the new church stood the old one. Vince unlocked the door. It was like walking into a cool space where a bomb had gone off. It was rectangular and the two side transepts had been walled over in Masonite with a door in the centre, all unpainted.

'The one on the right is the sports' teacher's office and the one on the left is the store room.' He unlocked the storeroom door. 'They are up there.' Vince pointed to three large cardboard containers with *'Kellogg's Cornflakes'* stamped happily on the side and two smaller cartons that were once the recipients of beer. 'Your ecclesiastical clothes are up there. You can get them down later.'

'But what's this big wall in front.'

'Behind that is the sanctuary of the old church and off to one side is a large sacristy which has a door to the outside, and this Eddie uses as a tool shed.'

It was when they re-locked the store room and turned back that Emmanuel saw the huge organ and choir loft, stretching right across the back of the church.

'Hey, it's great!' was his immediate response. The balcony of curved cast iron contained a huge organ in the centre and above it a rose window in what he thought were gaudy colours like the windows of the main nave area, now the all-weather physical education centre, with coloured painted lines all over the floor. The windows, over the years, had had a great deal of the coloured glass broken and had been replaced with clear glass, so they had the effect of teeth, but missing every second one. The wire netting nailed onto frames to cover and protect the glass from over-anxious students with balls did nothing to make the interior any happier.

'Vince,' asked Emmanuel, 'am I wrong or is the space in the old church here bigger than in the new one?'

'You're right, yes. Usually, they build new churches when they want larger spaces, but here, for some bizarre reason, the new church is a bit smaller.'

Emmanuel glanced again at the proud organ loft that he noted had a door with a chain and padlock at the bottom of the little stairway. He also noted, just before leaving, that the whole church was pine lined and so was extremely dark, but it had a very decorative ceiling that was vaulted with ornate cast iron supports that spanned the broad ceiling in three girder-like constructions which obviously supported the roof.

They stepped out into the bright sunlight and headed toward another relic of the past that Vince had the back section of as his office. If the old church was in a terrible condition, what had been the original Canonica, this grand weatherboard home, where Monsignor Christie had been resident so long ago, was almost totally vandalised. It must have once had a veranda that encircled it but it had only one part left across the front. The front was now a language computer centre and the other rooms were the art rooms. The small rooms that must have been little bedrooms or service rooms were used as storerooms and one of these served as Vince's office. The main school stretched across the front of the block, leaving only space for a car to pass between it and the new church. This block was also in weatherboard but in a very jumbled layout. Obviously, as rooms were required, they were just built to the same design each time but independently placed so it seemed as though someone had just built them wherever it was convenient without an overall plan.

The children now began to arrive and a buzz of noise swelled into yelling, shouting and screaming. Someone pushed Vince's office door open as he was showing Emmanuel something on his computer. 'Oh, sorry! I'll come back. I have something for you to sign.' With that and a sharp glance at Emmanuel he left, closing the door with a slam.

'Well, Eddie's a dream,' said Emmanuel sarcastically.

'Not exactly. That, believe it or not, was not Eddie.'

'Who was it then?' Emmanuel retained the image of an overweight man in his mid-forties with a tee shirt that was well stretched across his stomach, the reverse of it showing a well-washed *'Peace'* sign that must once have been red but with the constant washing had been reduced to faded orange; and a very plump face with a reddish beard going grey at the chin, a moustache and long, straggly red hair that was anything but dense in the region of his forehead; a peculiar red nose and tiny gold-rimmed glasses like those of John Lennon, marking him out in this day and age as a born-again hippy.

'That, Emmanuel, is the Headmaster!'

'Vince, this whole scenario is worse than a horror movie. Why on earth don't you just bail out and return to the Cathedral. You may just save your sanity.'

'Thanks,' was the only reply and they headed off across the broken ashfelt to the new church. Now the day was hot. 'But don't worry, you won't meet the worst until next week.'

'Oh, really? I can't believe it gets worse.'

'Unfortunately yes. Dolly and the Deacon are off this week for a line dancing competition in Sydney.'

'Wow!' was Emmanuel's blunt reply.

'Anyway,' went on Vince,' I'll give you the basics. It's not difficult. You see it every Sunday with Mons.'

Oh, Vince,' he replied, 'it's one thing to see a Mass being said, but it's totally another being part in it.'

'Don't worry. If there is a problem, I shall simply whisper what to do.'

After three run-throughs, Emmanuel basically had sorted out what was necessary on Sunday morning, and felt confident that he would forget it all, but with Vince's prompting he would get through it. By this stage, the morning had progressed and as they headed back to Vince's office he said, 'Get the boxes down from the store room and sort it all out. You need a cassock and a cotta. I leave it up to you but they will probably have to be cleaned. I believe those boxes have been untouched for years.'

'Thanks, Vince,' Emmanuel smiled, 'you're a dream. Vince headed back to his office.

Emmanuel looked about him in this strange landscape and was jolted as one of the bells rang from the tower of the old church, rather than the new. So it was that when Anthony Howes built this new church, his finances – or his wife's finances, as it was well before the steeple he had projected was built – the old bell tower in the original church continued to toll school times, the Angelus and all Sunday Mass times.

It was then that two oddly dramatic situations occurred at St. Bridget's, after Vince returned to his office. Within moments the same faded hippy, the headmaster, swung in.

'I have spoken to the staff and the Deacon,' he pronounced, 'and all are in agreement. Just sign.'

'What?' asked Vincent.

'That from tomorrow, all this shit about school uniforms is finished.'

This had been a real problem at St. Bridget's. Half wore uniform, the other half did not and the whole look of the school was simply confusing.

'We are behind the times, man,' he said to Vince. Calling him 'Father' was something that he found most aggravating.

'And if I don't sign?' asked an arrogant Vince, which was most unlike him.

'There will be a full school strike and I shall resign.'

155

Vince didn't even wait a second. 'I accept your resignation and the treasurer will pay into your bank account all moneys owing to you, plus your holiday pay.'

At that very moment, his telephone rang. 'Yes, yes, on my way. I have to go. Mr. Ryan is dying and I must be there.'

Vince snatched a well prepared black bag, grasped his coat and rushed down the corridor, out into the hot morning sun, into his car and off to the hospital to administer the last rites to Mr. Desmond Ryan.

To say the Headmaster was surprised at Vince's immediate action was an understatement. He and the Deacon had administered the school for well-nigh ten years or even eleven. He didn't quite remember, but to be discharged like this . . . And where the hell was his side-kick, the Deacon? Line dancing with Dolly in Sydney, the fucker, he thought.

As Emmanuel walked through a sea of yelling children, it being morning break and the tuck shop was inundated, he saw that the sports mistress was in firm control. He headed toward the old church to sort out what was necessary to retrieve from the cardboard boxes to wear on Sunday morning, and noticed a tiny boy sitting all by himself on a bench, swinging his legs back and forth. All the rest of the students were in pairs or groups, but this little boy was not. Why he was, and the repercussions later as a result of it are simply history.

'Hi!' he said and sat down beside him. He was like a miniature person, very tiny, with skin like silk, a pair of very skinny legs protruding out of a pair of ill-fitting shorts and with a shirt that had obviously known better days.

'Hello,' was the response from a face that was crowned with a mass of golden curls. The eyes were enormous in a honey green colour, with a fully-formed mouth and nose but it was the enormous eyes, with exceedingly long lashes in a strong blonde shade that gave this little boy a quality that was all his own. Emmanuel noticed that he put one foot on top of the other to cover up the fact that the left foot of his black sandshoe had a hole in the toe. He seemed uneasy and

Emmanuel didn't feel much better. He felt that he had intruded into this child's world but as he was now seated beside him he wasn't quite sure how to extricate himself from the situation.

'My name is Emmanuel,' he said, quietly. 'What's yours?'

The boy looked at his feet. It seemed that he was most preoccupied in covering the hole in the toe of his shoe. ''I'm John,' he said in a whisper and then he turned and looked into Emmanuel's electric blue eyes. 'It's not, really,' he added and again glanced at his feet.

'Do you want me to keep a secret?' asked Emmanuel.

'Well, you see, my real name is Giovanni, but at school they make jokes about it, so they all call me John.'

Emmanuel felt his heart go out to this miniature person. He thought in his own way that he was also suffering and so he drew nearer. 'Have you had something to eat?' he asked, basically trying to move the conversation along. The quiet response was, 'No.'

'Why? Aren't you hungry?'

'Sometimes,' was the clipped reply, 'but if I eat some of my lunch now I have nothing to eat at lunchtime.' He stared at his right foot that was covering the left.

'Why don't we see what the tuck shop has?' asked Emmanuel and the tightness of Giovanni's shoulders and the movement of his blonde curly head from side to side and his eyes not moving from his tiny feet showed that there was a problem.

'Why don't we see what's left in the tuck shop?' repeated Emmanuel, and in a voice that was below a whisper came the reply 'I don't have any money.' He refused to look at Emmanuel.

'Now, listen, as your grandparents and mine are Italian, we are more or less related.'

'Are we? Really?'

'Exactly. And as Father is my brother, it means he is also related to you.'

'I didn't know priests were allowed to have brothers.'

Emmanuel smiled. 'Oh yes.' His glanced sideways at this tiny boy and went on in a very authoritarian voice. 'Well, if you're my relative and Father's, do you know that every morning recess you are entitled to a free cake at the tuck shop?

He turned his head, not being sure what the word 'entitled' meant. Emmanuel felt stupid. He had used a word that had alienated the boy. 'You know,' he said, starting the conversation again, 'that your free cake is always waiting for you in the morning?'

'Really? For me?' The response was ecstatic.

'Of course. You and Father are relatives.'

'Oh gosh! Really?' He was so excited.

'Come on. Let's see what you would like,' and they headed off, hand in hand, for the tuck-shop.

It was chaos, even though the sports mistress, a certain Miss Ainsworth, was supposed to be in control. There were two lines and much jostling for position. Emmanuel and Giovanni fitted into the shorter line. Just before they were about to be served, an overweight, red-headed youth approached in the smartest new tracksuit and track shoes that were elevated at the heels so that when he walked tiny battery lights lit up, altogether an expensive get-up for a child at a primary school. This child pushed in front of them and demanded to be served, pushing Giovanni back into Emmanuel quite forcefully. Emmanuel had a short temper and if he saw what was his definition of wrong he always exploded. He leant over and grasped this fat lad and dragged him back.

'Get your hands off me!' he retorted arrogantly and then looked at Giovanni, now very firmly against Emmanuel and not at all sure that this tuck shop venture was really going to be worth it. Emmanuel was furious, and said to the lady serving that as Giovanni was first he would be served first.

'Well, look,' she said, 'we'll just sort Barry out first.'

'Oh no, we won't,' argued Emmanuel. 'This boy was first and that's it!' but to Emmanuel's surprise, Barry went ahead with his demand.

At this stage, the whole tuck shop, staff and students, were waiting for a showdown, and they were not unhappy at the result. The slap was audible and the sharp language from Emmanuel was heard by all. There was dead silence. He grabbed Barry by the throat. 'If,' he growled, in a most threatening way, 'you ever push in front of my friend again, I shall give you the thrashing of your life.'

Foolishly, and to save the situation, Barry thought to save his face by attacking on a racial level. 'You wogs are all the same.'

He didn't quite finish the sentence as the second blow from Emmanuel was much more determined than the first and he fell to the ground.

'Now, which cake would you like?' Emmanuel just ignored Barry blubbering and hauling himself up, then moving quickly away. Giovanni was so tiny and at six years old he could not even see up to the top of the counter. Emmanuel lifted him up in his arms as the sports mistress hurried forward.

'What's up here?' she asked.

'Just a moment,' Emmanuel responded. 'My friend and I haven't decided on our cake.'

Giovanni swung one arm around Emmanuel's neck and glanced at the assortment of cakes that were arranged by price and glanced at Emmanuel who was very aware of a mop of golden curls against his cheek. He saw that Giovanni had pointed to the least costly of them all.

'Oh no, my friend. Father would be very cross if you didn't take the best. Remember, we are all sort of relatives – always remember that.' So a large cake with pink icing, filled with jam and cream was removed from the counter and placed in a bag. Emmanuel lowered Giovanni to the ground. 'Put it on my account,' he said in a forceful way. 'Every week, Father or I will settle the expenses. A cake of this type is to be ready for Giovanni every day. Do you understand me?'

The bewildered helper said yes.

'I am the Sacristan here, so keep an account for me.'

'Yes, Father, certainly,' came the response.

Emmanuel felt a slap on the back from Miss Ainsworth. 'Well done, Sacristan, well done. If I had done it, there would have been a court case. Well done and very well deserved.'

Emmanuel turned. 'I trust you'll help Giovanni every day?'

'Consider it done. The helpers and I are right here. And Barry flattened!' She broke into gales of uncontrollable laughter.

'Would you like half?' asked Giovanni.

'No thanks, handsome. It's all yours. But before autumn is over Father and I will take you for a boat ride. How does that sound?'

Giovanni turned his head, with cream all around the corners of his mouth. 'You are the nicest man I have ever known,' he said, munching into the other half of the cake.

They sat there until the bell from the steeple rang, announcing the next lesson before lunch and he said he had to go to class but was happy because it was art and he was very good at it. So they parted, but not before he gave Emmanuel a hug. 'Thank you for the cake.'

'Just you remember that you must collect one every day or Father and I will be very unhappy. And remember we are sort of relations.' Emmanuel watched the tiny figure rush across the broken ashfelt in the direction of the old Canonica, which now housed the art school, but not before the two of them waved to one another.

Emmanuel turned and crossed toward the old church to retrieve the cardboard cartons. He entered into a din he couldn't believe. The old church had been well designed acoustically and with twenty youngsters yelling and screaming as they pursued a basketball it was deafening.

With the key given to him, Emmanuel opened the door and found he needed a ladder. He went to find Eddie to get one and Eddie was anything but co-operative. The simple exercise took basically what was left of the morning.

'Take them all to Father's office, please.'

'Take them yourself. I am not paid to do this work,' was the reply.

'I would be very interested to know exactly what you are paid to do and believe me I shall check with Father.'

'Please yourself,' was the arrogant reply as Eddie stalked out into the main church, dragging the ladder behind him. Emmanuel took the boxes one at a time to Vince's office but as he was locking the door it was Miss Ainsworth again who congratulated him on handling Barry. 'I would have flattened him many a time,' she said, 'but the administration here is all for 'make love not war'. Have you ever heard of anything so stupid?'

Emmanuel said no, he hadn't.

'By the way,' she added, smiling, 'the backhander was a beauty,' and laughed. The shrill sound on her whistle sent a sharp message to stop the game. 'He's a nice little guy, John, or Giovanni, call him what you will. He comes from a really poor background. Every time the Father gets a job they fire him. You know the system – last goes first. It seems to be the story of his life. Some people just don't seem to win.'

'Who is this Barry creep?' Emmanuel asked.

'Oh, don't you know? Mr Sacristan, you are going to be the hero of the school! The bastard you gave two good slaps to – and I must say the second was really good – is the bully of the school. Between his parents and the Deacon he has a charmed life. This is probably the first time anyone has dealt with him like this. Good on you, Mr. Sacristan. Oh, by the way, if it gets to a court hearing, I'll promise before all the saints I didn't see anything.' She laughed. 'Oh, I forgot – his name is Barry Howe.' Emmanuel said thanks and took the last of the smaller boxes into Vince's office.

The church bells sounded the angelus and a scraping of chairs could be heard as the children stood and recited it. Emmanuel remember when he was at school he loved the angelus, as it signified an hour's break from what he believed were tedious lessons.

As Vince had not returned, he headed down the street to the Higgins mansion, 'Shannon', and was happy to see Mary's car parked in front. He knocked on the door only to have a uniformed maid show him into the large drawing room.

'Darling, how are we? How was the first day at school?' Mary laughed.

'Very eventful!' he replied and was introduced to Nancy first, who thought him adorable and so handsome, then Sarah and her lacklustre husband, then Philip, who just gazed in wonder at this new creature called Emmanuel. A knock on the front door announced Vince, who came through and Emmanuel noticed that Mary addressed him now as the others did, as Father. As no one knew exactly where Emmanuel fitted in, the Higgins automatically addressed Vince as Father.

'Well, a busy morning for you too?' asked Sarah.

'Absolutely,' replied Vince, as the drinks were handed around on a large silver tray by the maid. 'Oh, Nancy, old Mr. Ryan has passed on. I went this morning to the hospital.'

'I'm glad,' she said. 'He had suffered terribly with that cancer.' Then they moved on to other subjects. Emmanuel was surprised that they all accepted death so easily. Apart from Richard he had had no contact with it but here no one seemed really concerned. The conversation was about the funeral and other minor things, but that was that.

'Well, Father, you look like the cat that has just caught a mouse.' Nancy smiled at him.

'Well, you're right.' He took a deep breath, as everyone waited in silence for the revelation. 'I have accepted the resignation of the headmaster.'

'Hooray!' went up in a shout, leaving Emmanuel a trifle confused, and needless to say all the conversation was now around that subject and who was going to replace him.

'Darling,' said Mary, 'you said you had an eventful day as well.'

'Yes, I made friends with a tiny boy called Giovanni and by the way, Father, you will be debited five cakes a week.'

'Oh, will I?' he responded, looking at Emmanuel. 'So that was your excitement?'

'Not quite. I flattened a student at the tuck-shop.'

'You did what?'

'Yes, and I must say it gave me great pleasure.' He recounted the whole story of Giovanni. 'Oh, and by the way, in case you are interested the boy I flattened goes by the name of Barry Howe.'

Vince gasped. Nancy thrust her glass into Sarah's hand, moved quickly across the room and kissed Emmanuel. 'You are wonderful,' she said. How splendid! First day at work and the Sacristan flattens the school bully. How fabulous!' She kissed him again.

'Well, 'Mary joined in, 'not a bad day's work – Headmaster fired and bully flattened. Sounds like a step forward for St. Bridget's.'

'Mrs Higgins,' Emmanuel began.

'Darling, the name is Nancy. Please.

'Thank you,' he carried on. 'Can you tell me why there is not a fund to help students like Giovanni whose parents have obviously fallen on hard times. I don't think it is fair or Catholic.'

'What are you talking about?' Mary came in first. 'St. Bridget's Benevolent Fund has been operative since the school began in 1848.'

'Be that as it may,' he replied, 'how come Giovanni comes to school like that and with a hole in his sneaker that he is embarrassed about?'

There was a deathly silence.

'I didn't know the fund even existed,' said Vince. 'Who administers it?' He glanced at Nancy and then at Mary.

'I'm not sure,' Nancy answered, 'but, just a moment,' and she left the room.

'No, no,' could be heard as a reply to the telephone in the hall, then Nancy re-entered and rang the bell.

'Yes, Mrs Higgins?'

'Lay another place setting. Mr Simon Thomas is joining us for lunch.' The way she said it Emmanuel was not sure whether it was to sit with them or that he was going to be served on a large silver salver with an apple in his mouth.

Before they went in to lunch, which was now late, Emmanuel said to Mary and Vince that he was going to take Giovanni to buy him some proper shoes. 'Are you coming with me?' he asked Mary.

'Absolutely, darling. A boy in need. We shall get all the things for him at White's. They stock all the sizes in uniforms for St. Bridget's.'

'Well, it's a pity there's not some sort of order in the school. Half of them are in uniform, half out and look at that Barry creature, in an expensive track suit and shoes, flaunting himself.'

'This is now to stop,' said a stony-faced Vince. 'In fact, that is why the headmaster has left us, over this issue of uniform.'

'Not before time,' chimed in Nancy.

The treasurer, Simon Thomas, was welcomed in and everyone moved to the large dining room, but today, much to Mary's annoyance, Michael was not present.

'Believe it or not he is doing some work,' was Sarah's bland comment.

The first course proceeded as usual but the electric undercurrent was there. As the main course was being served, Nancy began in dulcet tones, 'Simon, what can you tell us about the St. Bridget's Benevolent Fund?'

Simon immediately cleared his throat and reached for his glass. 'It's like this . . .' he began.

'Do go on,' urged Mary, rather patronisingly.

'The money that you collect goes into a separate bank account as it always has and is used to aid students who find school fees and other associated expenses extremely difficult.'

'If that's the case,' interrupted Emmanuel, 'how come Giovanni has no uniform or what passes for a uniform and sneakers with a hole in the toe?'

'My position, Mr. Lampedusa, is to collect from Mrs Higgins the money that the – how shall I say ? – the more well-to-do Catholic families donate each year to help the less fortunate. I keep an account record of the donors and the amount given. It is then banked and there my job finishes.

'But,' asked Vince, curious, 'who has access to this account? I have never heard of it and I have been here a year and six months.'

'The headmaster and an allocated member of the ecclesiastical staff.'

There was silence, but only for a moment before everyone chorused, 'The Deacon!'

'Yes, I am afraid so. The last priest gave him complete authority over this account and he was to use it in a benevolent way to aid students in financial trouble.'

'How much is in the account?' Nancy asked bluntly.

'I haven't checked the account for some time as it is not in my jurisdiction, but I can let you know tomorrow. By the way, Mrs. Higgins, the pork is delicious.'

'Thank you' replied Nancy and glanced at Vince. 'If one cent has not been used wisely we shall call in the police.'

'Let's see what's in the account first,' Vince answered. 'Remember, I have just accepted the resignation of the headmaster.'

'Must have been a shock to him,' the Treasurer chuckled with an obvious sense of satisfaction.

'Emmanuel, what was in the boxes?'

'No idea, but if you can discharge a headmaster I can tell you the next on the list is dearest Eddie.'

'Oh, him!' said Nancy. 'He should have gone out with the rubbish years ago.' And again Mary noticed a smile from ear to ear from the Treasurer. Obviously at some time he had caught the wrong end of the stick from both the Headmaster and Eddie. He was just waiting for them to receive their just rewards, but if it be known it was the same Treasurer, complimenting Nancy on her pork roast and smiling and chatting to all, now considering himself in the inner circle, who ultimately held the secret key, but for the moment he kept his peace. It was Nancy who sensed that the Treasurer knew a great deal more about the running of St. Bridget's than he now chose to tell.

'Well, go along,' said Nancy to Sarah's husband Bill, 'and take the gardener with you and bring back the boxes. Hurry up. Give him the keys, Father.' So an overweight, peculiarly lazy Bill, with the gardener and a wheelbarrow transported the boxes to Nancy's drawing room, with Bill having held the gate open whilst the gardener and he made three trips in the scorching February heat.

'They're all here,' he said, handing the keys back to Vince and immediately retiring to a small sitting room to watch the TV news with a whisky in his plump paw. But if watching was the name of the game, it was Philip who gleaned the most. He watched the power play of a new member of this group and in his mind he likened Emmanuel to a Siamese cat – same eyes, same air of aloofness but aesthetically perfect. As usual, his eyes rested on Vince whom he firmly believed was the most important person in the world.

The boxes were opened by Sarah with a table knife and the contents with the smell of time and mould spilt out into the room. The first large box emptied its contents in one spillage due to its being turned upside down and there were the most beautiful albs imaginable.

'Good heavens,' said Vince, 'if I had known that these were here I would have worn them.'

'What's under the polyester?' Emmanuel asked. Vince turned his head and stared at Emmanuel. 'Be careful, little brother.'

'Oh, always.'

The second box offered what Emmanuel needed, cassocks, but some in terrible condition.

'Try this one on,' suggested Sarah and it was so short as to be laughable but the third one was perfect and in good condition but missing many of the buttons.

'Simple. We take the buttons from the short one and transfer them to this one. Easy,' said Sarah. 'I'll have the maid do it this afternoon and have a rush job done at the dry cleaner late this afternoon.'

The box that contained things that everyone was interested in was the large one with the chasubles in all the ecclesiastical colours but all needing repair and cleaning.

'Well, Father, there is no excuse now,' said a smiling Emmanuel. 'Let's see if we can both do something for the 11 o'clock Mass on Sunday.

Vince narrowed his eyes. 'Let's see,' he responded, slowly.

The last of the boxes held the contents for altar boys, everything in miniature that the server wore. It was going back through the lace albs that two spectacular cottas were discovered. These are worn over a cassock and only cover the upper part of the torso; the lace falls below, covering, as one might say, the wearer's private parts.

'Leave it all with me,' insisted Nancy. 'I just happen to know someone in town who can repair or re-silk these vestments. What colour do we need for this Sunday, Father?'

Vince thought for a moment and then said it was violet.

'Good. It's just musty. It will be ready. Oh, I wouldn't miss this for the world. I can't wait to hear what the Deacon says when he gets back and realises we are using proper vestments. Oh, what a scream!

'Father,' added Mary, 'why don't you use altar boys? They did once, here at St. Bridget's, didn't they, Nancy?'

'Oh, but of course.'

'When I came here there was no provision for the use of altar boys and, remember, there had been a scandal in Melbourne about altar boys, so I didn't do anything. And the Deacon refused to have them, saying they took too much of his time training them, and when they finally got the knack of it they were old enough to join the local Sunday football team, so they were gone. But there is no reason why we can't train them again. That must surely fall under the jurisdiction of the Sacristan, wouldn't you say?'

'Absolutely,' Nancy agreed.

'Thanks, Father!' said Emmanuel, slightly sarcastically. The conversation moved back to Barry Howe and Emmanuel's handling of him.

'Fabulous!' was Sarah's comment. 'I can't bear him. I'm sure it was him who scratched all the side of my car with a key.'

'He sounds quite something,' added Mary. 'Can we book him in for a lobotomy?'

'I'm quite happy to pay for it,' was Sarah's final quip and as it was now half past one everyone rose from the table. Nancy told Emmanuel to leave all the boxes of things with her and she would get his dry-cleaned and the cotta's laundered for Sunday.

Vince was about to leave when Emmanuel asked whether, as they had no headmaster and Vince was in charge, he could have permission to take Giovanni from his lessons during the afternoon and organise a uniform for him.'

Vince embraced Emmanuel in front of everyone. 'Sure,' he said, and smiled.

'Come on, Mary, we are off to outfit a little angel.'

'I'm all for that,' she laughed. They walked back to the school with Vince discussing what sort of new head of the school they wanted.

'We shall advertise and see what we get,' replied Vince,' and you, little brother, can help me with the interviews.'

'Ready and willing, but remember, let's get rid of Eddie. He's the pits!'

Emmanuel went to the door of one of the classroom, knocked and entered, explaining that he had permission from Father to take Giovanni from class. 'Certainly,' was the response: the whole staff was now very agitated as Father, it seemed, was now on a power drive of change after eighteen months of accepting the status quo. Having dismissed the force behind them, this now only left the Deacon as a buffer zone between them and the parish priest, plus his now new supporter, who in his first day had become part and parcel they thought in dismissing the head of the school, as well as dealing Barry Howes a blow which all agreed was a good idea but which none would ever have had the courage to carry out.

'Come along, Giovanni,' Emmanuel urged with a smile. 'Father says you can come with Mary and me for an adventure.'

'Oh,' he replied, as he stood up, with the whole class watching in silence. Emmanuel took his hand and they went out of the classroom, which then buzzed with excited suggestions of what was going to happen to the boy. As the late headmaster had been dismissed due to his own arrogance and this was due to the issue of abandoning school uniform, Vince suddenly took it upon himself to deal directly with the problem. He printed up a sheet and had the office girl run off a copy for each student. making the school's policy precise and emphasising the use of school uniform. 'We have had and we shall have a continuity of St. Bridget's in every form and that means the acceptance of a common dress code for all, no matter what the financial status is at home. In the case of any parents who find themselves in difficulties concerning this, they are to contact me immediately as a charitable fund exists to help all the students at this school.' There was no messing about with this policy and a folded copy of it was handed to each student to take home, before the school day ended.

'Come along,' urged Mary with a smile, 'shoe shop first'. Giovanni, who seemed even tinier between the two adults, entered Clement's shoe store, a shop that could be called, according to Mary, dreary at the best, but they stocked school shoes if not much else. She glanced about, not seeing one pair of denim-covered high heels, which obviously meant Dolly shopped elsewhere.

'May I help you,' asked a middle-aged woman with spectacles.

'Yes,' said Mary, taking over. 'We need a very good pair of school shoes for our lad.'

'Certainly.' In an instant she returned with three boxes of shoes of approximately Giovanni's fitting. After two tries, he was fitted with the right size while Mary who noted his darned socks. A lump rose in her throat. 'By the way,' she said gently, 'we will also have a black pair of sneakers.' She glanced at a rack of children's shoes with alarmingly bright publicity, the type of Adidas and Nike sports shoes but in miniature. 'And we will have a pair of those as well. Which design would you like?' she asked the boy, who was captivated by a magic world he had never ever experienced. But much more was to come for him. With Emmanuel, he selected a pair of sports shoes with red and green stripes on the side, Giovanni declaring they were the nicest shoes he had ever seen.

'Is that all, Mrs, O'Shanassey?' asked the woman, as Mary handed her credit card across the counter.

'Yes, thank you.'

Then they went off to White's, the only department store in this small town, with Mary swishing in, followed by Emmanuel and Giovanni. The entire staff suddenly seemed to come to attention. 'It's Mrs. O'Shanassey,' was the whisper that flooded through the store.

'Oh, Mrs. O'Shanassey, what may we do for you?' asked a very obsequious middle-aged man.

'We're looking for a school uniform for Giovanni and a few extras.'

'Certainly, Mrs. O'Shanassey'

Mary was well known in this small town and had an enormous amount of social clout. The stores that dealt with Bantry did very well and they were very careful not to ruffle the feathers of someone who paid exactly at the end of every month without any problems, especially the local supermarket that had a very good relationship with Bantry, in particular the wine and spirit department.

'What may we do for you exactly?' asked a certain Jerry Hadcock. They knew this was his name as the little badge on his shirt declared it for all to see.

'Oh, a uniform? But of course, Mrs. O'Shanassey.'

Mary was getting a bit tired of having her surname repeated quite so often but bore up, with Emmanuel giving her a wink. The uniform was organised. 'Now give me four shirts, half a dozen underpants and six pairs of black socks for school and –'here she stopped - 'Giovanni, darling, would you pick out six pairs of coloured socks that you like.'

When the box of socks was lowered to his level he had a great time deciding exactly what he would like.

'I think a few polo shirts and some other shorts would be the thing, don't you?' asked Emmanuel, so used to Angela picking up the bill.

'But of course, darling,' replied Mary, which had the staff gossiping for weeks about Mrs. O'Shanassey's new boyfriend who couldn't be over twenty five at the most. And they had a little boy with them. Now what was happening, they wondered? Within the week every household was exchanging the information, exaggerating it to the point of its being ridiculous.

Mary's car drew up in front of a very modest house with a very excited Giovanni.

'Come this way,' he called. 'Daddy, Daddy!'

A man rounded the angle of the house. 'Giovanni, what's wrong?' he asked, moving quickly to his side and looking at Emmanuel.

'Oh, Mrs. O'Shanassey, I don't understand what's happening.'

'Daddy, look!' answered Giovanni, with one hand on his waist, lifting his left leg into the air. 'Look, aren't they nice?'

'Yes, they are great. Why don't you go and tell your mother we have guests?' At which Giovanni sped around the corner and into the house. 'I don't understand,' his father went on, looking at the bags of clothes and shoes. 'I can't pay for this. I am on unemployment benefits and I have no way of paying for all of this.'

'I don't remember asking you for money,' said Mary, realising that John O'Keefe was very embarrassed.

'Do come in,' he said, and they all followed him in through the back door directly into a small, spotlessly clean kitchen and through to the living room.

'How do you do, Mrs. O'Shanassey,' said Veronica O'Keefe. 'Giovanni tells me you have been shopping.' Before she could continue, Mary raised a hand. 'Giovanni, do you have a piece of paper.'

'Yes, Mary. Just a minute.' Both parents rose to correct Giovanni's bold us of the Christian name.

'That's fine. Giovanni and I are on familiar terms. Thank you, darling.' She took the sheet and wrote on it 'One daily paper and the largest ice cream possible for Giovanni'. Darling, I saw when we came around the corner that there is a shop that sells newspapers. Would you get me one, please?' She pressed a $10 note into his hand and he ran off, slamming the back screen door behind him.

'Let's make one thing clear,' Mary went on. 'These few things are the least I can do. Everyone falls on difficult times and it is the duty of others to help.'

'Mrs O'Shanassey,' said John O'Keefe, 'the uniform is fantastic. Giovanni is going to be the happiest little boy in the world but I am afraid it's not going to be much use to him. This is the last term for him at St. Bridget's. We simply can't afford the fees. I know they aren't terribly high but it's right beyond us just now.' He looked at his wife. "You see, when Giovanni was born and that was –'

Veronica indicated that they should all sit down, and carried on the story herself. 'I had seven miscarriages and then thanks to the saints Giovanni was born. He was the smallest child ever born in the local hospital and arrived a month early. He lived in an incubator for almost two months. I'm not afraid to say that it cost us everything we had. We had to take out a loan to pay for it all but we have the most wonderful child in the world.'

'Just a moment,' interrupted Mary. 'I, and most of the more secure Catholics in this district, as well as the larger Catholic businesses in this town, pay into the Benevolent Fund of St. Bridget's and this money is there precisely for this purpose.'

'Mrs O'Shanassey,' John began.

'No, I won't have it. This fund was well supported by my husband's family and the Higgins family and you obviously know Nancy.' A nod indicated that they indeed knew the most import matriarch in Sitwell. 'Well, now, that is all settled. Oh, by the way, this is confidential and the clothes are just a little extra to show our appreciation of you sharing your son with us. Wouldn't you agree, Emmanuel?

'Certainly.'

A bang on the screen door announced Giovanni's return. The chocolate and ice-cream smeared on his lips spelt out quite clearly that Mary's message had been well understood. Giovanni handed her the newspaper and the change, which she returned to his open palm.

'You keep it, Giovanni. Perhaps you can place a little of it in the collection on Friday.'

'Oh gosh,' he said, looking at what was in his hand, something extremely rare.

'By the way,' she went on, 'Emmanuel has promised Giovanni a ride in our boat.' Emmanuel picked up on this immediately, especially the word 'our'. 'So do you think that before summer is over Father could collect him one Friday evening and he could stay with us at Bantry and we could bring him back when we come to Mass on Sunday morning. Let me know if that's convenient.' And with that she stood, as did Emmanuel.

'Thank you very much,' was John O'Keefe's comment, and with that Giovanni disappeared, only to return with a sheet of Art paper and a painting of his of a red dog.

'This is for you,' he said, looking at them both. 'I think it is very nice, don't you?'

'Darling, it's exquisite. I shall have it framed next week, but you haven't signed it.'

Here he looked confused. 'Put your name on the bottom,' his mother urged him. 'And yes, Mrs O'Shanassey, whenever it's convenient for you we would both feel very happy leaving Giovanni in your care.

'Thank you so very much,' replied Mary and with that they left, this time by the front door, a door that was obviously rarely used, Mary with slightly damp eyes, carrying a sheet of drawing paper with a red dog painted on it.

CHAPTER SIX

The Deacon

CHAPTER SIX

The Deacon

'Darling, I will have another. Thanks.' Mary and Emmanuel were sitting in the drawing rook at Bantry, waiting for Vince to return. 'Well, darling, for your first day I would say you have done extremely well, flattening Barry Howes, making a life-long friend of Giovanni, and Nancy is absolutely mad about you.'

'All in a day's work. But why is the whole place so ugly and run down? That I just don't understand.'

'Well, sweetie, I hope you are not under any illusions that when I arrived at Bantry it was in this condition. It was terribly run down.'

'Oh, talking of 'run-down' or fallen down, can we have a look at the ballroom before Vince gets back?'

'Certainly. Let's look now.' But before she had even got to the door the telephone rang. 'Yes?' Oh, I'm afraid you have it all wrong.' She turned to look at Emanuel. 'It is us that are the grateful party. You see, when Giovanni is a well-known painter, the gift of the red dog will be worth millions, so it's a fair swop. But thank you for calling and I do hope to see you at Mass on Sunday. Now, do give me your telephone number. Thank you. Goodbye.' She hung up.

'Mrs O'Keefe?' asked Emmanuel, as he linked arms with Mary and walked down the long, gracious hall.

'Yes. She had assumed we had only bought him his basic uniform but apparently when she unpacked everything she was clearly surprised at the other clothes. You know, Emmanuel,' she said in a very serious voice as she stopped to face him, 'I feel so content – or should I say totally satisfied that I was able to do that small thing today, and the purchase of the clothes for Giovanni I know has given me greater pleasure than I shall get when Paul restores the fountains. Does that make sense?' She looked directly at him. He moved forward and embraced her. 'I think you are fabulous,' he said, and they stayed like that for a moment. It was then he realised that under this tough social façade and smart repartee was hiding a soft, sentimental Mary.

'This way, darling.' From a drawer in a hall table she extracted a key. At the end of the corridor was a pair of doors. She unlocked them and one squeaked open. Although late afternoon, it was still possible to see clearly in this vast space. Emmanuel was amazed that for twenty years or so this room had remained in such a condition. Half the ceiling or more likely a third of it had collapsed and was spread over half the floor. When one looked upwards one could see the beams and supports that held the slates in position. The celling was ornate – or what remained intact was ornate, a flat centre section was supported on four sides with a huge coved section that surrounded the room with huge swags of fruit and leaves and in the centre two vast plaster ceiling roses with metal hooks in the centres where once large chandeliers must have hung. But it was the space that was overwhelming. There were very few private homes in the district with a ballroom of these dimensions. On one side were four windows symmetrically placed and these were still hung with ornate curtain arrangements in shreds, with gilded carved pelmets over the top. The rest of the wall space was marked out with panels in wallpaper above a wainscoting and in most of the panels were hooks. These obviously at some stage held paintings.

'Where are all the furnishings?' Emmanuel asked.

'They are all stored in the two rooms behind the chapel, where they have been for years but Paul took the two big chandeliers away months ago to electrify them so we will just have to wait until he gets the plastering done and up everything can go again. But I have no idea what I can use it for.'

'Oh, come on. I think I have just heard Vince's car. He is late.'

They closed and locked the door, then headed back to the drawing room to meet Vince as he swept in through the front door.

'I will strangle him!' announced Vince, in an assertive way. 'I have just had him.'

'Drinks time!' cried Mary, realising Vince was furious. 'Now, darling, who is to be strangled?' They sat down with a glass in their hands.

'Eddie,' he replied, narrowing his eyes. Mary asked what he had done this time.

'He has flatly refused to clean the school, empty the rubbish bins or clean the yard as he is commiserating with his friend the headmaster at the local hotel. For that reason I am late. The whole staff had to get out and do the work.'

'Vince,' suggested Emmanuel, 'this is the only opportunity you may have and certainly before this Deacon gets back. Call him at once and fire him. You have this right. You are in charge.'

'That's fine,' Vince replied, 'I almost did it this afternoon, but if I fire him who at such short notice is going to replace him? The staff have chipped in tonight but I am certain they will not do it tomorrow.'

Emmanuel gave a broad smile, as did Mary, and they leaned across and clinked glasses. Vince looked totally bemused. 'What's happening?' he asked.

'Do you have the number?' Emmanuel teased, with Mary joning in. 'Oh, the number, well yes, I'm sure I do and won't it be a surprise.'

'I'm sure,' replied Emmanuel, enjoying the game. 'This calls for great celebrations, wouldn't you say?'

'Oh, definitely. It's such a pity the ballroom isn't finished. We could have had an inaugural ball.'

'That's right. And we could have displayed the precious painting at the same time.'

'The red dog? So Matisse, wouldn't you say?'

Vince was totally confused and had no idea why they hadn't grasped his dilemma. Mary stood up and went to the phone, dialled a number, spoke for a moment and then turned to Vince.

'Father, your new groundsman is waiting to speak to you.'

Vince walked across the room in a daze: nothing made any sense at all.

'Oh, said Mary, before handing the telephone to him, 'his name is John O'Keefe.'

Vince spoke for a moment and made arrangements to see him and explain his work schedule the following morning, then hung up, but before leaving the phone, from his jacket pocket he pulled out his telephone diary and dialled a number. Eddie's cell phone rang and when he answered it was with the voice of someone who was having quite a drink along with the headmaster.

'Whada you want?' Eddie spat.

'You have completely reneged on your responsibilities.'

'Get fucked,' was the slurred reply.

'Fine,' came the stern response from Vince. 'I would suggest you continue drinking with your friend for as long as you wish, as it gives me the greatest pleasure to fire you. The Treasurer will pay your wages up to this morning and your holiday pay will be added to it.'

'You can't do this to me. I'll just see the Deacon and that'll fix you.'

'You can drink with the Deacon as well, as far as I am concerned, but put a foot on the premises of St Bridget's except to attend Mass and I shall call the police. I hope that is clear.'

Whatever Eddie's reply was, it was obviously loud as Vince held the receiver away from his ear and without any more ado put it down. He returned to Mary and Emmanuel with a grin like a Cheshire cat. 'But how did you know about this John O'Keefe?' he asked.

'Oh, simple,' replied Emmanuel with a slightly superior look. 'We met an angel today and he informed us of everything.

'A what?'

Mary broke into laughter and explained everything to him.

'Do you realise,' Vince said, later during dinner, 'that I have fired two people in one day?

'And only one to go,' added Mary, with a vicious smile.

The next day saw a very nervous staff watching from the staffroom window Vince showing John O'Keefe what his set tasks were to be, and were so surprised that by lunchtime the years of scrap paper that littered the boundary fence were cleaned away and the burner belched smoke for the rest of the day. After school had finished, Vince called a staff meeting for ten minutes. He hated them, as he always said in these meetings absolutely nothing was ever resolved and they went on interminably. 'This meeting,' he began,' is going to be very short and I am not interested in discussing anyone's point of view. If you have a problem, see me in my office. The advertisement for the position of head of this school went into all the local papers this morning and I, with the Sacristan, will interview these applicants. We have a new groundsman, John O'Keefe, whose son is at St. Bridget's. If any of you wish to terminate your contract, come and see me before Friday. Oh, by the way, all the rubbish or junk that is just not used or ever will be is to be given to Mr. O'Keefe to remove to the tip or burn. Is that clear? The whole school is in terrible shape. Good afternoon.' He left for his office, where he collected his briefcase and departed, leaving a perplexed staff but one that knew very well things were about to change. Or were they? They discussed it amongst themselves.

'Let's just wait until the Deacon gets back.' So they decided to become spectators in a show down that was to begin on Sunday morning, when the Deacon returned, but they were very disappointed, as a telephone call notified all that Dolly and the Deacon were held over in Sydney due to a mechanical problem with their car. So it would be Monday or Tuesday when he returned to a depleted number of supporters.

Bolstered by the knowledge that Nancy Higgins had seen fit to invite him to lunch, and he was sure the invitation would be repeated in the future, the Treasurer, Simon Thomas, who was usually known as a bit of a mouse, took it upon himself to enter, without permission, and with a master key, the Deacon's office. From a bookcase on one side of the room, after a little searching about, he withdrew six volumes of accounts, all bound in green, and with nothing printed on the spines. When he opened one, he knew he had found what he was seeking. He laid out the first book and then checked that all the rest were in chronological order, then slipped them into a large blue carrier bag with long handles. Then he re-arranged the book case shelves, so there was not a trace of a vacant space where the six volumes had once stood. He locked the door, looked up the hall to make sure no one had seen him, and passed Vince's office, the door of which was closed. He could not be heard, but he tiptoed out of the back door where this blue carrier bag was placed on the passenger seat and hurriedly made for home.

As everything happened so quickly, and in one day, Simon also thought to strike while the iron was hot, but he knew he would never have had the courage to do what he had done had the Deacon been present. Even to have demanded these volumes from him was something he would never have thought to do. He did indeed look like a mouse, almost a cartoon mouse, constantly moving his head from side to side as if unsure of something or if in fact perhaps he had forgotten something. At sixty two years of age, he had gone on early retirement in order to concentrate his whole life on St. Bridget's. He had been married once, for a very short period and then his wife disappeared, leaving him for another bank teller, and the two of them had fled to finer fields. He had sold their home, giving her half and moved back to his parents, where, if the truth be known, he felt much happier. He was physically quite short and the thing you noticed first was his extraordinary rapid movements. He did not do anything slowly. If Simon had to pick up a pen, it was done in a flash. He wrote quickly, in a beautiful but spidery hand, but this was becoming a thing of the past. This little mouse, like everyone else, had a computer screen in front of him and as he adjusted his ever-present gold spectacles his head turned like a machine, producing a product, as he copied onto his computer every page from these six volumes. He headed his computer page with the dates and the title 'St. Bridget's Benevolent Fund' and well into the night this little grey-haired man with gold-rimmed spectacles bent over his computer like a character in a Dickens novel. He began the transfer of data that was going to give him the information that would not only project him forward socially as regards Nancy Higgins, but also lay a trap for the one person he disliked most in this world.

All week, Vince had been on hot bricks, ever since Emmanuel's first day, when he had given Barry Howe two decent slaps. He knew there was going to be trouble, but oddly nothing happened. It has often been said that bullies are cowards and in Barry's case this was true. For him to admit to his parents and on a power basis his grand-parents, that he had been publicly disciplined for an act of arrogance was something he knew would work against him, so he kept his peace. But if there was one person he now was afraid of and hated, it was the new Sacristan and one look in the school grounds sent Barry in the other direction, using his total vocabulary of expletives to show what he thought of Emanuel.

185

'You were very good,' said Giovanni. 'You are very clever,' and laughed as he held Emmanuel's hand after Mass on Sunday morning, as he and Vince came out after disrobing to the front of the church where there were still on this warm morning a large number of church attendees exchanging local news, better known as gossip. One of these people was a man who went by the name of Samuel O'Connor, but was always known as Sam. He was a tall man with a big round face which at the bottom hung in folds which cascaded around his neck. His reddish greying hair, a pair of bright green yellow eyes, like a cat's, and a big, slightly reddish nose gave him almost a cartoon appearance. But he was as much part of Sitwell or the district as Mary or Nancy. His wife Annie was mercilessly thin and as tall as a telegraph pole. No matter what she wore it always had the appearance of having been picked up two sizes too large from a charity bin. Her thin, bony face and two very soft blue eyes immediately proclaimed her character.

They were all chattering on together but it was Sam who noted the tiny boy with his hand in the Sacristan's.

'You know, Sacristan,' he began, 'this morning we probably saw the best Mass we have seen for years. Wouldn't you say so, Nance?' She loathed being addressed in this way.

'Yes,' she replied, 'but this is only the beginning.'

'Well, I hope so. And, Father, I have been meaning to ask you what the hell you are going to do with this bloody architectural mess here?' But he was interrupted by a voice. 'What are you talking about?' asked Anthony Howes, who was more than curious about the shift of power at St. Bridget's.

'It's a bloody mess. The whole place. The Protestants must be dying laughing at this shambles.'

There was an eerie silence as if someone had revealed a most inner secret in public.

'What would you know about architecture?' exclaimed an irate Antony Howe. 'All you do is breed dogs, it seems.'

'Listen, Howes, my knowledge of architecture, if this monstrosity in front of us is your concept of fine building, makes me Palladio.'

Mary and the others began to smile broadly. Anthony Howes had an Achilles' heel and that was criticism. He could not cope with it and became spiteful. 'Go back to the bloody awful house you live in and we shall blow this monstrosity up on Monday morning.'

Anthony left in a huff with Betty following up as she was having a discussion with a friend of hers about the Canadian mixed foursomes for next Saturday at the Sitwell golf club.

'Well, little man,' he said, looking at Giovanni, still with Emmanuel's hand in his, 'what sort of a dog do you have?'

Emmanuel noticed the same awkwardness as the first time he met Giovanni, where he put one foot over the other to cover the hole in his shoe, but today in his new shorts, shirt and shoes he was as good as the rest and felt it, but it didn't take much to undermine his confidence, especially if there was money involved, and having a dog is one thing, but keeping a dog fed well is totally another.

'I don't have a dog,' he said softly and Emmanuel felt something inside him that wanted to tell Sam to just shut up, be quiet and not make things more awkward for him. It was Nancy who beat them all to the punch. 'How do you expect a lad of six years old to feed his new dog?' and then she winked at Sam. They had been friends for a life time; local tongues had always put more to it but they were two people who with a look, a wink or a frown could pass a whole message to one another without a word.

'Well, well,' said Sam. 'Next week, the Sacristan and you are coming to lunch on Saturday. Is that all right?'

'Giovanni held Emmanuel's hand tighter. 'I think so, 'he said, summoning up his courage.

'Good. You see, I have a litter of pups, the best, you know, King Charles spaniels, the royalty of dogs.' Giovanni could only respond with 'Oh'. 'I'll let you have a choice and, you know,' as he bent down, 'the supermarket will give you free tins of food for him.' He stood up again. 'Won't they, Nance?'

'But of course. They are royal dogs.'

'Really?' Giovanni said, his eyes wide open. 'Emmanuel, a dog! A man is going to give me a dog!' Then he seemed very embarrassed at his own enthusiasm and moved back against Emmanuel.

'Giovanni,' he said to him. 'I have been speaking to Father and we have decided –' Vince turned his head in Emmanuel's direction, knowing that no discussion about anything important had taken place – 'that you are going to be our first altar boy.'

'I think it will be very hard for me,' he replied.

'Not at all,' Sam chimed in. 'I was an altar boy when I was young and now you are going to be an altar boy. I think a dog is a nice present.'

'Oh, it is.' Giovanni was overwhelmed but unsure whether a dog arrived before or after you became an altar boy. Everyone laughed at his genuine confusion. His parents remained in the background, amazed that their little son had captivated what was considered the Catholic backbone of society in this district. They knew that it had been his new-found friend called Emmanuel, the Sacristan, that had completely changed Giovanni's life and also, now, theirs.

'Now,' announced Mary, 'back to Bantry. 'Don't tell me, Sam. that you can't make it or you know how cross I can become.'

He laughed. 'Would we refuse an invitation to Bantry?' and laughed again.

'Mr and Mrs O'Keefe, you are also on my guest list.'

'Oh, Mrs O'Shanassey, I think we should be fish out of water, but thank you so much,' said Veronica.

'I won't hear of it,' Mary retorted. 'You must come.'

'Perhaps another day?' She smiled.

'Well,' said Emmanuel, 'you know you are always welcome.' She said thank you quietly. 'But if you won't join us, may we take Giovanni and when Nancy and the others return to Sitwell they will bring him to your front door.'

Veronica smiled again and held Emmanuel's arm. 'He would love it. He is always so alone. Yes, that would be fine.'

'Come on, then, handsome,' Emmanuel joked in a theatrical way, 'off to Bantry.'

'And don't forget,' added Sam, 'next Saturday Ferron for your dog.'

So Giovanni was swept away with this group of people, with John and Veronica just watching as the tiny blonde boy suddenly from not having any friends had in less than a week gained Mrs. O'Shanassey, Nancy Higgins, Samuel O'Connor, the Lampedusas, both Priest and Sacristan, all vying for his attention, Giovanni with one hand in Emmanuel's and the other in the hand of a very sizeable man called Sam, telling him that he was very good at painting dogs and that he had given Mary and Emmanuel a painting.

'Oh,' said Sam, where's my painting, then?'

'Well, I will have to do it in class next week,' he replied. 'I haven't got any paints at home.'

Nancy felt a lump rise in her throat. She knew the story well from Mary, and interrupted, 'Oh, Giovanni, you must come to my painting class. I have only one friend who paints with me and I am sure Philip would enjoy your company as will I.'

He looked at her and turned his head a little to the side, then bit the bottom part of his lip.

'Darling,' Sarah joined in, 'Nancy has tubes and tubes of paint and hundreds of brushes and pieces of paper.' She bent down to him. 'Darling, you must help Nancy use up the paint, otherwise it will all go hard and she will have to throw it all away. We wouldn't want that, would we?'

'No,' he said, with his eyes wide open, 'we wouldn't like that.'

Whilst everyone was organising cars, a very stiff Anthony Howe noticed a lot of competition for a boy he had never seen, whose father was now the cleaner and caretaker for St. Bridget's. He thought the whole thing stupid and so like them all, but it was Sam who won and with a large cushion from the back seat folded in two, Giovanni was just able to see out of the front window of the large black Bentley as they passed through Sitwell and on to Bantry, talking about King Charles spaniels.

'You can't believe how stupid they all are,' Anthony Howes repeated to his wife and extended family. When they were all safely indoors he asked, 'Barry, do you know the new caretaker's son?

Barry steered clear of a comment that might just end him up in trouble. 'No, he's in Grade 2. I don't know any of them,' and moved to the dining table. He retrieved a piece of cheese.

'I think Father is behaving quite unnecessarily and the moment the Deacon gets back I shall have a word with him and get it all put straight.

'Well, he is in control,' offered his son Sean, who was the exact opposite of his father, tall, broad shouldered and thin, just like his mother. Barry was his only child and his wife, Lyn, just ate and talked non-stop, the result being her weight. She simply doted on Barry and he, being cunning, played it for all he could manage.

Anthony Howes's architectural practice was in the next big town: Sitwell could never have supported an architect's practice, and his son, Sean, was a partner in the firm. If the truth were known, Sean was not convinced that the new church of St. Bridget was of any architectural merit at all.

The Deacon was not unaware of the developments in his absence. His cellular phone had rung continually and he was anything but pleased. He saw the events as Vince waiting until his back was turned and then striking at two members of his back-up team who were now out. He was most concerned that a new caretaker had already been appointed without his stamp of approval. He had made quite a secure base in his ten year stint at St. Bridget's and with the last priest firmly wound around his little finger what the Deacon said went. It was a foolish use of power and as a result many of the parishioners loathed him, especially his superior way of speaking to them. Many of the ecclesiastical laws and by-laws the Deacon manipulated to suit his own ends, working on the assumption that no one at Sitwell had any idea of Canon Law, and on that point he was correct.

'Come along,' cried Mary as everyone alighted from their cars and walked towards the house. 'Mary, it looks fabulous.'

'You have done so much work,' Sam's wife, Annie, commented

'Goodness,' said Mary, as she linked arms through Sarah's. 'How long is it since you have been here?'

'Ages, I think. I don't remember the last time. Look at that!' Annie brushed her unruly hair to one side and looked in Sam's direction. The other two women turned to where Giovanni was holding court, with Vince, Emmanuel and Sam laughing. 'If Sam had given that much attention to his two sons they might despise him just a little less,' she said.

'You think Sam has a problem,' commented Sarah. 'Bill and Michael would be lucky to pass one word a week to one another and you can bet it's sarcastic.'

'What's wrong with these men that they can't relate to their sons?'

'It's the same with Emmanuel and Salvatore, although in the last eighteen months with Richard things became so much better. Angela didn't help much,' Mary said, 'but this anti-social behaviour is just perpetuating.

'My eldest son has a girl and a boy but he doesn't seem interested in them at all,' was Annie's comment. 'It's as if he has done his duty dynastically and has just turned off. God help his wife. And look at Sam now, totally infatuated by Giovanni.'

'He's a very special little boy,' said Mary.

'Oh, I don't mean any harm to him, he's wonderful and Sarah has explained his very difficult background. It's not Giovanni that's worrying me, it's Sam. I don't think he would ever think of taking his grandson out for a drive as he has done today with Giovanni and I know for sure my son would and does consider it hell to be with Sam for more than ten minutes.'

'It's the same drama day in day out with Michael and Bill,' said Sarah. 'Oh, talking of Michael, where is he?'

'He's in Melbourne and has been all week. Nancy had some legal documents to deliver to a solicitor and was terrified they would go astray in the mail, so Michael was despatched and is staying with friends for a few days, I believe.'

The three women entered the coolness of the house to hear from the library intense conversation. The women looked at one another and headed in the direction of the room. Here was Nancy holding court with Giovanni. 'His tail is a bit long, I think.'

'Well, I think he looks like a fox.'

'Oh no, Sam, he is definitely a dog,' at which everyone laughed. Drinks in the drawing room and everyone moved there, with Giovanni still holding hands with Emmanuel.

'The house looks spectacular,' said Annie.

'Well, it has everything to do with a good decorator and my money,' laughed Mary.

After lunch, at which every subject was touched on, especially the Mass they had just attended, ('About time, Father. Good work!' was Mary's comment) they all ambled down to the river via the three large terraces and at the bottom moored to the little pier was the boat. Giovanni was overwhelmed but terrified to go on board. It was only in Vince's arms that he allowed himself to be transported aboard. With Vince and Emmanuel, it chugged up the river for about half a kilometre and returned as the others at on the lawn enjoying a breeze coming off the river. The staff dutifully refilled all the glasses.

'I have steered the boat,' Giovanni exclaimed excitedly, 'and we went for a big trip, didn't we, Father?'

'Yes, we did and I am sure you will be a good sailor.'

'Yes, I will,' he replied determinedly. 'When I have art this week I shall ask the teacher if I can paint a boat.'

Nancy smiled and with her digital camera took photos of everyone with Giovanni, and of course the boat. She was not going to be behind any art teacher when it came to painting Mary's boat. And so it was that a tired but very happy little boy sat beside Nancy as Bill drove them back to Sitwell.

Monday morning did not see the arrival of the Deacon, who was still driving somewhere between Sydney and Sitwell, listening to Dolly complaining yet again about the fact that he had two left feet, as well as about her concern over the situation at St. Bridget's. His conceit was such that although he found all these changes annoying, he never thought it would alter his lifestyle at all. But Monday morning at ten saw in Vince's crowded office four people and the Treasurer, Simon Thomas, who seemed to be in charge.

'You asked me about the St. Bridget's Benevolent Fund. Well, I have taken it upon myself to take the six volumes dating from 1848 and transferred all of it onto my computer, a long job, of course.' he started, adjusting his spectacles, 'but we're at a good point.'

'Well, what has happened to the money?' asked Nancy.

'You might well ask,' replied Simon.

'How much is left?' Vince enquired.

'Exactly eight hundred and twenty two dollars. You see,' he went on, turning and looking at a confused Emmanuel, 'the money is in this account to spend on children who have financial difficulties, so if most of the money is gone, this is good, as it means that the recipients have been helped.'

There was silence. Vince had an odd feeling that Simon had information that was going to be most painful.

'So everything is all right?' suggested Nancy, moving to leave.

'Well, not exactly.' Nancy sat down again and told him to get to the point. 'In the past, the student's name and amount with the use of the money and date were recorded, and this was done religiously – oh, pardon the pun –'

'Get on with it!' Nancy was beginning to lose her patience.

'Well,' he continued, adjusting his jacket and not very pleased with Nancy's highhandedness, 'it appears that for the last nine years this procedure has not been followed. We have no way of knowing where the money went or what it was used for as all that is shown in the register are deductions.'

'Who signed for them?' asked Emmanuel.

'This I am now going to have to go to the bank for, to demand all the dates.'

'I suggest we call in the police. Foul play!' cried Nancy.

'May I say something?' interrupted Simon. 'What if, and of course this is only an if, somebody had the last priest sign the cheques and then somebody cashed them and the money just disappeared into his pocket?'

'The Deacon!' Nancy shouted. 'A new car every three years – you don't get that on a pension.'

'Just a moment, Mrs Higgins. There are three possibilities as I see it: one, the headmaster, as he administered the power to decide who was to be the recipient of the money; two, the Deacon, and three the previous priest. Now, I don't think we need to rush into things just yet, as I still have some work to do at the bank, but let's just wait for a while. Oh, by the way, sign these forms and it will now only allow Father to sign a cheque for the amount and it must be counter-signed by you, Mrs. Higgins, as the president of this worthy Benevolent Fund.'

Everyone looked at one another. He was right, the Treasurer, there were three suspects and they still had to do a little detective work themselves to find out who were the recipients of all the money over nine year period and why it had not been entered into the ledgers as in the past.

'Well, there is enough money left to pay for Giovanni's school fees for this year, so when the new cheque book is ready, Father and I will sign the amount over into general revenue.'

'Certainly, Mrs Higgins, no later than Thursday.'

'Keep the ledgers safely, Simon,' advised Vince. 'I would hate to think that they just went missing.'

'Exactly', agreed Nancy. 'When you are finished with them, bring them over to Shannon and I will lock them in my safe.'

'Certainly, Mrs Higgins. What a good idea! It will take me only a few days more to complete transferring them on to a disk.'

'Well,' said Emmanuel, after the others had left, 'it's very Miss Marple, wouldn't you think?'

'Yes, unfortunately,' his brother agreed. 'It's very worrying. This sort of thing is not the public relations one needs. Oh, do you know, since I put the advertisement for a new headmaster in the papers I have received five applicants. I have said that you and I will interview them on Friday after the children's Mass. Is that all right with you?'

'Sure. It's not a problem. I won't come in again until Friday as there isn't much to do, and it's so damn depressing. The only highlight is Giovanni.'

'Yes, it's not exactly an invigorating environment.'

Dolly and the Deacon had arrived back late on Monday afternoon and were invited to dinner at the Howes's residence in Sutton Drive. Dolly took over, explaining non-stop how everyone had thought her so spectacular. Anthony Howes let the conversation go on for a while and then ushered the Deacon into his study. Having offered him a drink, he then demanded to know what he planned to do about the Priest suddenly taking it upon himself to fire and hire apparently without the school board's permission.

'Well, it's a delicate one,' smiled the Deacon, 'but the over-riding say does belong to the parish priest.'

'Really? I suppose that means he could sell the whole of St Bridget's lock, stock and barrel.' Anthony Howe slammed his whisky glass down.

'I think that would need the Bishop's permission and as the Bishop and I are on such good terms we don't have to worry.'

'Worry? Try telling that to the ex-headmaster and Eddie.'

'Yes, that is a very nasty problem, that one.'

'And it seems that the new Sacristan has a finger in the pie.'

'Oh, don't worry on that account. I am his superior and I'll have him knocked into shape in no time. It's such a pity Father didn't decide to get rid of that Miss Ainsworth, a nasty piece of work.'

The Deacon and Miss Ainsworth loathed one another. She saw him for exactly what he was, someone using the Church as a support for his social gain and said so loudly.

Tuesday morning saw the Deacon early for once and having seen Vince's car parked in front of the church he decided to strike.

'Good morning, Father,' he said, in a patronising way. 'Now what's been going on here while I have been away?'

'You will note very carefully,' said a stony-faced Vince, 'that as parish priest of St. Bridget's I shall determine policy here, not you. If you have any complaints, we shall see the Bishop together. Is that clear?

'Perfectly.' The Deacon realised very quickly that the dynamics at St. Bridget's had changed radically.

'Do you have the estimates for the repair to the church roof?' asked Vince.

'More or less,' came the arrogant response.'

'Have the quotes on my desk by the end of this week.

'What's all this about a new headmaster? I am sure that we can all patch up our differences. Len (the previous overweight hippy headmaster's name) has been here for years and really has this school at heart. He understands everything here better than anyone.

'Too late, Deacon. I begin interviews with the Sacristan on Friday. If he wants to re-apply he may, but personally I should consider it a waste of everyone's time.'

The Deacon moved from side to side, obviously needing the cigarette that was rarely out of his hand – in fact the two fingers that supported the usual cigarette were stained a rust colour from the nicotine. 'As the second most important ecclesiastic here, it should be my position to interview the candidates for this post.'

'Are you deaf?' asked Vince, in a superior way. 'I said that I and the Sacristan will do the interviews and if a staff representative is required Miss Ainsworth can sit in on them.'

'What would she know?' the Deacon spat.

'Is that all?' asked Vince. The Deacon, without saying goodbye stalked out and into the school yard where he immediately lit up a cigarette.

Vince and Emmanuel pulled up in front of the church on Friday, the last day of the school week, talking about the interviews after Mass.

'Good morning, Father, good morning, Emmanuel,' John O'Keefe greeted them. 'Giovanni will be very happy today.'

'Why?'

'Well, he hasn't seen you this week and so he thought you had gone away. I told him you hadn't but he has been a bit worried.' And at this point a tiny boy ran across the school yard and flung his small body into Emmanuel's arms. He lifted him up and kissed him.

'I thought you had gone away,' he said, with his arms still wrapped around Emmanuel's neck. The other students were arriving, noticing this strange sight, as did the Deacon from his office window.

Emmanuel lowered the boy to the ground. 'Nancy tells me your altar boy clothes are almost ready, so when you go to paint with her and Philip tomorrow you can try them on.' Giovanni beamed, hugged Emmanuel again and then left with his father, explaining to him that he really knew Emmanuel had not gone away.

At nine o'clock sharp, as Mass was about to begin, with Emmanuel dressed to serve, Vince in a cassock and lace alb with a chasuble courtesy of Nancy, and Emmanuel in cassock and lace cotta, a sharp cry came from the Deacon. 'What's all this nonsense?' He pushed rudely past Emmanuel. 'I am in charge here.'

'Past tense,' was Emmanuel's sarcastic reply.

'Have you got those three quotes for the repair of the roof on my desk?' Vince asked, knowing full well he had not.

'I will just change for Mass,' replied the Deacon, changing the subject.

'You will do exactly as your superior has demanded,' thundered Vince. 'You are not required here this morning as I have a server. Get those quotes now or it will be me telephoning the bishop about disobedience.'

The Deacon was black with rage. Never had he been treated like this, his ecclesiastical duties ripped out from under him. His ultimate power base was in assisting at Mass and letting everyone assume he had the same power as the priest.

Mass began but it was a pair of sneaking eyes belonging to the Deacon, who had noticed from the back door that all the work he had done in eradicating as much ceremony as possible from the Mass, bringing it down to the level of the people, as he thought, had been overturned in less than a fortnight.

'Please come in.' Emmanuel ushered in the first applicant and they all sat around a table in the library, which had been vacated for two hours. Vince looked at Miss Ainsworth, still decked out in sports clothes – in fact he wondered if he had ever seen her in any other sort of attire. The first applicant was a tall, thin man of about 35 to 40 years old. He gave a resume of his experience, but his lack-lustre appearance and casual dress sense tended to fit him into the category of the previous headmaster. They asked the usual questions, what he thought about discipline, uniform, school achievement standards, and then asked what he thought would happen if he were given the job. His opinions were so wishy-washy that it was impossible to be sure what he wanted to do at all. It was during the second interview, with a girl in her thirties, that the Deacon swept across the library and sat down. He began to take over, speaking about a more modern approach to education. Emmanuel placed his pen on the desk. 'Deacon,' he said, sharply,' if you would like an interview for this position, please wait in line with the others.'

Again, black with rage, he defiantly sat there. 'Move it!' said a smiling Miss Ainsworth, 'or it will give me the greatest pleasure to personally- but of course with Father's permission – throw you head first into the school yard.'

The Deacon was just about to tackle her verbally but the pushing back of her chair, and given that she was considerably bigger than he was, made him decide retreat was the only way. The slamming of the library door announced his departure. The young girl was most confused as the interview continued.

It was the fourth applicant, a woman in her mid to late forties, in a tailored suit but carrying the jacket due to the hot weather, who seemed to have what the three of them wanted. After asking the usual questions, they summed up in a moment. They were talking to a traditional teacher but also one with good ideas on evaluating each student to get the best out of them. Vince asked her did she have any questions.

'Oh yes,' Brenda Wade said, 'I have a few. Firstly what is the ecclesiastical role here in educational policy?'

'If you're asking about administration of the school, basically none. That would be your task. If at any time you needed my help, I am here.' She nodded her head.

'May I ask why a school situated in the middle of the country has no playing fields, just this small space around two churches covered in ashfelt?'

'You may well ask,' Vince replied. 'I have been here a year and a half and even though Emmanuel and I grew up in the city I think we had much more green space, and as you see there is not even a tree.'

'So I see. And your long term plans for St. Bridget's School?'

'Easy,' came in Emmanuel. 'We plan to move the lot, lock stock and barrel to that field two doors down, a big space with lots of trees.'

'An excellent idea.' She smiled at him as Vince and Miss Ainsworth turned their heads to stare at him, totally bewildered.

'Oh, another question, if you don't mind. How do you think the staff would cope with a woman in charge? I see you have had men before.'

'Not always,' said Miss Ainsworth, taking over. 'St. Bridget's was originally run by the Sisters and so traditionally the administration, except for the last fifteen years, has always been female.' At this, Brenda Wade said her goodbyes and left.

'What field?' asked Vince.

'Yes,' said Miss Ainsworth. 'What the hell are you talking about? Do you know who owns that field?'

'Not a clue, but for the future what a great idea, don't you both think?'

'Emmanuel,' Vince said, 'it's a great idea but don't you think it's a bit presumptuous to jump the gun. We would never have that amount of money here to purchase the field. There must be at least two or three hectares of it. By the way, Miss Ainsworth, what about this piece of land?

'Well, years ago it was marked out for St. Patrick's College but obviously with time it was considered wise to build it in the next town, which is twenty times bigger than Sitwell, so the land was returned to the owner, one of the stingiest and tightest members of the community.'

'Really? Who?' asked Vince.

'Samuel O'Connor,' she replied. Emmanuel let out an excited yell. 'Don't get too excited, Sacristan. You will find Sam O'Connor a hard nut to crack.'

'Oh, not me,' he smiled broadly. 'A little blonde, curly haired boy of six years old is going to do it without any trouble at all Saturday lunchtime.' They both looked at him strangely. 'Giovanni and I have a luncheon engagement at Ferron. But don't we still have another applicant?'

Vince said yes and Miss Ainsworth pushed her chair back to go and ask the last applicant to come in. She saw the Deacon just outside the door in the yard, smoking. 'We'll do your interview on Monday. We are a bit busy today.' She grinned and turned around to show in a young man. Needless to say this comment to the Deacon was returned with a string of expletives.

The last applicant was indeed young, twenty seven, and obviously not lacking in self-esteem, dressed in a smart sporty way. He held the floor and was not bad-looking at all, thought Emmanuel. He spoke as if he were interviewing them and at a certain point Miss Ainsworth frowned and looked sideways, then banged her fist on the table top, much to everyone's surprise. Then she took over.

'Rob,' she began, in a very familiar way, 'I suppose you are right in to sportswear, seeing how well you are dressed. What do you think about school uniform?' This was the first time they had had the opportunity to ask him a question.

'Thing of the past!' he answered.

'Oh, so you and the Deacon hold the same opinion?'

'Yes, we were only talking the other night.' Then he stopped dead.

'I think that's all we need to know,' she concluded. Rob attempted to turn the conversation around but realised that he had been tricked into giving away his relationship with the Deacon. After another ten minutes of him explaining his talents he was bid goodbye.

'Very sharp, Miss Ainsworth.'

'Thank you, Sacristan.' This was the formal manner of address the two of them kept up all the time now, and Vince thought it quite odd. 'I suddenly remembered where I had seen Rob. You see, I have lived in Sitwell all my life and every now and again you just forget faces, like today. Then I remembered about six months ago a staff party and the Deacon and Rob were chatting together all night. Well, if you want my vote I would give the job to Brenda Wade.'

'So would I,' agreed Emmanuel. Vince also nodded in the affirmative. 'Well, that's settled. Brenda Wade begins on Monday morning. Thanks for your help,' Vince said to Miss Ainsworth.

'A pleasure, Father. I shall now be able to tell the staff that as their representative, it was a clean fight.' They all laughed.

'I should have liked to have seen you remove the Deacon,' Emmanuel continued, laughing.

'Oh, it would have been a pleasure to remove that worm.'

Saturday morning saw Giovanni delivered by his father to Shannon as arranged, for his first painting lesson with Nancy and Philip. She could tell he was a little nervous. 'Do come in for a cup of coffee,' she offered.

'Thank you, Mrs Higgins, but I have an appointment with Father at the church over roof problems, I believe.'

'Well, Mary and Emmanuel will collect him from here and take him to Ferron for lunch and then home again.' She smiled at the boy. 'Come along now. We are painting boats today.'

'Yes,' he said, with a smile, but even Nancy knew that this little man in front of her was much more excited about something he had always wanted, a dog. Nancy was surprised how quickly he learned. He had to be shown only once or twice and it remained in his mind. Giovanni found Philip for the first time in his life someone he could help but he did it in a manner that was non-judgmental and always constructive. To say Nancy was impressed was an understatement. She pronounced the lesson a great success and the paintings of boats were left to dry.

She had a room in the mansion set up as a studio and organising another place for Giovanni had not been a problem. He chatted on to both Nancy and Philip as if he had known them all his life and for the first time instead of being the spectator in life Philip began short conversations.

'I think your boat is nicer than mine,' said Giovanni, leaning over and looking at Philip's work. Nancy had taught Philip well. He was a very disciplined illustrator as opposed to painter, but for all parties his work was a success. Nancy kept every sheet of work Philip had ever done and with some she would insist he rework them. When she was happy with the result, they were window-mounted, ready for when she thought an exhibition of his work was appropriate. Not that she thought anyone would necessarily purchase it but for his self-esteem. And now he had a chatty little friend. Nancy was sure there would be space in this exhibition for him too.

'Mrs Higgins, Mr Lampedusa and Mrs O'Shanassey are here.'

'Show them into the drawing room. We shall finish here and be with them in a moment. Offer them a drink.' The last suggestion was unnecessary: everyone who finished up at Shannon finished up with a glass in their hand.

'Emmanuel, I did a painting of a fabulous boat. It's your boat, Mary.' Giovanni excitedly embraced Emmanuel and kissed him, and, to Mary's surprise, did the same to her, as Nancy came through the doorway.

'Well, Nancy, this is the first good –looking man I have had kiss me for years!' Nancy noted that for all this banter of Mary's she was very touched indeed.

The four of them went in Mary's car with Emmanuel driving. Ferron was exactly in the opposite direction from Bantry, and as Mary said to Nancy, she had not been there since Keven had died and that was at least ten or twelve years. 'It's exactly the same,' Nancy told her. Giovanni was sitting with the driver, again on two cushions and only just able to see out of the window as the seat belt held him lower. 'They need to spend some money on Ferron. Goodness knows, Sam has millions.' This was a piece of information that registered well in Emmanuel's brain. 'He just won't spend anything. His investments have been brilliant and I must say he has helped me enormously investment-wise.' Emmanuel thought of two well-to-do families! He thought like Angela: she had determined his whole life with the idea that whatever you do you do it well, and because Angela had the money she did. But it was the drive not to be afraid that Emmanuel had absorbed completely, so when he said at the interview for the position of head of the school that they would just physically move the whole structure, it was in fact Angela talking and Emmanuel just automatically assuming that because he thought it was a good idea and a just one it should simply happen.

The car swept through an enormous set of wooden gates with a two metre high picket fence supporting them up and carried on up the drive to a very large, red brick homestead with a veranda that surrounded it. It was large. The two enormous bay windows in the front were only the beginning of this architectural extravaganza.

'Hello, hello!' cried Sam, as he crossed the veranda from the open front door. They all alighted. 'Well, Mary, one week Bantry, the next Ferron.'

'Sounds good to me.' She laughed as the little boy, now free of his seat belt, rushed up on to the veranda of the homestead and threw his arms around an enormous waist. Sam knelt down and Giovani kissed him.

'You see, Sam, Emmanuel brought me to see you.' Both Mary and Nancy saw the tears forming and moved up with Emmanuel as Sam lifted the tiny boy into his arms and carried him in through the front door, completely ignoring the other three. Emmanuel winked at the other two and they all entered to meet Annie half-way up the hallway.

'How great you have come!' she said. 'I was sure at the last moment you would telephone to say you couldn't make it.'

'Not at all. Wild horses wouldn't have kept us away.' Mary was interrupted by Sam speaking to Giovanni.

'Would you like to see the dogs before lunch or afterwards?'

'Sam, can we see them now?' The two of them headed off hand in hand to the area where the puppies were.

Ferron was indeed a grand house built on one level, when there was plenty of money to show off a prestigious dynasty. One entered the broad hallway, punctuated at regular intervals by arches supported on freestanding Corinthian columns. Exactly halfway down this long hall it was intersected at right angles by two corridors to the right and the left, with the same arches and columns contuing down both sides. The furniture was Victorian and imposing but this vast house had a fine layer of dust – or was it time? – that gave it a slightly tired look, though grand at the same time. Mary always thought that Ferron was like a deluxe hotel from the nineteenth century.

They moved to one of the drawing rooms for a drink, to be greeted by one of Sam's sons, the unmarried one whom Emmanuel said later either seemed embarrassed or cold. His body movements were odd. Much later, before Sam and Giovanni returned, the married son and his wife made an appearance. Of these two Emmanuel had no opinion at all.

'You sit next to me,' said Sam and the obligatory cushions were found for Giovanni's chair.

The dining room was vast; even with the nine of them seated it gave the same sensation as if a tiny table was in the centre of a ballroom. This was one of the most splendid rooms in all Ferron, again columns and pilasters everywhere and all symmetrical. Two huge marble mantles with mirrors above glared at one another from opposite sides of the room that had red silk damask on the walls, which were covered with Victorian landscape paintings. The damask spread round into curtains and decorative seating near the bay window. The whole thing was like a period film set, except it was real. The ornaments, the red leather-covered chairs, of which there were thirty – who these days would or even could for that matter seat thirty people for meal, Mary thought? As the meal began and the wine flowed, Emmanuel decided to move in on his target, namely Sam.

'Did you play sport at school?' he asked.

'Yes,' said a buoyant Sam, making sure Giovanni had enough to eat. 'I wasn't good at football but a real whizz at cricket. Do you play cricket at school?' he asked Giovanni, the perfect opening. Emmanuel played his first card.

'How can he?' he said replying for Giovanni. 'There is no space, only asphalt.'

'What do you mean, no space?'

'Exactly what I said, no space. Over time the school expanded but Anthony Howes's extravaganza also ate up the space, so cricket is impossible – unless you play it in the old church.'

'That's bloody ridiculous,' Sam exploded. 'We'll have to fix that, won't we, Giovanni?'

The boy agreed, though he was rather confused.

'Well, we could offer Giovanni an opportunity for life.' Emmanuel smiled. It was Nancy who suddenly realised Emmanuel wanted something from Sam but couldn't quite work out what. But she was more interested than in what the others at the table continued to talk about. Nancy turned and watched Emmanuel engineer Sam into a corner, using Giovanni as bait. They didn't even have to wait until the deserts, and Nancy was amazed that this beautiful young man with electric blue eyes had managed to convince Sam to hand over a valuable piece of land to the school only so that a little boy sitting beside him had the opportunity to learn to play cricket. She smiled to herself and thought it was nice going for Emmanuel, not bad at all.

When lunch was over, Sam, Giovanni, Nancy and Emmanuel went out to the breeding section behind the stables for Giovanni to make his selection of a puppy. Sam gave him all the pointers to pick the finest of the litter, and Giovanni listened attentively, looking at the five puppies. But it was the littlest of the litter at the back that he spotted and whether he thought it was like himself at the back and forgotten – which could not now be said of him – but it was this puppy he picked.

'He's a little runt,' said Sam, 'but one hundred percent pedigree.'

'What does that mean?' Giovanni turned to look at Sam.

'Well, I suppose it's a driver's licence for life.' He laughed as he spoke.

'Oh, I don't think he will be allowed to drive a car,' said Giovanni seriously.

Sam knelt down and pulled Giovanni to him. 'You are the best young man in the world,' he said. Nancy and Emmanuel noticed Sam, before standing up, brushing tears away. And so, on the return journey home with a puppy in a large cardboard box with an old towel at the bottom, the new owner was the happiest young man in the world.

Sam had spoken to Emmanuel and said that he would send on Monday one of the many kennels that he did not need and John could give it a coat of paint and everything would be fine. The cardboard box with the dog inside was just too awkward for the boy, so as he carried the spaniel in his arms Emmanuel followed with the carton.

'Daddy, Daddy!' he called. 'Look Mummy!' The pair of them rounded the corner of the house to see Giovanni with a small confused-looking spaniel in his arms with Emmanuel following. 'Sam says he will send a kennel down Monday but you will have to paint it. So don't worry – Eddie kept gallons of paint at school. Use what you need.'

Time passed rapidly for Emmanuel. He had not forgotten Richard but the sharp edges had worn off and so the memory became softer but none the less he was sad and empty. At Bantry there was not much time to think about himself: if it wasn't one thing at St. Bridget's then it was a calm pleasant existence at Bantry. This was punctuated by short spells of time with Giovanni, who was now with Sam an expert on King Charles spaniels, hence the name of Giovanni's dog, Charlie. Emmanuel was constantly in touch with Angela and they chatted on more or less every evening.

'A waste of time,' was Mary's comment to Vince. He had offered, with apologies, the apartment behind the new church to Brenda Wade, as rental accommodation in Sitwell, as places were hard to find and expensive. She took it as temporary accommodation but found the heat difficult to cope with and so an air-conditioner could be heard whirring as one passed the apartment. Sometime after her appointment and the confusion of the records she attempted to put in order, a nasty incident occurred that saw her at her best.

It was a Wednesday and there was an early morning assembly in the old church. Everyone left their bags outside and gathered inside for the event. On this particular Wednesday, John O'Keefe had left, with Father's permission, to purchase cleaning fluids and paper towelling from the next large town, Bordan, as the prices wholesale were much more attractive. So when the assembly was over all the students collected their bags and went to class. At lunchtime Miss Ainsworth, while crossing the yard early, noticed Giovanni in tears. She immediately swept across to have him fling his arms around her sobbing.

'What's wrong, Giovanni?'

'Someone took my lunch and my lunch box.' He was inconsolable. This had happened before but never to Giovanni. Miss Ainsworth looked up to see Emmanuel and Vince heading off to Nancy's, as it happened to be Sarah's birthday lunch.

'Come here!' she shouted to a young girl. 'Go and get the Sacristan now.' The girl was overwhelmed at the responsibility and rushed across the yard, just as Vince and Emmanuel were closing the gate.

'Now, Sacristan, now! It's an emergency!' cried the young girl; the two men turned in the direction of Miss Ainsworth and a sobbing Giovanni. The moment the boy saw Emmanuel coming towards him he ran in his direction, crying, 'Emmanuel, someone took my lunch box.' The tears flowed as Emmanuel held the tiny frame, heaving with a sort of fear, in his arms.

'It's OK. You come with Father and me for lunch. There's no problem,' he said, attempting to calm him down. But he was not to be calmed.

'My lunch box. Mummy bought it for me a week ago. It has a dog on the top.' The tears began again.

Miss Ainsworth had a face like stone. This had happened before. The doctor's verdict was that Barry Howes's testicles were not ruptured but were severely bruised when he had taken Polly Anderson's lunch box.

She had decided to take the law into her own hands – or perhaps her good quality leather shoes! But it wasn't the lunch that distressed the boy, it was the lunchbox his mother had bought for him, and he was so proud of it, probably all of three dollars worth. If you have very little in the way of finances, this is quite an investment. 'Mummy will think I lost it. But I didn't. I was very careful.' Again, in Emmanuel's arms, he burst into tears.

'Miss Ainsworth, I leave it to you,' Emmanuel informed her, sternly. 'I shall call you on your mobile when we get settled. Will you inform his teacher he may be late back from lunch.'

'Certainly, Sacristan. Leave it to me.'

Emmanuel left with Vince and Giovanni in his arms in tears as they went down the street to Shannon for the birthday lunch. They noticed a big black Bentley out in front as well as Mary's car. Vince rapped on the front door. 'Father, come in!' and he entered behind Emmanuel.

A very overweight Samuel O'Connor swept past all of them to find out what had happened, but Giovanni was implacable. All he could say was, 'Mummy will be so cross. It's my new lunch box.'

Emmanuel handed him to Vince. 'Just a minute,' he said and went to another room to call Miss Ainsworth. And someone else on this day just gasped at this beautiful blue-eyed young man that had a tiny boy in his arms and wondered seriously how to find himself in the same situation. Emmanuel shouted out to Nancy that Giovanni was joining them for lunch and would be back in a moment before disappearing. Sam made every overture possible to halt the tears and on his knees found two tiny arms wrapped around his very solid neck. If Giovanni felt this terrible sense of loss so did he.

Ten minutes later Emmanuel returned after Miss Ainsworth 'put out the word' and sure enough Barry and his gang had emptied or were in the process of emptying the contents of Giovanni's lunch box on to the asphalt. Barry had not heard Miss Ainsworth coming up behind him.

His friends had, but froze in terror and so he wasn't' aware of what was to come.

'His father will clean it up,' he said, in an arrogant way as he emptied the entire contents of the lunchbox onto the asphalt. The open-handed slap was so forceful that he fell to the ground at once, only to be pulled up by his collar and sent to the ground again.

'This time, Howe, you will pay for this.' Barry was walking around in a circle, dazed. 'You will go and see the headmistress. NOW!'

This was the scene as Emmanuel arrived, putting his hand on her shoulder to comment, 'Great going!' He saw that she was white with rage. She bent down to pick up the lunch box and lid, then handed it to him. 'Pick up everything on the ground now!' she screamed at Barry's friends, 'and put it in the bin. Do you hear me?'

'Yes, miss, yes, miss.'

'If you ever touch anyone's lunch box again, I will have you expelled. Do you hear me?' Her voice was hysterical and Emmanuel had never seen her like this. He tried to calm her down, but she just said it was OK and asked him to take Giovanni's lunch box. 'I hate this Howe child.' She walked off towards the Headmistress's office, ready to make real trouble for Barry.

With the lunch box in hand, Emmanuel hurried back to Nancy's, not wanting to keep everyone waiting for lunch. As he entered the drawing room, Giovanni freed himself from Sam and threw himself into Emmanuel's arms.

'Oh, my lunch box!' and began to settle down. Nancy collected it, but not before the boy had taken the green lid with the head of a dog printed on it to show Sam, who could do nothing but hug him. The maid removed the lunch box, washed it and placed it as Nancy had instructed in the very centre of the large sideboard where it sat surrounded by one of the finest collections of silver in Australia.

Emmanuel whispered something to Giovanni, who, still with red eyes, crossed the room and stood on his tip-toes to kiss Sarah 'Happy Birthday. She hugged him. 'That's the nicest hug I have ever had,' she said, smiling. And at that Nancy bid everyone take their places in the dining room.

Mary watched like a hawk as Michael, who had returned from a long stay in Melbourne, watched the beautiful Emmanuel with the little golden-haired boy seated between him and Sam.

'My mother would have been very cross if I hadn't come home with my new lunch box,' the boy said, seriously, to Sam. Sam O'Connor's mind drifted for a moment. In that sea of high quality silver on the sideboard the only thing this little boy held of any value was a plastic lunch box with a green lid and a dog's head on it, all of three dollars' worth, he thought. Then he glanced at Giovanni tucking into lunch and looked again at the box. Suddenly he saw that the value of the box far outweighed the precious collection of silver that surrounded it.

CHAPTER SEVEN

The Treasurer Makes a Move

CHAPTER SEVEN

The Treasurer Makes a Move

'Wait outside!' said Brenda Wade to Barry, as she called Miss Ainsworth into her office. In less than five minutes Barry Howe was handed an envelope but not before Brenda Wade explained to him in the crispest of details what would happen to him if he ever did anything like it again to another student. He wasn't so afraid of Brenda Wade. Why, wasn't it only the other night at home his grandfather and the Deacon were saying that she would not last long, but of Miss Ainsworth he was genuinely terrified. After the severe dressing down he was handed the envelope to take home immediately and told not to return for one week – suspension!

On his way home he ripped open the envelope and read the contents that explained that his anti-social behaviour was not acceptable at St. Bridget's and this was far from the first problem with him. His father was to come to the school and explain the situation first thing tomorrow morning with the letter returned and signed. Barry tore the letter into shreds and cast the pieces into the street, then went off to the playgrounds off Main Street. But unbeknown to Barry and at Miss Ainsworth's insistence, Brenda Wade telephoned Sean Howe to explain that a letter had been sent home and he was suspended for a week and that that would go on his record. She wished to see Sean the following morning at nine. So when Sean arrived home furious at what Barry had done, the boy refused to acknowledge that he had been given a letter. Sean lost his patience and a sharp slap resulted, only to have his wife and grandparents supporting Barry rather than the proper cause. This only went to make the situation in the Howes's house even more electric as the relationship between Anthony Howe and his son Sean was degenerating day by day and the work situation for Sean was becoming untenable with his father constantly interfering in every project. All living together in the large house did not help.

After Vince and Giovanni had returned to school with Giovanni clutching his precious lunch box the company moved to the drawing room for coffee and drinks. Michael saw what he honestly believed was a glimpse of paradise. Emmanuel sat beside Sam, both still furious about Barry Howes's treatment of their little boy. Mary saw it first, sitting beside Michael on the divan. His gaze never moved from Emmanuel. Michael's usual sharp repartee was silent, much to Nancy's surprise and Sarah's relief.

'He's the most beautiful boy in the world,' said Sam.

'Yes,' agreed Michael.

'Wrong boy, darling,' smiled Mary.

'Oh!' and with that the afternoon that had begun on such a sad note ended happily, especially for Michael. It was almost as if Emmanuel hadn't noticed him. He had, but the over-riding problem of Giovanni and everyone's concern had overshadowed the meeting. Mary was certain in one way or another contact had been made and it was only a matter of time before things would be up and running.

On the subject of up and running, the St. Bridget's Ball was looming and the committee to organise it was now being formed. A date was finally arrived at which suited all. So at eight on a sultry Thursday evening a very small group seated itself in the school library which boasted the most awful turquoise colour. The Deacon took over, explaining that the past formula had been a great success and he would take it upon himself to organise yet again the St. Bridget's Ball. The Treasurer looked about the room of no more than eighteen people, including Vince, Emmanuel, the Headmistress and the ever-present

Miss Ainsworth, as usual in a tracksuit. Simon Thomas stood up. 'I feel, Deacon, that you are out of order. A vote must be taken by the members present to decide on an overall organiser, and that has not been done..

'It isn't necessary,' snapped the Deacon, spinning around and glaring at Simon. Then, with a sheet of paper in his hand he began to read out all his ideas.

'One moment, Deacon,' Simon began again. 'What is your definition of 'a great success'?' Simon's neat appearance, his constant attention to his gold-rimmed spectacles almost gave him a feminine appearance. All his movements were darting. He never did anything slowly, unless he was baiting a trap.

'What's that comment supposed to mean?'

'As Treasurer of St. Bridget's, I can tell you that the last five Balls you, Mr. Deacon, have organised, have cost general revenue money. In the past the previous priest signed the cheques to cover the loss but I see no reason why the general revenue of St. Bridget's should cover your personal whims to go line dancing.' He smiled – or that is what Emmanuel mistook it for.

'How dare you insinuate that I have organised these events for my own gain.'

'Oh no, Deacon,' Simon continued, standing up, 'you may see it as a gain socially but for the funds of St. Bridget's it has for five years been a colossal loss.'

Vince interrupted. 'Do we have a nomination for organiser this year?'

'Certainly,' came a strong voice in the direction of Miss Ainsworth. 'I think this line dance thing with Dolly and the Deacon is a self-indulgent wank!' The Deacon tried to interrupt. 'Can it! It's my turn now,' she went on, sarcastically. 'Every year it's a bore. People stay away in droves.'

'That's not true,' the Deacon interrupted.

'Oh no? When was the last time the O'Connor family, or the O'Shanassey group attended one of these charades?'

There was dead silence and Vince noted to his surprise that the Treasurer had a grin from ear to ear.

'Now, I shall continue, having been so rudely interrupted.' The muffled comment from the Deacon was obviously not a favourable term, aimed at Miss Ainsworth. He was furious. It had never crossed his mind that anyone would have opposed him, so to organise his friends to vote for him was something he thought unnecessary.

'We need new ideas and someone with a fresh outlook. I nominate the Sacristan,' Miss Ainsworth went on.

'And I second it,' said Brenda Wade.

'Let's put it to a vote,' piped up Simon. 'All in favour?' The entire room, except for the Deacon and Emmanuel, raised their hands.

'Fine, fine, an almost unanimous vote. I now declare the meeting closed and we'll all wait for the Sacristan to report back in a week or so. Congratulations, Sacristan.' Nearly everyone applauded.

'But, Vince,' said Emmanuel, while driving back to Bantry, 'I don't know anything about organising a ball. I can't do it.'

'Of course you can. With Nancy on your side I'm sure it will be a great success. You just have to think of a theme.'

'Oh great! Perhaps you and Dolly can give a floor show!'

'Come on, Emmanuel. Where's your creativity?'

'I don't have any. This Ball is supposed to work. What if it loses money again?'

'Yes, that's the last thing we want, especially as the school has to be moved - every cent is now important.'

'Oh, why me?' asked a dejected Emmanuel.

Nancy had a parcel for Mary and as she wasn't coming in to Sitwell she walked down to the school just as lessons finished to leave it with Vince. As she came to the old Canonica, the bell rang and the students poured out of the art school section, yelling and screaming. Nancy waited until the hordes dispersed before entering to go down the corridor to Vince's office. She glanced into a most disorganised art room and at the back was Giovanni alone.

'Nancy!' he cried out and ran forward to kiss her.

'What are you doing here alone?' she asked, rather worried.

'I am waiting for Daddy. He finishes half an hour after the students go home, so Father said I could paint here while I wait for him.'

'What a good idea.'

'Hmmm,' he sighed, 'look, it's really bad.' He showed her his painting of Charlie. 'It doesn't look like him at all, does it?'

'Well, not quite,' she said, honestly. 'Why are you painting Charlie?'

He came up very close to her and holding her arm said, 'Oh, Nancy, it's a secret.'

'Really?

'Yes. you see, the other day at Mass, Sam told me he was having a birthday party and he has invited me and I thought I would paint a picture of Charlie for him, but it isn't working and I don't think I could buy him anything.' He looked down at the floor. 'I still have two dollars and thirty five cents. It's the change Mary gave me when I brought her a paper and I got an ice cream. I did what she said and put

221

a dollar in the plate at Friday Mass but I don't know what to buy Sam for two dollars and thirty five cents so I decided to paint Charlie. But it's not very good.'

Nancy felt the corners of her eyes beginning to sting. 'I have an idea. When you come to me on Saturday morning, I will show you how to paint Charlie in record time, as Sam's birthday is only ten days away.'

'Oh Nancy, that would be really good.' He screwed up his sheet of artwork and went to wash his plate and brushes. Nancy went down the corridor to give the parcel to Vince and chatted on about the coming St. Bridget's Ball until Giovanni joined them. When John O'Keefe came looking for him, he saw Nancy and Vince talking with him, with Giovanni sitting on Vince's knee. As Nancy left the school enclosure, she telephoned the local library and spoke to the head librarian, closed her telephone and continued walking down Sutton Drive, into Main Street. Halfway down was the Memorial Hall with the library on the left. The line of birch trees attempted to disguise the mediocre architecture. She swept in to find a table covered with books on dogs.

'Well, she asked, 'what have you found?'

'I think, Mrs Higgins, this is what you are looking for.'

'Yes, that's exactly what I want.' She took the book to the desk, had it stamped and set off in the direction of the newsagent. Here she had three colour photocopies taken of page forty three, then started off for Sutton Drive. As she passed a gift shop with a sale sign in the window, she glanced at the front and noticed a basket with five or six frames, all at five dollars. She entered for the first time in her life and went toward the basket.

'Oh, Mrs Higgins,' came the surprised sound from behind, 'may I help you?'

'Are all the frames the same price?' she asked in a rather superior way, and when told that they were she said, 'I'll take this one,' after she had lifted them all out and selected a very decorative reproduction frame with swept corners. The gilt, or fake gilt, was harsh but she sought the form, not the colour. From her purse she took five dollars in coins, and placed them on the counter. The girl asked if she would like a bag.

'No, thank you,' she said, grandly, and went out into the street with a very visible gold frame on one arm and a hidden Cartier bracelet on the other.

The following day saw a very interesting power play at the Higgins home, as Vince had a pastoral visit. He was not present. Bill, being Bill, Nancy thought it wiser and saner to simply send him lunch on a tray in front of the television set, so with Philip not present the three of them had lunch at one end of the vast polished table with Nancy obviously head of the table and Sarah and Michael either side.

'Well,' she remarked, 'what do we think is happening for the St. Bridget's Ball this year?' obviously baiting Michael.

'No idea, and I'm not interested,' he replied, determinedly.

'And I suppose you ae not interested in Sam's birthday party.'

'You have got it in one.' He stood up before the dessert was served and had crossed only half of the grand space before he heard Nancy speak to Sarah.

'I wonder which table Emmanuel will be sitting at?'

'Oh I haven't a clue, but I am sure he will enjoy Sam's birthday, don't you?'

As one woman winked to the other, 'Oh yes,' said Nancy, 'in fact I am taking Giovanni out to Bantry tomorrow night for Emmanuel to continue his swimming lessons. So nice to see the boys having a good time together in the pool.'

Michael stopped dead in his tracks and very slowly turned around. Not one word was said and lifting his hand he came back and sat at the table.

'We have been having such good weather,' Sarah said.

'Oh, haven't we,' chimed in Nancy. 'I am sure the Ball this year will be such a success with such a young, good-looking man at the helm. Oh, I am so looking forward to it.'

'Oh, so am I.'

'Ha, ha, ha!' was Michal's response.

'Dessert or another drink?' teased Nancy.

'A drink.'

'I suppose I could call Mary and see if she was prepared to lay another plate for dinner but you do know how protocol is these days.' Nancy feigned concern and Michael said nothing, but it was noticed that the drink was consumed rapidly.

'Well, well, what shall we do?' asked Nancy, raising a jewelled hand that included the obligatory glass.

Needless to say, the following evening, directly after school, Emmanuel, not having hit home base in Sitwell, waited for Nancy and Giovanni. To say he was surprised when Michael also tagged along was obvious. They all went to the pool, with Emmanuel in the water at what seemed to be the hottest time of the day. Giovanni automatically took his clothes off, which amounted basically to shirt and shorts, and pulled on his bathing costume. He went to the edge of the pool as Nancy and Mary moved to the pavilion for a drink.

'It's too deep for me,' said Giovanni, who had a fear of water. Two very well-tanned olive arms covered in the lower part in soft black hair lifted him off the edge and into his arms. Mary noticed an audible sigh from Michael. She leant over very closely to him and whispered, 'Next time, it could be you!' It wasn't quite a smile but she took it for an expectation of the future, in Michael's mind not the distant future. After a drink Michael changed and joined them but couldn't believe one could possibly in this life come so close to perfection. He was annoyed that Emmanuel spent all his time with Giovanni, even if two or three glances were real. After the prolonged swim, they changed and went in to dinner. By this time Vince had returned and conversation picked up. Oddly, Michael, for the first time in his life, felt out of it.

Mary by this stage had had the painting of the 'red dog' framed in a scarlet mount and a fine gold frame and it sat proudly on the library table on a miniature easel. To all effect it could have been signed 'Picasso' or 'Matisse'.

'What am I going to do for this damned Ball?' lamented Emmanuel as they ate.

'Well,' said Giovanni, 'you should have a different dog for every table.' There was dead silence and everyone looked at him. He suddenly felt awkward and turned to Emmanuel and then Mary. 'If there are lots of tables, you can have lots of dogs,' he said. Emmanuel gazed at him, perched up on top of two cushions as if he had never seen him before. In a moment, to everyone's utter surprise, he stood up, grasped Giovanni from his chair and in his arms began to dance around the table with the boy laughing.

'Exactly! Exactly! Dogs! That's how I'll do it. Dogs! Giovanni, you are wonderful.' As he kissed him, 'Half his bloody luck!' thought Michael as they whirled around and around.

'I think the pair of you should sit down and finish dinner.' Mary was worried that the excitement might upset Giovanni's digestive system.

When seated again, Vince was the first to confess. 'I've missed it. I don't understand.'

'Nor I,' Michael added. Neither Mary nor Nancy said a world, being old hands at this type of social whirl. 'Well, how do we go?'

'Like this,' Emmanuel answered. 'Each table will have a huge photographic blow-up of a different type of dog on a metal stand and base. Around the neck of each dog I shall place a series of coloured ribbons, for example blue for a poodle, red for King Charles spaniels, green for Alsatians and so on. Everyone who comes to the Ball must wear something that is the same colour as around their dog's neck. It's fabulous! Giovanni, you are a genius.'

Giovanni looked a little confused but accepted the acclamation anyway.

And so what might have been a non-event, the St. Bridget's Ball, with clever publicity and local one-upmanship, offered tickets at double the price. The minute that the locals realised that the King Charles spaniel table was almost booked out, and that a group from the football club had taken twenty seats for the bulldog table, and everyone had to wear something yellow, it just did not stop.

'Oh, it appears,' said the Treasurer,' that you seemed to hit on a formula. I am with the staff on the Pointer table. I can't think what I can wear that is beige, but I am sure I shall sort it out, Mr. Sacristan. I will forward the money for any initial expenses and you can return it to me after the Ball. Don't worry. Keep an account sheet and we'll sort it all out later.'

So a band and a disc jockey were the makings of a brilliant evening. The raffle this year was considerable in size, as opposed to the past of two chickens, all mounted up to something everyone at Sitwell was talking about and it was not just the Catholics who joined in the fun. It was everyone and it was the dog theme with a colour that had everyone on their toes. The decision to have no line-dancing this year upset no one except Dolly and the Deacon, who sat at the Chihuahua table with the Howes, their colour being lilac. The wind-up to the evening was electric with everyone having a good time and expectations were high.

The Ball began at eight o'clock but this was not before a little adventure had begun at nine in the morning, when Giovanni was dropped off by John in front of the Higgins' mansion and as usual he found reaching the knocker difficult. The maid, after greeting him, took him directly to Nancy's studio, where she sat at a large table with Philip on her left. After the usual pleasantries she began to explain to Giovanni what he was to do, much to his and Philip's amazement.

'Now,' she began, showing him her photo copy of a King Charles spaniel, 'do you think it looks like Charlie?'

'Oh yes. Charlie is now growing very fast.'

'Good. Now what part of the photo do you think is the most difficult to paint?'

He turned his head to the side and closed his lips tightly. 'The head is the hard bit.'

'Good.' With that Nancy took the photo and with a set square drew a square around the dog's head. She then took a Stanley knife and cut it out. On a piece of prepared squared art card she placed the photocopy of the missing head of the dog and at the corners where the photo had been cut placed in the angles tiny pencil points. She then took glue, pasted it on to the back of the picture of the head of the dog and carefully pasted it down on the art card.

'Now, Giovanni, take a piece of tracing paper and trace everything left on the photo without the dog's head.' He duly did this. Philip watched mesmerised, waiting for a miracle and it slowly happened. The parts of the King Charles spaniel that were missing were traced around the face of the dog and with strict instructions Giovanni copied the pieces that were missing from the photo.

'Too dark, darling. Watch carefully.' Little by little, in this intense lesson, Giovanni began to fill in with tempera paint all the bits that were missing around the face. Because the face was a photo, the rest seemed also to become a photo and little by little Nancy, refusing to accept anything but a copy of the photo with a hole in the middle which was firmly attached to the art board the painting began to emerge. Giovanni had never concentrated so much in his whole life and it seemed he couldn't make an error and if he did the photographic face in the centre being dominant visually, it was what one saw before anything else. Three intense hours which to Giovanni seemed only twenty minutes and he couldn't believe what he had produced. He was ecstatic.

'Look, Philip,' he said, 'it's very good.'

'Yes, it is,' Philip replied and ran his hand across his forehead.

'You will have to come to me this week after school and your father can collect you from here if we are to finish it for Sam's birthday.'

'Oh yes. Daddy can find me here after school.' Then he stopped. 'Nancy, how much does a frame cost?'

'Well, it depends.'

'It would be nice to have a frame for Sam. My red dog looks very good in a frame.'

'Well, I think it's not going to be too expensive. I'll have a look around.'

'Don't forget,' he said, proudly, 'I have two dollars and thirty five cents. Do you think that will buy a frame for Sam?'

'Oh, sure to, sure to.'

The night of the Ball was warm and clear, just the beginning of autumn and the Memorial Hall was packed. Everyone was excited, well not everyone. The Deacon thought the whole thing childish, but apart from him everyone entered into the fun. Some people even wore dog masks and the colour theme was something everyone could enter into, even if it was only a tiny coloured ribbon pinned onto a jacket lapel. But it had taken Mary and Nancy (and as a team they could be most formidable) to convince Veronica to attend. She was with John on the staff table and the colour was beige, the dog a pointer. These canine images were approximately a metre high on equally high metal

sands and covered with ribbons around the dogs' necks. Mary and
Nancy had organised that Giovanni could attend for half an hour,
then Nancy's maid would collect him and he would sleep at Shannon.
He would be returned in the morning. It was Mary who knew why
Veronica was exceptionally reticent to attend and called past the
O'Keefe home the Thursday before the Ball. Mary looked again at the
surroundings. They were situated at the very end of Rose Street. Once
there had been a railway system that had come to Sitwell. Now it was
disused and there were two railway workers' cottages, of which one was
inhabited by the O'Keefe family. To one side and behind, spread out
amongst rusty railway lines, was a vast unkempt space that had once
served the town. The look was, according to Mary, forlorn; all the tall,
dried grass, the fallen down sheds, the old piles of sleepers rotting in
the grass with the occasional lizard that basked in the last rays of the
summer sun.

She knocked on the front door. 'Oh, Mrs O'Shanassey, please come in.'

'Thank you,' Mary replied with a smile. 'I must apologize.'

'Good heavens, Mrs O'Shanassey, for what?' Veronica looked
confused, showing her visitor to a chair.

'Well, it seems we have commandeered your son.'

'Oh,' she laughed, 'he is the happiest boy in the world. John and I are
so grateful. You see, we haven't been able to show him the lifestyle you
have so kindly shared with him. The loan makes it very difficult for us.'

'What loan?' asked Mary, very surprised, as she placed a large bag on
the other chair.

'Well, we didn't think we could ever have children and so when
Giovanni finally came along, because initially he was so small he
caught every illness as he had a very low immune system. John was
working then, but we had to take a large loan to cover all the expenses.
Perhaps it's just as well we did. I don't think they would see us as
good collateral now.' She smiled. 'And so with a job or without it, the

loan has still to be paid back. We took it for ten years. You see, Mrs O'Shanassey, the doctors told us he wouldn't live beyond three years old, so we took out a biggish loan to make things as good as possible for him – and look, he is now six years old. The saints do hear prayers.'

'Yes, they do,' Mary replied softly. 'How long have you lived here?'

'All our married lives. The rent is good, so we can keep our heads just above water. We are not complaining.' At that moment there was a bang on the back screen door and Charlie ambled in. 'I'm sorry, Mrs. O'Shanassey, I'll put him out.' She stood up.

'No, it's not a problem for me. Besides, I haven't seen Charlie for a while. He has grown.'

'Yes, he has. Giovanni loves him. He sleeps in a cardboard box at the side of his bed. We tried a kennel but neither Giovanni nor Charlie thought it was a good idea. They go for a long walk every night in the old railway paddock.'

'Isn't it dangerous?' asked Mary.

'I don't think so. No one uses it. Charles chases the odd cat or lizard and I can hear Giovanni calling him back. Oh, I must say –'and Mary was aware that at this moment Veronica was unburdening her soul and sat quietly to listen. 'Thank you so much for the opportunity you have offered Giovanni to learn to swim. John took him to the local swimming pool but he was terrified and cried but it seems your nephew, the Sacristan, has a way with him.' Here she stopped and looked at her clasped hands. She slowly lifted her head. 'Giovanni loves him very much,' she said, and then remained silent.

'He's a very easy little boy to love,' Mary said, 'and I speak for Nancy Higgins and Samuel O'Connor. We find him adorable.'

'I was so surprised that Mr. O'Connor gave Giovanni Charlie. I know how much he sells them for and the box of dog food every week I collect from the supermarket. It is all very kind, you know. This is probably the best time we have had in our lives, thanks to Father and yourself offering John the job at St. Bridget's. He loves it.'

'Father tells me he is very popular indeed.'

'Thank you.

'Now, this is for you, and I won't hear no. You see, you have a better figure than I have and once I used it. Now it's time to share it with someone else, the same as you are doing with Giovanni. It's not easy to share love. At times you feel as if you are taking second place but if love is real there is never a loss.' Mary stood up and handed Veronica the large plastic bag. 'If you share Giovanni, this can only be seen as a minute part of what he gives us.' She shook hands and Veronica saw her to the door. As Mary got into her Mercedes, she noted the bleak expanse of the old railway sidings with long yellow grass and a look of abandonment. She placed her foot on the accelerator, genuinely glad to be away from the place.

So on the night of the ball Mary noted, across the hall floor, John and Veronica, with Veronica in a beautiful silk cream frock with a beaded top. She smiled to herself. Needless to say the King Charles spaniel table, with the colour red, saw an amazing gathering of people. Nancy had a burgundy frock which she thought appropriate to touch up with a beautiful diamond necklace and matching earrings; Sarah also had on a scarlet silk satin frock and was suitably jewelled; the men wore red bow ties or red ribbons in their lapels and even Sam managed a big red bow tie with an oversized handkerchief in red hanging out of his jacket pocket. Annie said later, 'It's the first time I have worn these,' touching her throat, 'for twenty years. I felt completely silly going to the bank and getting them out.' What she had retrieved from the bank was a heavy Victorian necklace in gold, pearls and diamonds, quite sensational, with matching earrings and bracelet.

But stars are always stars: with Vince in clericals on one arm and the beautiful Emmanuel on the other, Mary arrived fifteen minutes late to a full hall with all eyes upon her. She looked radiant. She had had all her hair swept up and her ruby red paper taffeta frock with a train swept in, but it was the jewellery that everyone spoke about for months. The setting was old-fashioned but the rubies were large and of good quality, totally surrounded by diamonds with matching earrings. Yet it was the long, matching evening gloves that gave her the look of a film star. The King Charles spaniel table had, right at the centre of one side, a small chair with two cushions and here sat Giovanni in his new black shoes, black shorts, white shirt and Nancy had asked Michael to get him a little red bow tie. This he did willingly, realising that Giovanni was the inroad to Emmanuel and as he remembered him in Mary's swimming pool he probably would have climbed Mount Everest if Emmanuel had been at the top.

So it was an excited Giovanni who rushed forward to greet the three of them and there was a round of applause for Mrs O'Shanassey, the Parish Priest and the organiser, Emmanuel, looking splendid in a dinner suit that Angela had dispatched from Melbourne by express courier.

You look beautiful,' Giovanni said to Emmanuel, 'and so do you, Mary.' She smiled and thanked him. It had been a long time since a Ball like this had taken place in Sitwell and the young found it genuinely great fun to be able to dress well. For the women it had meant a line-up at the hairdresser's. The jokes about which dog you were this evening had galvanised not only the Catholic community. The tables were on sale to anybody who wanted to come and have fun and dress up, especially as all the profit was to go to the establishing of St. Bridget's re-located school. Giovanni crossed the floor to the table where his parents were sitting.

'Mummy, look! Michael bought me a tie.' He held his head up proudly, showing the red bow tie. 'It's nice, isn't it?'

'It's very smart. Did you thank Michael?'

'I think so,' he said with a frown.

The dancing began with a slow foxtrot. Mary and Emmanuel were the first onto the floor and swept around with everyone watching, then one by one everyone rose and in a moment the floor was packed. The age group 25 to 35 had never seen an evening like this. They had all been to weddings, but this was different. Here everyone was the bride and groom and the experience was wonderful. The Deacon and the Howes were at the lilac table and Dolly, it must be said, threw her lot in, even if the Deacon sulked for most of the night. In a skimpy frock, Dolly danced with everyone, laughing and joking together. The Howes started off stiffly but soon joined in the fun, even Anthony Howe, which made the Deacon suffer all the more.

'Come on, beautiful.' Emmanuel lifted Giovanni into his arms. It was the contrast of one so dark and the other completely blonde that caused many to pass a comment.

A little after the half hour Nancy's maid had made her appearance and that signified for Giovanni more or less the completion of his evening. In Emmanuel's arms he bent down and kissed everyone and then, passing Michel, placed one arm around his neck, the other around Emmanuel's to support him. 'Thank you for my tie. It is very beautiful.' Michael bent around and kissed him. Giovanni had claimed another who thought him just great. Emmanuel allowed him down. He crossed the floor and said goodnight to the Headmistress and Miss Ainsworth, not, this evening, in a track suit, and then to his parents. He walked back across the noisy dance floor to say goodnight to Vince.

'I have spoken to Father,' said Mary. 'Come on.' She being tall and Giovanni so short they cut a comic act as they danced alone around the floor with the orchestra playing. When they had done their round, Mary kissed him good night as the entire hall began to applaud. He held Mary's hand and made a bow to which the applause was louder. Two more proud parents could not be found in Sitwell.

The Ball was hailed as a great success and those who stayed away because they could not get tickets, it being sold out, were quite jealous of the event, genuinely feeling they had missed out on something.

Sunday, after Mass, at which Giovanni was now assisting, the conversation was only of the Ball. A woman approached Emmanuel.

'Do you think that the dachshund table could be yellow next year? I have a beautiful yellow gown.'

'I'm sure I can manage something,' he smiled.

Monday morning saw a buoyant Treasurer sweep into Vince's office. 'Oh, Father, we have done very well, very well indeed. We have never earned that much money in one evening. Our Sacristan has really hit the target.' He showed Vince the balance sheet with the profits. 'Now, father, I feel I must have a serious word with you.'

'Really?' Vince looked surprised.

'Yes, Father, and I am afraid you are going to have to trust me.'

'Listen, Simon, on the ecclesiastical side of the administration you are the only one I trust.'

'Thank you, Father. It is indeed an honour to work with you.' He spoke in his flowery way. 'I have spoken to the Headmistress and she is in agreement. You see, I cannot see the point of waiting until next Christmas to move the school. The next term's break is coming up shortly and it is for two weeks. St. Bridget's at the end of the year breaks up one week before the government school. I am recommending that we give our students three weeks break this term and they finish the same time as the government schools for Christmas.'

'But can we possibly be that organised in just three weeks?'

'Oh no, Father. We must start now with the plumbers, carpenters and electricians at once.'

'But who is going to do all the architectural designs for the council?'

'Don't worry, Father. It is already finished. You will just have to wait a little while and all will be revealed.'

The Treasurer had indeed been doing his homework and Vince was in fact the last man on his books. The moment Simon knew for a fact that Sam was donating the land, the next day he had called Sean Howe and asked him to come to see him. This being done, he took him to the old Methodist church and explained that this was to be the central block for the new school and the classrooms were to be arranged symmetrically right and left of it but recessed so it left room for a veranda which would link the whole structure, instead of the shambles one now saw. 'Of course, Mr. Howe, I do not expect you to issue Father with a bill for this work. That would be unthinkable.' After the interview with the Headmistress about Barry's anti-social behaviour and the clear statement that if anything like it happened again she would automatically expel him, Sean was out for as good public relations as possible.

'How did you manage to get the old Methodist church?' he asked.

'Oh, you see my cousin is a property developer. Now that villa units are the thing the old Methodist church stands on a very sizeable block of land and so they would have to pay to demolish it. It has become a generous gift to St. Bridget's.'

'But why don't we just move the old church? It would be so much easier.'

'Oh no, Mr. Howe, that is another situation all together.'

So in the shortest time possible the town council had passed Sean's plans and even before the title deeds were passed to St. Bridget's from Sam's estate, work had begun by plumbers and builders putting in concrete sumps and in all it was on its way. But not before the Treasurer and Sean Howe held a tape measure from the boundary to the beginning of the building, which to Sean's surprise the Treasurer insisted on checking three times.

The staff were told that the next term break they were all to be on call. The three empty classrooms that were used for storage of old office equipment and desks were emptied out completely and so a vast tarpaulin at the side of the church began to rise like a mountain as more and more furniture was eliminated and the other classrooms began to prepare for the physical move.

'We shall leave the Canonica,' said the Treasurer, who had suddenly taken over. Everyone had thought that Vince was instructing the Treasurer how to organise things but it was exactly the reverse. The removal company was only fifty kilometres away so they agreed to move the church in two different sections. The old Methodist church slowly moved up Sutton Drive in two goes, around the corner and on to the new site. Later in the afternoon the front half was re-joined to the earlier part and the two empty classrooms were placed in position. The rest awaited the term break.

While this was taking place, Nancy and Giovanni were busy painting the background around the photo of the spaniel and Giovanni was elated. 'No, it's not the right colour. Have a better look. That's right. A little more yellow. Very good.' This was half an hour every night after school. The moment school was finished Giovanni rushed out of the gate and into Shannon, where Nancy and Philip were waiting. The effect of using the centre part of the photo glued to a board and tracing and painting the rest around it from what was left of the photo generally worked well, but with Nancy leading the way it worked very well. Friday night it was finished and if Giovanni was pleased so was Nancy. The moment he left with his father to go home, chatting on about his masterpiece which Nancy insisted he see, to say that John was surprised is an understatement. She took the painting and glazed it. In the morning, when it was dry, she put it in the frame she had purchased at the gift shop, giving it a bit of a rub so it looked a bit older. Saturday morning at eleven and in his smartest clothes, Giovanni, accompanied by his father, arrived at Shannon and both were invited in to see the masterpiece. When glazed it was almost impossible from a distance to separate the photo from the painting and in the gilt frame the effect was spectacular. John was very impressed indeed and left Giovanni with them as they were all off to Samuel O'Connor's for his birthday lunch. Giovanni sat in the back seat between Michael and Nancy. Nancy had wrapped the present and he had written on the little card. He asked Michael if he would hold the picture for a moment and reached into his pocket. He handed Nancy two dollars thirty five cents. She looked quite surprised. 'It's for the frame,' he said.

'Oh, darling, it didn't cost that much.'

'Really?'

'Oh no,' she said, regaining her composure. 'You owe me thirty five cents.'

'Is that all? It's a very nice frame.' He was rather confused.

'I will tell you a secret, but you must not tell Sam. I bought the frame in a sale.'

He just nodded, as Nancy handed his two dollar coin back, which he returned to his pocket. Michael handed his painting back, which he held very tightly as if someone was going to spirit it away. Nancy noticed Sarah blotting her eyes in the front seat.

Mary and Emmanuel were already there. Vince had parish work to do and said if he could make it he would, but not to wait for him.

'Emmanuel!' cried Giovanni and swept up for a kiss.

'Half his luck!' thought Michael, who shook hands with Emmanuel and engaged him in light conversation.

'Come in, everyone,' called Annie, and they were ushered into the large drawing room. In a moment Sam's ample frame joined them. 'Happy Birthday!' everyone cried and handed him their gifts. Giovanni held back and waited until he had opened all of them.

'Sam, this is from Charlie and me.' He handed him the package and stood back to watch, as did everyone. 'Oh,' was all Sam could say as he reached out to hold Giovanni's tiny body in his broad arms, and the tears flowed.

'Well, let's have a look,' urged Mary. Then, 'Good heavens, it's divine!'

The compliments came from all quarters. 'I think it looks like Charlie so you won't be lonely without him.'

Samuel O'Connor was tough. He was also hard. He never allowed anyone any quarter. He was in charge and that was it. But somehow a tiny boy of six had slid in under this iron façade and found a very sentimental adult called Sam whom he loved very much. He saw Sam the same as Nancy or Emmanuel. They could do anything and they were always there for him, not so much to help him but to protect him and this was what gave him the courage to push ahead now, not remain in the background. With Nancy showing and teaching him how to paint it was an avenue that at school stood him out as someone with a real talent and as a result his self-esteem at school began to rise.

Sam immediately removed a painting of roughly the same size from the wall of the drawing room and hung Giovanni's painting of Charlie. Although the painting he removed was of considerable value, to Sam the painting of Charlie was worth a million times more.

Michael was surprised at the effect the boy had on all this group and while Sam and the boy went out to have a look at Charlie's brothers and sisters, Nancy related the story of the two dollars and thirty five cents. 'I thought he would spend it on himself,' Mary said, softly.

'Is that all he has?' Annie blew her nose loudly. 'I am glad Sam's not here or he would be in tears.' She wiped the corners of her eyes.

While this was happening, Michael, whose chair was next to Emmanuel, leant over and rested his hand on Emmanuel's shoulder. Emmanuel chose to ignore it or so it seemed to Michael, who couldn't get started with him. Their relationship was still quite formal and Michael didn't like it, but he put up with it as he basically didn't have an option.

Emmanuel had stayed in Sitwell on Thursday. He rarely did this, but Vince asked him to help with sorting out some accounts ready to hand on to Simon the following day, and which he just had not had time to deal with.

'Oh that! I'm not sure. I'm afraid you will have to ask John O'Keefe if the order has actually been delivered.' With that Emmanuel went out into the yard to find him.

'John!' he shouted, as he saw him emptying his bin into the burner. He joined him.

'There's a copy of that in the caretaker's room,' he offered, so Emmanuel crossed the yard, chatting on about Giovanni's painting of Charlie. The caretaker's room was in fact the old sacristy and they went in together.

'It's a damn sight larger than the mouse hole we have,' he commented, looking about. This had been Eddie's office and storeroom for years and as John said he had almost filled a skip with the rubbish in it. It was a fine space, with a high ceiling that was coved, all lined in pine but painted in ghastly bright blue. The old drawers were still in place which once held the chasubles and folded albs. Two windows opposite one another completed this symmetrical arrangement but at one end there was a door which obviously led into the old church.

'Does the door open?' asked Emmanuel.

'No idea. It's locked, but perhaps one of these keys opens it. I only found them the other day as I was clearing out Eddie's collection of pornography from the bottom drawer. There was this bunch of keys. I haven't had time to try them.' He handed Emmanuel six old-fashioned keys, tied together with a piece of string.

'Let's look,' suggested a curious Emanuel, so key after key was inserted into the lock but to no avail, when suddenly the last one turned in the lock and they pulled the door toward them, first having to move a large carton of paper hand towels.

They entered into a strangely lit area which was obviously the sanctuary. It was completely dark. The large end window had been boarded up to save it from the ever present threat of a ball.

'I can't see a thing,' said Emmanuel, brushing a cobweb away from his face.

'Just a minute,' John replied and returned with a light on the end of a long electric cord. He plugged the socket into a power point, switched on and the two of them stared in amazement. It was enormous, this architectural form in front of them. The noise and ever-present whistle of Miss Ainsworth could be heard clearly from behind the false wall of struts and masonite but it was the huge high altar that was overwhelming. It wasn't gothic in form, as neither was the church. It was an eclectic structure that had columns and arches. Somewhere on top was a sort of tiny temple with a dome and it seemed to be marble or perhaps painted marble. Everywhere there were gilt lines or simply gilded cornices. The sheer size of the structure was overwhelming. 'My God,' exclaimed John 'how many years has this been locked away?' as Miss Ainsworth's whistle summonsed her class to silence.

'I've no idea,' replied Emmanuel, shaking his head. 'John, would you go and get Father, please.'

John left him andEmmanuel walked about as far as the electric lead would go, glancing in awe at this hidden structure.

'Wow!' was Vince's comment. 'Eddie always told me the keys were lost. Not bad at all.' In a harsh light, the pair of them moved back and forth, looking at every part of it. 'Turn the light over here,' Vince asked. Emmanuel turned his back on the altar. In front were several steps and a platform very close to the altar. At the bottom were the altar rails. Everything appeared intact but with only harsh electric light it was difficult to grasp exactly the whole concept of it as the shadows distorted angles. Vince's sixth sense told him that for the moment they should keep quiet about it.

'What's all this at the sides?' John asked, glancing at raw timber pieced together at strange angles.

'Pull it forward,' suggested Vince, now holding the light as Emmanuel and John balanced a huge structure and dragged it a little away from the wall.

'Oh, it's a side altar, I think. There's another, Father, on the other side.

'Well, we do seem to be complete. Listen, not a word about this for the moment. I don't want the Deacon putting an oar in here.' John agreed and they went out, locking the door behind them, with Emmanuel rolling up the electric cord. John offered Vince the keys but he said, 'No, you keep them safe.' Vince and Emmanuel walked back chatting on about the find, only to see the Treasurer lightly move across the broken asphalt which was no longer littered with papers and orange peel. He went into the old sacristy for a word with John; the Treasurer, after a few minutes, came out. 'About five, you say? Perfect. We shall be there,' and hurried off across to where he had parked his car. He sped away, leaving behind an extremely puzzled John O'Keefe.

'I could be in Sitwell at 4.30 tomorrow,' came a sharp retort to the Treasurer's request.'

'Oh, but you must, Mr. O'Connor. It is a matter of the utmost importance.'

'Simon, what's wrong?'

'I'm afraid I cannot possibly tell you over the phone. It is far too confidential. Shall we say 4.30 in front of St. Bridget's? You will never regret this, Mr. O'Connor, I promise you.' So with a lot of cursing and carrying on Sam telephoned Nancy to find out what was happening.

'I haven't a clue,' she told him. 'I had Simon here for afternoon tea yesterday and I must say he asked me the strangest of questions, quite odd, but he is organising the change-over of the school quite well. He has drafted everyone into helping. He has turned out to be quite the taskmaster. Listen, why don't you drop Annie off here, do what you have to do with Simon and stay to dinner? We can eat early. It's not a problem. Ok, settled. I'll see Annie at 4.30. Bye!' She hung up and went to the kitchen to give instructions for the evening meal.

At 4.30 Annie went into Shannon and the black Bentley was left parked in front of the house. Sam then ambled down to St. Bridget's to find Simon waiting.

'How good of you to be so prompt,' he smiled.

'Well, what's the mystery?' Sam asked.

'Oh, just this way.' Simon led Sam to the two houses that stood between the church and the new school premises.

'Well, you have made progress,' Sam commented in surprise.

'Absolutely, but it is these dwellings that I want you to look at.'

'The answer is a definite no. Do you understand me? No!'

'Oh, Mr. O'Connor, I do hope you will hear me out.' Simon spoke in a hurt way.

'Oh, get on with it.'

'You are the owner of the land that these two houses sit on. The larger one was originally the house for the Sisters and the other, I believe, was either the caretaker's or someone's.'

'So?'

'Well, we – and here I speak for St. Bridget's – are the owners of the houses and you the land. An agreement arrived at well before our time.'

'So?'

'Please come with me.' Simon withdrew a set of keys from his pocket and they went into what had been the Sisters' residence, a generous three bedroomed weatherboard house with a very large living room but all in poor condition, especially the primitive bathroom and kitchen, but generous in space. It had not been lived in for at least fifteen years and only recently had both the buildings been cleared of dense overgrowth., They looked about and then they went to the smaller, two bedroomed house, both in the same style, verandas across the front, trimmed in decorative cast iron but in a shocking condition, as Sam said.

'How right you are, Mr. O'Connor, and this is the fault of the previous administration. Goodness knows how poor Father has coped with this mess.' He closed the door with a slam. 'Right, now we can go to my car, I think.'

'Where are we going?'

'All will be revealed. Oh, do push the seat back and place the basket on the back seat. Thank you so much.' Simon continued in his flowery way. Sam was horrified at Simon's driving. He obviously knew only one speed – fast. He braked sharply at corners and took off at an alarming speed, overtaking anything in front. From the little country mouse, behind the wheel of a car Sam was convinced he was a maniac and was genuinely concerned for his safety. They turned into a poorly maintained road and bumped down the half-made street.

'Where the hell are we?' he asked.

'Oh, Mr. O'Connor, this is Rose Street.' The name meant nothing to Sam and the car came to a sudden halt outside a small house.

'Out we hop,' said a buoyant Simon. 'Oh, do hand me the basket. Thank you.'

'Well,' said Sam, looking at the bleak landscape.

'You see, Mr. O'Connor, St. Bridget's received from my cousin the old Methodist church for our use as general hall and physical education centre.'

'I'm aware of that,' snapped Sam.'

'My cousin has also at a government auction purchased all this land as well. He plans to develop the Methodist church area into villa units, not very smart I think personally but there is a market for them, it appears. On this site he will do the same but he will begin here in three months' time and redevelop this area in three stages.'

Sam now had no idea what he was doing there.

'That would mean, Mr. O'Connor, that the first things to be demolished would be these two houses here.' Sam looked at him. There was more to this and then all of a sudden he heard a cry. 'Charlie! Come here! There could be a snake.'

Sam spun around as if he had received an electric shock and in the tall, yellowing grass was Giovanni, laughing and playing Charlie.

'What's going on?' Sam demanded.'

'Mr. O'Connor, the O'Keefe family are resident in the better kept house here. They pay the rent they can afford but in three months whey will be evicted.' Simon stopped and then played his trump card. 'You own the land next to St. Bridget's. We own the houses but at the moment as we are moving the school we are without funds to renovate them. My idea is this: you have the funds to renovate them. The smaller one would be let to the headmistress and I will open a separate account for her weekly rent to be deposited and this will be paid to you until such time as all you have spent on the property with interest is returned. The larger of the two houses you will decide on the rent and I feel it would be a fine thing if Giovanni was able to take Charlie to play in the newly developed school grounds with trees and lawns rather than take the risk of stepping on a tiger snake here.'

There was no answer. Giovanni had seen Simon's car and now recognised Sam. 'Sam, Sam!' he cried and raced forward, followed by Charlie in hot pursuit, thinking this was a fine game. Giovanni threw himself against Sam. 'Sam, hasn't Charlie grown?' he asked. Sam bent down, picked him up and kissed him, with Charlie jumping all over him barking. Simon noticed tears roll down Sam's face and he knew that this was the sign he had been waiting for.

'Come along, you two. I have a basket of cakes and your mother has a cup of tea for us.'

Sam couldn't even have described the interior of Rose Street. He was busy talking and laughing with everyone, as Giovanni sat next to him, eyeing a large box of cakes that Simon had thought would be the fitting end to a successful business venture with Samuel O'Connor.

A breakneck drive deposited Sam in front of the two run-down houses. As he struggled out of Simon's car, he looked at the two properties. 'Oh, Mr. O'Connor,' said Simon with an odd smile, 'I believe these are now your responsibility.' He handed him the two front door keys. 'I am positive that with your influence in Sitwell, this project should be finished well before the three month period. We don't want any mishaps on the unkempt space behind Rose Street.' With that he hopped into his car and literally sped off, sending gravel and dust from the side of the road everywhere.

'Well,' asked Nancy, 'what was the mystery?'

'None,' came the reply, 'but I have to go out again in a moment.' He glanced through Nancy's telephone book, and said, 'Yes,' in reply to something on the telephone and then, 'No, now. I'll see you there now.' He hung up. 'You girls keep going. I'll be back for dinner.'

Once again, Sam entered the bigger of the two houses but this time with Sean Howe beside him. He asked him how much of the necessary work needed a council permit. 'Well, we shall need permission to connect these houses to mains water and they will definitely have to be restored but it depends on the alterations you want inside.' Sam looked around. 'This small room here can be a bathroom, plus the other one a new kitchen and that back wall where the old tank was joined, that space added to the kitchen; French doors to a large decking at the back; the rest is up to you. When does the Council meet again?

'The end of next week.'

'Have the plans ready for approval then.'

'Just a minute,' said Sean, 'that's really pushing.'

'I'm paying,' Sam spoke sharply, 'and all good quality stuff – no shit. And remember, I am employing *you*, not your incompetent father.'

There was dead silence. 'I will start on renewing the roofs tomorrow,' Sean replied.

'I can see they leak. And the minute the permission is approved next week it's all stops out. I don't care if you use a hundred men on this job – get it done as quickly as possible. Do you understand me?' An almost exhausted Sean said he did, knowing quite well that Sam was going to be a particularly difficult client. 'And the other house, Mr. O'Connor?

'Whatever you want,' Sam said in an uninterested way as he walked around the bigger house again. 'Hm, yes, french windows and broad decking. Mind you, none of this skimpy stuff. I will be down to check on the details and just remember, if there is an incident at Rose Street, you are to blame. Here!' He threw Sean the two sets of keys. 'It's your responsibility now,' mimicking what Simon had said to him earlier.

He walked back to Shannon feeling particularly happy and in his heart he knew why. That could not be said for Sean, who puzzled all the way back up the street. What on earth had a problem at Rose Street to do with him?

The next day the telephone rang at Bantry. 'Hello, Mary, it's Sam.'

'What can I do for you?' she asked.

'Mary, you said you had your interior decorator here this weekend.' She added that she believed there would also be a plastering company.'

'How long is he here for?'

'Three or four days. Why?'

246

'Will you bring him to Sitwell for me? Give me a ring when you're both free. Thanks, Mary.' He hung up. What on earth is Sam on about, she wondered and then sighed. 'Oh, what a bore!' She walked toward the drawing room where she sat down. It was Friday so Emmanuel was at Sitwell and in four weeks it was his birthday. Needless to say, Angela had invited herself and Mary had extended the invitation to Kerry and Salvatore. Oh, why can't Angela come down with malaria, she thought, and as she sank back into a chair her telephone rang again. 'Darling, just press the brass button.'

A smart car, followed by a removal van and a large truck made their way down the very imposing drive.

'Paul, darling, how are you?'

'Exhausted! I'm sure it's hotter in the late afternoon here than in the city.'

'You should have been here three weeks ago, sweetie. Vince and Emmanuel lived in the pool'

'You're right,' he said with a smile. 'I should have. Darling, this is the plastering company we are using and believe it or not they are only thirty kilometres away. Let me show them in first and then we can get going. Oh!' he yelled at the removers, 'put the fountain down here and the other is at the other side of the house. Be damn careful of the chandeliers. Mary, they have, for some reason, been a nightmare to electrify without seeing the wiring, but we finally made it.'

'I knew you would, sweetie. Oh, I have a favour to ask you.'

'Anything.' They went into the house arm in arm.

'A good friend of mine wants to see you but for what I don't honestly know. Forget it, darling! Sam is what you would call over-weight and married, not that the latter has ever stopped you.'

'Mary, how can you say such a thing!'

'Easily, darling. I know you. And I must introduce you to the most beautiful young man in the whole world. You will adore him.'

'I'm ready!' he laughed.

'Well, you'll have to get on line behind Emmanuel and Vince.'

'A family affair, is it?'

'He has golden curls and big green eyes and he is the most lovable six-year-old in the world. Come along and I'll show you his work.' She took him into the library, while her staff served the men drinks on the veranda. Paul stood at the door and looked at the red dog.

'Mary, it's divine. What do you mean, a six year old painted it? It's naïve but great. I love his tail. He looks a bit like a fox. This kid's a genius.'

'Well he is now in hand with Nancy, painting a surprise for Emmanuel's birthday, so let's keep it a secret.'

'Consider it done.' He smiled and looked again at the red dog. 'Mary, would you lend me the red dog?' She wanted to know why, as she had become for some reason very territorial about it: apart from Sam she was the only one to have one of Giovanni's paintings.

'Listen,' he replied, intently. 'Do you remember Gerry Sidler, the gallery dealer? She is having a big exhibition of naïve art. It's her big show for the year and I know this would be just what she is looking for because it's just so immediate. May I give her a call?'

'Yes, but it's strictly on loan.'

'Perfect. Now, come on, guys, let's see the bomb damage.'

From the strong and constant use of expletives, it was obvious that this was not going to be an easy job but from the fallen pieces it was possible to make a mould and reproduce the broken ceiling in sections.

Paul left the plasterers in the room, still exclaiming and arguing about the restoration.

'Come along,' he said to Mary. 'Now listen, it's impossible to get two matching cast iron fountains but these are the right height and are similar. Besides you can never see them together, so what's the problem?'

Mary looked at the huge fountains in pieces on the lawn and then something swept back over her so that she didn't hear anything Paul was saying. All she could think of was a very hot February afternoon and a little boy with a hole in his black sandshoe, very baggy shorts and a darned sock. She knew the money spent on Giovanni, which was barely a fraction of what these fountains were going to cost, gave her a greater sense of investment and something much more than just helping, compared with what these fountains would ever give her.

CHAPTER EIGHT

Preparation for Change

CHAPTER EIGHT

Preparation for Change

'Darling, it's Friday night, so when you see your boys off we'll have a drink and then go to Sitwell for dinner.'

'Why?' he asked, rather confused by the social arrangements.

'Because it's Friday.' She looked at him.

'Really?'

'You see, Vince stays with the Higgins Friday and Saturday nights – parish pressure. Emmanuel has been in with Vince, helping him today, so I generally join them Friday evening. We have dinner at Nancy's and then Emmanuel and I return here. I presume that's satisfactory for you?'

'Absolutely!' Paul smiled. 'Oh, I have all the fabric you asked me for.'

'Oh, how divine, darling! Nancy will love you for life.'

'Well, she may not. You see, to find violet or black silk damask is impossible. Who uses it? But as I had some cream silk damask left over from a job I cut the length in half and had half dyed purple and the other half black. I must say the results are quite good. I may just do something like that for a job I have coming up.'

Mary telephoned Sam to say that they were in Sitwell that evening and could he make it? The answer was an obvious affirmative. 'Bring a note book or pad, sweetie. I have no idea what Sam wants but be prepared, just like a good little scout.'

'Ha, ha!'

Mary's Mercedes drew up in front of Shannon. As they alighted, Paul noted a black Bentley parked quite close by.

'Come in, Mrs. O'Shanassey,' said the maid and they were shown into the drawing room.

'So you're the decorator,' said Sam, briskly.

'Yes,' said a determined Paul, 'and what exactly is your problem?'

'Come with me,' he instructed. 'The others haven't arrived yet.' Trouble at the school, it seems.' And as fast as Paul had entered Shannon he exited it.

'This way!' came the directions of a very determined, overweight man. 'I want it good, you know.'

'I'm sure you do,' exclaimed Paul, not having any idea where he was going. At the end of Sutton Drive they crossed the road and ended up in front of the pair of houses that were in the process of having new roofs fitted.

'Come in,' said Sam. They entered from the back door that was not locked. 'Well?' he said.

'Well what?' Paul was confused.

'Well, how long would you take to furnish this house?'

'What, with everything?' He sounded surprised.

'Yes, everything, but really nice.'

Paul looked about. The spaces were comfortable and generous and he noted a lavish use of marble in the two incomplete bathrooms Sean had started at once. 'You're talking soft furnishing?'

'I think so,' Sam said, rubbing the side of his chin. 'Beds, curtains, carpets and furniture where it's needed. When can it be finished?'

'Hold on, big boy! I'm not sure what the hell you want.'

'I have no idea,' replied Sam, 'but it must be really nice.'

The notepad came out and sketches and measurements were taken, with Sam holding the end of the tape.

'What about the colour?' asked Paul.

'Up to you, but nothing too bright. You can ask Giovanni tonight what colour he would like his bedroom to be, but I think basically neutral colours for the rest.'

Paul said 'OK' and they went from room to room. It was question after question, with Sam simply saying yes or no.

'Are you sure you have it all?' he asked, concerned. 'Oh, how about swags above the living room curtains?'

'Don't you think that's a bit pretentious?' Paul asked.

'Not if it's done well,' Sam said in a superior way. 'You see, Giovanni likes them.' By this stage Paul was convinced that this Giovanni was Sam's lover, and as he knew, via Mary, that Sam was married this was to be a deluxe love nest.

'I can do it but to do it well it's going to cost.'

'Do it!' Sam's was a sharp reply. 'Now, let's go through it all again.'

Paul now for the third time went through every room, re-checking light fixtures, the carpet, the furniture, the curtains, the crockery, the glassware, the chandelier which had to have a dimmer. It didn't stop. Sam had not forgotten one single detail, and then he sprang the trap. 'When can you deliver it?'

'Deliver it? You haven't even finished the kitchen or bathrooms, let alone the painting.'

'Today is Friday,' retorted Sam in a sure manner, 'so that gives us Saturday, Sunday, Monday and Tuesday, so we shall be ready for the carpet on Wednesday and I shall expect the rest finished for the following Monday.'

'Come on! That's impossible.'

'No, it isn't. Call your workrooms now and get them going. I'll pay overtime for you but get going and just remember if Giovanni is bitten by a snake, it's your fault.'

This last comment Paul lost completely, his head so full of this colour with that, the divan, the two-seater divan in a room called Giovanni's with the television on a low table. Paul's head was spinning. In fact, when he returned to Shannon he asked for a quiet space to re-work all these ideas and then began to phone everyone he knew to pull it together in breakneck speed, not honestly believing it was possible. But he was not stupid, Paul. He knew exactly what he had in his storerooms and on the floor in his showroom and his mind was working like a threshing machine to use everything he had with an alteration here and there to make a very handsome profit. It was rare a client gave a decorator a free hand and Paul was out to profit by it if Sam wanted everything more or less by the following Monday week. Now where the hell were those beige silk curtains a client had refused to take? And the burgundy ones that had been made too short? Paul returned to the drawing room and was correctly introduced to everyone. Vince and Emmanuel arrived at roughly the same time as Michael, who had been out. Paul saw two opportunities and was certain he wouldn't refuse either.

'Hi!' said Emmanuel and swept across to kiss Paul. 'You look great! What's been happening in town?'

The green slither swept up Michael's spine and the jealous colour was almost obvious in the colour of his eyes. He wondered what it must be like to have Emmanuel kiss you, but was totally surprised when Paul kissed Vince and then him. 'Well!' he thought.

'Another drink?' suggested Nancy as the maid moved amongst them with a tray. Then Paul witnessed something that he considered the most amazing thing in his life. The knocker beat out a call and the maid went to attend to it.

'Come in!' she cried. 'Everyone is here.' She was speaking to someone who entered the imposing corridor escorted by a maid, a tiny boy with a mop of golden curls. Paul stood back and watched the men move forward, holding him and kissing him. He was definitely the star of the evening, with Nancy, Annie and Mary chatting on to him as if he was an adult, not a child, but it was Sam that surprised Paul most. His summing up of Sam was of someone who always got his own way and was probably extremely selfish. Yet there he was with a little six year old boy hand in hand with him, talking about a dog called Charlie. Mary smiled at Paul, who now seemed confused, but a look again at Michael managed to pick him up, as he knew from experience Emmanuel was well out of his reach. Paul found the evening to be almost surreal in the sense that this tiny boy held the whole table at his fingertips. After the noise became louder and louder and the evening wore on, Paul saw a tiny boy get down from his chair and sit on Emmanuel's lap and to his surprise everyone just accepted it and kept on chatting. In all Paul's life he had never known Emmanuel other than self-centred. He thought him without doubt the most exotic creature on God's earth but in all the time he had known him resident at Angela's he had never seen him show any concern except for Richard in his whole life. It was a six year old boy whom he thought, without a doubt, loved Emmanuel very much and he was certain it was reciprocated equally.

As the night wore on, a little head of blonde curls nestled in against Emmanuel's neck.

'Mary, may I have your keys?' She passed them across the table. 'Come on, beautiful, it is past your bedtime.'

Good heavens, thought Paul, is this really Emmanuel? Giovanni passed around the table and kissed everyone goodnight and when his duties were almost finished he was whispering something into Nancy's ear.

'Of course, darling, of course.' And with that Emmanuel swept him up into his arms and they made their way to Mary's Mercedes. By the time they arrived at Rose Street, Giovanni's head was nodding and after parking the car he carried the boy to the front door and knocked. It was immediately opened by John.

'I have a very sleeping young man,' he smiled, and Veronica moved across to take him and carry him to his bedroom.

'Will you have a drink with us?' John asked. It was phrased in such a way that to refuse would be an insult.

'Certainly, I will. Love to.'

'Is a glass of white wine OK?'

'Perfect.' This was the second time Emmanuel had been to Rose Street and in all honesty he wasn't keen on the surroundings of the empty railway sidings in the night, which gave it a ghostly feeling from the past. Charlie came up for a pat, obviously missing his master.

'I'm sorry,' said Veronica. 'Giovanni has asked if you will give him a goodnight kiss.'

Emmanuel rose and Veronica escorted him up an extraordinarily narrow passage to a small room which was quite warm. He sat on the edge of a very rudimentary bed with a cardboard carton beside it and an old towel in it.

'Goodnight, beautiful,' he said, sitting on the edge of the bed and then kissing a very sleepy boy. Giovanni looked at Emmanuel and reached out to put his thin arms around his neck.

'I love you, Emmanuel,' he said very slowly.

'And I love you,' Emmanuel replied, kissing him, 'and always will.'

With that a head decked in golden curls rolled over and in a matter of seconds was asleep. This was obviously the sign for Charlie to follow suit. He hopped into his box and curled around and closed his eyes.

Veronica led Emmanuel back to the living and kitchen area after turning off the light. He sat down and took a sip of the wine. There was a silence and it was Veronica who broke it. 'Thank you for looking after him this evening,' she said. 'He adores being out with your friends.'

'He is more adult than child,' he replied in a matter of fact way. 'He fits in to any group.'

'Only adults,' John joined in. 'He has no friends at all at school, none. He is always alone. We are a bit worried.'

'I wouldn't be,' Emmanuel smiled reassuringly. 'Between Nancy, Mary and Sam, not to mention Father, he probably doesn't have much space for others. And I forgot Charlie!' They all laughed.

Emmanuel finished his glass of wine and stood up. 'You should be very proud of him.'

'We are.'

He kissed Veronica goodnight and shook hands with John. He went out into a warm late autumn evening. The eerie shapes cast by the fallen sheds and stacks of sleepers did nothing to make him feel that this was a good place to live in, low rents or not.

Saturday saw great action at Bantry, not to mention St. Bridget's. Nancy and the others in the Catholic community had insisted that everyone rally around the moving of the school and so whippersnippers, lawn mowers and chain saws were the music to which the women made copious cups of tea and coffee, served with sandwiches, cakes and lots of good cheer. The large area was now basically cleared and the big potholes were being filled with truckloads of soil, the voluntary workers hard at it, levelling it all out. The lower limbs of the trees had been removed and prefabricated seats that encircled many of the trees were now in position. This preparatory work had been going on since Sam had given the OK for the property ownership to be handed over to St. Bridget's. The development of it all was being controlled by John O'Keefe and overseen by the Headmistress and Miss Ainsworth, who were most complimentary about the progress of the two classrooms and the old Methodist church now in position.

Work internally on these structures went ahead at full steam. One of the classrooms – and they were all roughly the same size – was being furnished as the new library and here the Headmistress laid down the law. Nothing kitch was the cry, so instead of a bright orange carpet and turquoise terrylene curtains the carpet was burgundy with tiny beige triangles and this look came with co-ordinated curtains in burgundy. The orange carpet and turquoise curtains did not make the transfer across and so for the last two weeks of the school term the library was closed and the librarian, with a wheelbarrow, began moving all the books across to their new home.

'It's becoming very co-ordinated, the look!' laughed Emmanuel.

'Yes, not bad at all,' was Vince's reply.

But if there was progress at the school, Sam saw the progress on the old Sisters' residence as pitifully slow and Sean had to bare the brunt of his constant complaints. Paul also found Sam's impatience to be very annoying and said so. Sam's retort that he was paying had no effect on Paul at all. 'Yes, he's an arsehole,' Paul said to Mary. 'Totally unreasonable. He expects me to decorate a whole house in a week and make it more or less Versailles.'

'Do have another drink, darling.' They settled back into comfortable chairs after Paul had sent the plasterers off after a day of sweating and cursing. He went on about how Sam was wanting things that just couldn't be pulled out of a hat when the phone rang.

'Just a minute, darling.' Mary picked up the phone. 'Oh no!' then after a short while, 'Yes, I will explain everything. I am so sorry. He must be very distraught. Do give him my condolences.' She hung up and walked back to her chair, then sat down, looking Paul directly in the eye.

'Well, what's happened?

'Your life, darling, is now to become very complicated.' He lent forward. 'Listen, you have probably caught bits and pieces of the conversation about your work – not with me, darling, but with Sam. You see he has just lost his best breeding dog, a wonderful male called Manuel.'

Paul looked at Mary as if she were talking about breeding pterodactyls. 'Mary, what the hell are you talking about? He straightened his legs and relaxed back into his chair.

'Well, it appears that Manuel escaped from his enclosure and twenty four hours of seeking failed to locate him. Three hours ago he was found dead.'

'I'm sorry,' Paul commented, not knowing what else to say.

'The worst of it is that the vet says after an autopsy that he was bitten by a snake. Oh God, I hate them. They really do make one's skin crawl.'

'Mary, I have lost the plot. How does Manuel being bitten by a snake affect me?'

So she began the story from the beginning, of how Emmanuel had discovered Giovanni, and the following events that bound him into their company. She even related the story of the lunch box with the dog's head on the lid.

'I would fucking well kill that Barry,' Paul said. 'I loathe bullies. We had one when I was at school, a vile bastard.'

'Well, you can now see how Giovanni affects all of us.'

'But hang on,' he interrupted. 'What's this story got to do with me?'

'Can you keep a secret?' She smiled and explained why Sam was so intent on having the house decorated so he could move Giovanni as quickly as possible from the tall grasses and the piles of sleepers from the old railway siding as he was very concerned that when Giovanni and Charlie went for their nightly walk in this place they might just disturb a snake which might not find either Charlie and especially Giovanni pleasant company.

'Why didn't he tell me?' asked Paul.

'Sam is Sam,' she replied. 'He wants this to be the surprise of a lifetime for the little boy, but now, with this snake episode, he is going to be impossible.' She wasn't wrong.

'We'll manage it,' he said and picked up his mobile phone to make several calls, the general gist of them all being that it was now an emergency.

The painters were getting the worst end of Sam's tongue as the carpet layers were due in the following day. 'Just do the fucking skirting boards and then you can do the rest with plastic over the carpet. Come on!' he yelled. To say that the painters removed him from their Christmas card list is an understatement. So while Sam raged about the house, now, with at least fifteen men working in different areas, another odd little drama played itself out in the Headmistress's office.

'I don't know how you cope,' said Simon, looking at a rainbow painted in crude primary colour that glowered behind Brenda Wade's desk, and two huge posters of the Rolling Stones that she had half removed from the opposite wall. 'It's just so tasteless,' he went on, sipping his tea. 'But the library is almost complete and it's just so smart.

Brenda said, 'I have given strict instructions that no poster work is to be pasted onto the walls. I personally can't bear it.'

'Nor I,' cooed Simon. 'Some work in frames, yes, but that's definitely it.'

A knock on the door heralded Jan, the art mistress, in her usual Indian outfit with extraordinary tasteless jewellery according to Simon.

'Oh, Brenda, isn't it just fab? Robbie's got a transfer to Sydney and the salary is almost double. It's great.' The two of them looked at one another. 'I'm so sorry but I'm leaving just before the big move. I'll stay until the end of this term, which is two weeks.'

'That will be fine,' said the Headmistress.

'I'll give you a hand with the interviews for my replacement. No one knows the ropes here like me. After all, I have been here twelve years.'

'That won't be necessary,' said Brenda, in a clipped voice.

'I shall have your salary and holiday pay transferred into your account on the last day of school here,' added Simon in a very efficient manner. A figure in a very washed-out saffron printed outfit closed the door and went out into the cool autumn morning. She was stunned. 'It's as if they are dismissing me,' she thought, 'the bastards.' She crossed the school yard and encountered her old supporter the Deacon, to whom she related in exaggerated tones about almost being thrown out but the thing that annoyed her most was that they, the administration, would employ someone without her aid or guidance and this bit hard, so for the last two weeks of work she was completely obstructionist alongside the Deacon.

263

'Oh dear,' remarked Simon with a smile, 'we must advertise at once. I shall leave that to you and Father. Well, well, three down and only one to go.' A very broad smile crept across his face. Brenda wondered whom the Treasurer saw as the last to go.

With all the activity and preparation to move the school in only two weeks, Vince was genuinely surprised at the enormous voluntary work force aiding and preparing for the event. Who would have thought that Nancy Higgins and Sarah would be making cups of tea and serving sandwiches and cakes, joking with the locals? Mary put in one day but decided that was it.

After an advertisement was put in the local papers and word of mouth trumpeted the news, sixteen applicants telephoned for an interview for the vacated art teacher's position. This time the interview panel consisted of Vince and Emmanuel as before but now with Brenda Wade on Vince's left. The interviews began on the Tuesday of the following week but the Headmistress insisted that they were not held in the new, smart library but in the previous computer room across the hall from the Art Room. The interviews began directly after school finished and they were able to find out what the applicants thought, what their aims were and then they were shown the Art Room. It was particularly repetitious, with all the applicants not giving too much away lest it limit their possibility of getting the job. At six thirty, the three of them were feeling the strain; the same questions repeated again and again were becoming tiring and the hedging about aims and what they thought was constant throughout. Number fifteen was a young man of about thirty four it seemed, well dressed and as Emmanuel thought, the only one he would have been interested in and he wasn't thinking on an academic level. Vince asked the young man, Jonathan Wise, where he had worked before and he replied at a school about forty five kilometres away.

'Why have you decided to apply for the position here?' asked Brenda.

'Simply because the new headmaster finds my philosophy of teaching unacceptable,' he answered.

The three of them looked at one another. 'I don't understand,' said Vince.

'I am a traditionalist. I believe certain skills must be taught but Len has other ideas.'

'Just a minute,' interrupted Emmanuel. 'Len?'

'Yes. I believe he was here before he accepted the new position. I was on the staff representative panel and I voted against employing him, hence my situation now.'

'But who would think of employing Len?' asked Vince.

'Well, you should know, Father,' Jonathan replied, looking Vince straight in the eye. 'I believe you wrote the reference.'

'I most certainly did not,' said Vince sharply.

'Well, I read it. It was positively glowing and it was signed Ecclesiastical Representative of St. Bridget's, Sitwell.'

There was a deep sigh and the three of them looked at one another. 'The Deacon, the rat!' muttered Emmanuel. Vince cleared his throat and looked at Emmanuel. They spoke for a few more minutes, then as they had for all the applicants took him across the narrow hall to see the Art Room.

'I'm sorry,' Jonathan Wise said. 'I couldn't possible work under these conditions.' He moved about, opening cupboards full of junk, cardboard, paper and other objects all jammed in together. 'Why is the sink so high and there is only one?

'We plan to alter all this. There is an empty classroom in place, ready to be totally designed for the next term. If you take this position, would you be prepared to work through the school term break with the architect so everything would be ready for the new term?'

'Certainly, but I simply could not work in these conditions.'

'Father, Father!' came a shout and Sean Howe rushed into the old art room. 'Sorry,' he said, not looking at anyone. 'Father, the iron worker wants a hundred dollars to make the cross to go on top of the old Methodist building. It's the best I can get.'

'Hello, Sean.' Sean spun around and saw a figure silhouetted against the only window in the room. As his eyes adjusted to the light he saw a face he knew very well.

'Jonathan!' he exclaimed, and went forward formally and shook hands, but Emmanuel noticed the hand was held much longer than is the usual custom. 'What are you doing here?' he asked.

'I'm applying for a job as art teacher.'

'Really? Well, the very best of luck.' Then, for some reason, he blushed.

'Sean and I went to St. Patrick's together,' Jonathan explained.

'Well, we have one more interview to go,' said Emmanuel. 'Why don't you take Jonathan over and show him what will be the new Art Room, Sean. He has a good idea about multiple sinks at low levels.' Brenda and Vince turned to look at him in surprise.

The three of them returned to the other room for the last interview, trying to show a certain amount of enthusiasm and even before they had spoken about the prospect for the position the three of them knew that number fifteen had the job.

Sean stepped out into the late afternoon light. He had been in no hurry to go home, due to a screaming match that had occurred last evening. Yesterday, whilst crossing the school yard, now littered with every form of crate filled with things to be set up in the new school system, he witnessed something that totally horrified him. He saw a little girl walk across the asphalted area toward a bin in order to throw her orange peel in when suddenly he saw a young, over-weight boy run up behind her and push her to the ground. As she fell, she slid, grazing both her knees badly and began to cry but before he could do anything a shrill whistle was heard and Miss Ainswoth was seen hurrying forward. Barry decided to retreat but in great fear of Miss Ainsworth and not looking where he was going ran headlong into the edge of a large wooden crate. He slid to the ground with a deep scratch that was bleeding. Sean watched, transfixed. This was his son! Brenda Wade had said he was anti-social and here he was in front of him, acting like a lout. Miss Ainsworth helped the little girl up and took her to her room, where she administered first aid. She had deliberately ignored Barry, obviously hoping death might occur as a result of bleeding! Sean shook himself and hurried across the yard to help Barry to his feet.

'You cretin!' he screamed and with that loud shout a large number of the volunteer workers stopped and watched. 'Go and wash your face,' he demanded. 'I have a good mind to send you to a reform school.'

Barry sulkily walked off to be joined by his two equally nasty friends to wash the blood from the cut. But this was not the end of it. In fact it was just the beginning. So when Sean arrived home that evening to see everyone making a fuss over poor Barry it really was the straw that broke the camel's back. His relationship with his wife was electric. He now couldn't bear to be in the same room as her, constantly talking and eating.

'You!' he cried, as he entered the living room; although they had a large apartment attached to the house at the back they always ate with Anthony and Betty, as Sean's wife could not be bothered to cook. And alone, she had no one to chat with. 'You! Barry, you should be horsewhipped and I might just do it,' he shouted. Betty took her whisky and sat down. She had told Sean not to work with his father and absolutely not to marry Lyn but a pregnant woman! Betty had seen this relationship go from bad to worse but had been unable to do anything. After Sean refused her advice she knew in herself that eventually this evening was destined to arrive so she sat back as a passive spectator and watched. He was not what you would have called beautiful; the correct adjective was 'handsome'. He hadn't changed much from his school days, the all-rounder, good at sport and a fine academic. His Head Prefect look still remained with him; he was tall, with a head of wavy, dark brown hair, deep brown eyes, a strong nose and a very sensual mouth. Just under it was a cleft chin. His broad shoulders were evidence of a sporting background. He had large, strong hands and he tanned easily, so at this time of the year his face and arms were very dark.

'As from now, Barry, your pocket money from me is finished.'

'How can you be so indifferent?' complained Lyn.

'You,' said Sean, spinning round as she put her beer can down, 'have been so intent on feeding this fat child to the point where he is now obese – do you hear me – obese! Just like you, he should be on a low carbohydrate diet and no pocket money to buy the rubbish sold at the tuck shop at the school.'

'He has a right to enjoy life,' she retorted, swinging into the argument.

'Oh yes, but at whose expense? So he can steal boys' lunches, push girls over in the playground? What a fine son we have!'

'It's just playfulness,' added Anthony, deciding as the patriarch that he had better have his say.

'Playfulness? Oh, charming,' Sean spat out. 'He is a bloody delinquent and you call it playfulness. And by the way,' as he turned in a menacing tone on Barry, 'tell your mother and grandparents all about your homework.' There was a silence, and Barry, in an arrogant way, moved over to his grandfather, knowing very well the powerbase in this house. 'He doesn't do homework.' He moved over to Barry and seized him by the arm.

'Don't! You're hurting me.

'Hurting you? I should like to throttle you, you cheat!'

'Don't speak to him like that,' shouted Anthony, in a superior way.

'He *pays* – do you hear me – he *pays* other boys to do his homework and we, we are the fools. We give him the financial means to do it.' By now Sean was really worked up. 'You,' he said, turning on Lyn, 'you're an appalling example of a mother. You eat and talk non-stop and when he wants food or money you willingly give him both. What child at St. Bridget's has approximately thirty to forty dollars a week pocket money? Some of them have none. Do you hear me, Barry? None. And from me you will not receive one cent, I promise you. And don't any of you get too worked up about Barry enjoying the new St. Bridget's school because I for one am prepared to make a bet he doesn't get through the next term. Expelled!' he yelled. 'And just see, my overweight son, how that is going to help you make it to St. Patrick's? I am totally ashamed of you.'

'Well, what sort of a father and husband are you?' spat Lyn unwisely. 'Let's take the father first. Hopeless!'

'You're right, absolutely hopeless. That is because every time I turn my back in this house after disciplining this cretin I have three equally stupid fools rushing up to comfort him and another five or ten dollars ends up in his fat hand to corrupt him or buy someone or something. If the three of you wish to continue, that's fine. Tonight, I am totally finished with him, and on the subject of husband' –Sean was now black with rage - 'perhaps I should ask what your role is as mother. It seems that my mother is the one responsible for this fool, Barry, not you, flopped down like a hippopotamus in front of the television day in day out. Husband? If you're talking about money, you're well provided for. If you're talking about sex, forget it.' Years of pent-up thoughts and tiny hates were manifesting themselves in this volcanic eruption. 'Apart from the foolish – or 'stupid' is probably the word I am seeking – first time I had sex with you and you assured me you had taken precautions. You see how stupid men are.' He spat at her. 'And if I hold my hand up and count the number of fingers, that's approximately the number of times in my whole life I have had sex with you. Your overweight problem is ridiculous and if you think making love to someone who belches after drinking too much beer is romantic, forget it. I am finished with all of you. You have all undermined me with Barry so I wash my hands. He is all yours.'

'How dare you speak like this in my home!' shouted Anthony, beginning to stand up.

'Oh, sit down, you fraud. I've had enough of you as well, always the big architect about town. You are incompetent, your vision is zero and that hideous structure at the end of Sutton Drive is living proof of your 'talent'.'

'Get out of my house,' Anthony screamed.

'When I am ready. And by the way, I shall leave you and Barry and your architectural firm, you see,' he went on with a smile. 'As from next Monday I begin work with Thompson & Kelly at Bordon. So, good luck in your training with Barry. You're going to need it.' He turned to leave the room, then turned back. 'Oh, Lyn, you can go to hell.' He left, slamming the door.

The air was electric but a car leaving via the front drive made it very clear that Sean was not sleeping in Sutton Drive this evening. The conversation between Anthony and Lyn went on for hours. Betty excused herself and sat alone in the kitchen, looking around her. She felt completely numb. It had to happen, she realised, but she was shocked that it affected her so badly . . . Barry was her grandson and she knew everything Sean had said was true. They were responsible for Barry's antisocial behaviour to a certain degree. The money had been easy and as a fat bully he had profited. They had all known this, but closed their eyes to it. But to lose Sean was for Betty the most harsh of blows. She loved him dearly and now she realised that in her passive non-resisting way of always smoothing things over she was also partly responsible for his leaving. She had never had a lot of time for Lyn but she was the mother of her only grandson. Then she thought this equation through: she had, in effect, by not taking a stand – and she knew she could have – traded Lyn and Barry against Sean. She now knew passionately she had made a terrible mistake.

The last interview over, Vince was tired and Emmanuel oddly buoyant. 'Emmanuel, will you go and ask Sean what time he is here in the morning, please.' As they picked up their sheets of paper, Vince smiled. 'You can tell Jonathan, Brenda, as he's under your jurisdiction.'

She thanked him and said she was sure they had made a wise decision. 'I must confess I was very embarrassed at the state of this art room. I have had quite a lot to do but I should have looked more carefully. It's in a terrible state.'

'Don't worry. I think this is a thing of the past,' he replied.

Emmanuel walked across to what was to be the new art room. He got as far as the veranda which was already in position and went to go in but something held him back and his large blue eyes saw through the quarter-open door two men in one another's arms. He returned but not before telephoning Michael.

'Why don't you come for dinner? Vince and I are leaving now. You can come for a swim if you like.' 'Great' came the reply and a very elated Michael notified Nancy he was eating at Bantry that evening. He left the room humming a very jaunty tune.

'You never called me. You never said anything,' said Jonathan. 'You just disappeared.'

'I've been a fool. Last night I dismissed my family, son and wife. I guess I shall not see them again and you know what?' he asked, sitting down on a crate. 'I am perfectly happy and even happier now that I have seen you again.'

'Sean, there isn't going to be a second mess up. Is that clear?'

'Yes, yes,' he repeated, looking down at his feet. 'Do you hate me?'

'No, Sean, if you love someone completely, hate doesn't come into it but disappointment and rejection do.'

271

'She was pregnant,' Sean said softly.

'You could have come to me like a man and told me, instead of slinking off like an animal as if you were then too embarrassed to tell me. How do you think I felt?'

'I'm so sorry. It appears I have fucked everyone's life up.'

'No, Sean, only your own.'

Jonathan walked slowly around the empty room, looking at spaces he wanted to change.

'What do I do now?' asked Sean.

'You look in a mirror and ask that question and if you're honest with yourself you will find the answer. Where are you living now?'

'At the local motel.'

Jonathan moved back and put a hand on his shoulder. 'I am living, or for the moment I have my things, in my aunt's house on Pierce Street. She is holidaying in Queensland for still another month.' A strong hand came up on top of his.

'How could I have been so stupid to think I could fit into a world of social behaviour that I don't believe in?'

'It's been a very expensive lesson for you,' replied Jonathan, as Sean rose and held him in his arms.

'Can you ever forgive me?' Sean asked, looking into Jonathan's eyes.

'Only, Sean, if you are braver and face the future in a more honest way. Then I cannot only forgive you, I can love you, for the rest of your life.' They kissed.

'Why don't you get your things from the motel?'

'I haven't anything to collect. I left Sutton Drive like this last night. I haven't even a toothbrush.'

'Funny about that! I just happen to have a spare one.' He smiled. 'Call back at Sutton Drive. Don't be afraid. You have made your stand. Collect your clothes and things and I will be waiting at 27 Pierce Street. Then we shall work out our future living arrangements. What do you think?'

'Like old times,' Sean smiled.

'Not quite. This time we must have one hundred per cent honesty.'

'I promise.'

'I shall hold you to this promise. And something tells me that this time it's going to work.'

Betty saw Sean's car enter the drive and after a quarter of an hour drive back out again. A feeling of finality swept over her but if Sean's future looked brighter Betty the following morning was to see storm clouds as she had never seen in her life.

'I think it is very good,' said Giovanni, leaning forward and looking intensely at a painting in front of him, with Nancy frowning as she adjusted her spectacles, something she was never ever seen with in public. What the two of them were looking at was the painting Giovanni was doing for Emmanuel's birthday. On that warm day now, some months ago, when in Vince's strong arms Giovanni had experienced his first boat trip at Bantry, Nancy had taken many photos and there had been a splendid photo of Emmanuel with Bantry in the background. Nancy had, with her Photoshop, printed this photo up and taken three copies, of which she was exceptionally pleased with the clarity. As she had done for the painting of Charlie, she again cut the upper torso of Emmanuel from the photo and adhered it to a stiffened art board, then the surrounds were traced on and the work began. This was obviously much more difficult than the painting of Charlie and so some pieces were redone several times but it was starting to come together. Every night after school, Giovanni was seen rushing down the street to Nancy's for half to three quarters of an hour's work while John finished his duties but now, with the moving of the school, his duties were much more.

Sam slipped an envelope into John's pocket one morning and said that was for the work he had done cleaning up around the two houses and if he had the time next Saturday there was still some work at the larger house.

'I can't believe it,' Paul said to Mary. 'There isn't a plumber to be had. They all seem to be at the school. How am I going to put these fountains up?' He sounded in despair. 'I hope I don't have to bring someone up from Melbourne. This is crazy.' But his usual plumber he used in Melbourne, with an assistant, were, after a day's pleading, en route to Bantry, with Paul muttering about local cretins.

Jonathan decided the only things he could use from the old art room were two large, beautifully panelled cupboards that had been painted in an array of shades with stars and moons over the top.

'The answer is 'no'.' said the art mistress sharply; 'I happen to be in charge here, even if it is for only two more weeks and they stay where they are.'

'She said what?' asked Simon in amazement. Having heard from Jonathan and Sean that they had the painters at their disposition and planned to get as much done as soon as possible, he moved quickly in the direction of the art room but this morning it was to be the second drama for him. Earlier in the morning he had passed by the old Methodist church, now looking much healthier, being totally repainted, and he had seen the head painter, a vast man called Heinz, painting the front door a shade of purple. No, he thought, puce was the colour.

'What do you think you are doing?' he shouted. Heinz looked up from his work in paint-stained white overalls.

'What I've been told to do.'

'Oh? Really?' answered Simon, sarcastically. 'And who do you think pays you?'

Heinz put down his brush and his huge form swung around. 'Now listen to me.'

'Oh no. You listen to me. You have been instructed to paint the whole complex plus the two houses cream with white trim and with black high gloss doors. Am I correct?' Simon narrowed his lips.

'Yes, but the old guy with the beard said to liven the place up a bit with purple.'

'Well, he is not going to pay you. I am, as the Treasurer, so just get a cloth with some turpentine and wash this hideous colour off and do exactly what you have been instructed to do. If you have a problem, see me. If I have any more of this inappropriate colour work I may just hold off paying for sixty days instead of our agreed thirty.' He stormed off in search of the Deacon.

'Trouble, boss?' enquired a young apprentice as he rounded the corner to hear Heinz using a string of expletives.

'Listen,' Heinz shouted, 'don't change any colour code here unless the little queen in the gold glasses says so and don't listen to the old pensioner with the greybeard and moustache.'

Simon would have been horrified had he realised how he had been described, but his fury was evident as he stalked across the school yard to finally locate the Deacon having a cigarette in the shade.

'You are totally beyond your jurisdiction, Deacon. It is the Parish Priest, me and the Headmistress who will decide the formulae for the new school.'

'What are you going on about?' the Deacon asked, offhandedly.

'You may just find, Deacon, that your expense account is unable to be paid due to these works and obviously as a good Catholic you will accept that.'

'What the hell is this all about?' he replied, drawing heavily on his cigarette.

'You heard me. You have a pension independent of this salary, so watch it very carefully,' he threatened. 'One more interference in the school's moving and I shall telephone the Bishop's secretary to say we don't have the funds to pay you. And, Deacon, if you think purple is an appropriate colour I think your will find Heinz has a large container of it but be careful, he may just pour it all over you.' He stormed off, only to be intercepted by the architect, explaining that the art mistress was being difficult. He was generally the real mild-mannered mouse but to ruffle his feathers as the saying goes produced a very different type of animal. Simon, still in a rage about the Deacon interfering, swept up to the art room door with an extraordinary din going on inside. He flung the door open and with the banging of it returning to the door jamb the noise died down a little.

'Be quiet!' he screamed in his high pitched voice. 'Not a sound!' The room fell into an eerie silence. 'I will see you,' he said, looking at the art mistress, 'outside now.' As she crossed the room, the noise began to rise. 'I said 'Silence'!' he shouted and the class suddenly returned to their work, not daring to look up. The slamming of the door as the art mistress stepped outside was the signal to the students to remain in complete silence, even if they looked at one another in sheer disbelief that in an art class you could not yell and scream.

'It has come to my attention,' began Simon, yet again adjusting his gold-rimmed spectacles, 'that you are being completely obstructionist in our move to the new site. I give you two options only. You give one hundred percent co-operation or with Father's approval you will be fired for disobedience. That will save the school one and a half week's salary. Or you can pitch in and help. Which is it to be? Oh, by the way,' he went on patronisingly, 'to be fired means no references.'

'Do what you want,' she replied, pushing past him. She was most surprised to find she had been handled in the same way.

'You will empty those cupboards now, as I shall send Heinz and his team over to collect and have them painted. And, dear art mistress,' he said in a vicious way 'I mean *now*.' He walked out of the old Canonica and yet again went to Heinz to give him instructions about the two large cupboards.

'Well, Mr. Treasurer, what colour would you like them? Pink or orange?' This he said with a smile.

'Oh, it's not up to me. You must ask either the architect or the new art master.' And he walked off.

'You can't win in this place!' said Heinz under his breath and called out to his apprentice to get a couple of volunteers and 'get the fucking things out and sandpaper them and undercoat them'. Then he wiped the violet paint off his hands and sought the new art master for further directions.

'I can't believe it,' said Simon, having a cup of tea with Brenda. 'Really, she has worked – or should we say entertained - herself here for twelve years and now has decided to make things difficult for us. So ungrateful! I am totally shocked.'

But there was a large group of people working as volunteers and others professionally paid who were very careful of this neat little man in gold-rimmed spectacles who had just assumed the authority to run the whole show: the more there were showdowns, the more his authority was seen to be absolute. He never did anything major without first convincing Vince that financially it was best for the parish.

The next morning at the Howe residence in Sutton Drive Anthony showered and had breakfast. Betty sat opposite him in silence, sipping her coffee. She had slept badly last night and the whole of her past had come back. It seemed to haunt her. She knew that Anthony had married her for her money and after a few years she managed to push this fact into the furthest reaches of her mind, but where was she now, she thought? The only thing or person she truly loved was her son, Sean, and as a result of not being more supportive, or perhaps attentive, to him, knowing his marriage was a disaster and not taking a stand in his favour, yesterday he had left her for good.

'I'll be late home this evening,' Anthony said. 'A troublesome client.' At that very moment Barry bounded into the room for breakfast.

'I need ten dollars for things at school,' he said, even before saying good morning.

Betty looked up. 'No,' she said. She knew it was too late but stuck to it.

'But I need it, grandpa,' he wailed and Anthony put his hand in his pocket.

'I said NO,' screamed Betty, hysterically. 'Don't you two understand anything?' There was dead silence and as stupid as Barry was, his native cunning saw the bank doors closing in front of him.

'Betty,' said Anthony, 'I don't feel that a scene in front of Barry is going to help anything.'

'Don't you?' she replied quietly. 'You have misunderstood everything, Anthony, and I suppose I am also to blame. If I had cut the money stream off to you, as I am now doing to Barry, I wonder what our life would have been – divorce, I suppose.' She looked into her cup of coffee. 'Get your mother to make breakfast and prepare you for school,' she said, in a studied way which made Barry think it was probably wise to acquiesce at this point. He disappeared. 'Great, isn't it?' she said, looking at Anthony. 'He didn't even say good morning. Just interested in getting a handout.' She stood up and went to the stove to refill her now empty coffee cup. Anthony had never seen her like this and oddly felt afraid, but why, he wasn't sure. One thing he did know was that he wanted to be as far away as possible from her at this moment. He said a quick goodbye and fled. His blue BMW was seen streaking up the drive. She looked over at where he had been sitting and picked up the newspaper. Underneath was his cellular phone. Why she did it she didn't know but she opened up his messages and aimlessly looked at them. She was about to return it to the table when she suddenly went rigid. 'Dear Ant confirmation see you at the apartment at 1.40 today 25ᵗʰ March love as always yours B.' She sat down with a thud, only to hear Anthony's car returning. She quickly turned off the phone and returned it under the newspaper, drinking her coffee in gulps. The front door opened with Anthony calling, 'Oh, I forgot the phone. I'll see you later this evening. Bye.' He seized his phone and the slamming of the front door said it all.

'Who the hell was B? So these late nights, having to stay over in Bordon because of early appointments the next morning meant there was a mistress. She thought about it for a moment and was very surprised she didn't feel anything, no loss, no emptiness, absolutely nothing. The only loss she felt was Sean. He had been the only one each day to give her a kiss and welcome her day with a good morning, but B? Who was this B person, she wondered? She moved to her bathroom, undressed and showered and as she turned the water off and reached for a towel it came to her: B – Bronwyn, our dearest Dolly. The four of them were always together. Why hadn't she seen it? How blind can you be? She dressed as usual in a polo shirt and trousers, then walked back through the cavernous house full of small rooms which she suddenly hated. She picked up the telephone and sure enough Dolly answered. 'No, I can't make it this afternoon. I have an appointment in Bordon, but I will see you this weekend.' She hung up and then phoned a real estate agent to ask if the Villa Unit No. 6 on Manoka Street was still vacant. The answer was they were trying to let it but the address made it difficult. 'Don't let it. I have someone who will come in for the key this morning,' she said, hearing a rap on the back door.

Lyn waddled in and before she even opened her mouth Betty took over. 'You will hire a taxi truck and transfer everything you own to 36 Manoka Street Unit No. 6. You will collect the key at the real estate office. Just leave all of Sean's things and take all of yours and Barry's and get out! I shall give you until six o'clock this evening, then I shall have all the locks changed here.'

Lyn looked at her in amazement. 'I always knew you would support that fool,' she said, unwisely.

'Do you hear me, or are you deaf?' came the sharp reply.

'He can't even do it. It's a miracle I became pregnant.'

'No, Lyn, that is called a fucking disaster. Now move your giant arse and get going because if there is one thing of yours here after six o'clock this evening you will find it on or about the rubbish bins. Remember it's rubbish collection this evening.'

The forceful closing of the back door made it very clear that war boundaries has been determined.

Betty ran her hand through her short hair and looked about her. She had wasted almost forty years of her life and for what? A husband she never slept with, who only drew heavily on her bank account. On that point she called the bank and said she would be down in fifteen minutes. It was a simple process on the computer and the signing of two sheets of paper to cancel payments on Anthony's credit card and block him from touching any of her still vast financial resources. The thing she could not understand was why she was not furious with Dolly when she looked logically at the situation. It was fine and perhaps Dolly had done her a favour but the thing that did bite into her was every time Dolly and the Deacon had been guests in her home Dolly and Anthony probably had thought they had been so very, very clever. She sat in her car, having left the bank, not having any idea what to do. She just stared out of the window into Main Street.

She must have sat there for twenty minutes, feeling the necessity to go somewhere, but where? As from today, she was completely alone and this was not a scenario she thought was going to be pleasant. Then slowly, ever so slowly, she began to see hope. She saw an avenue and knew whatever it cost, morally or financially, this was the way to go.

She pulled out and drove back down Sutton Drive, following a taxi truck and smiled to herself as it turned into her drive. She continued on and parked in front of the church and got out. She looked about and saw a vast army of young and old carrying the last boxes of books to the now completed new library. She walked about confused and finally saw Vince. 'Father!' she cried, and hurried toward him.

'Mrs Howe,' he smiled. 'May I help you? The volunteers are being marshalled by Simon. He has turned out to be a genius at personal organisation.'

'Lucky him!' she responded. 'Father, do you know where Sean is?'

'I'm not sure, but if you follow the line of people with boxes of books, the second building up is the new art room and this morning they have managed to get two second-hand stainless steel sinks. I assume they are organising the installation.'

She thanked him and hurried off in the direction of the building, bypassing this human chain moving the last of the things into the school library. She stepped up onto the veranda and went to where one of the ladies helping had directed her. She knocked on a closed door, only to have Sean open it while another young man was on his knees at the other side of the room stacking packing cases to lift the new sinks to the correct height.

'Hi!' he said. 'Come in. It's chaos here and in less than a week and a half it will be worse.' He smiled as he saw a different Betty, a resigned person, not necessarily happy but not completely out of the game. 'Jonathan, I should like you to meet my mother.' Jonathan stood up, brushed his trousers down and walked over to her.

'I'm pleased to meet you,' he said.

'Likewise,' was the clipped reply.

'Sean, I have something to tell you.' She looked at Jonathan, who started to leave.

'No, not this time,' said Sean. 'Mum, this is my companion, lover and above all my friend. Somehow or other we are going to make it together.'

Because the last two days had been so traumatic for Betty, this latest piece of news fell short of revolutionary and she just smiled. 'Well, it seems my proposition affects both of you. Lyn is leaving today with Barry for one of my Villa Units in Manoka Street and so is your father. He apparently has an apartment in Bordon. Did you know?'

'No,' he replied, shaking his head.

'I shall call him this afternoon and send all his things across. So that now leaves me with this house in Sutton Drive alone.' She was speaking quietly and sat down on an upturned crate.

'I'm sorry,' said Jonathan.

'Don't be,' she answered. 'It's probably a blessing.' She looked about the empty room. 'So you are the new art teacher I have heard about.' Here she stopped and looked at both of them as if she did not recognise either. She stood up and began to walk around the empty space. 'I went to school here at St. Bridget's. I loved it. We had a great sports mistress. The Sisters were quite strict but in a funny way we really liked them. No matter what happened in your life you could go to the Sisters' house and ring the bell if they weren't here at school. They were always there, yes, always there and always ready and willing to help.' She was looking out of the window now as the line of people moving the last of the books were laughing and joking, but all helping. Then she spun around like a spring and titled her head. 'Where are you both going to live?' she asked, excitedly.

'At the end of the month we shall have to decide,' Sean replied. 'As from last night we are at Jonathan's aunt's house on Pierce Street but she is back at the end of the month, so a decision will have to be made.'

'I have a deal,' she said very quickly. 'The pair of you can take over Sutton Drive. The apartment at the back is sufficient for me. Oh, I know,' she said, seeing Sean about to interrupt. 'You can have carte blanche to completely redo the house in and out. Mind you, to make it fit into a streetscape with Shannon across the street is surely a test for any architect. What do you say? And besides,' she went on with a funny smile,' this is a small town and tongues wag, but my son living at home with his mother and' – here she turned and looked at Jonathan – 'and his handsome friend is sure to confuse everyone. And just think, Jonathan, you can walk to work every day. Think about it, boys, and tell me what you decide.' As she reached the door, she turned. 'Oh, drinks after work and dinner. Jonathan, do you like seafood?' His nod was a confirmation, and Betty left the room, closing the door behind her, leaving Sean completely amazed at his mother's approach to his relationship with Jonathan.

'The house is a disaster,' said Sean, 'but it's not impossible to totally remodel it. What do you think?' He sounded uncertain.

'I am all for your mother. Let's confuse the locals!'

If Dolly was off having a passionate fun time, the Deacon most certainly was not. Vince had called him in to explain about the reference that was obviously written on St. Bridget's letterhead paper, giving a glowing reference to Len.

'Sit down,' Vince demanded, and explained why he had called him in.

'I am entitled to write a reference for whom I please,' the Deacon replied arrogantly.

'That is correct, but not on St. Bridget's paper and without my permission. I have called the school and explain my position. This is the last time you do anything like this, do you hear me?' Vince's voice was rising. 'The school is now going to review Len's appointment and you should be very careful that the Bishop's secretary does not hear of this. I believe he takes a very dim view of misused ecclesiastical power. Now get out!' He returned to his work as the slamming of the outer door made it clear that the Deacon had been routed again. Vince crossed the yard on the way to have a look at the library, now with all its books installed.

'Father!' shouted John. 'May I have a word?' He saw John had a broken picture frame in his hand but the glass was intact. 'Father, this was behind the cupboards in the art room when we moved them outside. Do you need it?'

'No. If you can use it, take it. I am sorry it's broken.'

'Oh, I can fix that. It's for Giovanni.'

'Well, in that case it's a pleasure.'

John thanked him and disappeared in the other direction.

'Oh, Father,' came a cry. 'Such progress!'

'Yes, you have done very well.'

'How kind of you to say so,' Simon beamed. 'I can't wait until the end of next week and everything is in position. Oh, what joy!'

'Yes, it certainly will be a relief. Oh, what have we to decide about the old church and the Canonica?'

'Oh, Father, please, please leave these two buildings in my hands, I beg you.'

'Sure.' Vince was slightly overwhelmed with Simon's performance. With that they went off to check the new library and to see what was happening in the new art building.

'Very nice. such an improvement,' commented Simon, and they then moved to the new art building to see two large panelled cupboards standing on a plastic sheet, having been given an undercoat.

'I never realised they were such fine cupboards with all that rubbishy art work all over them. They appear to have quite good storage capacity,' Vince remarked. 'Simon, how exactly are our finances going?'

'Well, Father, I am pleased to say, with all the volunteer workers, we are in a very good state. I think if we are all careful, we should come out of this change-over not owing a cent.'

'That's fantastic. You really are a whizz in the financial department, a hundred per cent on target.

'Not quite,' was the quizzical reply.

Friday night saw John collect Giovanni from Shannon as usual and drive him home to Rose Street. Giovanni saw in the back seat a picture frame and asked what it was for.

'Father gave it to me, so you can put your photo in it.'

'Oh yes,' he beamed, 'that will be nice.' He chattered on about school until they arrived home. The moment the car was in the drive Charlie dashed out, jumping all over Giovanni. 'Get down, Charlie. I will change and we can go for a walk.

'Only along the side of the road,' warned his father, 'and not in the paddocks behind the house. They are too dangerous. Do you hear?'

'Yes, daddy.' He raced around the corner into the house to change and then out with a lead to take a very excited Charlie for a walk.

What he did not see was a very red-eyed Veronica who waited until John had come in. She showed him a letter that had arrived in the post. 'Have a look,' she said, quietly and reached again for her handkerchief. 'What on earth are we to do?' She began to cry, while John, after reading the letter, stood up and put an arm around her.

'Listen, we have come this far. Remember the doctors told us Giovanni wouldn't live past three years old. He is now six. I have a permanent job. We shall make it. We have to, for Giovanni's sake.'

The letter that had Veronica in tears was an eviction notice that stated they had one month's notice to leave the house due to financial expansion. The work was to be accelerated at Rose Street and so the work teams would be in in exactly one month, for which, owing to such short notice, this last month's rent would not be collected. The letter apologised for any inconvenience.

'Where are we to find a rent like this in Sitwell?' she asked.

'I don't know, but I will speak to Father tomorrow morning. Perhaps he knows of something. But let's not upset Giovanni too much.' He was still holding his wife, who was still in tears.

Then he disappeared and returned with a little hammer and three long thin nails. 'Would you wash and dry this, please,' he said, handing her the glass from the wooden frame, which had the new nails firmly embedded in the corner and the glass and its old cardboard backing cleaned down. He went into Giovanni's tiny bedroom and removed a photo from the wall, being very careful not to damage the corners whilst removing the selotape. The photo of Emmanuel with Bantry in the background that Nancy had taken fitted neatly in the frame. He re-hammered the tacks back into position and then they both went up to Giovanni's room. He hung it on an existing nail in the wall. Veronica sighed. 'It truly was Giovanni's lucky day when he met Emmanuel. He has come on in leaps and bounds.'

'Yes, he has,' John agreed. 'Who would have thought our son would be a guest at Bantry, Ferron and Shannon? He really has made it.' He laughed and so did she. 'This will work out, don't worry. Everything else has.'

'Oh, John I am in no doubt that we shall find something, but the rent is going to be much higher and there is still the loan to pay back.'

'Yes, that loan goes on strangling us.'

CHAPTER NINE

The Change Begins

CHAPTER NINE

The Change Begins

Saturday morning saw John drop Giovanni off at Shannon and begin work at the big house beside the church. Every cent now was important to him and Samuel Osborne was quite generous in his payments, but it was a much quieter Giovanni that entered Shannon this morning.

'Good morning, darling. I think your painting is going very well. We should almost finish it today. Remember it's Emmanuel birthday next Friday and there is going to be a big party at Bantry. Nancy saw him bite his bottom lip. She knelt down in front of him. 'What's wrong, Giovanni?'

He put a hand on her shoulder and bent over to whisper, 'We haven't got a house anymore and Mummy has been crying.'

'What do you mean, you haven't got a house?' She looked directly at him as she spoke.

'I am not sure,' he replied, 'but I am very frightened. I think Charlie is, too.'

Nancy stood up. 'Where's daddy, darling?'

'He's working next to the church.

She rang the bell and when the maid arrived told her to give the boys something to eat and drink. 'I will be back in a moment.' She quickly change her shoes and headed out down the street, only to see a taxi truck pulling out of the Howes's drive with Anthony Howes's car following it. How odd, she thought, and turned to see yet another removal van, but a considerably larger one, with a Melbourne address on the side of it, not to mention a black Bentley parked in front of the church. Good heavens, she thought, what's happening? 'Sam' she shouted, as the removers and two women moved in and out of the bigger of the two houses, with Paul yelling instruction to everybody. 'Sam, come here for a minute.'

'Can't it wait, Nancy?' he called back.

'Certainly not,' came the sharp response. Nancy was not used to people speaking to her like that, especially friends. Sam came out of the front door as the men were trying to take a velvet divan in.

'Move it, mate!' shouted one of the removers and Sam stepped back, then out onto the veranda. Nancy explained what she had heard from Giovanni and said to Sam that he was quite upset.

'The bastards! They said three months. Thank the saints Paul has got everyone going. Where is Giovanni now?'

'At Shannon.'

'OK. I'll speak to John and then I'll call you on your mobile. Then you bring Giovanni down here.'

'Very well, but it all sounds very mysterious.' Sam had been very secretive. She knew him only too well. This house had something very concrete to do with a little boy with blonde curly hair.

An hour passed, with Sam walking about as if he were on hot bricks, watching everything. Paul felt like telling him to disappear. 'Give me another half hour,' Paul asked, and Sam moved out to the back garden area, where John was clearing out the last of the rubbish from behind some bushes. Paul's yells of 'Not there!' and 'Be careful!', 'Where the hell is the electrician – the light fixtures are ready to install,' echoed around.

'I'm here, what's your problem?' came a very butch voice.

'I don't have one, but you will if these are not connected in half an hour. You said you would be here an hour ago.'

This was the banter which became more electric as time went on.

'John,' said Sam, 'can I have a word with you?' John came over and sat on the step of the decking as someone walked past them with teak furniture for the decking area. 'Just in time! With my frame, getting down's OK, it's getting up that's the problem.' He laughed as they went to sit on the new chairs. Now, what's this about the house in Rose Street?' he asked.

'How did you know?' asked John.

'A little bird spoke to me.'

'Well, we had no idea that anyone was going to develop the old railway sidings so soon and last night we received an eviction order for the end of the month. I am waiting to see Father, to see if he knows of a house at a low rent in Sitwell. I have a good job here but it's the loan that kills us. If I can get a small house on a low rent, that would be fabulous.'

'I see. I need you to do me a favour.'

'Anything. Your gift to Giovanni has changed his life. He is a bit of a loner, but with Charlie he is the happiest boy in Sitwell.'

'Thanks. Now, don't ask me any questions, but would you return to Rose Street and bring your wife here. We may be able to solve your accommodation needs.'

John said he could go at once and disappeared up the side of the house, leaving Sam looking from the elevated deck at the view right over the new school playing fields, with large trees shading the edges. He got out his cellphone. 'Nancy, will you bring him down now,' he said and hung up. He walked back through the house; he had done it a thousand times but this time, the electrician took his ladder back to his van and a large crash was heard as the removal van's back doors slammed shut and were locked. A roar of an engine meant they were off.

Sam looked at Paul. 'Well, there is still some fine tuning to do but it is certainly liveable.'

'Come with me,' answered Sam, and they walked through the house, admiring the curtains, fittings and the rest, with Sam giving Paul the whole story of Giovanni. Paul looked at this overweight man who had given him a very rough time putting the house together in record time, and it all became clear. Sam was not paying for this house for the O'Keefe family: he was paying for it only because he loved Giovanni.

'Stay,' Sam said. 'You can explain everything better than me.'

'Here we are,' came a cry at the front door, and Paul opened the screen door to Nancy and Giovanni.'

'Sam!' he called, and ran up the carpeted passage and into Sam's ample arms. 'Sam, what are you doing here?

'Well, I am waiting for your parents.'

'Why?'

'It's a secret.'

'Hm.' Giovanni had his tiny hand on Sam's.

'Do you like this house?'

'Oh yes, Sam,' he said enthusiastically as Sam showed him around.

'Look here.' And there was a generous bedroom and off it a bathroom all done with marble tiles.

'Oh, Sam, it looks like Ferron.' Nancy and Sam began laughing.

Paul as yet had not seen Ferron so he missed the funny comment. 'In here,' he said as he saw John and the woman he assumed was his wife. They entered the house.

'Oh, good morning, Mrs Higgins,' they said, surprised to see her. 'Good morning, Mr. O'Connor.'

'Paul will give you a look around. We will wait on the decking area.'

'Sam, if I stand on the chair, I can see the new school grounds.'

'Do you think Charlie would like it here?'

'Oh yes, Sam. He doesn't like walking along the road. Daddy says the paddocks are very dangerous. They have snakes and things that are not good for Charlie.'

'Well, you see that wooden gate? When you live here, you can open that gate directly into the school grounds and you and Charlie can run and play.'

'But Sam, I live at Rose Street.' Then he frowned. 'Well, I'm not sure where I live now.' He looked at Nancy for some reassurance.

'I think you must live here,' she smiled, 'then it isn't far to come and paint with me.'

'Oh,' he replied, not at all sure what was happening.

'Here we all are,' Sam said. 'Good. Now, you have seen over the house. What do you think of it?

'It's a palace,' answered Veronica.

'Giovanni, come here.' Sam sat him down at the table on the decking, with all the cushions under him so he could put his arms clearly above the table top. Everyone watched, John and Veronica having no idea what was happening.

'Here is a piece of paper. Are you good at arithmetic?' asked Sam.

'A little bit.' Everyone smiled.

'Well, here is a pen. Now when Mary gave you two dollars and thirty five, did you think it was a lot of money?'

'Oh yes, Sam. It's a lot of money, but I have only got two dollars left and I am going to buy a frame for my painting for Emmanuel. Nancy is going to get one.' He motioned for Sam to come close so that he could whisper. 'But it won't cost a lot of money because Nancy knows where there is a sale.'

'Clever Nancy! Right, let's get this finished,' he said forcefully, with everyone, especially Paul, very curious as to how this game was going to end. 'Write down two dollars fifty cents and now write the same thing underneath. Right. Good boy. Now add it up.'

Giovanni put one arm around the top of the sheet so no-one could see his work and then he showed it to Sam. 'Perfect. That's correct. Now hand the sheet to your parents.'

The boy climbed down and it was then Paul realised how tiny he was.

'I don't understand,' puzzled John, with the piece of paper in his hand.

'Well, Sam explained with a broad smile, 'Giovanni has handed you the sum that you will pay weekly as rent on this property for as long as you remain tenants here.'

They looked at one another and Veronica burst into tears. 'But this can't be true,' exclaimed John. 'Five dollars a week for a deluxe house at the end of Sutton drive. The house is beautiful.'

'Thank you,' Paul responded. 'We aim to please our clients.'

'Now, all that is settled,' Sam interrupted, 'what about a cup of tea? Nancy, we'll leave John and Veronica here. I believe you have a secret painting to finish?'

'Don't tell anyone, will you, Sam?'

'Not a soul. Come on, Paul. Oh, sorry!' He pulled a set of keys from his pocket. 'I'm assuming you will take the offer?'

'Oh yes,' John replied. 'It's a dream come true.'

'Glad you like it. Come on, Giovanni. We have to talk business about stud fees.' When Giovanni looked at him blankly, he went on. 'I think Charlie should earn you quite a lot of money.'

'Do you Sam?' he said in amazement. 'But I still have two dollars left.' With that Sam picked him up as they walked up the street, leaving John and Veronica walking from room to room, John still with the piece of paper in his hand that showed the addition of two dollars fifty to two dollars fifty.

With only two weeks or less, Marry was whipped in to making decisions. With house guests there was no problem in the mansion, but Angela? What was she to do with her? 'She is such a bitch,' she said to Paul. 'I can't believe I have to suffer her for Emmanuel's birthday.' She drained her glass. 'Another, sweetie?'

'Well, at least you won't have Vince complaining about the odd fountains, and if I may say so, if this weekend is going to be a disaster why not bring in a catalyst to diffuse it all?'

'What are you talking about?'

'How about our blond bombshell?' Mary looked at him, obviously not grasping the point. 'He's called Giovanni, but I believe we're seeing him next Wednesday evening for a deluxe event at dear Mrs. Higgins.'

'Listen here, Paul, if you dare return to Melbourne before all this is over I shall never speak to you again.'

'Come on! You have Emmanuel to assist you.'

'Past tense, it seems,' was her comment, followed by a grin. 'Isn't it interesting that love manages to survive everything?'

'I wouldn't bet on it,' he answered, dryly.

The week moved on and it was the Wednesday morning of Nancy's special dinner party. She generally managed with a delicious ease to extract cash from pockets and was so willing to accept cheques for the St. Bridget's Benevolent Fund, which was now, according to Simon, at a low ebb. The evening was black tie and anyone who was anyone was invited. Those that weren't just bitched. This year Nancy had a special draw, and as the guests swept into Shannon and were shown to the flower-filled drawing room, a tiny boy with gold curly hair in shiny black shoes, black shorts, a white shirt and the tiniest waistcoat and black bow, helped serve hors d'oeuvres on a small silver salver and was constantly back and forth to the kitchen for replacements. Giovanni chatted with everyone but as the night wore on moved close to Emmanuel and Vince. Now there was also another man very close to Emmanuel, and Michael reached down to lift Giovanni up into his arms.

'You have been working for hours,' he said.

'There is a lot of people,' the boy replied and then reached out for Emmanuel to take him.

'I think you had better sit next to me,' Emmanuel smiled. A grasp of his hand obviously meant that Giovanni thought the same thing.

Sam and Annie arrived late. 'Logistics,' explained Sam: 'Puppies,' added Annie.

'Sam,' exclaimed Giovanni, 'do you have new puppies?' Sam said that there were five and that Giovanni would love them, as he came over and kissed him. Although Giovanni was still being held by Emmanuel he threw his arms around Sam's neck.

'So, Giovanni, it means that Charlie is an uncle.'

'Really? Oh, I must tell him.' This caused a certain amount of laughter from the guests closest to them and with that they were directed into the large dining room with Giovanni still in Emmanuel's arms, telling a lady he had never seen before that Mary had the nicest boat in the world and he had been on it with Father. With everyone seated, the meal began. Nancy had the table out to its maximum, seating, closely, thirty one people. Most of them had one thing in common, the capacity to give and Nancy was out for the maximum generosity. After the main course the noise and chatter was silenced with a teaspoon on a glass, but surprisingly, although everyone looked towards Nancy, as head of the table, it was Mary, who, looking at Sam, took the floor. 'This is Nancy's evening and being out of order I am speaking first.' She looked about as the Treasurer yet again adjusted his spectacles. 'I haven't had a great deal to do with this fund. I donate and hope it is going to help. This fund has fallen into a situation where it has been abused. We have all given but careless administration has seen the money not go where it should.' There was dead silence. 'Father and the Treasurer have righted this situation and we are now in a position to guarantee that every dollar you give will end up serving its correct purpose.'

'May I interrupt?' said Samuel Osborne, and everyone turned in his direction. 'Mary is right. There has been a mishandling of the funds in the past but I would like to say the amount that remained in the fund was sufficient, with Father's and Nancy's signature, to make, or should I say, offer, this wonderful young man here an education at St. Bridget's. If nothing else in this world, I, and I am sure you as well as Mary and Nancy, should be and are the proudest group in all Sitwell.'

There was a round of applause as Emmanuel drew Giovanni toward him. Everyone there that evening had heard the hard luck story and the fact that he was there, serving food and now eating with them, was the first time they had a tangible show of where their money had gone. Vince slowly stood up. 'We don't always succeed in the things we want in life but the fact that Giovanni and other students like him have the opportunity, thanks to your generosity, makes this world a better place.' He sat down amid a great round of applause.

'Well, it's my party and I am the last to speak. We are now well in control of the finances and with the new headmistress and Father we can go on helping those whose families find themselves for one reason or another in trouble. But let me just point out one thing,' she went on in her authoritative voice. 'This little man sitting here didn't originally receive help from the Benevolent Fund. It was the spontaneous generosity of Emmanuel and Mary, who took it upon themselves to help a little boy from St. Bridget's who to everyone else was invisible. This should be a lesson for every one of us.'

There was a deathly silence and then the clapping began. Giovanni was very confused about it all and was not sure exactly how he fitted in, but the smiles he received assured him everything was all right.

'I know it's your show,' repeated Samuel O'Connor and smiled at Nancy, 'but Annie and I will double the highest donation offered this evening.'

There was a round of applause with comments such as 'Be careful, Sam!' and 'What about that!' as everyone knew of his tight hold on money, but very few people knew of the old Sisters' residence next to the church, fully decorated and fitted out and being offered to Giovanni and his parents for only five dollars a week. Nancy was very proud to take Vince and Simon a large number of cheques. Never in the history of St. Bridget's had the wealthier Catholics given so generously.

The next morning the oddest thing was that just short of leaving Shannon and in very high spirits, Nancy was told by the maid that a lady was in the front drawing room to see her. She duly entered, to be absolutely overwhelmed at the woman, who rose to greet her.

'I am sorry to interrupt your morning,' Betty began, 'but things for me are now upside down or changing anyway. I would have posted it but it seems a bit silly as I live just across the street. The event you had last night was to raise money for the Benevolent Fund: I should like to make a contribution.' Nancy, to say the least, was totally surprised.

'Please, sit down,' and she rang the bell. 'Tea or coffee?'

'Coffee, please, black.' The maid disappeared and there was an awkward silence. Then Betty began, 'You won't have to view the monstrosity across the road much longer.'

'Really?'

'No. Anthony's gone, as have Lyn and Barry, but it seems I am the winner after all.'

Nancy said nothing, but looked at a woman now in her late fifties who was about to readjust her life. 'Sean and his friend, or companion,' she hurriedly corrected, 'are going to live there. I am going to take the large apartment at the back. It's fine for me.'

'You are indeed fortunate,' Nancy commented, loathing Anthony Howe, 'that Sean and his friend are going to share their lives with you, for, you see, in the long run that's what it's all about.'

'Yes,' Betty replied, as the maid offered her a coffee and Nancy tea, 'I was thinking of helping at the school but I guess I would be considered a bit out of it all.'

'Not at all,' said Nancy softly. 'We are going to need all hands on deck at the end of next week when we move the school into its new position. I don't mind saying that I, quite to my surprise, like serving tea and coffee to the helpers. It's strange, I didn't think I would. Mary's not

299

keen on it but I like it. Giovanni promises he will help with the sugar,' she added, laughing.

'I have heard about him,' Betty said. 'Sean told me a terrible story about his lunch box.' She looked down into her coffee cup in silence.

'It's past now,' Nancy reassured her slowly, 'and he is well protected and in a safe haven.'

Betty sighed deeply. 'It's difficult to start over again. I guess there are lots of fools like me.'

'We're all fools in one way or another,' said Nancy kindly. 'The most important thing is not to dwell on it. You are going to have Sean and his friend live with you. I would say that that is extremely positive and you might just be surprised at how well things work out.'

Betty thanked her and reached for her cheque book in her bag. 'How much have the others put in,' she asked.

'Well, Sam O'Connor and Annie doubled the highest donation.'

'I'll match Sam's O'Connor's cheque.' Nancy reached into her bag, sorted the cheques and handed Betty Sam's cheque. She copied the amount, filled in the particulars and signed it.

'That's very generous,' she commented.

'My pleasure,' said Betty and rose to go.

'I'll come with you to the gate. I am off to see Father now.'

As they reached the big cast iron front gate at Shannon, Nancy smiled. 'Well, I shall look forward to seeing you next week. I need someone to help me cut sandwiches.'

'I'll be there.' Betty smiled and turned to leave as Nancy laughingly asked, 'Any chance of removing that front fence of yours?'

'I think Jonathan said the same thing, so it will have to go.' She walked off across Sutton Drive into a house to be fully renovated, and although she was the only person in it, it didn't feel empty.

'Good heavens, that's a fabulous amount of money,' was Vince's reaction. 'We can now help the Marshall girls.'

'And who are the Marshal girls?' asked Nancy.

'Two girls of six and five. The family have been in financial difficulties for a long time. I'm afraid he drinks a lot but with this money the girls can be transferred back to St. Bridget's from the Government School for next term. I must call Mrs. Marshall.'

'Oh, Mrs Higgins,' Simon greeted her as he swept into Vince's office. 'Thank you for a splendid evening last night. Quite an event, if I may say so.' Vince handed him a bundle of cheques. 'Oh my!' He scanned the amounts, not to mention the signatures. 'Well, we have done well, thanks to you, Mrs Higgins.'

At that moment Emmanuel entered as he was in Sitwell that morning, which was unusual, it being Thursday.

'I'll leave you here,' said Vince. 'I want to show Nancy the new library.' They departed. Simon sat down as did Emmanuel in Vince's cramped office.'

'How did the donations go?

'Splendidly, absolutely splendidly. We seem to be really going ahead with Father at the helm. I have put off the meeting for the costing of the repair of the church roof until the school is up and running, then with that done we shall know exactly how much money is left in our accounts. Well, I must be off to put these cheques in the Benevolent Fund and do a little more detective work. Goodbye.' He rose and briskly made for the door.

Emmanuel looked out of the window, aimlessly, at the enormous quantities of materials, equipment and school furnishing, all under huge tarpaulins, wondering when this move would ever be finished.

That weekend, the last before the move and Emmanuel's birthday, saw Giovanni at Bantry with Emmanuel and Michael, sailing up and down the river. That Friday evening Emmanuel had organised a surprise dinner on the boat for Mary and the four of them, without Vince, as he as usual remained at Sitwell each weekend. With much laughing and drinking, a splendid relaxed evening was had by all, highlighted by local gossip. At about ten o'clock the boat was moored at the pier and everyone climbed the terrace steps, Emmanuel with a very sleepy Giovanni in his arms. Once inside, he was changed and put to bed.

Mary let the boys talk on and retired. When she rose early next morning, Saturday, the plasterers were still at work in the ballroom. When she had looked out to see if they had arrived, she noticed Michael's car in the same position as the previous evening. 'Well, well,' she smiled to herself and made for the breakfast room only to hear a loud cry announcing that Giovanni was up and about as well. He joined her for breakfast.

'Mary, do you think they will keep my painting I gave you for a long time?' he asked in a worried tone, having seen the empty easel on the library table.

'I am not sure,' she replied, 'but it will be back at Bantry soon.' He nodded his head but a certain amount of doubt remained.

After breakfast they went to see the progress in the ballroom. Except for one small corner section it was finished and today they promised completion, so that the painters could be in the next week and the chandeliers hung.

'Mary, it's very big in here,' the boy said, looking about the totally overwhelming space. They moved outdoors into the warm autumn sunshine.

'Hi!' came a cry from the upstairs balcony.

'Emmanuel, how did you get up there?' asked Giovanni.

'I flew up,' he laughed.

'You can't fly. We are going to see the dogs.'

'OK. I'll see you later.' Emmanuel moved back through the French doors into his bedroom. He sat on the edge of the bed and a hand reached out to hold his arm. Emmanuel took a deep breath as if it signified the closing of a chapter in his life, then he leant over and kissed Michael.

'Will you stay today, then we can all go back to Sitwell early Sunday morning, if you like.'

'Sounds fine to me. I'm beginning to like Bantry.' With that Michael reached across and pulled Emmanuel on top of him.

'I've never felt so complete,' he said. You're wonderful.

Emmanuel did not reply but a kiss was the obvious sign that he too had also enjoyed Michael's company and although things were calm, a base had been established for future development.

There is an odd saying that things happens in threes. Whether this is true or not the Deacon was about to experience three blows that he was not to recover from. He was, as usual, completely and arrogantly supreme in his mind as to presume the moving of the school was entirely his idea, as well as the renovation of the two houses beside the church, the larger one for the O'Keefe family and the other for the headmistress, who was ever so grateful to escape the hot box beside the new church that she was attempting to live in. He began to put the word about that he had had to battle Father but that he did it single-handedly for the benefit of the parish. It did not take long before this news spread back to all, especially Vince, Nancy and Sam, who were furious, especially Vince. The Deacon attempted to wriggle out of a dressing down by Vince, saying it was just that his popularity was so high the parishioners naturally assumed the work and planning was his. Vince's loud voice obviously conveyed to the Deacon that this was just rubbish and one more word about his 'hero routine' and he would call the Bishop at once.

The Bishop was called but not by Vince but by an irate Nancy. The incident occurred on Sunday morning at eleven o'clock Mass. The sermon had been preached to a full church. This also annoyed the Deacon, as Vince was an extremely popular man and as a result of eighteen months' hard parochial work the dividends were seen in a full church. The time came in the Mass for the distribution of the sacrament and it was at this moment that the Deacon made his first of three mistakes.

Vince and the Deacon were totally opposed to one another on the question of distributing the sacrament. Vince served the sacrament to those who came forward to receive it and placed the host on the tongue rather than handing it to them. The Deacon occasionally would refuse the sacrament if he thought that for some reason it should not be given. There had been many heated debates about the Deacon refusing the sacrament to what he called mentally disabled people. There were two lines receiving the sacrament this Sunday and as Vince was more popular needless to say many parishioners preferred to receive the host from a real priest rather than a deacon. Vince's ciborium was empty and he returned to the tabernacle for more hosts. At this moment the Deacon, who had no-one waiting for him in his line, immediately moved over and began distributing the host. Nancy was cross. She had to receive it from the Deacon, but when he refused to allow Phillip to receive it and told him to sit down, Nancy was outraged. They went back to their pew and sat down. Nancy was shaking with rage. The Mass finished and Nancy and Phillip remained in their pew as everyone stood up and left. As Vince came around the corner with Emmanuel and Giovanni, Nancy stood up and in no uncertain manner demanded that Phillip be given the sacrament as he was every Sunday. Vince called Phillip over and Emmanuel returned from the sacristy with the key for the tabernacle. Vince unlocked it and distributed a host to Phillip, but while this was happening Nancy saw the Deacon sweep out to the front of the church to take the credit for the Mass. She turned suddenly and followed him out. He hadn't even time to reach for his cigarettes when Nancy attacked him verbally. All those about to leave stopped and crowded back to watch and listen.

'You fool!' Nancy screamed. 'How dare you go against what your superior has instructed!'

'Now, now, Nancy,' smiled the Deacon.

'It's Mrs Higgins to you,' she snapped loudly. By now a great part of the congregation decided to stay and watch the fray.

'Come, Nancy, you know my stand on the disabled.'

The forceful slap sent the Deacon's cigarette packet to the ground, spilling in all directions, and his glasses spinning of in another. 'I shall, Deacon, be calling the Bishop's secretary. Mind my words, you haven't heard the last of this.' She stormed off with Philip, Sarah and Bill following. Sarah later said she was overwhelmed at her mother's forceful way of dealing with the Deacon. Vince and Emmanuel left the church later and found the congregation still present and speaking rapidly with a certain amount of laughter.

Nancy did indeed on Monday morning call the Bishop's secretary, but not before she had put in a call to Monsignor Christie, who after a few minutes and listening to Nancy's excited comments of 'constantly undermining Father', also put in a call to the Bishop himself, as they were old friends.

Towards the end of the following week the Deacon received a letter from the Bishop to say he was temporarily suspended from his contract until such time as he, the Bishop and Father Lampedusa made an appointment to speak to one another. A copy of this letter, with a series of suggested dates for a meeting, was forwarded to Vince, who could not have been happier.

This was the big weekend school holidays had started. The school, or the main part of it, was to be moved and it was Emmanuel's birthday. The Wednesday before the Saturday night festivities at Bantry saw Salvatore driving Angela and Kerry to Bantry with, as usual, Angela in control of the conversation.

'You know,' she said, 'I haven't seen Nancy Higgins for at least three or four years, although we are in regular telephone contact.' She related Nancy's dealings with the Deacon. 'He sounds a loathsome type of person. I do hope the Mons can sort this out. I don't want the boys having more trouble than they need.'

Paul had been well used by Mary, wanting the ballroom finished, though he knew she would never use it. When he first took on the restoration of the room, he had taken the shredded curtains and pelmets back to Melbourne and these had been re-made and were ready for installation. When he arrived on Thursday in a small van with the electrician and several enormous packs of curtains in plastic bags, the painting had just been completed. Before starting work, he joined Angela, Kerry, Salvatore and Mary for lunch, and they all began exchanging gossip.

'Mary, the place looks wonderful,' said Salvatore, who with the group had done a tour of the house and gardens the previous day. 'I can't believe it. You have done so much work on the place.'

'Oh, not me, darling. Paul has done the lot.'

'I have noticed,' commented Angela for the second time, 'that those ghastly old fountains have been replaced.'

'Yes.' Mary smiled artificially. 'You and Vince can talk about them all night. He also hated them.' This comment cut the fountain subject dead, much to her satisfaction. It didn't matter what the subject, Angela always had a way of turning it, and not always in Mary's favour. Later, while walking with Kerry in the garden and then down to the pier, Mary said she would be quite happy to drown Angela as the highlight of Emmanuel's birthday party. It was then that she explained to Kerry the great change that had come over him.

'But he seemed so cheerful last night at dinner,' Kerry replied. 'We remembered him only in tears at Richard's death.'

'It has everything to do with love,' Mary told her.

'Is he in love?' Kerry asked, as they sat down in the autumn sun on a green cast iron garden bench.

'Oh yes,' Mary relied positively. 'He has two lovers.'

'What?' Kerry turned sharply and stared at Mary.

'His first love is an Irish-Italian called Giovanni – his mother is of Italian origin. Salvatore will love him, as we all do – blonde with green eyes and all of six years old.' Kerry gave a sigh, and Mary went on to tell the story of Giovanni, how through his introduction to Emmanuel life had changed for both of them.

'Emmanuel did what?' exclaimed Kerry.

'Yes, he flattened this Barry Howe kid right on to the asphalt. Apparently Emmanuel was seen as the hero of the day. Then we went and bought him a new uniform, shoes and some clothes.'

Kerry reached over and held Mary's hand. 'I am very proud of both of you.'

'He's turned out to be a very important little man in our lives. Sam O'Connor can't live without him – do you remember Sam and Annie?'

'Only vaguely.' So Mary recounted Giovanni's entry into Sam's life and the pleasant consequences of it. 'He often comes out here, either one night a week with Vince or for the Friday and Saturday with Emmanuel. He is in love with the boat. Can you believe it? Emmanuel is teaching him to swim.'

'I can't believe it. Angela and Emmanuel were the original founders of the King Herod society,' at which they both laughed. 'Oh, by the way, if only you had been with us on Wednesday, when we arrived and Salvatore swept down the drive with all the urns restored along the drive up to the front of Bantry. Angela was, I am sure, pea green with envy.'

'Hopefully,' was Mary's reply, with narrowed eyes.

'But you said that there were two lovers. Who's the other?'

'Michael Higgins, it appears. It took some doing but I am very happy with the results. In fact last Friday Emmanuel and Michael organised a surprise dinner for me on the boat and Giovanni was the captain. It was quite divine. I have honestly no idea what I did with my life before Vince and Emmanuel and now Giovanni took me on. Oh, by the way, Vince is also mad about Giovanni. He carries him everywhere. He is so tiny you won't believe it. And the stack of catalogues on the library table, with the now returned 'Red Dog' on the front cover of it! Gerry Sidler rang me on three occasions to try to get me to sell it. She said of all the paintings in her big exhibition this year of naive art the red dog by Giovanni was the most talked about. Isn't that divine? And to think he gave it to Emmanuel and me as a spontaneous gift. Oh, so divine!'

'What's Michael like?' asked Kerry

'Well, if you want the look, it's international tennis player. His personality is great. He has the ability to make everyone laugh and feel totally relaxed and I am certain that this positive point in his character is helping Emmanuel enormously. Oh, just in case you wonder, he is crazy for Emmanuel.'

'Well, it appears that the Mons's recipe for instant recovery has worked.'

'So it seems,' Mary agreed. 'Vince and Emmanuel are here tonight but their daytimes are one hundred per cent dedicated to moving the school on Saturday. After Mass on Sunday they should be free. Come on, let's see how Paul has marshalled Salvatore and my staff to refit the ballroom. You know, Kerry, if it looks all right, I might just have the birthday dinner in there. What a good idea!'

'I'm sure the staff are not going to agree.'

'Oh, don't worry. I have hired two extra girls for these few days so everything will be fine.'

They turned and headed back toward the house, arm in arm, with Mary suggesting various methods of shortening Angela's life. 'Here they are!' cried Angela herself, as she took over as the hostess of Bantry. Vince's car pulled up followed by another. He alighted first and went to the back door of his Mercedes to retrieve a gold-haired little boy in his arms as Emmanuel got out of the driver's side. The other car held Sarah, Michael and Nancy, so it turned out to be a party before a party.

'Well, Father, who is this young man?' asked Angela, having previously greeted all the others.

'My name is Giovanni and I am six years old. I have a King Charles spaniel called Charlie,' he answered her, all at once summing up his life-story.'

'Well, I believe you are a painter.'

'A little bit of one. Nancy helps me.'

Vince lowered Giovanni to the ground and gave him a kiss. Because there were people he didn't know, he moved immediately to Emmanuel and held his hand. If Kerry was surprised that her sons had taken an emotional interest in this tiny boy, Salvatore was without words.

'You look like Father,' said Giovanni, looking at Salvatore, who smiled at him. 'Father has taught me how to sail the boat. I am very good now.'

Mary interrupted. 'Nancy, would you like to take your student and the others to the library? I think there is something to see.' They all followed Giovanni into the library.

'It's back,' announced Giovanni proudly. 'I painted that, but,' he hesitated, 'his tail is a bit funny.' Everyone laughed. Beside the little table easel stood a stack of catalogues of the naïve exhibition with the red dog on the cover. 'Oh!' was all he could say. He moved back to hold Mary's hand and beckoned her to come close. 'Mary, can I take one home for Mummy and Daddy?'

'Certainly, darling.' Then to Angela's utter surprise she picked him up, sat him on her knee, reached over and took one of the catalogues and a pen that was nearby. She opened the front cover and told him what to write, and so in the first one is was 'To Daddy and Mummy, love Giovanni' then 'To Nancy, with all my love, Giovanni' and so on. Everyone had an autographed copy. Giovanni was elated.

They moved through to the drawing room where drinks were served.

'We only have one more day at school and then we go on holidays,' he proudly announced to Salvatore.

'Won't that be nice?' he smiled.

'Charlie and I can play all day.'

'Are you good at sport,' Salvatore asked, falling under Giovanni's spell.

'No. The others push me over all the time so I just sit and watch. I don't like sport,' he added softly.

'How's the ballroom going?' Michael asked, as Nancy and Angela were chatting ten to the dozen.

'Well, let's have a look. I have left Paul to it. He has had Salvatore with him all afternoon and the electrician and the staff. Let's see.' With the exception of Nancy and Angela they all moved down the broad corridor and it was Kerry who noticed Salvatore's broad hand on Giovanni's little shoulders.

'Wow!' cried Emmanuel. Everyone just moved into the vast room and looked about. No one was more overwhelmed than Mary. 'Darling,' she said to Paul, 'you are a genius. It's divine. How did you know where the paintings went?'

'Easy.' he smiled. 'Someone drew a plan on a piece of paper and numbered all the paintings on the back. Lucky us!'

But it was the pair of chandeliers that were the dominant feature of the ballroom, together with the mirror and paintings.

'Emmanuel,' Giovanni asked, with a frown, 'what is a ballroom for – Mass?'

'No, darling. Come here.' He bent over, held him and as he began to hum a tune, Paul moved to a small cupboard that was set into the panelling in the wainscoting. He pressed a pre-selected button and music sounded from an invisible orchestra. Emmanuel and Giovanni moved round the floor in time with it, laughing. When they arrived back at the group, Emmanuel handed Giovanni over to Mary, Salvatore and Kerry swept around the room and in a very dramatic movement Emmanuel offered his hand to Michael. So when Angela and Nancy arrived, having heard the music, they saw two couples dancing slowly around this vast ballroom.

There was much rowdy conversation over dinner, with Vince explaining to Salvatore and Angela the dynamics of moving a school. At the end of the evening a very tired little Giovanni, in Michael's arms, said goodbye to everyone, with his Red Dog catalogues clutched firmly in his hand. He was chauffeured back by the Higgins to Sitwell but he was fast asleep in Michael's strong arms in less than ten minutes.

'He's a great little guy,' said Salvatore to Emmanuel. 'Seems like nothing ever worries him.' Over another drink, Emmanuel told them the terrible tale about his lunchbox being stolen and how upset he had become.

'I would have thrashed the bastard,' said Salvatore, in a very aggressive way. Vince, Mary and Emmanuel realised that the little boy had collected another heart to his credit.

* * * *

Friday saw lunch at Nancy's and, in the evening, dinner at Ferron, at which Giovanni joined them to celebrate the beginning of his school holidays. Paul was also invited and it was here that he saw one of the most opulent Victorian houses he had ever seen, corridors lined with columns, huge rooms furnished or over-furnished with the most beautiful things and the collection of magnificent paintings Sam's grandfather had amassed were overwhelming. Paul's eyes never stayed on one thing for more than a moment, as there was something else nearby equally spectacular. 'Come this way,' and they all followed Sam into one of the large front drawing rooms with a large, magnificent Arthur Streeton landscape over the marble fireplace. As they were about to sit down, Sam beckoned them to look at the finest painting he owned and in a five dollar frame was Giovanni's painting of Charlie. It was so evident to everyone that he was so immensely proud of it that they all saw that he was about to burst for joy. As they sat down and the conversation began, Giovanni moved across and lent over the arm of Sam's chair to whisper in his ear with a big smile and little giggles between the words.

'Sam,' he began, 'Charlie likes the new school grounds.'

'I'm glad.'

'You see, Sam, there are lots of trees.' He began laughing softly. 'He likes to piss against trees.' He burst into laughter, and Sam's big arms swept him up in his and he kissed him.

'You are wonderful,' he laughed, with tears in his eyes.

'So are you, Sam,' was the spontaneous reply.

Saturday morning saw both Vince and Emmanuel leave early for Sitwell to oversee the moving of the school, which left Mary and her staff the day to organise the large dinner party for Emmanuel's birthday. Salvatore, Angela and Kerry went off to Sitwell and then to Shannon for lunch. This was perfect for Mary as she and Paul set about organising the evening's events.

The moving of the school was almost an anti-climax. A huge truck moved the first classroom that had been disconnected from the electricity and water the day before. It was effortlessly, or seemed effortlessly, placed in its new position. Most of Sitwell came and went, watching this well-organised move. There were no mishaps: it went like clockwork, much to Vince's relief and Simon's. And not having the Deacon dashing about as comic relief helped no end. The truck had started its transportations at six-thirty in the morning and by a quarter to seven in the evening the last school room was placed upon its concrete stumps, to a large round of applause from all who were watching. 'Father,' said a most content Treasurer, 'I feel we can say we have done it.' He smiled and gave a sigh. 'Now I shall begin marshalling the troops to paint and put everything back together. Oh, I have heard,' and here he laughed, which was rare for Simon, 'there have been very strong words between the Headmistress and the fifth grade teacher about the curtains in her room. Do you remember them? Hideous things, in primary colours, with alphabets all over them. The sort of thing that they sell as bed linen for infants, not at all suitable for St. Bridget's.'

'And who won?' Vince queried, smiling.

'Oh, the Headmistress, of course.' At which he dashed off to speak to someone about putting in new channel and curbing.

This time John and Veronica O'Keefe were unable to refuse Emmanuel's invitation to his birthday party and the large group assembled in Mary's drawing room for pre-dinner drinks. A very nervous little boy held a package all wrapped in silver paper with a silver bow, waiting for the others to give their gifts to Emmanuel first. Finally it was his turn and he walked up and very gently handed it to him. Emmanuel knelt down, with everyone watching, and began to open the parcel. The silver ribbon fell to the floor; Giovanni retrieved it and held it in his hand. Then Emmanuel opened the paper that Nancy had folded around it. He just stared at the little painting and tears began to form. Emmanuel was not given to showing emotion – anger, yes, he had a very short temper, so Salvatore for the first time saw his son in this state with the little boy in his arms and a head of golden curls against his cheek. 'It's so beautiful, and so are you,' he said, looking again at the painting and realising that the two dollars that Giovanni had left had gone into purchasing the frame, his last money just for him, and the tears flowed again. Michael's hand on his shoulder gave him the courage to slowly stand up and use the handkerchief he was offered. Then he bent down and picked Giovanni up in his arm and slowly moved in a circle.

'This is the most wonderful present I have ever had in my whole life,' he whispered to the boy. There was another man present who knew exactly how Emmanuel was feeling, as he had felt exactly the same when he had received his painting of Charlie some months ago now. The painting of Emmanuel was a fine piece of work and it had taken him a long time, with Nancy's aid and his own patience, to complete the little masterpiece. Now glazed and in a little gilt frame the effect was very professional. The painting was handed from person to person and the comments were equally flattering.

Giovanni lent close to Emmanuel's ear: 'I might do one for Father but I shall have to ask Nancy.' He spoke in a very business-like way.

'I love you very much,' said Emmanuel.

'I love you too,' came the reply, as, led by Vince, everyone began to applaud.

'Now,' announced Mary, 'Giovanni and Emmanuel will lead us to the ballroom for dinner.' They all looked at one another, but just before they left the room Paul made an announcement: 'I know it's Emmanuel's birthday but I have a little something for Giovanni.'

The boy looked excited as a rectangular, flat parcel was handed to him. He was ever so anxious to open it and there it was, a needlepoint picture of Charlie from the nineteenth century in a fine gilt frame.

'Oh, look!' he cried excitedly to Emmanuel and then the group. He moved quickly over to Sam. 'Sam, look, it's Charlie. All in dots. It's very beautiful. Mummy, look!' A quiet word from Veronica sent him scurrying back to Paul whom he kissed and said, 'Thank you very much. I shall hang it in my bedroom.'

The large group moved down the corridor to two closed doors. In from of them, Giovanni took one door, Emmanuel the other and the guess were overwhelmed at the splendid scene laid out for them.

In the centre of this vast room was an extraordinarily long table, covered in a white damask cloth with candelabra, flowers, beautiful china, crystal and an enormous quantity of silver – a shimmering vision for a birthday party no one was to forget. For Giovanni it was like being taken right inside a Harry Potter film and being the star. Veronica and John fitted in well, even if Veronica was nervous. She and Annie chatted on for some time and John's honest, down-to-earth approach endeared him to everyone. Mary noted Giovanni seated on Salvatore's knee, talking to him, and wondered if Vince and Emmanuel when they were young had received the same attention at home.

The next morning saw everyone at Mass. The empty site around the two churches and the very dilapidated canonica were extremely sad, with even more of the asphalt broken up under the weight of the removal truck.

'Goodness, we do have a problem,' remarked Nancy, glancing at the site.

'Not at all, Mrs Higgins,' argued Simon in a flowery way. 'I feel we are on the correct road to recovery.'

'Really? It looks like a bomb went off.'

'Never fear! Before you know it, it will all be in place.' Nancy glanced at him and went into the church.

But if the church yard looked a forgotten heap the house diagonally opposite Shannon followed suit. Betty had given her son the finance to do exactly what he wanted with Anthony's 'masterpiece'. The first thing he did when his plans were cleared by the Council was to demolish the extraordinary roof system of different levels and replace them with a common roof line that was not covered in red tiles but in grey ones resembling slates. The huge front windows, which took the full afternoon glare, were removed and small-paned glass French doors opened out onto a newly constructed veranda which shaded the front of the whole house. The huge decorative section of rough-cut rock which Anthony had seen as a serious architectural feature of the house was demolished, including a huge fake parapet wall of rock which concealed a chimney. From an architectural statement that had nothing to do with the streetscape the large monstrosity began to take on a very passive face in creams and whites and to Nancy's utter delight the front fence she so loathed was demolished and a tallish picket fence and gate system was installed.

But if the exterior was mainly dressing down the structure, the inside was a nightmare. It was here that Jonathan and Sean discussed for hours how on earth to put together an interior that was viable and this required time and money. The latter was not a problem, but time was, as Sean and Jonathan had to be out of his aunt's home on Pierce Street, so they moved into a shambles of builders' equipment, half-demolished walls, a very rudimentary bathroom but the two very contented lovers folded one another in their arms each night, knowing for sure that this was going to be the love affair that would carry them through their lives together.

Betty was genuinely surprised at how much easier her life was. She was often out with them socially and quite often they ate together. When asked at golf where and how Anthony was, she always replied, 'I have no idea,' which generally stopped the conversation. Behind her back the local tongues wagged as in any small country town, but gossip being gossip it was also noted that she was dressing in a less masculine way and taking the art teacher in as a boarder to help Father out was indeed a very charitable thing.

The major change to the interior of the house was the demolition of the fireplace wall in rough rock and the rebuilding of it in brick and rendering it in plaster. The addition of a simple black marble fireplace as Jonathan said, 'did the trick'. So, little by little they began to haul it all together with a very contented neighbour who, without Anthony Howe always making things difficult for Nancy at the Council. She requested the removal of the shrubby native trees and the return of an avenue of plane trees that had once been there, as well as a line of them in front of the new school and church. Hurdles are meant to be hurdled, and finally Nancy, pulling strings, won and the whole of Sutton Drive, from Main Street through to the end where the church property was, was also planted with young plane trees.

But although Sutton Drive was now returning to what the inhabitants thought it should be, tree-lined and smart, with major work on the go at the Howe residence, there was still a major eyesore at the end of the street, and here, no matter how Nancy pushed, the Treasurer held firm. He knew what he was doing and she would just have to wait. 'All will unfold,' he told her, though he was not quite so sure about the unfolding. He had been over the bank records many times, because the Benevolent Fund had been a simple but separate account. It had never, until recently, with the change to Nancy and Vince as co-signatories, ever been on computer, so it became even more difficult to gain the information he sought, even though the bank manager had allowed him access to all the old records, which he had photocopied. It was the last nine years of finance that were just impossible to trace where the money had gone or how.

The following week saw frenetic activity at St. Bridget's, with an enormous number of volunteers digging trenches for the plumbers, carrying building equipment, levelling playing fields, laying in a little cricket pitch and the obligatory football oval, much reduced, with Miss Ainsworth overseeing all. A large tennis court-sized piece of asphalt was laid and in the following weeks would see lines of different colours defining boundaries for different games.

If one was a crow flying over the top of St. Bridget's school, one would have seen an architectural mass that was shaped liked a capital E with the centre stem being the old Methodist church, now the physical education centre for Miss Ainsworth. The rest of the shape was the classrooms, which made up two courtyards. Here the volunteers, under instruction, laid a brick area. The whole complex was surrounded by a veranda system, designed by Sean to unify a very ordinary structure into something reasonably smart. So those three weeks saw the school painted inside by helpers and outside by professionals and a team of inexhaustible women providing lunch, tea and coffee all day, laughing and genuinely enjoying the opportunity to help. It was in this group that nearly every day Nancy met Betty and little by little the years of bitterness, or rather indifference, dissolved. Even so, Betty had told no one, not even Sean, who the other woman was. She just waited to see how things worked themselves out with Sean and Jonathan before she made a move, a very public move.

So when the three week period was up, a fine, well-dressed school was waiting for its uniformed pupils. Brenda had managed in this three week period to galvanise her staff into a group where their aims were all pointed in the same direction. The new computer section had been totally upgraded, as had the art room and the library. In fact Brenda wanted more than an aesthetically pleasing building: she also wanted and demanded results, so the staff, seeing her pitch in with the rest of them, changed their minds about her. It had been dead easy under the old regime of Len and the Deacon: if you were on their side, life was simple; go against them and your contract might not be renewed, as in the time before Vince when the Deacon had managed to control the previous priest without much trouble at all. Now things were different.

Emmanuel crossed the broken asphalt to Vince's office, as that had remained in the old Canonica, only to find the front room (which was now empty of classroom materials) covered in photocopied documents and Simon on his knees moving one against another.

'What are you doing?' Emmanuel asked.

'You may well ask! Somewhere in this sea of paper is the answer to our lost money.'

Emmanuel knelt down and looked at the sheets and Simon tried to explain as simply as possible what the problem was. Emmanuel glanced at the many sheets spread over the floor. It often happens that if you look for something so intently you never find it. This was the case with Simon, who was so determined to locate the money which he had a plan to use that he never saw the obvious.

'Simon, why are there two accounts here? I thought you said there was only one account for the Benevolent Fund?'

Simon turned his head and looked at Emmanuel as if it was the first time he had ever seen him.

'What do you mean?'

'Look, this sheet has the account number 0025-3715 and this sheet has the number 0025-3115. The seven has been changed for a one or vice versa. Which is the Benevolent Fund's number?'

'The first one, 0025-3715.'

'Well, what's the other one?'

Simon adjusted his gold-rimmed glasses, reached over to his coat on the chair, pulled out his telephone and phoned a friend of his at the bank and waited. 'It's not on the computer, I'm afraid,' he said. 'Yes . . yes . . really? Thank you ever so much, Lois.' He waited a few moments. 'I can't tell you how eternally grateful I am to you. Good bye.'

'Well?' asked a curious Emmanuel. 'What's happening?'

'It appears,' Simon began, standing up as did Emmanuel, 'that there is a second account with a number very similar to our account. Some moneys went into our account but the major amount has gone into the other. And who do you think has access to the other account? You're right,' he went on very determinedly, 'the Deacon. And I am willing to bet that he was helped in this scheme by an assistant in the bank who just happens to be Dolly's brother. Just charming! So that's how they did it and the previous priest just signed the cheques, never knowing how much was even in the account as the Deacon kept all that administrative work to himself. Now, Mr. Sacristan, what do we do now?' He gave a wicked smile.

CHAPTER TEN

St. Bridget's completed

CHAPTER TEN

St. Bridget's completed

'I feel the correct thing would be to inform the police,' said Simon.

'How much money do you think will be returned?'

'Very little, I should think. Just imagine, if this was an issue for the taxation department they would sell Dolly and the Deacon up, even their holiday house.'

'What holiday house?' asked Emmanuel.

'Well, Dolly and the Deacon have a holiday house right on the esplanade at Brentwood, but a house like you have never seen, so tasteless, so very 'them', even if the position is good.'

'Mr. Treasurer,' said Emmanuel with a straight face, 'what if we were to convince the Deacon to sell the holiday house and transfer the money into our general account?'

'To 'convince', Mr. Sacristan! That does sound a little like blackmail.'

'Yes, exactly,' was the reply.

'I am ashamed that I didn't think of it first,' grinned Simon.

'You have a cousin who is into property development, don't you?' Simon said he did, and Emmanuel went on, 'Well, get him to go and a have a look at it and see if he is interested. Then he can give us a price so we know where we are going.'

'Good thinking, although it is so hideous I am positive that he would only be interested in the land value. You see, the house was designed by guess who? Anthony Howe. It's on two levels; the top one is all glass but above the windows is an approximately two metre high space in vertical weather boards. Dolly or the Deacon has had every board painted an alternate colour, pink, green, pink, green. And if that wasn't bad enough, they then painted a forest of wrought iron in the same manner. So tacky!' He said this in a very superior way.

'Mr. Treasurer, you get me the information and I will do the rest.'

With that Simon gathered all the paperwork up from the floor and then sat on a crate to dial his cousin. 'No, no,' he insisted, in a very calculating way, 'this is extremely urgent. Besides you may just make a lot of ready money quickly . . . very well, tomorrow afternoon. And remember, keep this to yourself. Goodbye. Well now, we wait until tomorrow afternoon.' Clutching his papers, he made off toward his car in the street.

A second blow was about to strike the Deacon, and a third was not far behind. It was the first day back at school for the St. Bridget's pupils and strict regulations were read out by the Headmistress about acceptable behaviour and the care of their new school. There was still a lot of planting of shrubs and trees to be done, but the interiors were completed.

The following day, as school was dismissed, a very excited Simon sought out Emmanuel, who was with Vince. 'May I have a word with you, Sacristan?' The two of them walked over to the old church. 'You won't believe it,' he began excitedly. 'My cousin said that as it is a deep double block, the house could be demolished and he could get eight deluxe villa units on the site. And – wait for it – how much do you think he will pay?'

'No idea.'

'Two million dollars cash into the church funds as soon as the papers ae signed – two million dollars! I had no idea the land was worth so much. Oh, this will solve all our problems. Well, Mr. Sacristan, this is now your responsibility.'

'I shall need a copy of the two account numbers, the name of Dolly's brother, the church account and the telephone number of the chief Sergeant at the local police station, and your cousin's number.'

'Give me ten minutes.' Simon dashed back into the Deacon's old office and, in the neatest copperplate handwriting that one would expect of him, copied out all the information needed, folded up the sheet and inserted it into an envelope.

'Excuse me, Father. This is the letter you asked me for, Sacristan. I shall see you all tomorrow.'

While driving back to Bantry, Vince noticed that Emmanuel was nervous and asked why. 'Oh, nothing,' was the reply, but over dinner Mary also noted an uneasiness in him. The next morning Vince left early as usual and later Emmanuel left in his car.

'I hope there's no problem with Michael,' was Mary's concern. 'I don't remember Emmanuel so nervous.' But if the build up to this encounter did not find him totally confident, face to face was another issue. Both Emmanuel and the Deacon had hated one another at first sight and nothing had changed either of their opinions, so when the front door bell rang and the Deacon opened it to Emmanuel he knew there was trouble.

'Keep it short. I am going out in a moment,' he said, in an arrogant tone and showed him into the kitchen area. 'What do you want?'

'I have an envelope for you. I thought I would deliver it personally as I know how you like to keep your private life just that.'

The Deacon snatched the envelope and withdrew the sheet. To say he was shocked was an understatement. He blanched white and immediately lit a cigarette. 'You can't prove a thing,' he spat out.

'Oh, but we can, now,' said Emmanuel, moving into the game. 'I believe the charges carry a seven year jail sentence.'

'No one will believe you.'

'I'm sorry but you're wrong. You are at present suspended from your contract as Deacon, pending a meeting between Father and the Bishop. I am sure, with a certain amount of pressure from the police, your wife's brother will spill the beans. I think that's the expression. You see, the silly thing you did was put the second account in your name, not his, so you will take the entire blame.'

The Deacon was like a caged animal. He walked backward and forward across the kitchen floor seeking a way out.

'We have you, Deacon, but there just might be a way out of the seven year jail sentence and the public scandal.'

He stubbed his cigarette out in his saucer and lit another. He looked sideways at Emmanuel. 'What's the deal?'

'No deal. You will do just what I say and no one will know a thing about your dishonesty.'

The Deacon stroked his short grey beard and adjusted his glasses. 'What do you want?'

'The telephone number second from the bottom. You will ring now and accept the offer for your beach house. This man will be around with his solicitor today to finalise the deal.'

The Deacon looked arrogantly at Emmanuel as if nothing made sense.' 'Why should I sell my beach house?'

'Simply because the money will be deposited not into your account but into the church account, all of it, and that's it. Now, you have exactly two minutes to call the property developer or I shall call the other number at the bottom of the page and we shall hand all the documents over to the police. I also believe this involves the taxation department as well.'

'Bastard!' was the Deacon's comment but he picked up his mobile phone, spoke to Simon's cousin and made an appointment for two hours hence, as the solicitor was at Sitwell due to a problem to be resolved in Rose Street. Emmanuel stood up and went to leave. As he reached the front door he turned sharply. 'Oh, I forgot one little thing.'

'Really?' came the Deacon's sarcastic reply.

'You will cancel your contract as Deacon at St. Bridget's owing to stress and ill-health and that letter will be on the Bishop's secretary's desk within three days. Good morning, Deacon.' He moved out into a crisp late autumn day, with brilliant sunshine. He was unaware until he was in his car that his hands were shaking. He drove back to St. Bridget's ever so glad to see Vince's car was not there and parked his before going to the Deacon's old office, where he found Simon huddled over an old-fashioned electric radiator which he upset as Emmanuel came through the door.

'Well, what happened?' Simon asked, righting the radiator.

'Done. Telephone your cousin in two hours and check that the papers are signed, then the money is St. Bridget's.'

'Wonderful. Two hours? Oh, did you tell him how much the property was worth?'

'No and perhaps if you call your cousin now tell him not to tell the Deacon until the papers are signed. He's cunning, is the Deacon.'

'Yes, but not cunning enough.' Simon put the call through to his cousin, who told him he had done him a fantastic deal and that the least he could do was buy Simon a new car.

'How kind! But what if I was to send you an account for a little less for the restoration of the church organ? Would you be terribly upset?'

'Go for it, Simon. It will be a pleasure. I am going to make a killing out of this. Bye!'

Simon paced up and down the little office.

'Stop!' cried Emmanuel. 'You're making me nervous!'

'Oh well, come with me! stated Simon, and they headed across the broken asphalt to the old church. Simon opened the door with a key and they went in. 'If . . . . . if the Deacon signs and the money is ours, this will be renovated at once. I have five companies just waiting for my phone call this morning and now the organ renovation is to be paid for.' They looked round the interior and the word 'bleak' was appropriate. There was only the left-over rubbish that Miss Ainsworth did not need in her new domain and it strangely smelt abandoned, forgotten or out of date. They walked around, talking about improvements until Simon's phone rang. He literally jumped. 'Yes,' he said in a tense way, and just listened, with Emmanuel now becoming very nervous. What if he had not signed this all over into the church funds but had decided to keep it and run? It was an equation Emmanuel had not thought of. Simon closed his telephone and looked at Emmanuel with a straight face and whispered, 'We've done it! Who said blackmail was a dirty word?' He began to laugh. 'The Deacon will get a shock when he comes back.

'Oh, but he won't be coming back.' Emmanuel smiled.

'What are you talking about? There is twelve months left on his contract.'

'He has decided to resign his contract due to stress and ill health.'

'Clever you, Mr. Sacristan. Two birds with one stone, I believe the saying is. I must leave you now. I have a million things to do, but congratulations, Mr. Sacristan. I couldn't have done it, congratulations.' He dashed out, leaving Emmanuel looking around and wondering what this structure would look like when it was totally restored, and to his surprise it happened much more quickly than he expected, as two of the five companies before twelve o'clock were seen off-loading scaffolding at the side of the old church. It was obvious that a new tin roof would be in position very shortly.

When Vince returned from pastoral work and noticed scaffolding rising around the old church and ladders against the old Canonica, he phoned Simon. The only response he got was 'It is all totally under control, Father. Don't worry.'

'I don't know what's happening,' Vince said to Emmanuel over dinner. 'Simon won't tell me anything.'

'Oh, he knows what he's doing. Don't worry,' replied his brother, smiling.

Later, Mary drew Emmanuel aside to ask whether everything was fine with Michael. 'Perfect,' was the reply and he kissed her before heading off to bed, following what could be described as a busy day.

Simon had waited a long time for this moment. He had always been under the heel of the Deacon and the previous priest, and now he was free. His fantasies of restoring the old church had resulted in an enormous folio of names and addresses, telephone numbers, everything that, should a miracle occur, he was one hundred per cent ready for. So his phone rang all day. He called in quotes for the re-glazing of the windows; the plasterers were already taking measurements as were the electricians. It wasn't just the old church: the Canonica was also to be restored. Simon was like a bee. He danced all day around the edge of the honeycomb, making sure that every angle was just right.

The next day he took Vince and Emmanuel aside and explained to Vince what he was doing. He said that the new church was in such bad repair that it wasn't worth wasting money on, but he held back two pieces of information, one being the blackmail for the money to do this renovation and another tiny piece of technical information in case he encountered a last thrust of power from the Deacon and Anthony Howe.

'But can we pay for all this?' asked Vince.

'Certainly, Father, but I think a certain discretion about it would be a good idea until the meeting is scheduled for the debate about the roof on the new church.'

'But surely that isn't necessary now?

'Oh, but it is, Father, oh, but it is!' he reiterated. Vince shook his head and said that as Simon had virtually single-handedly moved the school and it looked fabulous he was not about to doubt his capacity to handle this project, especially as he loathed the Anthony Howe building. 'Come with me, please, gentlemen,' so Vince and Emmanuel crossed to the old church and entered to a sea of workmen. Simon signalled to the foreman and in less than fifteen minutes the huge masonite wall that covered the sanctuary was ripped down to the sound of hammers and the occasional expletive, with just some of the upper stays still in position. It was now possible to see what Vince and Emmanuel had seen with John some months ago.

'Emmanuel,' said Vince, 'go and get Nancy. I think she will enjoy this moment.' He disappeared, leaving Vince and Simon watching the last pieces of timber crash to the floor. Then they started on what had been Miss Ainsworth's office, then directly opposite the store room. An enormous quantity of broken Masonite and structural timber was seen being hauled outside and dumped in a heap.

'No, no!' cried Simon. 'Put it all over on the grass area. I have the Council coming in this afternoon to remove all the asphalt.' Vince looked at Simon. 'Happily the Council need this for filling this month.'

It was with the demotion of the three walls that the floor plan of a giant Latin cross became apparent, but the overwhelming effect was from the enormous architectural high altar, topped with a dome, supported on eight columns, where the Blessed Sacrament would have been placed for all to see. A bang behind Vince made him turn around as a workman bumped the cornice with a length of timber. Nancy, with Emmanuel, followed in after the workman's exit. Her left hand moved to the side of her face and she just stared ahead, then to the two side transepts now being stripped of shelving, that had previously served for the office and storage zones. She said nothing, but stepping over the debris moved closer to the front and in the morning light saw, silhouetted, this huge altar, as the morning sun was rising., She turned to say something to Vince and then saw the organ and choir loft, and a workman unscrewing a rustic gate that had closed it off to students.

'There were burgundy velvet curtains behind the cast iron balcony in my day' she said quietly.

'And they shall be returned. I have them on my list,' said Simon in a confidant voice. 'We are going to plaster over the pine lining. It's the only way. It will give the church just the elegant light touch it was missing. I am sure you agree,' he said, looking at an astonished Nancy.

'Oh yes,' she answered, looking all around her. 'Of course.'

He had not missed anything. The front room of the Canonica that had been the language laboratory and computer centre was taken over by Simon with papers everywhere. Restorers were in for quotations and he drove a very hard bargain. He wanted the best for St. Bridget's but at the lowest price possible. He manoeuvred in every possible way, calling in old debts and openly exploiting a competition between tradesmen until he got the price he wanted. Then he was like a dog at the heels of a prowler, pestering them to watch the standard of work and finish as soon as possible. As Nancy reminisced with Vince, Emmanuel saw two men begin to remove the window frames, having first removed the bird wire that had protected them from the students' over-enthusiastic ball throwing.

'I do hope, Mr. Treasurer, that that ghastly yellow, red and blue glass is not to stay.'

'Oh heavens, no! Come this way, Mr. Sacristan.' Emmanuel enjoyed these formal games with Simon, even if it unnerved others, including Vince. 'Look,' he went on, pointing to a window in the old sacristy which had one broken pane but had all the border glass intact. It was acid etched on the palest green, a border of shamrocks. 'Terribly appropriate, wouldn't you say?'

'Were all the windows once like that?'

'I think we can say yes.' Simon smiled. 'Those primary colours are insupportable. They moved back, hearing a crash as yet another wire window guard fell to the floor.

The progress was amazing, as that afternoon a truck laden with all the window frames, damaged and otherwise, headed off to Melbourne to a studio that promised the completed glass and frame restoration in four weeks. Two young students from the Melbourne School of Painting and Decorating arrived and immediately began the work of repairing and repainting where necessary the High Altar, and the two side altars which were now in position. From behind the side altars, when they were removed in order to be re-installed, six cardboard cartons were found, packed full of a very rustic set of nativity figures and animals.

'Good heavens,' exclaimed Emmanuel, 'Angela has an exquisite collection of nativity figures. These are very rustic and quite big. Look, the mice have eaten most of the garments away. What a shame!'

'Oh, I believe that as Sacristan it is your responsibility.'

'Thank you, Treasurer. You are most kind,' retorted Emmanuel, rather sarcastically.

'You do have six months before we shall need them, and I am sure you will do a splendid job. Do give me a call if you need some finance.' He moved away and gave a startling yell at a workman about being careful when working near the organ.

Emmanuel had a workman move the boxes to the old art room for the time being as it was necessary to clear everything out of the church that didn't serve as the scaffolding for the plastering was to go up the next Monday. By that stage the twenty seven new cement stumps would be in position. The church bell sounded the completion of school and Giovanni, as usual, raced down to see if Emmanuel was still there. He never took Charlie to play in the school grounds until he was certain that all the pupils had left. He saw Emmanuel's car out in front of the church and set out to find him. As he entered the Canonica, assuming he was with Vince in his office, he saw him on his knees, pulling battered figures out of boxes.

'Emmanuel!' he cried and threw both arms around him and in kissing him almost knocked him off balance.

'How was school today?'

'OK. I sat and watched sport. It's a bit boring. But what are these for?' he asked, picking up a figure that was obviously supposed to be a wise king. Emmanuel explained what they were. He then helped Emmanuel unpack the boxes. There must have twenty figures and lots of broken animals. The costumes were indeed rudimentary, with glue stains and drawing pins holding old bits of cotton in position.

'Mummy makes these dresses,' he said.

'Really?' asked Emmanuel in surprise. 'Are you sure?'

'Oh yes. A lady from Melbourne sometimes sends a doll in a box and Mummy fixes up the dress and things.'

'Why don't we go and see your mother?' Emmanuel suggested, standing up and swinging Giovanni onto his shoulders. 'Watch your head!' They went off across the yard, up the street and rang Veronica's front door bell.

'What a pleasant surprise! Come in.'

'No, I want you to come with me for a minute, if you don't mind.' Veronica removed her apron, saying there was no problem, and Emmanuel lowered Giovanni to the ground. They re-traced their steps and went into the Canonica. Veronica was shocked at the state of the old art room, with paint-splattered walls and broken plaster work.

'Don't worry,' laughed Emmanuel. 'Simon is going to re-plaster the whole Canonica. The lath and plaster is in a shocking condition.' She looked down at the large group of figures.

'Giovanni tells me you restore these figures.'

'Well, not exactly. When I could get the work I used to restore them or if they were in a really terrible condition I'd re-construct costumes for antique dolls. Every cent helps!' She smiled. 'But there hasn't been much work for a while. John is very good at re-carving the damaged pieces. He once made an entire arm for an antique doll.'

'How much would you charge to do this lot?' he asked, with Giovanni trying to make a sheep stand up.

'I wouldn't charge. After all you have done for us it would be a pleasure, but I'm afraid you would have to supply me with the materials and the designs you wanted. You would have to find someone to repaint the face and hands, as these are in a very bad condition. What are they constructed out of?'

'I think,' he replied, ' they are *papier maché*, wood, string, a bit of everything, but as for re-making the faces, there must be a plaster resin that can be used.'

'He is standing up,' laughed Giovanni: a camel on three legs stood only for a moment, then fell over. 'He is missing a leg, the poor camel,' he said, in a very concerned way.

'Look, leave it with me. I have to go to Melbourne for three days next week and I will come back with the reference and materials and then I will have a chat to Simon.' With that, after a kiss, Giovanni and Veronica headed home to a very impatient Charlie.

'How many metres, sweetie?' asked Paul on the phone to Emmanuel.

'No, I don't think metres, but it's for a nativity scene.'

'You mean half-metre offcuts in silk taffeta, if they're going to be the sort of thing Angela has?'

'Yes, that's it. And little ribbons and fine braids. Where shall I get them?'

'Oh, don't worry. I have a garbage sack at the studio filled with bits and pieces. They are all yours, but it will cost you.'

'Oh?'

'Yes, when you are town you must have dinner with Anthony and me. That's the deal. I shall have it all packed up for you. See you next week, sweetie.' Emmanuel hung up, thinking, 'Hmmm!' and closed the Canonica before heading out to his car. At that moment, he saw Jonathan Wise, the new art teacher about to cross the road.

'Jonathan' he shouted. 'Can I speak to you for a moment?' So he returned to the Canonica to show him the figures. Jonathan was not blind to Emmanuel's very good looks and those strong blue eyes that seemed to see straight through him.

'You mean, to paint the faces and hands and some of the animals when they've been repaired? Sure, it's not a problem. Don't tell me St. Bridget's is going to have a Neapolitan nativity scene?

'You've got it in one. You may have to help me with the background scene – trees and rocks and such.'

'It will be a pleasure to help you.' He smiled and the smile was returned. Michael had told Emmanuel that he thought Jonathan was much more than just the boarder across the road from Shannon: after this brief encounter, Emmanuel was certain he was correct.

Emmanuel was expected in Melbourne the following week. He had work and things to collect from Monsignor Christie for Vince and three days in Melbourne was not such a bad idea, he thought, as he pulled out onto the freeway, heading for Melbourne. He was very aware that in the six months that he had been at Sitwell he had fitted in there and felt comfortable. It was definitely different, living with Mary, from living with Angela. With Angela it was all go, restaurants, the races, charity events, theatre, but with Mary it was totally people-orientated, families not so much in the classic sense but limited groups of people who supported one another, even if they were completely indifferent to their own, such as Samuel O'Connor, with two sons he barely spoke to but who was in love with the little boy of six years old who shared his love for spaniels. Emmanuel puzzled this over and over again. It was not that one lifestyle was better than the other: they were just different, he finally decided.

His three days in Melbourne were frenetic and on one of the evenings he and Angela joined Paul and Anthony for dinner, with lots of laughter and drinks, Paul now able to share in the Sitwell jokes, as he had spent so much time at Mary's, working.

'I think you are going to get a call soon from the Treasurer,' said Emmanuel, smiling.

'Why?' Paul frowned.

'Well, he has this idea that when the Canonica is finished he will ask the parish to donate suitable, appropriate furniture for re-furbishing it and that's where you come in.'

'Really? How?'

'You, being an outsider, can select the pieces and then have them installed.'

'I see. I get bitched for not taking Mrs Somebody's dining table because I have selected another. Oh, it sounds like feeding Christians to the lions.' Everyone laughed.

'I believe the Treasurer is going to leave the entire furnishings, curtains and everything in your very capable hands, as he has heard via Nancy that Mary thinks you are divine.'

'How right she is!' he laughed. 'Oh, don't forget those two black plastic bags. I hope they do the trick.' Emmanuel thanked him. 'And how's our little artist?'

'He seems a genius in the making,' said Anthony. 'I think we should be buying now, don't you?'

'Perhaps,' replied Emmanuel, tilting his head to one side.

The next morning saw Emmanuel in Angela's room which held her Neapolitan nativity scene. As she passed the door she glanced in, imagining that this private moment was somehow for Richard, but he turned as he heard her footsteps and called her in. To her surprise he began to ask her all sorts of questions about the figures and their setting.

'I can lend you several good books with very good photos, if you like.

'That would be great.'

'Emmanuel are you looking forward to the year being finished and being back in civilisation?'

'Yes and no,' he answered. 'I really like Bantry and I have discovered I have a brother I really like. I never knew Vince well as a child. He was much older than me and it's nice to have a brother re-discovered. I never thought I would ever fit into the church routine and be able to serve with Vince but I can and I like it. It was fun teaching Giovanni.'

'You love him very much don't you?' she said slowly.

'Yes, I do and when my year is up I should like to take him to Paris with us. Would you mind?'

'Not at all. He is adorable. I must say I was very surprised that Mary had taken to him.'

'He is very loveable and just so fragile you want to hold and protect him. He loves Vince and to go up the river with him in the boat is the tops for him. He doesn't have any friends of his own age, only adults.'

'Lucky boy!' she said, not explaining her comment.

'So we shall see. After Christmas I shall probably for a while do half Sitwell, half the time here. I just don't know.'

'Well, there's six months left to work it all out, so don't worry. Paris will still be there.' She hugged him.

The final evening before he returned to Sitwell he had dinner with Kerry and Salvatore and the conversation he had had with Angela was aired again. Emmanuel gave the same replies and asked after his paternal grandparents. Salvatore said all was well but Mario had drifted away from the family circle a bit and he rarely saw him. He then asked about Giovanni and said if he was having a show of his work he would like to buy one.

'Good heavens,' laughed Emmanuel. 'It seems everyone wants a painting by Giovanni.'

'That's easy for you to say,' his father replied. 'You have a beautiful portrait by him – it's a really very competent piece of work.'

'Oh, Mary said to tell you that you are always welcome to come and stay a Bantry, so perhaps you could discuss a painting with the artist himself. I believe he is now doing a secret painting of Vince, but I haven't seen it. Nancy and Giovanni keep their work very hidden away.'

'And Michael?' asked Kerry, having been well informed by Mary.

'I like him a lot. It's a very different situation from Richard. I don't suppose any two relationships can be the same but with Michael I seem to be very happy and this relationship keeps changing all the time. It's not as fixed as with Richard, because I don't live full time with him. Each time I see him there are different facets to his personality that I discover, so I shall see. I have realised that although I speak to him on the telephone, I am very aware that I am in Melbourne and he is a long way away in Sitwell.' He looked into his half-empty glass and noticed the neck of the bottle as Salvatore topped it up. 'Thanks,' he said, smiling.

'You know you can bring Michael to stay here whenever you want,' said Salvatore.

'I'll see what he is doing,' he replied, smiling again.

The next morning, he said goodbye to everyone, and the Mercedes sports swung out and headed for the freeway. Emmanuel was very aware that he felt very happy and his mind ran over what he was going to say to everyone. Then it struck him, quite hard, that he had missed them, Vince, Mary, Nancy and especially Giovanni and Michael, Sam and Annie, yes, even the Treasurer. This was a totally new experience for him and the feeling as he came closer and closer to Sitwell, and especially to Bantry, prompted him to telephone Michael to join them at Bantry for dinner. It was a complete feeling of belonging to a place and to the people that he had used in a certain way six months earlier to form a bridge that he was able to cross after Richard's death. He had crossed the bridge, thanks to this group and he could not think of a single reason to return to his old lifestyle, as luxurious as it had been. As the big gates swung open at Bantry and his car nosed its way down the urn-lined drive, the huge red-brick mansion with verandas loomed up with a new fountain spouting water all around in the late autumn winds. He was immensely happy to embrace Mary and honestly say he had missed her.

As the mild autumn continued, Simon became more and more agitated as he was afraid that with the onslaught of winter it would slow up the work. Up the street this was also a major concern, as the new roofing system was not completed on the Howe house, even if enormous visual changes had occurred. The interior was altered completely from a myriad of small rooms. Sean had demolished walls to make larger spaces with more elegant proportions. All the internal stonework had been removed and Betty said quite frankly that she had no idea how she had lived in the original structure for so long without seeing anything wrong. The look the boys sought was an international one, a mixture of European and Asian art and artefacts together, and as both Jonathan and Sean had the same likes and tastes the house became a soft, harmonious series of spaces tastefully decorated.

Today, as Sean slumped down in a comfortable chair, he was feeling anything but harmonious. It had been a day in which he had had to face facts, and the facts were extremely hard to take. After lunch at St. Bridget's, Miss Ainsworth's class entered the new physical education hall, changed into their shorts and tee shirts with large logos of the school on the left-hand side in red and black, the school colours. A whistle blast had them all lined up and it was then that she noted a very red-eyed Peter Kelly with a very nasty bruise on the upper part of his leg, which he kept rubbing.

'All out onto the court,' she shouted, but went directly to Peter to find out what the problem was, as she realised he couldn't play volley ball when he was limping. The moment that her hand touched his shoulder he began to cry. She knelt down in front of him and asked him what was wrong and in between sobs he informed her that Barry Howe had beaten him up and taken his lunch money. A white rage began to rise in Miss Ainsworth, who told him to dress. She immediately telephoned the Headmistress, who arrived post haste.

'Have you had anything to eat?' Brenda asked softly; a shake of the head determined that he had not and with that she left with Peter hand in hand in the direction of the tuck shop, where the volunteer ladies were cleaning up. A quick explanation of the situation saw Peter sitting at a bench with the ladies reheating a lunch in the microwave for him. Brenda now called Sean and said she wanted to see him urgently with or without his wife. Barry was sent for and he sat on a chair outside her office in the little corridor, quite happy that he had escaped an English lesson. Sean was at home, supervising the new bathrooms with the plumber and in fifteen minutes was seen coming through the main door. There he saw Barry swinging his legs back and forth as if nothing was wrong. Sean was followed by Lyn, who made a big fuss of him and the parents were duly shown into the Headmistress's office.

'I am aware of the enormous work you have offered the school as architect,' began Brenda' but this latest brutality I am not, under the circumstances, prepared to tolerate.'

'Oh, boys will be boys,' piped up a now very overweight Lyn.

'Are you aware,' Brenda went on, looking daggers at her, 'that your son beat up a boy younger than himself, driving his boot into his side and upper thigh, causing serious bruising and this was so he could extort Peter's lunch money? Remember Peter went without lunch whilst your son probably ate more sweets.'

There was a knock at the door and Miss Ainsworth entered, determined to make an end to Barry one way or another. As she had passed him on the chair, he cringed in genuine fear as she came over and grabbed him by the front of his jumper. 'You've had it, Howe!' she spat. 'This time you are going.' She thrust him violently back into the chair. Now Barry was worried. The thought of Miss Ainsworth thrashing him was becoming a strong probability and being a thug and a coward he was afraid.

Miss Ainsworth entered the office in her usual tracksuit with a whistle hung around her neck and Brenda noted her eyes were narrowed. After brief introductions she made it crystal clear what she thought of Barry and his appalling anti-social behaviour. Sean said absolutely nothing, with Lyn doing all the defending. Then he stood up. 'What do you suggest we do?' he asked, looking at Brenda.

'I will not expel him, on one condition, and that is that you transfer him as of today to the state school. I can call the headmaster as I know him well. Now, if you like?'

'That's really unfair,' protested Lyn.

'So is beating up boys younger than you,' retorted an icy Miss Ainsworth.

'Make the telephone call, please,' said Sean.

'What sort of a father are you?' snarled Lyn, sarcastically.

'I am as incompetent as a father as you are irresponsible as a mother.'

There was a deathly silence while Brenda rang and spoke to the headmaster. She hung up and looked at Sean and Lyn. 'He will begin school tomorrow at the state school off Main Street. Just a moment.' She reached into her filing cabinet and pulled out a form. There was not a word said whilst she filled it out. She put a school stamp on it and signed it, then handed it to Lyn.'

'It's all your fault, all of this!' Lyn spat at Sean.

'Listen to me, Mrs Howe. If it were not for your husband's generosity to this school I would have cheerfully signed not a transfer sheet but an expulsion order. Do you understand the difference?' she asked, staring at her. 'Collect your son, tell him to collect his things and leave.' She signalled for Sean to remain. The slamming of Brenda's door made it quite clear that Lyn thought this was a set-up and her poor son the victim.

'I'm sorry, Sean,' Brenda said – they were on first name terms, 'but this is the best I could do.'

'I appreciate that. If in the future someone checks the records, transfer can mean anything; expulsion is deathly clear. Thanks, Brenda.' She just smiled.

'I believe you have been called in to assist Simon?'

'He is one of the few people in this world that do not need assistance, just reassuring. Thanks again.' He turned and left.

It was an elated Miss Ainsworth who returned to take over her class from a helper. A shrill whistle blast had everyone in line waiting for the next order.

'Here we are,' Jonathan said, handing Sean a drink. 'It can't have been too pleasant in Brenda's office today.' Sean, looking downcast, admitted that it was not. 'Look, Sean, I have been in the teaching business all my life and my experience is you get terrible parents but you also get terrible children, and sometimes neither has anything to do with the other. I taught Barry but only for one or two lessons and although he is your son,' he went on, moving to sit beside Sean, 'he is out for trouble. He is generally described as a smart arse but if it's any consolation he is about to enter a different kind of school where his peers are just as rough and tumble, so perhaps his education socially is just about to begin.' Sean sighed as he looked at Jonathan. His prophecy of Barry not lasting a term in the re-located school had come true and he felt heaviness settle on his shoulders. And how right he was! A black eye in the first week made it very clear to Barry that there are bullies and thugs in every school.

But this afternoon, Jonathan witnessed something odd at school. The class that Giovanni belonged to was having sport and Jonathan had only a small class due to three quarters of them having computer lessons. As the rest of the computers had not arrived, he took the seven students for art to deal with the overflow for a few weeks. In his classes silence was the rule, but today a whisper was heard here and there. He looked aimlessly out of the classroom window and saw a little boy sitting on a bench, swinging his legs back and forth while the other students played sport with the ever-ready whistle for foul play. Later, after the class, he was sitting in the staffroom just having made a cup of tea when Miss Ainsworth bowled in. With her cup of coffee she sat down beside him and he asked her why Giovanni was sitting alone and not playing sport?

'He's my biggest problem,' she replied. 'He is so small and so fragile that it doesn't matter what I do or how I watch him he is always pushed over and hurt.'

'Who's pushed over and hurt?' came a voice from behind them. They looked up to see Brenda, also there for her tea break.

'Giovanni,' said Miss Ainsworth. 'He is the most adorable person in this world.'

Brenda looked at her; it was most unlike her to pass a flattering comment about any student. 'He is our resident artist,' smiled Brenda.'

'Really?' queried Jonathan.

'Yes. Just a minute.' She went out and returned with the catalogue with the red dog on the cover. When he opened the front cover he saw a dedication in a very junior hand 'To my Headmistress, love Giovanni'. 'It's the nice gift I have ever received from a student,' she said proudly.

Jonathan looked at the catalogue again. 'This is a very upmarket gallery,' he commented in surprise.

'Yes, it is. Mrs. O'Shanassey and Emmanuel are the owners of the red dog painting. She told me that there had been three offers to purchase it at the exhibition at quite high prices but she refused to sell it. It must look quite something among the Streetons and Longfellows at Bantry.'

'Miss Ainsworth,' said Jonathan formally, 'and with your permission,' he added to Brenda, 'instead of him sitting all alone outside for the sports period why can't he come to my class. I only have the seven students from the computer class.'

'I've no objection,' said Brenda.

'Nor I,' added Miss Ainsworth. 'He is just not cut out for sport, so it's better that he develops his talents in other directions.' She did not notice a big grin that swept across Brenda's face as if she knew a very big secret.

School had finished for the day and Miss Ainsworth made for the supermarket where she chattered with friends and then headed home.

As she put her hand in her pocket a wave of exasperation swept over her. 'Damn, damn, damn!' she shouted, realising that she had left her telephone in her jacket pocket in her office at school. A stern word to the cat and she dumped her supermarket bags on the kitchen table, got back into her car and sped off to school to retrieve her telephone. As she parked her car, she noted Mr. Sam O'Connor's black Bentley parked in front of the church but took no real notice. Then as she rounded the veranda, going in the direction of the hall, she heard excited voices. She turned left to see Brenda's light on in her office and then in absolute amazement she looked out on this warm late autumn afternoon and saw Giovanni with a little cricket bat in his hand, Vince at the other end of the pitch, Sam O'Connor bowling a tennis ball, Emmanuel fielding, and Michael at the stumps. Every time the ball was hit, Charlie had to make a decision whether he chased Giovanni or the ball.

'Run, Father, run!' came a little excited voice.

Miss Ainsworth sat on the edge of the raised veranda flooring and just watched. 'They are wonderful, aren't they?' Miss Ainsworth spun around. She had not heard Brenda come up behind her. Miss Ainsworth just shook her head. 'It's Giovanni,' she said quietly, 'and with his court. You see they play cricket every Wednesday night after school, the five of them, for about three quarters of an hour. They love him very much.'

'I can see that,' Miss Ainsworth replied. 'I would never have guessed – and Father as well.'

'Yes, he loves it. They all do. Emmanuel said that, like Michael, they hated sport at school and yet here they are playing together, with the boy. Unfortunately, with winter coming, these Wednesday evenings are going to come to an end until spring.'

'I don't see why,' said a determined Miss Ainsworth. 'I have an indoor cricket set and the pitch is laid out on the floor. When the weather is bad they can play in the hall. I'll set it up before I leave. It's not a problem. I just can't believe it – and Sam O'Connor!

'He adores Giovanni. I spoke to his wife the other day and she said that if anyone made life difficult for Giovanni they would answer directly to him.'

The match finished, the equipment was placed in a canvas bag carried by Emmanuel and Michael; Vince swung Giovanni up onto his shoulders to the cry of, 'We won, Father, we won!' They walked across the field and in through the back gate of John and Veronica's where an abundant afternoon tea awaited them.

'What sort of light fixtures are you hanging?' asked the electrician.

'Well, I know what I want - but the cost!' lamented Simon.

'Oh, you should give the hotel in Brentwood a call. It's to be demolished and a new three storey building is to go up.'

'What's that got to do with me?'

'Haven't you ever been in the ballroom?'

'Once,' admitted Simon, 'for a very down-market wedding. The food was inedible.' Then he spun around. 'The chandeliers, you mean. Are they for sale?'

'I suppose so. Everything else is.'

Simon got on his telephone to locate the number. He said good afternoon and the electrician listened to the very flowery prose as Simon edged his way to the subject of chandeliers. 'Oh, I see. The six go together. Hm. I take it from that comment that they are not sold. Tomorrow at nine would be fine. Thank you ever so much.' He hung up. 'Will the ceiling take the weight?' he enquired in a business-like way, then turned to leave the almost completed interior.

The local parishioners knew that there was a good reason that the old church had been renovated but for what purpose remained a mystery. The Canonica was now completed on the outside and looked quite splendid. The old asphalted area had been cleared and planted as a lawn with trees and the nativity figures had been moved yet again as the plastering now began in earnest in the Canonica. For Simon, the real problem was the windows of the church. They had taken much longer than expected and he was very nervous, as although huge sheets of plastic covered the openings a strong wind and heavy rain would definitely see the new plaster and paintwork marked.

'Good morning,' he said, looking every bit the provincial businessman in a collar and tie. 'I spoke to a lady yesterday afternoon about some light fixtures.'

'Just a minute, mate. I'll get my mum.'

Simon looked about him at a splendid 1850s hotel about to be demolished. Vandals, he thought!

'It was me you were talking to,' said a voice behind him and he swung around to face an extremely hard-faced woman of about fifty five or sixty with long blonde dyed hair, shortish, with an enormous bust-line that was balanced by a large backside all in stretch black lycra. 'I wonder if she does line dancing,' he thought. Her long, false, mascaraed eyelashes seemed like small brooms and he wondered how she saw through them. The very heavy make-up in an odd shade that looked as if she had been lying under the grill for some time, with pale whitish pink lipstick all added together: he decided she was a mess.

'Oh, how do you do? How kind of you to see me at such short notice.'

'Come and have a look. I am telling you now I am selling them all together. I don't want to get left with one or two. I am not stupid.' Simon decided it was unwise to chase that subject.

As the vinyl padded doors swung open he realised that the whole hotel from the fifties on had been bastardised and very little of the original Victorian fixtures was in place. But there they were, three down one side and three the other. They were enormous, but he doubted seriously that these were the original light fixtures. He assumed, correctly, these were indeed 1950s copies of earlier, grander chandeliers and at the time of installation in the Esplanade Hotel must have cost quite a lot.

'How much do you want for them?' he asked, dropping the niceties.

'I want six thousand dollars for the lot.'

He feigned shock. 'Really? That's quite a lot for the church to find.' He moved closer to them. 'They are big. I would have said too big for a domestic interior and six of them obviously just couldn't be used.' He looked around, then turned slowly, like a cat that had seen its prey. 'I'll give you five thousand and that includes all the matching sconces. The cheque can be cashed immediately.' The woman fluttered her false eyelashes as if by a miracle they were going to show her a sign. 'And obviously we shall take the responsibility of removing them, this afternoon.'

She gave a weak smile and narrowed her lips. 'I am only doing this because they are going to the church.'

'What name shall I make the cheque out to?'

The moment she left the room, he called the electrician to bring the large van and two cars full of volunteers at once, with plenty of packing. 'Hmmm,' he thought, 'I never thought of sconces through the church. Silly me! And look, we must have how many?' He counted twenty four in this large, forlorn room that had once been the centre of entertainment for well over a century.

Simon went and had a look about Brentwood more from curiosity to see Dolly and the Deacon's love nest by the sea. He was shocked. It was in such bad condition; paint was peeling and the garden as such was overgrown with prickly pear and weeds. He then gave himself an early lunch and waited for the electrician and helpers to transport the goodies home, as he saw it.

Mary announced over dinner that she was going to Melbourne for three days and was taking Sarah so the boys would be well looked after by the staff, as for two of these days Vince was in Sitwell. Emmanuel took it upon himself to invite Michael for this period. It was at this time, alone in Bantry, that both of them realised that they had much more in common than they thought. Just being alone allowed each to look at the other in an entirely different way and the walks in the garden and then back to the open fire in the library seemed almost perfect.

Emmanuel stood up and pulled back the curtain to gaze out on the front garden with a fountain having great deal of trouble keeping the water at an even flow due to the wind that had come up. 'I love being here,' he said, turning around to face Michael. 'I just adore Bantry. It's a world all by itself, a private domain that you don't have to share with anyone. When I first came here, about seven months ago, I couldn't believe the loneliness this place represented but you see I was the bearer of the loneliness, not Bantry, and now I realise that this is probably the most generous place on earth.' He sat down beside Michael, facing the blazing logs in the grate. 'I know what you mean,' Michael replied. 'You feel safe here. At my family's you don't; it's always confused and noisy, with people always arguing. That's why I live at Shannon with mum and Nancy. My father doesn't count. He disappeared away light years ago. He doesn't even think. With the whisky and television, we never talk – there isn't any need to.' He stopped and looked into the fire. 'You are the most exciting person I have ever met in my life.' He reached over and held his hand.' Wouldn't it be wonderful if we could just stay here at Bantry for the rest of our lives?'

'Well, you know, Michael, stranger things have happened.' He reached down to kiss him.

Mary had gone to Melbourne for several things. There was an financial dealings to check and she had to see her solicitor as well as do the usual shopping with Sarah and Kerry. Over dinner the second evening at her home, she had invited Salvatore and Kerry, and over drinks before dinner with the rain teeming down she turned and addressed them both. 'This last year and a half have been the happiest in my life,' she said. 'First Vince and then Emmanuel. I never wanted a family but all of a sudden I have one, or perhaps I have found relatives that have developed into something we all need – real friends.'

'I can go along with that,' added Sarah. 'Vince staying at Shannon two nights a week and sometimes three has changed my life, not to mention Nancy's and Michael's. It doesn't seem really fair but you have done the hard work bringing up these boys and we're now profiting by it.'

'You never really hold children,' Kerry said seriously. 'You only have them on loan and when the time comes to hand them on you must, no matter how difficult it is. Salvatore and I still miss Wednesday nights when Emmanuel and Richard used to have dinner with us. Wednesday night is the loneliest night of the week – it's just empty.'

'If Nancy didn't think that everyone was at lunch on Fridays, I think she would believe the end of the world was nigh.' They all laughed, to break this moment when it seemed that Mary and Sarah had, in a social context, won, leaving Kerry and Salvatore the losers.

'This means,' said Mary, realising that Salvatore's silence meant he felt this badly, 'that you must come more often to Bantry. Why not at least once a month or every three weeks, just like your Wednesday night dinners of the past? It's up to you: come and share, that's what it's all about, sharing them. Oh, Salvatore, while I remember, I need some marble tiles. I have a medium sized bedroom that is rarely used and a funny half-pine lined dressing room off it. I plan with Paul to turn the dressing room into a bathroom so that when Giovanni comes he has his own bedroom and bathroom.'

'Well.' commented Kerry, with a smile, 'I didn't think you had any maternal instincts.'

'I don't, but I happen to love this little boy and so he is becoming part of Bantry. He loves it and especially the boat with Vince.'

'What colour are you thinking of?' asked Salvatore.

'Oh, Paul will telephone you. He said something about honey colour with tortoiseshell wallpaper. Sounds a bit exotic for a six year old but Paul has purchased what he said was the most divine set of steps for Giovanni to use at the hand basin and they have to have marble inserts re-done, so you see that's all to be organised before Christmas, as Giovanni will be staying for a while and having swimming lessons with Emmanuel.

'You are organised,' said Kerry.'

'Pretty well,' Mary smiled, 'now Emmanuel has Michael to support him. Shall we go in to dinner?'

Everyone was at Nancy's for lunch as usual on Friday but it was a special day, for Simon had had a team of volunteer workers with buckets of hot soapy water washing off twenty or thirty years of restaurant grease for two days and irate electricians who had to re-open the walls from behind to fit the twenty four wall sconces that surrounded the church as well as the side chapels and the high altar area.

'I don't know why you didn't think of this before the new plastering went up,' snapped the head electrician.

'Simply because I didn't realise that the chandeliers came with their sconces,' Simon replied grandly. However, that day they were all in place and the chandeliers were being lifted into their new positions with Simon constantly crying out to them to 'be careful'. Before lunch, Vince, Emmanuel, Nancy, Sam, Sarah and Annie witnessed from the floor the last chandelier being fitted onto its hook in the ceiling. Vince wasn't the only one who was surprised at the total effect on the church, now looking like an Austrian ballroom. Even Simon was a little nervous at the opulence but pretended that it was absolutely marvellous. The others just stared at the effect.

'Well, Father, I believe the honour is yours. This way, please, all the switches are in the sacristy.' Simon led Vince in. 'These are the dimmers, these large boxes with the dials. It thought it wise to install them now,' having at the back of his mind a vision of light as in a theatre. 'Well, Father?' He stood back, Vince flicked the switches and the applause out in the body of the church confirmed all of Simon's expectations. 'Oh, goodness, Father, I think they are just a little bright!' He returned and reduced the brilliant glow.

It was a few moments before conversation returned to normal. 'Father, it's magnificent,' said Mary.

'I'll say,' agreed Sam. 'I wonder what our boy will make of this.' He laughed and with that they turned and began to leave the church, only to be confronted by a very excited John O'Keefe.

'Father, Father!' he cried, and everyone for one reason or another expected a tragic situation involving Giovanni.

'What's wrong?' asked Vince, showing great self-restraint.

'It's this letter, Father. Look.' He thrust an envelope into Vince's hand. Vince drew the sheet out and read it. 'But this is fantastic.'

'But, Father,' he asked in a confused way as the letter was handed around. 'Who did it?'

'Doesn't it say?'

'No. Veronica called the moment the letter arrived but the company said they had come to an agreement with the person who paid.'

'Paid what?' asked Emmanuel, not understanding anything.

'The loan,' John replied, with tears running down his cheeks. 'The loan has been paid off by someone, but who?'

'You mean the loan for Giovanni?'

'Yes, it's all paid off,' he repeated.'

Vince smiled. 'Perhaps a prayer for this generous person would be in order, don't you think?' and he looked about at Nancy, Mary and Sam, or perhaps all together. Which one, he wondered? Everyone looked at one another.

'Come along. I don't want lunch getting cold,' said Nancy, breaking the tension. 'We are having the most splendid salmon today. Come on, Simon, we're waiting,' as he raced back and turned the lighting system off and the electricians took down the final scaffolding, swearing they would never work with Simon again.

At lunch, Simon was beginning, 'Well, did you like the windows, Mrs. Higgins?' He gushed on.

'Very much, but were they originally like that?'

Simon looked at Emmanuel who winked at him. 'I do believe so. You see as a sports centre for so long it was inevitable that the etched glass was replaced with just any old colour.'

'Oh, Father,' Simon began again, as soon as Grace had been said, 'I have called the meeting for the repair of the church roof for Thursday evening at 8.30. I don't expect it will take long.'

'But what's the point of the meeting? We shall be using the old church now.'

'Oh, but there is every reason. I am sure there will be standing room only.' Everyone looked around the table and it was Emmanuel who sensed that Simon had been waiting a long time for this opportunity.

'I still don't see the point,' said Vince.

'Please, Father, I think you will be very happy at the completion of the meeting.'

* * * * *

'No, no! Just rip it all out! I hate it!' Mary exploded to the builder and his assistant. The bedroom for Giovanni and this service room that interconnected with it had been stripped and Mary, having a look around, thought the space good but it was a dark room. The only window opened directly on to the upstairs veranda and was a very tall sash window that, when the bottom pane was taken to its highest point, one bent one's shoulders and head and stepped out onto the veranda. Just Giovanni's height, she smiled to herself. She turned to go when a cry of, 'Mrs. O'Shanassey, there's a door!' She turned and walked into this service room off the bedroom and the young assistant with a jemmy had sprung a door or part of the vertical pine panelling which was hinged and when he pulled it open forcefully, since there was no key, inside was a very shallow space, approximately one brick in depth, and there it stood! Mary moved quickly forward and seized a very moth-eaten felt bag standing vertically. 'Carry on,' she instructed and swiftly moved downstairs to the kitchen. She took a deep breath and withdrew from the dusty felt bag the chalice with the diamonds encrusted on it.

'Well, well!' she murmured. 'So this is where Alice hid it all those years ago. No wonder we never found it.' Oh God, she thought, I hope there's not Anne's body under the flooring!

The maid came into the kitchen and was surprised to see Mary there. 'Oh, Mrs O'Shanassey!'

'Take a great deal of care and clean this, then I will tell you what I want you to do,' Mary said to her.

Vince and Emmanuel were home early and made a dash for the veranda as the rain poured down. Michael's car followed them in. 'It's freezing,' said Emmanuel, pulling his coat closer around him. The three of them entered the house and moved to the library, to be greeted by Mary, who pushed the button and in an instant the maid brought a bottle of champagne and something hot to nibble.

'Busy day?' enquired Vince. 'How are Giovanni's rooms going?'

'Great. They have both been completely stripped and the plumber is here tomorrow. Paul has already sent his designs up here so they know what they are doing.' She smiled, but Emmanuel noticed it was an odd smile, and wondered why.

'If you'll excuse me for twenty minutes,' Vince said, 'I have a quick bit of work to do and then I'll be back.' He disappeared and Mary rose to move to the fireplace, placing her drink on the mantle.

'I need to speak to the two of you,' she said, in a very business-like manner. 'When I was in Melbourne, I went to my solicitor and I have completely changed my will. I have no children so I have left Bantry and all the investments to you, Emmanuel.' Here she paused. 'And Giovanni. If something happens to me before he turns twenty one, you are the executor and inheritor. You will keep everything intact to share with him, and on the subject of sharing I think you will find, Michael, that Bantry is big enough to have you here with Emmanuel for what's left in your lives. But I leave you this responsibility of Bantry and for Giovanni, and I expect you to honour my wishes. My solicitor will send you a copy as he has written it in much more detail.'

Emmanuel started to say something but words failed him. He stood and held Mary in his arms. 'Shall the three of us just keep this a secret?' she suggested, with a smile and looked over to see 'the red dog' on the table easel.

Sitting at the dinner table, their conversation was mainly about the point of the meeting the following night. 'It's a waste of time,' argued Vince. 'What is to be discussed?'

'I wouldn't miss it for the world. It's been the buzz of Sitwell all week.'

'But there's no point to it,' Vince insisted.

'There just might be,' smiled Emmanuel, knowing that Simon seemed very concerned that this public meeting should take place. Mary rang the bell and the maid brought to her an object covered in a tea towel. Mary thanked her and placed it between her and Vince. 'Vince,' she said, putting her hand on his, 'I have left Bantry to Emmanuel and Giovanni. It's also for your use as long as you live but Emmanuel will administer it. This is for you.' She whipped the tea towel away to expose the diamond encrusted chalice.

'I can't take this,' he said. 'It's worth a fortune.'

'Oh, but you must, Vince. You see, it's never really been mine. It's been hidden since Alice died. She had it altered to serve God and as that is your jurisdiction it is now yours. Be careful with it.' Smiling all the time, she went on, 'Well, that seems to have got everything in order. 'Oh, did I tell you (but not a word to anyone else, boys),' speaking very dramatically, 'that Nancy and I gave to Sam that afternoon that the Howe child stole Giovanni's lunch box five hundred dollars each? He added another five hundred and has been having the time of his life moving it all around the stock exchange.'

'What's it for?' asked Michael.

'It's a portfolio for Giovanni. Can you imagine that Sam, a multi-millionaire is having the time of his life building this up for him!'

'It's admirable,' answered Vince, turning the chalice in his hands.

'No, it's Sam's way of saying that he is also working for Giovanni. He could write him a cheque for whatever amount he wanted to, but this money is different. It's Giovanni's, and Sam feels that by him working at this little portfolio it's his genuine contribution to a little boy he loves very dearly, as we all do.'

Now the church was almost finished, Nancy collected all the re-silked Low Mass sets and placed them in the drawers ready for Vince, determined that the moment the Mass was returned to the old church the new polyester vestments that served in the Howe church would be done away with. It was approximately at this period that a large box arrived at Bantry addressed to Father Vincenzo Lampedusa and when it was opened Vince stared in amazement. Angela had had all the linen albs and cottas made up and had added all her collection of antique lace. The card inside read simply 'To Vince, with all my love, Angela'.

Simon's prediction was correct and at 8.30 the Howe church was packed and everyone who entered noticed large timbers supporting the ceiling beams of the church, where the water had been leaking in for years. At a table at the front sat Vince, Simon, Emmanuel and Nancy. Anthony Howe had been alerted to this meeting and said he would meet the Deacon at the church. His car swung into Sutton Drive and he noticed Shannon, looking as pristine as ever, then turned his head to look at where he had once lived. He stepped on the brake at once, only to feel a bang from behind. A young man got out of his car and began to abuse him for his careless driving. There was no damage except that Howes's rear light on the right side was completely smashed and not functioning. He apologised and pulled his car over to the side. Where had his masterpiece gone? Yes, gone! It just wasn't there any more, his masterpiece! He drove and with great difficulty found a parking place. He wondered why there were so many cars. He spotted the Deacon smoking just outside the front door and asked, 'What the hell is happening?'

'I don't know but if it's trouble it's sure to be the Sacristan and the Treasurer. Let's go in' as he stepped on his cigarette butt. They were at the back and Anthony noticed Betty sitting between Sean and another man, all talking together as Dolly waved to them from the side, where they joined her.

A ring of a bell announced the meeting was to commence. Vince stood and welcomed the packed church and then handed the meeting over to Simon, who was confidently ready.

'I have called this meeting tonight to clear up two or three issues and it is imperative that you all understand them clearly. The original church behind us is now ready for occupation. The last details have been completed, the organ restored and Mrs. Sullivan will once more take her rightful place in front of this splendid instrument. This building is to be demolished.

'Over my dead body!' yelled Anthony Howe.

'That, Mr. Howe, is easily arranged. If you lie three metres in from the water-stained walls, the demolition crew promise that half the roof system will collapse at once, due to the ends of all the beams being in a dangerous condition due to water infiltration.'

There was a gale of laughter. Then Anthony Howe, regaining his composure, began to attack. 'This building is a listed building. I have seen to that,' he stated smugly, as the Deacon nodded his head in approval. Got them, he thought.

'Wrong, Mr. Howes. This building can never be a listed building if it was constructed illegally initially.' He smiled in Anthony Howes's direction. 'For, you see, Mr. Howes, this building is two and a half metres too close to the street and according to building regulations it is illegal and as such is to be demolished. We start work tomorrow at 7.30 in the morning and in case the rest of you are interested,' he said, adjusting his glasses, 'the walls, according to the initial plans, in these hideous bands of stone and cement, should be solid. In fact when the demolition crew checked last week, the walls are all hollow.'

There was dead silence.

'This is all a plot to smear Anthony's name,' piped up Dolly.

'Really?' came a voice from the audience. 'You are a fine one to talk about plots.'

Vince went to stop this conversation, knowing it was going to lead to trouble but with the Treasurer's hand on one arm and the Sacristan's on the other, Vince remained silent.

The third blow for the Deacon was now at hand. Betty rose: 'This building was built with my money and foolishly I allowed Anthony to go ahead with it. But you, Dolly,' she spat, 'have been my husband's mistress for some years, it appears.' The silence now was electric, everyone waiting for trouble. The Deacon looked amazed as all eyes turned on him. 'I wouldn't worry, Dolly,' and she emphasised the 'Dolly', 'you have two penniless men and as far as I am concerned you're welcome to them.'

This brought a round of applause.

'Oh, you're so smart!' hissed Dolly. 'Because you have money you think no one else has. I happen to have a beach house worth at least two million dollars.' Dolly was clearly becoming furious.

'I believe, Dolly,' replied Simon, enjoying all this, 'that you are speaking in the past tense.

'What are you rabbiting on about?' she spat.

'Ask the Deacon,' he said and Dolly turned on the Deacon, who was stroking his grey beard and desperately craving a cigarette and a quick exit from this social dilemma. Then it crossed his mind and he spun on Dolly.

'You tramp!' he exclaimed.

'What the hell has happened to the beach house?' she shouted.

Vince was once more restrained as the Deacon mumbled something.

'You did what!' Dolly screamed. 'I'll kill you!'

'An excellent idea but not in here,' quipped Simon, and that had everyone laughing again; even Vince had a smile on his face. 'I do hope that this Sunday we shall see you all at Mass and I can guarantee a big surprise for everyone. I think that concludes the meeting. Thank you so much for coming, and we bid you a good evening.' He rang his desk bell, signalling the meeting was over. The noise was immediate and very loud, with everyone giving their point of view, mainly about Dolly and the Deacon. The demolition of the church did not seem to worry anybody.

Nancy pushed her way through the crowd to Jonathan, Sean and Betty. 'Please do come on to Shannon for a light buffet supper. Drinks are being served. I would be delighted if the three of you would join us.'

So the demolition crews moved in and in less than a fortnight the Howe church was just a vague memory in everyone's mind. The front of the old church was landscaped as before with a broad drive up to the front of it in white gravel, bordered either side by six Irish yew trees cut into cones, with a large double wooden gate either side of a single gate. All this and the tall picket fencing were painted in pristine white. The fencing system ran across the front of the church and Canonica, in front of the two houses and across the front of the school, giving the whole complex a unity it had never had in the past.

One Wednesday evening Miss Ainsworth, having been to a meeting after school at the State School and having a bundle of paper, decided that she would take them directly to school rather than home and back to school the next day. She drove up Main Street and turned into Sutton Drive, now lined with young plane trees that continued across the front of St. Bridget's. In the afternoon sun a gilded Celtic cross shone out from the top of the old church. She parked her car and with the bundle of papers under one arm opened the side gate to the school and rounded the veranda to hear voices. She looked across to the cricket pitch where the game with Giovanni, Sam, Vince, Emmanuel and Michael had just concluded. She noticed Emmanuel's arm around Michael as he shared carrying the canvas bag with the equipment inside with Sam, and seated on Vince's shoulders was Giovanni. She could hear Charlie barking and then she saw Giovanni bend over and kiss Vince on the forehead, and, knowing he was well supported by his strong arms, threw his tiny arms in the air and yelled, 'We won, Father, we won!'